THE
SANDERSONS
FAIL
MANHATTAN

ALSO BY SCOTT JOHNSTON

Campusland

THE SANDERSONS FAIL MANHATTAN

SCOTT JOHNSTON

ST. MARTIN'S PRESS
NEW YORK

First published in the United States by St. Martin's Press, an imprint of St. Martin's Publishing Group

THE SANDERSONS FAIL MANHATTAN. Copyright © 2025 by Scott Johnston. All rights reserved. Printed in the United States of America. For information, address St. Martin's Publishing Group, 120 Broadway, New York, NY 10271.

www.stmartins.com

Library of Congress Cataloging-in-Publication Data

Names: Johnston, Scott, 1960- author.
Title: The Sandersons fail Manhattan / Scott Johnston.
Description: First edition. | New York : St. Martin's Press, 2025.
Identifiers: LCCN 2025005252 | ISBN 9781250384782 (hardcover) |
    ISBN 9781250384799 (ebook)
Subjects: LCGFT: Humorous fiction. | Novels.
Classification: LCC PS3610.O3893 S26 2025 | DDC 813/.6—dc23/eng/20250220
LC record available at https://lccn.loc.gov/2025005252

Our books may be purchased in bulk for promotional, educational, or business use. Please contact your local bookseller or the Macmillan Corporate and Premium Sales Department at 1-800-221-7945, extension 5442, or by email at MacmillanSpecialMarkets@macmillan.com.

First Edition: 2025

To those who raise their hands and say "WTF?"

The tent stood still, soon to fall,
Echoes of gaiety, a closing chapter
They were gone now, the lovely people
None left to wonder what comes after

—Charles O. Littlewood
    (From *Fulminations of an Outsider*)

THE
SANDERSONS
FAIL
MANHATTAN

DROP-OFF

It was the first day of the new year at the Lenox Hill School for Girls, there on Manhattan's Upper East Side.

Ellie Sanderson's daughters, Ginny and Zoey, reluctantly agreed that she could walk to school with them, but only on the condition that she stop half a block away. Having your mom walk you to school was embarrassing even in middle school, but this was high school!

Ellie understood. As they neared Lenox, she let them walk ahead, trailing them the final half block, reluctant to let them go.

Finally, she stopped across the street and watched them disappear into the courtyard with all the other girls. It was, briefly, a sea of green tartan, and it made Ellie smile.

Her girls had grown into young women who made her proud. They were so different, those two—Ginny, self-assured and independent; Zoey, shy and kind—and yet they somehow fit together. She would lose them soon, a thought that intruded far too often in her idle moments.

After the last girls filtered in, Ellie was filled with a feeling of contentment. She lingered for a bit, trying to hold on to it. She couldn't know that not long from now, she would stand at this very spot, torn whether to cross the street one last time.

God, things can change.

THE MAYFLOWER CLUB

S he knew she should want this, and she did, didn't she?

Ellie was guided into a small lounge at the Mayflower Club and asked to wait for her host. She was ten minutes early, a habit inherited from her military father.

Manhattan was dotted with private clubs, most concentrated in Midtown and on the Upper East Side. A handful, like the Gotham and the Brook, remained staunchly all male. To legally maintain this status, conducting business was strictly forbidden, and briefcases were required to be checked at the front desk. Other clubs like the Metropolitan, the Knickerbocker, and the various university clubs, had long welcomed women into their ranks.

The Mayflower, though, stood out as one of only two prominent clubs with an exclusively female membership. Founded at the height of the Gilded Age by a prominent socialite who also happened to be a suffragette, the Mayflower was modeled on the venerable men's clubs of the era. Its graceful Neo-Georgian clubhouse occupied the better part of a block in a prime location on Park Avenue. Inside were dining rooms, guest rooms, a squash court, and other amenities. In stark contrast to its brother clubs, there was no bar, something thought unseemly for the fairer sex.

For women of a certain background membership was expected, although it was far from automatic. There had been a time when rejection was socially traumatic, the sort of thing that prompted families to decamp to less competitive cities. This period lasted, give or take, from the Lady Astor days to the 1960s (a time when social norms of all kinds were reconsidered).

Today, things were subtler. The rejected were not rusticated and invitations did not evaporate. But it was still a blow, an invisible mark. Everyone just *knew*, and the rejected *knew* they knew, and it followed them around in sub-rosa exchanges. *She was blackballed at the Mayflower, you know.*

No matter that it was all because some random dowager on the admissions committee had heard something from someone who'd heard it from someone else, and really the relevant *something* was twisted by the fourth retelling.

Damage done.

Ellie, waiting alone on a couch in the lounge, knew little of these things. The couch, while beautiful, was so stiff it seemingly sent a message: Guests should not get comfortable.

Sitting there with nothing to do, she resisted any urge to check her phone, knowing its presence was likely frowned upon.

Fishing for a way to pass the time, she picked up a copy of the sole book on the coffee table, the *Social Register*. Ellie had heard of it, vaguely, but had never seen one before. Wasn't it some sort of social arbiter? She associated it with another time—the 1950s, perhaps? Examining the cover, she read a peculiar phrase printed across the bottom, its pumpkin-colored letters set on a black background:

Look At Dilatory Domiciles Always To Ensure Accuracy

It was an odd sentence, she thought. For starters, they capitalized their prepositions. Odder still was the wording. A "domicile" was clearly a home, but didn't "dilatory" mean *tardy*? So, what was a "tardy home," exactly? Ellie opened the book and saw that it was a directory. She looked at a random entry:

Adams MR & MRS Gifford O (Swift Percilla M)
111 Duck Pond Lane, Locust Valley, NY 11560
(987) 574-5777
Summer: 45 Fox Run Path, Sharon, CT 06069
JUNIOR Grace E
at Friends Academy
P '69, Sm 71

It read like a society dog tag. Curious, Ellie checked the notes in the back. She found that *P* simply meant *Princeton*. She wondered what they put if you went to Penn, or gosh, Purdue. Would one suffer the indignity of multiple letters, like *Sm*? (That turned out to be "Smith.") The lone *S* was awarded to Stanford. She doubted very much that Louisiana Tech, her alma mater, got its own letter, but which college got proprietary use of *L*? None of the Ivies started with it. . . .

She flipped through to the S section. There they were, Will's parents, Jack and Beatrice Sanderson. Her mother-in-law went by Bitsy.

Even after three years, the ways of New York, particularly *this* New York, the Upper East Side, were still a mystery to Ellie.

She didn't care much, if she were being honest, for the neighborhood's social pretensions. But the Upper East Side was William's home. What she wanted, finally, was a place that was hers too. A place to finally plant her own roots and raise her girls. William had promised her as much years before. At age forty-two, it wasn't too late. That the place turned out to be New York was an accident of marriage.

So, however strange, these would be the ways she learned.

WELCOME TO THE BOARD

While Ellie sat patiently at the Mayflower, a group of twenty gathered around a large oak conference table just a few blocks uptown. They were not just any twenty, for the board of trustees of the Lenox Hill School for Girls wasn't just any board. Its members were people who *mattered*—people who attracted others like electrons to a nucleus, people who quietly enjoyed the unexpressed envy on the faces of others in their orbit.

They were corporate heavyweights, which here in New York generally meant Wall Street. Some media titans were also in the mix, of course, as well as lions of the legal world and NGO leaders.

They were, unfailingly, rich—rich because the main function of being on a school board was to write checks and solicit others to do the same. It was expected that board members would give at least $50,000 a year, and far more to periodic capital campaigns. Most had children at Lenox and would also pay full tuition, which for the school year just begun had risen to $70,000 per student in the upper grades.

The traditional role of any board was one of governance, but in recent years, that function at Lenox Hill had been largely ceded to the headmaster, more recently referred to as "head of school" lest there be any racial sensitivities regarding the word "master," which there most certainly were.

Despite the fact that Lenox was a girls' school, for much of the school's history the board had been male and as white as the underside of a flounder. The first woman wasn't invited to join the board until 1971. That was Dorothy McKibbin, who, then seventy-two, and having recently retired as president of Wellesley, could be counted on to not serve for long. But it was a start.

More recently, it was decided that the school needed to present a more inclusive face, so there were several board members of color. This new emphasis, perhaps long coming, was cemented after the previous head of school's somewhat infamous meeting with the Yale admissions people a few years back.

This was William's first meeting. Danish and bottles of Fiji water were on the table. He knew most of the others, either through reputation or school events. He saw one friend from summers in East Hampton, Tanner Elliot, down the far side of the table, as well as Morgan French, a Goldman banker. David was licking the remnants of his second Danish from the tips of his fingers.

As a boy, William had gone to Grafton, Lenox Hill's nearby brother school, although he'd left early to board at Andover. With talk of his success at Bedrock Capital, not to mention his penchant for writing large checks, the board wasted no time in tapping him to join.

There were many reasons William quietly regarded this as a moment of triumph, none of which had to do with the quotidian aspects of running a school. A Lenox board position was social currency, the kind you couldn't buy. Well, you *could*, but still. You were deemed a person of substance, an imprimatur that lurked just below the surface of any social interaction. The news would pass as effortlessly as a light breeze across dinner tables and grass tennis courts. *Oh, did you hear he's on the Lenox board?*

It also meant you had something others wanted, something more specific than status: pull with admissions. Outsiders—those not from Manhattan— could not possibly fathom the annual wave of panic attacks this process triggered through the naturally competitive East Side parental class.

Lenox Hill started in kindergarten, which meant applications were submitted when girls were all of four. If you weren't a legacy or a sibling, the admission rate was under 10 percent, a number that seemed to get lower every year. Lenox was now officially as hard to get into as Cornell, if not quite matching the other Ivies—yet.

But which kids to take? Since picking out the intellectual leaders of tomorrow from a bunch of four-year-olds playing with washable markers was effectively impossible, other means of divination became necessary. These were more involving of money and influence than whether little Brittany was a good sharer during the group interview. Ultimately, the process was a political and social one. Cozying up to a board member or two became an all-but-required part of the game.

At dinner parties and golf games, William knew his position would dance suggestively in front of others without so much as a word. Then those delicious moments would come, ones where he'd be pulled quietly to the side: *You know, Kathryn, my oldest, is applying to Lenox....*

Most important for William, though, was that the school was expected to step up for board members when it came time for college applications. This involved more than just recommendations because every girl got those in one form or another. It was the back-channel discussions with the right members of college admissions staffs, the kinds of discussions that quietly got things done. In this new era, the beneficiaries of these discussions were increasingly *not* of the Sanderson demographic, but William knew things still worked differently for board members.

It also wouldn't hurt that his wife, Ellie, was really coming along. She was on the upcoming Halloween benefit committee and in line to co-chair next year. This was a high visibility role and considered an honor. It had followed Ellie's serving on the Taste of Summer committee for the Central Park Conservancy, another coveted role that helped elevate Ellie's profile and, by extension, his.

William's oldest, Ginny, was starting her senior year, and college applications loomed large. Her record was impeccable, but it was best not to take chances. Every base would be covered.

And she was damn well going to go to Yale.

William sat there quietly, feeling this the prudent approach for his first meeting. He listened as Morgan French gave the fundraising update. The previous school year's annual drive raised over $4 million, and that, combined with the recent bull market for equities and alternatives, meant the endowment had cracked $200 million for the first time. There was polite applause around the table.

"Well done, all!" said Duncan Ruggles, the board's chair. Duncan had a patrician air with a perfectly aquiline profile. His gray hair was swept neatly back and held in place with outside agents. He presided over a hedge fund called Voyager, said to have $20 billion under management. William knew that Voyager's fees for the most recent year would have covered the entire Lenox endowment ten times over, but this was an observation he kept decidedly to himself.

"As you know," continued Duncan, "we'll soon be kicking off a capital campaign for our incredible new wellness center. Our vice chair, Judith Ramsey, will be taking the reins on that one. Judith, what's the goal?"

"Twenty-five million dollars. We'll announce when we have five million in pre-pledges."

William knew that's the way it was done. Never publicly announce until you have some private momentum. William had met Judith once or twice at school fundraisers but didn't know her well. She was a senior partner in litigation at Devlin, Shaw. He made a mental note to send Devlin some corporate business. It wouldn't hurt to make some allies around the table.

"Before I turn things over to Padma," said Duncan, "we have two new members with us today, and I'd like to give them a special welcome. William Sanderson joins us. He has two daughters, Ginny, a senior, and Zoey, a tenth grader."

"Thank you," said William, leaving it at that.

"We also welcome Barbara Selkirk. Barbara runs the Lucius Trust, where they are doing important work in educational reform, particularly in the area of social emotional learning. I think we'll all have much to learn from Barbara."

William had never heard of this woman, nor had he heard of "social emotional learning." If Barbara Selkirk had any connection to the school, Duncan wasn't mentioning it.

That was curious. Barbara sat there, stone-faced, revealing nothing. Later, William discreetly Googled the Lucius Trust and discovered it was affiliated with the United Nations. That was also curious, but not curious enough for William to investigate further.

"A warm welcome to you both," continued Duncan. "Now, I'd like to turn things over to our head of school, Padma Minali, who has some important updates for us, including news about a very special new student. Padma?"

WE'LL HAVE TO RELAX THE DRESS CODE

Padma Minali was finishing her third year at Lenox, having been hired away from a well-regarded private school in Seattle.

She'd had big shoes to fill, having followed the legendary Susan Latimer, or "Mrs. Latimer" to all who knew her, including board members.

A *fin de siècle* WASP with horn-rimmed glasses and a manicured bob, Mrs. Latimer had served forty-one years at Lenox, having started as an English teacher fresh out of Wheaton. She'd counted Duncan Ruggles's wife, Melissa, as one of the hundreds she had taught over those many decades. But, with the horrible events of 2020, the board decided to thank Mrs. Latimer for her service and look for a more "updated" image. A committee was formed, headhunters were hired, and a nationwide search produced Padma. Mrs. Latimer was duly feted en route to a slightly early retirement.

"Thank you, Duncan, and I'd also like to extend a personal welcome to William and Barbara. My door is always open. Before I get into it, I'd like to remind everyone that our annual Halloween Ball is coming up very soon. As you know, this is a significant fundraiser for us. This year's theme is called the 'Monster Mash.' Any involvement from those in this room is certainly welcomed and encouraged."

"I will state that a bit differently," said Duncan. "We expect everyone here to be involved."

"Thank you, Duncan. Last year, between ticket sales and the silent auction, we raised over half a million dollars."

"And let's aim to top that this year!" chirped Duncan.

"And top it we will, thanks to all of you. Changing the subject a bit, I think you all know that broadening our reach here at Lenox Hill has been a priority of mine and this board's for some time. I'd like to think we've been leaders in that regard among the independent schools, and in this light, I am pleased to report the student body is now forty percent BIPOC, up from fifteen percent just five years ago. We are making gains among the faculty, as well, although that's a somewhat longer process."

BIPOC stood for "Blacks, Indigenous, and People of Color," the term "minorities" having been deemed somewhat of a pejorative. William was pleased with himself for knowing this.

"But," Padma continued, "times continue to change, and it is our obligation to change with them. The very definition of *diversity* is an ever-evolving one and we must be sensitive to the idea of self-expression in whatever form it comes to us. In fact, more than being sensitive, we must be *embracing*. We cannot reap the rewards of diversity without being open to the forms that diversity may take. I'm sure you all would agree."

Padma let it hang there, waiting for a response. It took a few moments for the others to realize one was expected.

"Hear, hear," said Duncan Ruggles. Others murmured assent, effectively agreeing to whatever came next.

"With this in mind," continued Padma, "we are *so* excited to have a very special transfer for this year, one you've perhaps heard about. Joining us in tenth grade is Clover Hunt. Clover's persona is an unusual one, one with which you may not be familiar, but we are just so thrilled to have her here.

"Clover, who recently changed her name from Amy, self-identifies as *goblincore*, a growing subculture inspired by the folklore of goblins. The goblincore exhibit an appreciation for aspects of nature not typically regarded as beautiful. I'm reading now from a definition provided by Clover herself in her transfer application:

> *These aspects can range from animals such as frogs and snails to materials such as ground rocks and mud to fungi such as mushrooms. An important part of our culture is dress, with goblincore favoring a secondhand aesthetic of earth tones and oversized sweaters evoking moss and other flora.*

William wondered if this was some sort of elaborate joke.

"The goblincore," continued Padma, "are also one part of the growing movement of *eco-sexuality*, which consists of those who engage in romantic or sexual relationships with nature itself. The movement gained particular traction during the pandemic. But, importantly, embracing Clover also means embracing her chosen aesthetic, so I recommend a special-needs exception in the dress code so our new student can fully realize her right to self-expression."

Hearing about Clover Hunt, she of the goblincore, was not exactly what

William had been expecting in his first board meeting. Despite being possessed of, he fancied, an open mind, William sometimes had trouble keeping up with what he was supposed to believe. At that moment, if his thought bubble had been visible to others, it would have said, "What the actual fuck?" But the chances of his opening his mouth were approximately equal to one of his daughters solving cold fusion before the end of the week.

The others also seemed to be processing what they'd heard. The dress code—a blazer over a white blouse combined with green tartan skirts—had been unchanged for over a century. William wondered about the precedent this would set. Surely someone would say something.

He looked around the table. Maybe someone who'd been on the board longer. Damien Rutledge, for instance. He'd been on the board forever. He should say something! Finally, one of the others, Pete Richmond, spoke up.

"Um, are we worried about loosening the rules here? I mean, other students might decide they have to self-express, too, and who knows where that, you know, leads?"

"That's an excellent point," said Padma, "and I certainly share your concerns. That's why this is a one-off exception for now, and any other exceptions would have to be carefully vetted for authenticity. We don't expect many."

William noted that while Padma's words acknowledged she "shared Peter's concerns," the expression on her face did not.

Duncan took up the reins. "I think this is an excellent opportunity to demonstrate to the community our commitment to inclusiveness," he said, making it clear to the others how they were supposed to feel. A hand was raised. "Yes, Darlene."

Darlene Buckets was another newish board member. William didn't know her personally but certainly knew *of* her. Darlene had made a name for herself as a contemporary art collector and as a fixture in the society columns. Her husband was J. Townsend Buckets, the wealthy corporate raider, sometimes known as "Money" Buckets in the media.

"I can't say I know any goblincore," said Darlene, "but I think they sound fascinating, like an excellent *riposte* to our culture's unhealthy obsession with traditional forms of beauty."

William noted how Darlene's face, stretched like Glad Wrap, almost perfectly reflected the overhead lights. She seemed pleased to wield the word "riposte."

"So well said," observed Padma, "and I'm delighted you all agree."

They hadn't agreed or voted on anything, or even discussed it, but William knew decisions were often arrived at in such ways, in the meeting *before* the meeting, and then made to seem as though they had been agreed upon in the actual meeting, members tacitly coalescing around the dominant voices. He knew it was imprudent to question such moments, even if this did seem to be pushing Lenox Hill's traditional progressivism to a new level. He wondered if that was wise, but the thought vanished like a Danish within arm's length of David French. William was more interested in seeing the meeting wrap up. He had a lunchtime appointment with his personal trainer.

"I'd like to add," said Padma, "that I may have another, perhaps even more exciting announcement regarding our diversity efforts in the next few days."

"How intriguing," said Duncan. "Can you give us a hint?"

"Well, it's not finalized, so I don't want to jinx it, but I'm sure you will all be quite pleased."

ARMY BRAT

Tizzy was late, of course. She always was. Ellie still sat in the Old World surroundings of the Mayflower lounge.

Waiting there, the many pit stops of her youth seemed a distant memory. She had been Ellie Maddox then, Army brat, moving with her parents from base to base. Looking back, it was hard to differentiate them. It was all a blurry continuum of little Monopoly houses and dusty heat. Postings typically lasted two to three years, never long enough to feel like any place was home.

Ellie had been a gangly child, always like a fawn finding its legs. That, combined with a natural shyness, made her an easy target. It didn't help that she never fit in any of the tidy boxes kids liked to put the other kids into. She grew guarded, finding it easier that way, avoiding the bullies and also the pain of constant goodbyes. She developed a resilience that masked her loneliness.

Puberty was kind, at least, and gangly became gamine, if gamine could describe a girl on the tall side. Others noticed Ellie's beauty long before she did, and those long limbs, so awkward to her thinking, became the object of jealousy among the other girls. Later in life, her lack of self-awareness for her beauty or its effects on those around her would become one of her more endearing qualities. Ellie's eyes were a light green and hair a lustrous black. Her complexion was flawless and, to many, suggested a Mediterranean provenance.

She excelled at school, ultimately winning a scholarship to Louisiana Tech. Considering a career in teaching, she majored in education. After graduation, she moved to Atlanta to be near her parents, now stationed at Fort Benning. She worked days as a cashier at Starbucks while taking night classes at Georgia Tech, pursuing a master's in teaching.

It was there, at that Starbucks, that she'd first encountered a beguiling boy about her age who came in almost every day around the same time.

Boy. That's how she thought of him with all that sandy-colored hair he was constantly brushing away from his eyes. She knew his name was William because he had to give it with his orders. Every day, she'd write "Will" on the side of the cup.

She couldn't know that it was William who first noticed *her* and was immediately smitten. In those few brief moments he had to speak to her before the next customer's turn, he'd always make an effort to advance their exchange from the previous day. It became an odd, staccato conversation, drawn out over several weeks.

William was a junior executive at a fast-growing New York–based company called Bedrock Capital. They managed money for others, he said. This meant nothing to Ellie, but just the way he said it—*Bedrock Capital*—suggested it was supposed to. He was still relatively junior, so he was the guy who got sent out for coffee every day. He had privately bristled at this—at least until he encountered the comely cashier.

"Do they manage money for the Flintstones?" Ellie asked. (Ellie would return to that comedic well many times over the years.)

"Very funny. They're actually kind of a big deal."

Naturally, Ellie didn't register Will's interest in her, not at first. But soon she found herself looking forward to their daily ritual. What would he think to say in the fifteen seconds he had today? She thought his rhetorical efforts were cute.

They quickly established that neither was native to Atlanta or knew many people there. This became the basis of a bond, and after he asked several times, Ellie agreed to dinner.

Initially, as with all things, she was guarded, especially when it became clear that, for Will, Atlanta was a mere pitstop. She was determined to leave the peripatetic days of her youth behind her.

But as the weeks progressed, she would hear stories of Will's home and family back in New York, where generations of Sandersons—that was his very patrician-sounding last name—had lived and died. She was drawn to the permanence he conveyed. It was one of family and place, this despite being a thousand miles from home, and despite his efforts to seem dismissive of "all that." It was as if everything she longed for, he relished living down. She once pressed him about it and all he said was, "Legacy can be a burden." That was one of the few times he'd managed to annoy her.

Will casually emanated wealth by his very aspect, and a cynical observer might have said that this is what drew Ellie in. But that wasn't it at all. Ellie's life had felt untethered, and here was a man who, despite his casual dismissiveness of his roots, was anything but. He was far from home, but he knew where home was. If pressed for hers, Ellie couldn't say.

Of course, Will's boyish good looks didn't hurt either—the perfectly straight nose and shaggy blond hair. She associated those looks with preppiness but wasn't sure because she didn't think she'd ever met a preppy before. If she had to pick one word to describe Will—not just his looks but *William*—she might have said "effortless."

They dated, and Ellie gradually let her defenses down. It was an idyllic time, exploring the city together, biking the Beltline and going to concerts and Braves games on weekends, catching each other where schedules allowed on weekdays.

One day they'd planned to go on a picnic, but it rained. Will said to come over and surprised her with a fully laid-out picnic right there on the floor of his apartment. He played a CD of nature sounds for ambience. "And hey, no ants," he'd said.

It was a gesture that became something more. On their infrequent mutual days off, Will would often surprise her with another picnic. Sometimes, it would be conventional, in a park or by a riverbank. Other times, he'd catch her by surprise. Once he even bribed the maintenance guys at his office building and had a table set for two on the roof with its sweeping views of the city.

William decided that it would be easier all around if Ellie moved in with him, and besides, "You can save on rent." Expedience was not a persuasive argument for Ellie, and she resisted, but this only amplified Will's ardor.

A few months later, he dropped a bomb. Bedrock Capital, which was growing quickly, wanted him in Chicago. "Come with me," he said.

Ellie was devastated, thinking the choice impossible. She could stay and suffer the end of yet another relationship. Or she could go, starting over in yet another place, one which neither she nor William knew.

He had no choice, he argued. The firm wanted him there, and he was on a fast track.

"To what?" Ellie asked.

"Partner, of course. And we're doing good things, El. This is a firm that's really trying to make a difference."

After fretting for a few days, Ellie said no. She had to make a stand somewhere, and that's what she would do here, in Atlanta. But William said Chicago was just a brief stop, and New York would follow soon. They could make a forever home there.

"So, what? I'm supposed to follow you around like a homeless puppy?"

"No, like a wife. Marry me."

"What?"

William dropped to one knee. "I'm serious. I love you. Marry me. We'll do our time in Chicago, and then we'll make New York ours. You'll love it there."

And so she did, and they went to see the justice of the peace the next day, much to the chagrin of William's parents, who had always imagined a big, tented affair.

Chicago, though, lasted years longer than expected. William was doing well there and the firm was reluctant to have him leave. Ellie continued with her degree, but then Ginny and Zoey came along, and she became a full-time mother, catching glimpses of Will between his endless hours of work.

In little ways, Will began to change. It was a gradual thing, so gradual that Ellie hardly took note. He grew more serious, working even longer hours, and gone was the boyish sweep of hair—he combed it back now in the style favored by many of his colleagues. Hair gel kept it in place.

Gone, too, was the spontaneity. Ellie figured this was a natural consequence of children and middle age. As for the picnics, they became less and less frequent until they didn't happen at all.

The call from New York finally came, and with it another promotion, this time to run the Sustainable Investing Department, Bedrock's fastest-growing group. While it was painful to move yet again, this one would be the last.

They had been in New York for three years now. Ginny and Zoey liked Lenox, and things were going well for William at Bedrock. Ellie had made friends, and time was spent in East Hampton, where the Sandersons had long summered.

New York was the first place she'd heard "summer" used as a verb. She'd heard of the Hamptons, of course, and found them beautiful (if painfully crowded during the warmer months). The endless green lawns and privet hedges trimmed with geometric precision were so unlike the dusty bases of her youth.

And now, here she was, sitting on that stiff couch in a club where the ghosts of previous generations seemed to haunt the very halls. Ellie still felt like an intruder here in New York, but her uneasiness waned with each passing season.

She was learning the ways of this tribe.

Where was Tizzy, anyway?

TEA FOR TWO

Padma left the board meeting and walked over to Madison. She was meeting her predecessor, Susan Latimer, at a coffee shop called Ralph's. Padma discovered that it was short for "Ralph Lauren," and that it was inside his flagship store and not at all possessed of the hipster coffee shop vibe of her native Seattle. It felt like what it was—a refurbished mansion from a long-gone era. Buy a double-breasted blazer here, or perhaps just an expensive latte, and magically transform yourself into old money.

They were meeting for the first time, and she found Mrs. Latimer already there, occupying a corner table. Older and beautifully turned out, she sported her trademark horn-rimmed tortoise shells and classic white bob.

"Mrs. Latimer, so nice of you to take the time," said Padma.

"It's no problem, really. Of course, I have more of it these days, and I'm so happy to help in any way. And please, call me Susan."

"I was led to believe no one did that."

"Oh, don't be silly."

"Okay, Susan it is."

"So, how are things at dear old Lenox? I've tried to keep my distance, of course."

"Oh, please come anytime. Our door is always open to you."

"That's very kind, but Robert and I have been spending more time up in Maine. We have a little place up there. Prouts Neck."

"That sounds very nice," replied Padma, who'd never heard of Prouts Neck.

A waiter came and they ordered. English breakfast tea for Susan, and a mocha latte for Padma.

"I confess," said Susan, "that I was curious you called. I mean, after all this time. Is everything all right?"

"Oh, yes. All good. I was just hoping you might give me some background on something. I'm heading up to Yale tomorrow, to meet with Admissions."

"Ah, I see," said Susan.

"It's my first visit, and Duncan Ruggles suggested I reach out to you and get some background. I understand there's some history there."

This was true. It was often referred to as a "special relationship" by Lenox insiders, as if referring to the rich and complex diplomatic history between the United States and Great Britain. As head of school, Padma was expected to manage that special relationship, something she hadn't spent much time doing. The board could be counted on to sleepwalk through most things, but Yale wasn't one of them. She had to put in some time on it, or the board could become an irritant.

"Yes, you could say that," said Susan with a chuckle.

"I'd love to hear it, if that's okay."

Susan sighed. "Ah, Yale, they were the bane of my existence."

The waiter arrived with their orders. Susan took a few moments to steep her tea.

"The first thing you should know," she said, "is that Lenox was always considered a *Yale school*. Traditionally, all the great preparatory schools here in the East were aligned with an Ivy—Harvard and Yale, mostly, although Deerfield always fed Dartmouth, and Lawrenceville Princeton. All the others, Harvard or Yale. Groton and Milton, for instance, were Harvard schools. And by that, I mean if you went back far enough, say the 1930s, they would send around eighty percent of their graduates there."

"You're kidding," said Padma.

"Not at all. The big Yale feeders were Andover, St. Paul's, and Hotchkiss. Of course, Yale was all male until the sixties, so at Lenox we sent our girls various places. The Seven Sisters and so forth. Smith was popular, and Radcliffe, which hadn't yet joined up with Harvard. New York is a Yale town, though, and some of our graduates were married to very influential alums, so when Yale went coed, we established a powerful connection. They needed to scale up their numbers and they knew our program at Lenox was one of the utmost intellectual rigor. Our girls were prepared. It was a natural fit."

"Are you telling me we used to send eighty percent of our seniors to Yale?"

"Oh, no, nothing like that. By the sixties, all those pipelines had waned substantially. Even an Andover was probably down to twenty percent or so—still an enormous number. Our numbers were similar, at least for a time."

"What happened?"

"The Ivies chose, gradually, to pursue other priorities."

Padma couldn't help but sympathize with that. Yale had rejected her application years before, and it still rankled. She'd told herself it was a rigged game, an old boys club, much as Susan described. But in recent years Yale had transformed itself into something she rather admired.

And now here she was, the very face of an elitist school. The ironies abounded, she knew. Sometimes she yearned to be back on the West Coast, but she was an agent for change, and she'd sought out this opportunity.

"So, our numbers went down," continued Susan. "Well, they did for *all* our peers, but ours more than most. At one point, we didn't get a single girl in for four years running. Alarm bells went off with our alums and the board—oh, I can hardly do justice to the agita. It fell to me to right the ship, so to speak."

"So, what did you do?"

"Well, I went up there!"

"When was this?"

"About nine or ten years ago, I'd say."

Normally, Padma knew, college admissions staff came to *you*, but Yale had long scaled back, particularly from schools like Lenox Hill, from which they were sure to score multiple applications anyway. They just didn't need to travel anymore, except for occasional public relations jaunts.

"It wasn't my first visit," Susan continued. "Some years before I'd gone to see Walter Goodyear, the legendary dean of admissions back then. I remember I could barely spy him behind the piles of application folders. There was a deadness in poor Walter's eyes. He'd been at it far longer than most, rolling with each new wave of priorities. How many application essays had he read, so many sounding the same. Once, he said to me he'd take his own life if he read one more essay about how a two-week trip to build houses in Guatemala—at their parents' expense—gave a kid complete empathy with the world's poor. And there was this new trend, where every applicant seemed to have started their very own 501(c)(3), most not holding up to the slightest scrutiny.

"He told me once he couldn't go to parties, or if he did, he was evasive about his occupation. Otherwise, he was besieged, pinned in a corner all night, doomed to be lobbied by tiger moms or to answer questions about legacies or athletes or whether they really did discriminate against Asians. They did, of course, but he could hardly say it. All this is why you can't find contact information on any of them on the websites. Most admissions officers don't last very long, you know.

"Anyway, this time I was meeting with the new dean, Wilson Girard. The office had gone digital, so things looked far less chaotic. Wilson's still up there, but I suppose you know that. His office was sleek and clean with crisp postmodern art on the walls. But it was merely the illusion of order, you know, because those poor people are so overwhelmed."

Padma knew.

Currently, Yale was getting close to fifty thousand applications, most of which were highly impressive. They had to whittle that down to about two thousand, out of which they would expect fourteen hundred to attend. The simple math was that if each application were only given 5 minutes for an initial read, the task added up to almost 4,000 man-hours. With a staff of fifteen, that worked out to over 275 hours per man for first reads alone. Then came rounds of cuts, with staffers, each covering different regions, and each with their own ax to grind, bargaining over their personal favorites.

"There were the boxes," continued Susan. "So many boxes to be checked! Every varsity coach had recruitment slots, naturally, but the academic departments needed bodies, too, and the *Yale Daily* needed budding journalists, and the orchestra desperately needed a world-class bassoonist, and, God, the large donors were always screaming. . . . The list was endless."

Susan paused to sip her tea.

"I'm sorry, I doubt I'm telling you anything you don't already know. It's been an adjustment, spending most of my time in sleepy Maine after being surrounded by so many people for decades. It's nice to talk."

"Of course," said Padma, stealing a discreet look at her watch.

"I imagine," continued Susan, "Duncan Ruggles sent you here for the next part of the story."

"I honestly don't know, but I'd love to hear anything you think would be helpful."

"Well, I don't know how helpful it will be, but I'm happy to tell the tale."

ELLIE'S IN THE BOOK

Back at the Mayflower, Ellie was still thumbing the pages of the *Social Register* when Tizzy finally breezed into the waiting lounge. The mysteries of the *Social Register*'s nomenclature would have to wait for another day.

"El!" cried Tizzy, exchanging kisses with Ellie on both cheeks. "Sooo? What do you think?" She did a theatrical twirl.

"Your dress? I think it looks great."

"No, silly! I've lost four pounds."

"Oh. I didn't know you had any weight to lose."

Tizzy was rail thin, like many of the women Ellie met in Manhattan. So was Ellie, but the difference was she didn't have to work for it.

"Rick and I are going to the MoMA Ball at the Armory, and there's this dress I simply must wear. But it was either lose four pounds or hold my breath all evening. I tell you, Ozempic is a miracle drug. Everyone's using it. Let's go eat or, in my case, wave some food near my mouth."

Tizzy laughed at her own joke, and they made their way up the grand staircase to the second-floor dining room, where a light buffet was served every day from noon to 2:00 p.m.

Tizzy Addison was another Lenox mom. Ellie had gotten to know her through various school committees and countless travel soccer games. She had a girl, Piper, in Ginny's class.

As they entered the cavernous dining room, Tizzy leaned in and said, "So, a birdie told me you're invited to the Steins for dinner."

"How—?"

"Oh, please. People talk. And good for you! Their dinners are legendary. I hear his wine collection is the best in New York."

"I'm afraid I don't know much about that."

"About what? The Steins or wine?"

"Wine, but both, I guess. Casper is Will's boss, of course, but I've only met him a few times."

"Well, talk is Will is going places, a big promotion and all. That firm is hot as a pistol. What do they call it? Conscientious capitalism? Anyway, you must be sooo excited!"

"Will worked very hard for this, so I'm happy for him."

"Oh, honey, what about *you*? Your job is to spend, spend, spend. We need to get you into some couture."

"I don't know, Tiz. I don't see myself as a fashion plate."

"With that figure? Consider me your tutor. You're going to need to learn these things now that William is playing in the big leagues, and I'm here to help." Tizzy leaned in conspiratorially. "Whenever I want something from Rick, I just let him have some no-no hole."

"I'm sorry, some what?"

"You *know*, the no-no hole."

"I don't—" A look of realization crossed Ellie's face, which promptly reddened. These women were certainly different. "Oh," was all she managed.

"C'mon," said Tizzy, "let's go pretend to eat things."

They each retrieved soup from the large tureen and made their way to an empty table. "I love the consommé here," said Tizzy. "It has practically zero calories."

Tizzy chatted away. She was what William called a conversation dominator. He'd once said, "Next time we have dinner with the Addisons, make a mental note of how many of the evening's words are spoken by Tizzy. I'd say it approaches ninety percent."

It was probably closer to ninety-five today. This suited Ellie just fine as she tended naturally toward silence, a combination of shyness and fear she might say the wrong thing.

Around the room, amid the light clanking of soup spoons and gentle conversation, Ellie saw some familiar faces, many from Lenox Hill. "Tiz, thank you so much for having me," she said. "What a beautiful club."

"Well, it's about the people, you know, although I do spend more time in the spa than I'd care to confess. So, tell me," Tizzy said, shifting gears, "how's Ginny doing? Has she figured out where she wants to go?"

This was the all-consuming topic of conversation for senior parents everywhere, particularly at schools like Lenox.

"Ginny's always hard to get a read on, but we think she wants Yale. In fact, we're going up there this weekend."

"William is a Yale man, isn't he?"

"He is. And he's quite adamant about it. *All Sandersons go to Yale*," she said in a mockingly deep voice. "It's like it's some kind of birthright, but even I can tell things don't work that way anymore. Ginny knows it, too, and I think she's just protecting herself in case it doesn't work out."

"Oh, come on. Ginny's a star," said Tizzy. "She's a shoo-in."

"Well, that's nice of you to say. What's Piper thinking?" said Ellie, preferring to turn the conversation back in Tizzy's direction.

"Oh, gosh, that child doesn't tell me anything."

"Didn't Ginny tell me you all had been up to New Haven yourselves?"

"Oh, right," said Tizzy. "That was last year. Seems so long ago I almost forgot. Piper always has trouble focusing."

"Well, I'll be thinking good things. They always end up where they should in the end. That's what everyone keeps saying, anyway."

"Yeah, I've heard that one too. Usually from parents whose kids are at Wisconsin."

Ellie decided not to bring up her time at Louisiana Tech, a school that would never have a proprietary letter in the *Social Register*. Not that she was embarrassed. To the contrary, she valued her time there. But Tizzy might be embarrassed on her behalf and then say something like, "Oh, I hear that's such a fun school."

"So, I heard something," said Tizzy. "I mean, I'm practically bursting."

Ellie took another sip of consommé, wondering how Tizzy would take it if she wanted some actual food.

"*Well*, aren't you going to ask me what?"

"Oh, sorry. What?"

"A little birdie told me Lenox might be getting a midsemester transfer. A *special* one."

"Okay . . ."

"Ask why she's special."

Ellie wished Tizzy didn't require constant prompting.

"Why is she special?

"Because *she* is a *he*. It's a trans person, or trans kid, or whatever."

"Really."

"Really."

"That seems like a big step," Ellie said.

"That's just the way of it now. I hear Lenox is dying to make it happen. That's *entre nous*, of course. I just think she's so brave. I'm told her parents are bursting with pride over the whole thing."

"Oh, okay," replied Ellie, not knowing what else to say. She wondered if William knew.

"Anyway, on a different subject, I checked," said Tizzy, lowering her voice and placing a confiding hand on Ellie's forearm. "You're in the book."

"Is that good?"

"*Yes*, that's good. With all your committee work and William's new job and his family history and all, I'm very hopeful."

The "book" was the place where newly proposed candidates were posted, there to remain for a gestation period during which members could offer comment, anonymously or otherwise, to the admissions committee. To get to the book, a candidate had to pass an initial committee review, a step intended to weed out obviously flawed applicants.

Not that she'd tell Tizzy, but Ellie had never heard of the Mayflower before coming to New York. William encouraged her, saying, "All Sanderson women belong to the Mayflower." (Apparently, there were many things "all Sandersons" did.) She'd never thought of herself in those terms—a "Sanderson woman"—but it had a reassuring sound.

Ellie found all this a bit funny given the progressive flirtations of Will's youth, although by the time they'd met, despite the occasional Dead & Company concert, he'd already begun to construct an establishment résumé. It was a contradiction she had found appealing in those early days.

Lately, though, William had seemed more distant, and focused on his career to an almost unhealthy degree. That weighed on Ellie . . . but she knew how demanding his job was, particularly with his recent promotion. Ellie was determined to make him happy, and if joining the Mayflower was what he wanted for her, then that's what she would do. It wasn't a question of status— that had never concerned her—it was more about fitting in, becoming part of a whole. If the Mayflower Club made Will happy and helped her find her way with all these women, then that is what she would do. Planting roots was as much about friends as family.

"Earth to Ellie," said Tizzy.

"Sorry," she said, coming back to the present. "It's a lot to take in."

"You looked like you were somewhere else for a minute. Anyway, I probably shouldn't even mention it, but there's one tiny little fly in the ointment. A speck, really. There was some question on the committee, I'm told, about taking someone so soon."

"So soon after what?" asked Ellie.

"So soon after moving here."

"I've been here for almost three years."

"That's soon, at least by club standards. It can happen, of course, and please don't take this the wrong way, because you *know* I love you, but you're not what's considered a . . . conventional candidate."

"I don't understand," said Ellie.

"I'm sure it doesn't come as a shock that there's a bit of Old World snobbery inside these walls. You're known to these women, but you didn't go to Chapin or Spence or Lenox with them. They don't meet many women who grew up on military bases, and don't get me wrong, I'm *not* implying there's anything wrong with that. In fact, I think it's wonderful, we all do! It's just not the usual mold."

Ellie was taken aback. "Oh, I didn't realize. Listen, Tizzy, I don't want to put you in an uncomfortable position. It would be wonderful to join, but I don't want to embarrass you . . . or Will."

"Well, he's your ace in the hole, isn't he? The Sanderson name carries weight around here."

"I feel so stupid," said Ellie.

"Don't! I'm sure it will work out. It just might take a bit longer than we hoped."

"Tizzy, seriously, I can withdraw my name if this is going to be a problem for you."

"Absolutely not! This is all going to work out just fine."

MORE MAYA, LESS MILTON

Susan Latimer began to tell the saga of Yale.

"So, by my second visit," she said, "the winds had clearly shifted, and not in a direction that pleased many Lenox Hill parents."

"How so?"

"While it might not have been shocking for a big public school in Toledo or Little Rock, for a top independent school like Lenox Hill, the sudden dearth in Yale acceptances was enough to induce institutional panic. Almost overnight, the pipeline had vanished, with even generous Yale alums finding their children rejected, instead winding up at Middlebury or UVA or Wake. Fine schools but . . . not Ivies, and not *Yale*, you see. Old Blue parents were not amused, mostly vowing never to send another dime to New Haven. But more to the point, why were they spending tens of thousands a year on Lenox Hill if they weren't seeing results? The pressure mounted on us to *do* something. But what?

"And so I went, taking the train up to New Haven. I arrived unannounced, if you can believe that. It was a gamble, but I thought it might convey the perceived urgency. It was then I found out just how much Yale's priorities had changed, and those priorities did not include schools like Lenox Hill. I remember Wilson Girard saying, 'We look at Lenox Hill and what we see is an Upper East Side neighborhood school for rich girls. White ones.'

"'Well, that *is* who tends to live in our neighborhood,' I'd said. He told me Yale had recently appointed its first dean of diversity and inclusion—this was before they added the *equity*—and was moving in a different direction.

"So what did that *mean*, I demanded. Was Lenox Hill to be *ex*cluded by this new inclusivity? They didn't look at it that way, he said. It was more about *in*cluding those who hadn't been fortunate to have been included in the past. I pointed out that our girls were receiving one of the finest educations anywhere and they simply wouldn't find more qualified applicants. He said that was hardly the point. Your girls will survive just fine at other universities, he'd said.

"I remember being exasperated. I must have thrown up my hands and said, 'Help me out here because I am under a *lot* of pressure.' Was there anything I could do? Well, if he'd appeared arrogant, he got even more so. 'Do I have to spell it out?' he says. 'New York is a big, diverse city. Maybe you should reach out to other neighborhoods. Then maybe we can talk. Yale is about multiculturalism and opportunity now.'"

"So, what happened?" asked Padma.

"I remember thinking I was being dismissed, and I remember dreading the conversation I'd have to have with the board. I think I said something like, 'Is that it, then?' And then he said something that set Lenox on an entirely new course."

"What was that?"

"He said, *no*."

"He said no."

"Correct. He wasn't finished with me. I remember the conversation almost word for word."

"No," said Wilson Girard.

"No?"

"It's your curriculum too."

"What's wrong with our curriculum? We're quite proud of it. It has stood the test of time."

"Not relevant. Change it. Or don't. But if you care about having girls come to New Haven, change it."

"I'm sorry?"

"I looked at it recently online. The whole thing. It's so DWE."

"Sorry?"

"Dead White Europeans. Emily Brontë? Seriously? And who the hell bothers with Latin anymore?"

"Just tell me what you need, Wilson."

"More Maya, less Milton. Maybe hire a diversity consultant. All this comes from the top, Susan, so don't shoot the messenger."

"I found myself at a crossroads. Stand up for classical Western education or go with the cultural flow—a flow that was becoming a torrent. In the end, it wasn't a difficult decision, not if I wanted to keep my job. Lenox Hill became Yale's dancing bear, and I sold my soul, although I did manage to hold on to Latin."

No you didn't, thought Padma.

"So, we hired one of those diversity people," Susan continued, "and followed her advice on how to revamp our curriculum. We established an outreach program into Harlem, the Bronx, and elsewhere. We raised more money for scholarships and created affinity groups. We flew a Pride flag in the spring. It was all quite a change."

"And did Yale come through?" asked Padma.

"In a way. Our numbers did start recovering. The irony, though, was that the parents and board members who had panicked and backed the decision to change our focus . . . well, they didn't benefit at all, admissions-wise. Sure, our numbers rose, but the establishment kids weren't doing any better with Yale or any of the other Ivies. If anything, they were doing worse! It turns out that the Ivies just wanted the minority kids and were delighted to let the better private schools prepare them. This hadn't been the plan *at all.*"

"I'm sorry, you're saying this like it's a bad thing. Surely that's not what you think."

"You misunderstand me. It was a good thing. We needed to broaden our net."

"But . . ."

"But it was the pedagogy part that bothered me. It seemed like we were throwing the Enlightenment overboard, not to mention dumbing things down. Not all the new kids were up to Lenox's rigor, and there was pressure to make sure they got through. We had to take our foot off the academic gas, as it were. That always stuck in my craw. But, goodness, I couldn't solve every problem. I was told to improve our numbers with Yale, and that's what I did. That there were unintended consequences, well, that's just the way it goes sometimes."

Yes, thought Padma, and those unintended consequences had now fallen on her lap. Not that she cared in the least that the progeny of rich white families weren't getting into Yale—they'd had their way with Ivy admissions for generations—but she had to still at least pretend to be their advocate.

"Oh," added Susan, "if you're going up there, try to get Wilson out of the office. Take him to Mory's for lunch. That usually gets him to lower his guard."

"Mory's?" asked Padma.

"You'll see."

THE NUMBER

The next day, Padma rode the Metro-North commuter line up to New Haven, following Susan Latimer's game plan from years before. Except Padma had an appointment. Normally, Faith Collins, Lenox Hill's college counselor, would have made a trip like this, but Padma wanted to handle this one herself.

Wilson Girard's office, located on leafy Hillhouse Street across from the president's mansion, was just as Susan had described it. She mentioned in an email before coming that she'd never been to Mory's, and that she'd "heard good things." Wilson had immediately suggested setting up lunch. They made the short walk over, dodging an errant Frisbee or two along the way.

"You know, Yalies invented the Frisbee," said Wilson, tossing a neon-yellow one back.

"No, I didn't know." *Or care*, Padma thought.

"Back in the fifties, students loved the pies from Frisbie's Pie Company down the highway in Bridgeport. One day, some of them turned the pie tins upside down and started throwing them around and the Frisbee was born. So the story goes, anyway."

"Who knew?" said Padma.

"Who indeed? Ah, here we are."

They arrived at what looked like a small white clapboard house. Inside was a warren of wood-paneled rooms. The tables were all heavily carved with generations of Yalie initials as well as the crests for the many a cappella groups that would come and sing for their suppers (or drinks, at any rate). When a tabletop was fully carved, it was removed and bolted to the walls as a kind of commemorative art. Padma had seen the famous Whiffenpoofs sing once when they'd made a West Coast swing. They weren't her cup of tea.

What wall space remained was crammed with pictures of Yale athletes-past, all wearing the distinct letter sweaters, white with a blue *Y*. Padma found it odd that such a progressive school cherished a backward-looking institution like Mory's, but these East Coast schools all loved their traditions.

Wilson led them to a booth. After examining the menu, Padma ordered a salad and something called Baker Soup, along with a Hendrick's and tonic. She tended to be abstemious, but she was hoping Wilson would follow suit. As Susan had suggested, college admissions officers, at least the ones from desirable schools, were notoriously guarded individuals, and she was here to gather information. She suspected Wilson's inner chauvinist wouldn't allow a woman to drink alone.

Sure enough, Wilson obliged, ordering a Macallan's on the rocks, along with the rarebit.

"Rabbit?" Padma queried. "Where are we, King Arthur's Court?"

"*Rarebit*, not rabbit. Courtesy of the Welsh. Quite tasty, really."

"I'll take your word for it."

The bow-tied waiter returned with the drinks in no time.

"Thank you, Duane."

"Of course, Mr. Girard," said Duane, turning to see to other tables.

"Much of the staff has been here for decades," said Wilson.

Padma made small talk for a few minutes, waiting for the Macallan's to cast its pleasant spell over Wilson, who told a few war stories. He also complained about how the foreign kids, particularly the wealthier Chinese, had started hiring "consultants" to write their kids' essays from scratch. "And now we have AI to contend with, ChatGPT and such, on top of everything. The damn things have gotten to the point where they can write a decent essay."

Padma knew this was already becoming a problem at secondary schools as well, and software countermeasures were being used. Staying ahead of cheaters was effectively an arms race.

Wilson ordered another Macallan's. Ever so casually, Padma said, "So, how's this year shaping up?"

"Very well, or very rough, depending on one's perspective. We'll set another record, that seems baked in the cake. We can't even keep up with the foreign applications, and now that we're a free ride for anyone whose parents make less than seventy-five K, we're looking at record numbers domestically too."

"How are things shaping up for *us*, Wilson?"

"Oh. Applications aren't even all in yet, Padma. I don't know how to answer that."

"I know, but maybe we can speak in general terms."

"Ah, so when you say *us* . . ."

"I mean a school like ours."

"I think we have a good understanding, don't we? I assume you're aware of our priorities, institutionally?"

Padma did indeed, and she wholeheartedly agreed with those priorities. But if she was going to be an agent of change, she also had to keep her job. It was a fine line.

"I do, but what about . . . the others?"

"The others?"

"The more . . . traditional applicants. I do have constituencies I need to please."

"Ah, I see." Wilson took a long swig of his Macallan's. "I think you can guess. Got any athletes?"

As the Ivies made room for the foreign, the BIPOC, and the first-generation applicants ("first-gens"), athletics had become the last redoubt for most rich white kids in the admissions process. Not football or basketball, mind you, but there was still squash, rowing, golf, fencing, and the biggie—lacrosse. Each of these sports needed to fill a team, and most of the BIPOC kids didn't have access to a squash court or a rowing shell. Thus, in the Greenwich, Connecticuts, and the Brookline, Massachusettses, there was almost an insatiable demand for private coaches and expensive travel teams.

This was somewhat problematic for city schools like Lenox Hill. They didn't have the endless playing fields of the New England boarding schools like Andover or the suburban schools like Brunswick. Lenox Hill's outdoor teams were forced to take a bus for thirty minutes each afternoon to the open fields on Randalls Island, which lay in the noisy shadows of the RFK Bridge between the Harlem and East Rivers.

"You know that's a challenge for us, Wilson. A squash player or two, maybe."

"Hmm. What about specialists? Any musicians? Scientists?"

"Where are you with legacies these days?" asked Padma. The mere asking made her feel dirty.

"We're on the verge of phasing them out as a preference altogether. A vestige of another era. In fact, you could say we're already there, with some exceptions, of course."

"Those exceptions being kids who happen to be preceded by large checks."

"Hey, the endowment's only forty-five billion dollars. Someone's got to pay the bills."

"That was humor, I assume."

"Yes, humor. It wasn't funny?"

"It was a little funny."

"Yes, well, *you* try being funny after reading a hundred applications a day. Where is Duane?"

"Off snaring a rabbit somewhere, I imagine."

"It's not rabbit," said Wilson.

"Just baiting you there, Wilson."

"Ha! Good one."

Padma shifted gears. "So, it pains me, but I have to ask. . . . What's the number?"

Wilson knew exactly what she meant. The number was a mere rumor to most, but in certain circles, such as the corner booth at Mory's on a Wednesday afternoon after two Macallan's, it was a real thing. The number was what it cost to buy your kid's way into Yale.

There was a caveat, of course. Your kid couldn't be a dullard. The days of well-connected legacies gliding in with B-minus averages were decades in the past. A-minuses and 700s on all SATs were a necessary floor. Anything lower would drag down the class averages too much, which was unacceptable at any price. (Despite how much private contempt they held for it, even the most in-demand colleges were slaves to the *U.S. News & World Report*'s annual college rankings. SATs were a big factor.)

Still, if your kid met those academic thresholds, there remained a number, and it got bigger every year. It took a lot, after all, to move that $45 billion needle.

Wilson gave her an answer.

"Seriously?" asked Padma.

"Seriously. The money flows from Asia are off the charts. Mideast too. Russia was big for a while, but we have to be careful about them these days."

"Are these people sending their kids here?"

"Some, but a lot of them give money just to have their family names associated with us. The Arabs, in particular. They may not have kids in the pile, but they want a program or a professor's chair named after them. A Saudi sheik wrote a thirty million dollar check just last week."

"Wow," said Padma. "What did he get?"

"An endowed chair in Islamic Studies."

Yale was a brand of incalculable worth, and they knew damn well what they could get for naming rights or their precious admission slots. For the sheik, $30 million was probably a drop in the bucket, but it bought him instant prestige, perhaps also diluting the stain of some of his country's less savory pastimes.

"We also get about a billion a year from the feds, which is basically the cherry on top. So, you can see why catering to legacies isn't, ahem, a priority. An added benefit, between you and me, is that we don't have to care what our alums think about our approach to things and whether the football team is having a winning year. We pretend to care, of course, but we don't."

"I see," said Padma, who wondered what revelations a third glass of Macallan's might bring.

"You didn't hear me say that," added Wilson.

"Say what?" asked Padma with a smile.

"But, of course, some of our alums are wonderfully generous, so exceptions are made. You have any parents this year who play at that level?"

"Maybe. I've got a few private-equity daughters coming up. One has a dad at Bedrock."

"Well, I would think he's practically choking on money."

"I suppose. The kid would be fourth gen."

"Well, I told you what good that does. In fact, it's a borderline negative with most of my colleagues. Does she play any sports?"

"Not well enough for D1."

Wilson eyed the small amount of whiskey left in his tumbler. "You should know, even with a big number, there isn't likely to be room for more than one or two from a school like yours. One to two traditional candidates, I mean. If we're talking nontraditional, well, there's no real ceiling."

Padma knew this would make for an unpleasant conversation with William Sanderson, whom she was supposed to meet in a few days. The Sandersons had already met with Faith Collins, Lenox's college counselor, a few weeks before, and William had made it clear he expected Ginny to enroll at Yale. The sheer entitlement of it boiled Padma's blood, but she kept that to herself.

"Hey, if it helps, there's another number that will still get the kid's folder a hard second look. It helps, but it's far from a guarantee."

"And what is that?"

Wilson told her. Padma leaned back and sighed. "It's good to be king, I suppose."

"Well, it beats the eighties when I was an undergrad and the place was falling apart."

"Hard to imagine," said Padma. "Wilson, I need to get our numbers up. I know you spoke with Susan Latimer some years ago, and I want you to know Lenox *responded*."

"Yes, I remember. Your efforts have been quite impressive, but you must understand, we're under a great deal of pressure here."

"Pressure? You guys are Yale. You're the ones who *apply* the pressure."

"It may look that way, Padma, but we all have people we answer to."

"And who would that be? The students?"

Wilson gave Padma a crooked smile. "Absolutely. We're terrified of them. And hey, don't think I like any of this. Part of me misses the days when we took the class president who was also captain of the football team and a Westinghouse winner. Now you've either got to be a specialist or goddamn Greta Thunberg. That's just the way it is."

Wilson drained the last of his Macallan's. "Look, I shouldn't be telling you this," he said.

"Tell me what?"

"I think you already know we're prioritizing equity, but there's an institutional view, from our side of the fence, that schools like Lenox just aren't keeping up with the *kind* of equity that we're looking for in an independent school these days."

"Wilson, we don't disagree about any of this. Did you know we just accepted our first eco-sexual?"

Wilson flagged the waiter. "Duane, could I get some rice pudding? Make it two."

"I'm fine, really," said Padma.

"No, no, you really must try some. It's transcendent."

Padma relented and Duane came right back with two servings. Wilson started shoveling some in his mouth.

"So, remind me what those are again?"

"What?"

"Eco-sexuals."

"It's a newly revealed sexuality. They have relations with nature."

"You really *are* making an effort. But I suppose she's not a senior."

"No."

"I'll level with you. Here's what I'm up against—it's *perception*. The public perception, and the perception here in New Haven, is that schools like Lenox have not kept pace with the times, even if you say that you have. Appearances are everything. If you want better results from us, you need to move that needle. You're fighting a century-old reputation. For most of that time, that reputation worked for you. Now, not so much. Bottom line, you need to make a statement," said Wilson.

"What kind of statement?"

"Something bold. Right now, if you must know, our focus is on the trans. We need to get our numbers above Harvard's, but I don't imagine you can be much help there."

"Wilson, I'll be sure to take everything you said into consideration."

Padma choked down some rice pudding. She was Indian, and she knew what good rice pudding was. This wasn't it.

"Mm, it's delicious."

THE THIN EDGE OF THE WEDGE

The job of head of school was one that required the patience of Job. Patience with misbehaving or underachieving students. Patience with teachers, who always had complaints. Perhaps more than anything, patience with parents who all thought their child was the most special of all the special children.

Padma Minali was not a patient woman.

Oh, she could play the game, burying her agenda beneath a layer of materteral benevolence. But she burned for change. Big change, social change.

As soon as she was back in the city, Padma called Barbara Selkirk.

"I've just been in New Haven. Bump our offer. Whatever it takes."

Barbara agreed.

Wilson would get his statement.

The board was coming along, but she knew she could only force the pace as much as broader social pressures would allow. She was pleased they agreed to a dress code exception for Clover Hunt, but it was a baby step. She wanted to do away with Lenox Hill's dress code entirely. Blazer and tartans were an anachronism, a blatant expression of Eurocentric elitism, something that never would have been tolerated back in Seattle. Children needed creative outlets, and how they chose to present themselves each day was an important one.

The BIPOC girls, in particular, had their own cultural dress expressions, ones far removed from the lily-white Scottish roots of tartan plaid. Forcing the children to dress that way was just another form of oppression—one that had to be dismantled, she knew, with an active program of what had come to be known as "anti-racism."

She was making progress, and each small win made the next step that much easier. She spoon-fed the board in small digestible bites—although more recently political developments enabled her to accelerate the pace.

Revolutions took all forms, she knew. In this one, the battle lines were drawn up by culture and identity more than class, a tweak on the traditional

Marxist playbook. European thinkers like Gramsci, Foucault, and others gifted this to the cause when the proletariat hadn't held up their end, stubbornly refusing to seize the means of production. An inside game had become necessary, one that focused on institutions.

Guns or not, it was all the same revolution.

Centuries-old social constructs with their outdated notions of absolute truth and logical inference were being tossed on the scrap heap. Such thinking stood in the way of equity, and equity had always been the goal. It was almost as if the Duncan Ruggleses of the world were oblivious to what was happening. He and the other Lenox board members were conscripts in a war they didn't know they were fighting.

One of Padma's first acts had been to quietly ditch the Latin requirement. She was shocked to learn any school still had one. A dead white language! Its very presence was a deterrent to applicants of color. The Latin teacher, Mr. Gallup, made a fuss, but Padma arrived with a mandate, and use it she would. Mr. Gallup was now enjoying retirement, tooling around in a golf cart in The Villages.

Oh, there were a few parents and alums who pushed back, some of it taking the form of a Substack blog called *Undercover Mothers*, which had a growing following. Whoever they were, they were unwelcome reactionaries, hiding in the shadows. She suspected a current parent from Lenox was a ringleader. There would be hell to pay if Padma unmasked this anonymous coward.

She was reminded of a Lenin saying. "There are decades where nothing happens and years where decades happen." Or was it weeks? No matter. The point was that history was not a linear process, and social progress came in great, heaving lurches. The Movement played the long game, waiting for openings, *crises*, to present themselves. It was at such times true progress was made. Often, it was during times of war, the seismic social shifts disguised by the bullets and bombs of ignorant men.

Other times, though, it took the form of an inconsequential man, maybe even a small-time criminal choked to death by the police. Through such men history's hammer often dealt its blows. Had some bystander not thought to get out his phone and start filming, that man would be as forgotten today as a thousand other vanishing tragedies in the American story. But someone *did* take out a phone and someone *did* film it.

The Movement had its moment, and 2020 had been one of those years when decades happened.

The year before, 2019, a largely unknown academic published a book called *How to Be an Antiracist*. Its sales were modest, but by the next year white America desperately needed a how-to guide for absolution. *How to Be an Antiracist* vaulted from obscurity to runaway bestseller.

It was this cultural moment that Padma embraced, jumping at the chance to run one of the nation's most prominent private schools, for they were in the greatest need of absolution.

Over that long, hot summer of 2020, the curricula of elite schools everywhere, including Lenox, were retooled. Layers of historic oppression were dismantled. By July, Instagram was flooded with "Black@fill-in-the-name-of-the-school" posts, with anonymous accounts publishing vignettes of personal trauma. It was an eye-opener for many.

Of course, the revolution was about more than just black folks. People of color, while still a huge priority, were no longer alone on the front lines of the Movement. This was an opportunity for all marginalized peoples—the *othered*—to get their share of the American pie. The Movement was for the Clovers too, and Clover was just the beginning, the thin edge of the wedge.

This was where Padma would make her mark. She'd heard Wilson Girard loud and clear. Despite the fact that the school year had already started, there was one more transfer she was actively recruiting: a trans girl named Easter Riddle. Easter was at a local public school, but her parents wanted a change. Barbara Selkirk had been helping with the recruitment, which mostly involved throwing money at Easter's parents. The last offer was a full ride plus a generous allowance for transportation and other expenses. Brearley and Spence were the competition.

Easter, who until two months ago had been Richard, would be the first trans student at Lenox. She would be the first trans student at *any* girls' school in New York and it was damn well going to happen. Lisa Fleming, the admissions director, objected that Easter's academic record was not up to Lenox standards, but Padma overruled her.

Lisa was looking for work elsewhere now.

A new front had been opened, justice for the transgender. Padma knew how important it was to force the pace, to keep the reactionaries off-balance, adjusting to fights they'd already lost. How quickly trans rights had suffused the culture!

Perhaps the cleverest thing the Movement did was allow the other side to think that their concessions would calm the waters, that the "crazy radicals" would happily retire to quiet lives in picket fence America—just as soon the establishment agreed to that one last thing.

But that was many things ago.

There was no calming the water. Revolution was a permanent mindset, and new cultural exigencies were always waiting in the wings.

Padma marveled at their foolishness, those rich men and women so desperate to signal their virtue.

Something on television distracted her. It was on mute, but Sylvia Haffred was hard to miss. Haffred was an activist lawyer and prominent feminist. She had a knack for landing high-profile clients, ones that would conveniently land her in front of television cameras. Padma unmuted her monitor.

"The time has come for the power brokers of Hollywood to answer for their crimes. . . ."

It looked like another #MeToo situation. Padma quietly hoped the perpetrator, whoever it was, would suffer in hell. It was late, though, and time to go to bed. But before she did, she checked her email.

And there it was, a message from Mark Riddle, Easter's father.

Easter was coming to Lenox.

She would start next week.

A (PRIVILEGE) WALK IN THE PARK

Designed in 1858, Central Park was Frederick Law Olmstead's crowning achievement. Its 843 acres had expansive lawns, meandering streams, and picturesque lakes perfect for a lazy afternoon on a rowboat. There were sections of forest dense enough to make you forget you were in the middle of a mighty metropolis. Whatever elements of urban decay lurked outside its perimeter, the park retained its pristine appeal.

On this crisp fall day, Ms. Fincher's tenth-grade girls journeyed to the Sheep Meadow, one of the park's largest open spaces. Zoey Sanderson was in high spirits, and why not? It was Friday, the air was warm for October, and they'd been liberated from school early. They were only told they were there for some kind of exercise.

"All right, girls," said Ms. Fincher. "Attention please, quiet down. I'm sure everyone remembers Shonda Gomez-Brown from Equivision, who's been so wonderful helping us with our inclusion and anti-racism efforts. We're here today to participate in an exercise called a privilege walk. Shonda will show us how, and I just want to emphasize how important these exercises are. I know it's fun to be in the park, but no goofing around! Shonda?"

Shonda, whom all the girls called Hyphen Lady, practically bounded forward.

"Hi, girls, I'm so psyched to be with you today! Everyone looks so great. You are all proud and fierce women! I feel like we need a war cry to tell the world who we are, like Nubian warriors. Can I get a *whoop*? Let me hear it!"

"Whoop!"

"One more time but louder!"

"*Whoop!!*"

"Awesome. Give yourselves a hand!"

The girls clapped enthusiastically. "Yay, us," whispered Zoey to herself.

"Now, let's begin our exercise. You'll find this is loads of fun, but also, we just might learn something about ourselves. Everyone form a straight line facing me. Stand about three feet from the next girl."

The girls took a few moments rearranging themselves. Zoey found herself next to Clover Hunt, the goblin girl, whom she didn't really know yet. Most of the girls were steering clear, not knowing what to make of her. What made this girl tick? Zoey wondered. An empathetic soul, Zoey felt kind of bad, often seeing Clover eating lunch by herself.

In the coming handful of days, she would learn just how unnecessary those feelings of empathy were.

"Hey," said Zoey.

"Hey back!" said Clover.

She took in Clover's outfit. Today she wore a baggy brown sweater that appeared homemade on top of olive pants rolled up to mid-calf. Her hair, dyed several shades of green with streaks of neon, had some kind of twig ensnared in its clutches. The overall effect was that of a haphazard nest on acid.

"Okay, that's great, girls," said Shonda. "Next, I'm going to hand out some sashes." Shonda made her way down the line of girls. "What we're going to do is use these as blindfolds. So, if you would, tie them around your head and make sure to cover your eyes."

She waited while the girls fumbled with the different-colored sashes.

"I don't like purple," said one girl. "It clashes."

"The color of your sash doesn't matter," said Shonda.

"Can I trade with someone?" the girl asked.

"Again, it makes no difference. Please tie your sashes." She waited another few moments. "All right, is everyone good?" There were murmured yeses. "No peeking! Okay, I'm going to ask you a series of yes-or-no questions. Depending on your answer, you will either take a step forward or a step backward. Does everyone understand?"

"Not brain surgery," muttered Clover, making Zoey giggle.

"Okay, here we go. The first question is, are you right-handed? If the answer is yes, take one step forward, otherwise take one step back."

The girls complied.

"Next question. Did both your parents go to college?"

This continued for perhaps twenty questions. Among them:

Does your family own more than one home?

Have you ever attended a summer camp?

If you walked into a business and asked to speak with the "person in charge," would you expect that person to be someone of your own ethnic background?

During school breaks, does your family go somewhere on vacation?

"Now," continued Shonda, "without moving from your spot, remove your sashes."

Sight restored, the girls looked around and discovered they were spread apart, most having advanced far forward. One girl, a shy girl from the Bronx named Jemma Brown, was far back. For her part, Zoey was all the way forward. Interestingly, Clover was still right next to her.

"Did we win?" asked Clover, but only loud enough for Zoey to hear. This made Zoey snort with laughter, knowing very well that they hadn't.

"Is something funny?" asked Shonda.

"No, sorry," replied Zoey, struggling to keep a straight face.

Shonda turned her attention to Clover. She seemed consternated. "It's Clover, isn't it?" Shonda had been fully briefed by Ms. Fincher before the outing.

"It is indeed."

"Clover, honey. Are you sure you understood the rules?"

"I sure did, Shonda."

Zoey thought she detected just the slightest hint of sarcasm. If so, it was just concealed enough that Shonda couldn't be sure. Shonda considered the situation, wondering if Clover had been truthful, but decided there was little to be done, at least at the moment. Turning back to the group, she asked, "What do we think the purpose of this exercise was?"

Coco French immediately raised her hand.

"This exercise is called a privilege walk. It is meant for us to reflect upon how power and privilege can affect our lives, even if we aren't always aware of it."

It sounded like Coco had memorized that, Zoey thought.

"Suck-up," whispered Clover.

"You have no idea," answered Zoey.

Coco French, the prettiest girl in the class, was nothing if not an expert at gaming the system. The teachers loved her, as did most parents, but beyond the eyes of adults she was mean as a snake, the class bully. Somehow, though, she'd gotten herself elected class president. Probably some combination of fear and indifference on the part of her classmates, although she did have a worshipful posse that followed her everywhere. They called themselves the *BB Girls*, which, it was said, stood for "Blonde Bitches."

Back in middle school when Zoey'd been going through an awkward phase and carried a few extra pounds, Coco had asked Zoey to her birthday party. The invitation was unexpected, and Zoey was thrilled. She got a present and a new dress, having obsessed about both for several days. Ellie took her to Spring Flowers on Madison and they picked out a lavender dress with white polka dots. On the big day, present in hand, Zoey nervously rang the doorbell of a beautiful townhouse just off the park. She nervously smoothed her dress as she waited.

Damien Brody, a Grafton boy, answered the door. Was this a coed party? The potential presence of boys made Zoey even more nervous.

Damien, a grade above Zoey, was the subject of every adolescent East Side girl's fantasies, and needless to say Zoey had never exchanged a word with him. His brown mane always swooped just so, making for perfect "flow" as it fanned from beneath his lacrosse helmet. His green eyes were impossibly pale. Zoey's heart stopped for a moment.

"Yes?" asked Damien.

"I'm here for the party?" she said.

"What party?" said Damien.

"Coco's?"

He gave her a blank stare.

"Coco . . . French?" she added.

Recognition passed across Damien's face. "Oh, the chick from Lenox. Why would Coco French be throwing a party at my house?"

"This isn't her house?"

"No . . . it's my house," said Damien. "Who are you, anyway?"

It suddenly dawned on Zoey what was happening. The party, if there even was one, wasn't here. Beyond that, transcribing her thoughts would have been impossible, because none could have been articulated. Her mind became a swirling convulsion of inchoate shame, the kind no one can quite experience like a middle school girl.

"N-n-no one," she said. A speech impediment, one she'd outgrown three grades ago, reasserted itself. She willed the tears not to come, not yet. She felt her body starting to spasm.

"Hey, are you okay?" asked Damien.

Zoey turned and practically ran toward Madison Avenue. She turned the first corner, looking for any refuge, and ducked in the first doorway she came to, a boutique grocer called Butterfield Market. She made for an empty aisle where she allowed the tears to come.

There had, in fact, been a party. Coco's parents had rented Serendipity 3, the famous ice cream parlor, for the entire afternoon.

That Monday at school, Coco found Zoey and zeroed right in, making sure an audience of her posse could witness. "Doughy! We missed you! Where *were* you?" The other girls, having been in on the joke, cackled as a pack. They readily adopted the nickname Doughy.

Withdrawing into herself for months, Zoey avoided those first, uncomfortable dances with the boys at Buckley and Grafton, knowing Coco would be there, ready to inflict damage at the most propitious moment. It was a dark period, the kind that leaves a permanent imprint on a personality. She would carry it with her always.

Two years later, by the time they stood in the Sheep Meadow, Zoey still despised Coco French with the kind of ferocity only a teenage girl could muster. But shy by nature, she knew direct confrontation would see her the worse for it, so she made it a practice to avoid Coco and her hangers-on wherever possible. It was just easier that way and Coco, thankfully, seemed to have turned her attentions elsewhere.

The privilege discussion went on for a while. At one point, Shonda tried to draw poor Jemma into the conversation, asking her how the exercise "made her feel," but Jemma was so far back it was difficult to hear what she was saying. Zoey could tell she was horrified and felt badly for her. The whole thing seemed like an exercise deliberately meant to embarrass everyone involved, although the Jemmas of the world in particular.

Zoey tried to decide how she felt about her own position, positioned there on the front lines of privilege. She tried to gin up the requisite feelings of guilt, but it was difficult standing next to Clover, who seemed more amused than anything. Mostly, Zoey wanted the whole thing to be over.

But she did wonder about Clover, a girl who had made her laugh. Perhaps she was worth getting to know.

NEW HAVEN

Only a few days after Padma's visit to New Haven, the Sandersons also made the trip. William decided they would take the campus tour.

They joined a group of twenty or so and channeled through an archway with eight-foot iron gates, meant to evoke a portcullis. They emerged to a scene of unimaginable splendor, a large courtyard of manicured grass surrounded by a building of high gothic architecture, looking every bit like it might have been moved stone by stone from Oxford, or perhaps some Renaissance monastery. A pair of willows stood at one end. One could imagine Lord Byron, in another age, beneath their graceful limbs, summoning words of romantic poetry out of the perfumed air.

"This is Branford College," said the tour guide. "We call our dorms *colleges* here, which might sound funny, but it's one of those traditions we borrowed from the British. Branford was one of several colleges on campus designed by famed architect James Gamble Rogers in the nineteen twenties."

The group marveled at the scale and beauty of the setting, the turrets and spires, the weathered stonework and leaded windows, all set under a brilliant autumn sky. One woman bent down and touched the weedless grass, perhaps to see if it was real.

"Students get to live here?" asked another woman with a Midwestern accent.

"They do," said the guide, who sported a ring that dangled from her septum. "The rooms are all suites with common areas that each have a fireplace." She was almost relentlessly cheerful.

William, speaking to his family, but in a voice he judged just loud enough to be heard by the others, said, "That's my old room, right up there." He pointed to a leaded glass window on the second floor.

"The dining hall," continued the guide, "occupies the west end of the courtyard, and it has its own fifteenth-century Burgundian fireplace as well as an organic, locally sourced menu."

No one had the nerve to ask what a Burgundian fireplace was, although

William, the one-time history major, vaguely recalled it was a Germanic ref-erence. Sometimes he wished he'd paid more attention in college.

"In the southeast corner is Harkness Tower, which, at over two hundred feet, is the tallest structure on campus. In it is housed a fifty-four-bell caril-lon, which is played twice a day by a student guild. If you are still on campus around lunchtime you can hear a performance."

The group left the courtyard and continued its way through campus, the guide walking backward the whole time.

"To my right is the Beinecke Rare Book Library, one of dozens of libraries on campus."

The group gazed at the modernist structure, which featured a grid of veined marble panels on its sides.

"Beinecke's exterior walls consist of three hundred marble panels, each milled to a single inch. On a sunny day like today, the filtered light on the inside glows with an incredible amber color. Beinecke is open to the public if you'd care to take a look after the tour, but, sadly, I only get you for an hour, and we have so much more to see. Now, you're probably wondering about the building behind me that looks like the Parthenon. . . ."

The group floated along, taking in all the magnificence that centuries of rich donors could buy.

The Sandersons had been to Yale together a couple of times, but only to Harvard games out at the Bowl, both times making the day trip up from Manhattan. William gave faithfully every year to the alumni fund, with those donations ramping up as Ginny approached her application year, this year.

For Ellie, having attended Louisiana Tech, where dorms were made of cinder block, the tour was something of a revelation. She marveled at every courtyard, tower, and spire. She pondered passing students, wondering what miracles they had conjured to gain entrance to the kingdom.

Not that they *looked* special, she thought. In fact, they appeared a bit rag-ged, mostly in sweats, an odd contrast to the pristine campus, and not at all the Shetland sweater-wearing avatars of her imagination.

Almost echoing her own thoughts, Zoey said, "They don't look very curious to me."

It was a game they sometimes played called Curious or Not? It came from Ellie's mother, Ada, who always had a thirst for knowledge. She maintained that the entire world could be divided between the curious and the incurious. It turned out it was remarkably easy to discern, a call you could make after only knowing someone for a few minutes. Sometimes, at a party, Ellie would silently rifle through the others in the room, able to quickly deposit them in one camp or the other. Ada always maintained that you should find your friends among the curious.

"I don't think you can tell just by looking at someone, sweetie," said Ellie.

Ellie had been quite happy with her education at Louisiana Tech. She'd found it challenging, and the scholarship had been crucial. For her, education was what you made of it. But this, Yale, is what William wanted—no, *expected*—for his daughters.

Sandersons always go to Yale.

Ellie didn't have the same burning desire. She thought there were many schools worth considering, and not just in the Ivies, and certainly not just Yale. But if Ginny decided this was what she wanted, she would fight for it.

"Pretty great, huh?" said William. It was a statement more than a question, a prompt, and it was aimed at Ginny.

Ellie sighed, knowing this was the wrong tactic to use with Ginny. Reverse psychology was more effective, saying something like, "It's probably a reach, anyway." Despite having two of them, William's understanding of teenage girls wouldn't fill a thimble.

"It's okay, I guess," said Ginny, refusing to give her father any satisfaction.

They had already been to Cornell, Georgetown, Bucknell, plus that southern swing to Wake Forest, UVA, Richmond, and Duke, although William hadn't bothered with those visits.

Ginny was a standout student at Lenox Hill but also wasn't one to be told what to do. She might easily push back if she felt pressure to continue the Sanderson "legacy." But Yale's early application deadline was looming and Ginny was steadfastly noncommittal. Early applications, William reminded her, had a much higher acceptance rate.

Ellie suspected Ginny was just yanking William's chain by drawing this out. That would be very Ginny.

"What's the creepy building over there?" Zoey asked, pointing to a tomb-like structure with no windows.

"That's Skull and Bones," said William. "It's a secret society for seniors."

"Secret? Cool. What's in there?" asked Zoey.

"No one knows," said her father. "It's a secret," he added, smiling, whispering the last few words.

"Who belongs?"

"Nobody knows," said William.

"Cool," said Ginny. "Were you in it?"

"Well, if I had been, I really couldn't say, could I? What kind of secret would that be?"

"So, you *weren't*, then," said Ginny, never missing a chance to needle her dad.

He hadn't been, something that still rankled decades later. But no need to get into all that. "We'd better get going, or we'll be late for the game."

"Oh, football," said Ginny. "Be still my beating heart."

"C'mon, Ginny, show a little spirit!" he said.

William had decided to time their Yale visit with a football game to enhance the experience for Ginny and also lay the groundwork for Zoey. William knew how seductive it could be, with the marching bands and cheering crowds, all set in the grandeur of the sixty-five-thousand-seat Yale Bowl. He offhandedly mentioned that the Bowl had been the largest stadium in the world when it was built, and that the previous record holder had been the Roman Colosseum two millennia earlier.

Of course, this wasn't *The* Game; that would be Harvard a few weeks hence. It was the Dartmouth game—an important Ivy matchup, to be sure, but not *The* Game.

William had not been to anything other than the Harvard game since his graduation and was unprepared for what he saw: a near-empty Bowl. The announced attendance was 7,330, which, in the vastness of the Bowl, might as well have been two dozen. The student section, once full for every home game, was empty, a few stray pieces of trash blowing around like tumbleweeds. The scattered few in attendance appeared to be a mix of football families and hardcore older alums. Not even the New Haven locals showed up anymore.

William realized that coming to the game had been a tactical error. He had known of the girls' lack of interest in football, but he thought they might be engaged by the tailgating and the pageantry, none of which was in evidence. Noting that neither had looked up from their phones since the first quarter, he decided to cut their losses and get everyone back to the city.

He and Ellie had an important dinner to get to, anyway. They couldn't risk getting delayed in traffic.

740 PARK

There are many wealthy neighborhoods in modern New York. In recent decades, neighborhoods once unknown to the monied classes, neighborhoods like Tribeca and Nolita, had become the province of crypto barons and oligarchs alike. Even Brooklyn, its vast neighborhoods once home to New York's aspirational classes, was now beyond the financial reach of the vast majority of Americans.

But, for a certain sort, the discerning rich sort, the Upper East Side was still the ne plus ultra of neighborhoods. No, not those soulless canyons of bland condominiums near the East River but rather the stately neighborhoods adjacent to Central Park, where one found the prewar co-ops, their scalloped awnings having protected generations of wealthy from the elements.

The East Side was home to more "dilatory domiciles" than anywhere else—"dilatory domiciles," of course, being the phrase that so puzzled Ellie in the *Social Register*. Many were found on Fifth Avenue, which bordered Central Park. Their buildings were stunning, certainly, with their open views, apartments of West Side strivers visible over the green canopy of the park.

Nothing quite had the resonance of *Park Avenue*, though, which lay two blocks to the east. For at least a century it had been synonymous with genteel wealth.

It wasn't always.

Prior to the 1870s, the avenue had been a filthy place, with the soot-spewing cars of the New York and Harlem Railroad traveling up and down its length. In a stroke of genius, Cornelius Vanderbilt proposed lowering the tracks into a cut, which would then be covered by a park where dandied pedestrians could stroll in their Sunday finest, perhaps calling upon their neighbors. This new development was an immediate draw for the Gilded Age barons, who lined the avenue with mansions. Later, room was made for a new invention, the automobile, with a narrower, beflowered median remaining up the center.

With the roaring twenties came more people and a new invention that made it possible to house them: the elevator. The booming city could now grow up as well as out. Mansions on Park yielded to apartment buildings built in a classical style. Period fire codes, though, limited all residential buildings to 150 feet owing to the difficulty of fighting an elevated blaze. Thus, every building was built to exactly that height, or fifteen stories.

In 1927, the Municipal Dwelling Act allowed new structures to exceed 150 feet, but only if the higher stories had smaller footprints. A few new apartments, designed with graceful setbacks, were built to take advantage of the new law.

One such building was 740, which, of all the addresses on Park, had the grandest reputation. One of its first residents was John D. Rockefeller Jr., who lived in a duplex there until his death in 1960. Jacqueline Kennedy Onassis, née Bouvier, spent her childhood there. More recently, billionaires like David Koch, Woody Johnson, and Ron Perelman had called 740 home.

Little of this history was known to the Sandersons, although William certainly knew of its reputation. The Sandersons lived at 580, a few blocks south, in a "classic six." It was more entry-level Park Avenue, something they bought when they first moved. A well-respected building, to be sure, but William had been pondering an upgrade for several years, and now, with the news of his promotion, it seemed all but obligatory.

Despite William's prodigious earnings, though, 740 was not in reach, even if something had been available. They had an accepted offer on a four bedroom at 895, still an excellent address. At $12 million, it was a serious upgrade, and as an added bonus, 895 was much closer to Lenox Hill, close enough that the girls could walk to school in minutes. All that remained was board approval, which, in the Sandersons' case, would be perfunctory.

William and Ellie took a cab. It was only eight blocks, but the air was humid and it wouldn't do to arrive perspiring. William announced themselves to the doorman, who discreetly checked a list and then pointed them to an elevator, one of the last in Manhattan that had its own elevator man. He and the rest of the staff were dressed, improbably, like eighteenth-century British field officers, ready to charge once more into the breach.

Riding up, Ellie elbowed William in the ribs. "Yabba dabba do!" she whispered, giggling. She liked to kid William about the name of his firm, particularly when he got too self-serious.

"Not *now*," he said, under his breath, just as the elevator door opened. William was mildly surprised to see it open right into the foyer of the apartment.

This owed to the fact it was the only apartment on the floor, a rarity in New York.

This particular floor, and the one above it, were the realm of Casper Stein, the founder and CEO of Bedrock Capital, one of the largest money managers in the world. Tonight, William was the guest of honor, having just been appointed head of Sustainable Investing, Bedrock's fastest-growing division. Could a spot on the executive committee be far behind? That's when serious wealth became stupid wealth.

The money, even at William's level, was breathtaking. His base was $1.2 million, but that was an afterthought, really. Bonuses and profit sharing would typically be in the low tens of millions in a good year, plus there were options that might be worth a *real* fortune down the road. Bedrock's stock price had been on a one-way trajectory for years.

"Here they are!" cried Missy Stein in a singsong voice, gliding down the staircase from the second floor. Missy was seventy-year-old Casper's considerably younger second wife. Together they had a single child, Harper, who'd graduated from Lenox Hill the year before. Missy gave each Sanderson three kisses, alternating cheeks in the European style. "So good of you to come," she cooed, as if the Sandersons might have done anything else. "You know, Casper does so enjoy his outings with you at Dunehaven. Such a lovely place."

The Sandersons were members of the Dunehaven Club in East Hampton, where William was third generation. Occasionally, William arranged for golf outings there for Bedrock's bigger clients. It was a coveted invitation, and clients flew in from around the country for the occasion.

"Just happy to help the cause," he said.

Casper Stein followed his wife and settled for just one of Ellie's cheeks and then shook William's hand. Casper had the imposing presence that anyone who was worth eight billion seemed to have. Tonight, he wore a double-breasted blazer over a magenta Paul Stewart shirt, open at the neck.

Looking around, William knew better than to gape at the exquisite old English furnishings, the art, and, more than anything, at thirteen thousand square feet, the sheer scale. An understated compliment or two would be all that was expected.

William always had to force himself not to stare at Casper's hair, an immovable promontory atop his head. He knew the junior people at Bedrock would joke about what it might take to move Casper Stein's hair. An earthquake? A tropical storm? It also had a suspiciously uniform and unnatural color. Auburn? No, not quite. Burnt umber, perhaps. It was not, all agreed, a good look, but Missy Stein was the only person on the planet who could conceivably tell him that, and if she had, he hadn't listened.

"So good to see you both," he said. "Come in and meet everybody. Toby will get you a drink."

They were fourteen, in all, and William knew most by reputation. There were Cilla and Arthur Fenton, Cilla being a ubiquitous presence on the charity circuit. Her picture was featured frequently in the New York Social Diary, sort of an online society scoresheet. She'd clearly had work done, thought William, but the elegant contours of her face possessed a subtlety that Darlene Buckets lacked. Morgan French, his fellow board member, and his wife, Lily, were there too.

"If everyone would indulge me," said Casper, "I have a little dinner-party tradition. If you would follow me." He led them through several rooms until they came upon a glass door with a silver metal frame. "I confess to being somewhat of an oenophile, and this is my pride and joy, my wine cellar— although I suppose it's hard to call it a cellar on the seventeenth floor!"

Casper laughed heartily. William wondered how often Casper had made that particular joke.

"It has three chambers, each cooled to a temperature optimized to suit its occupants. The first is forty-four degrees, which is for the dryer whites. The second is fifty-five degrees—that's for more full-bodied whites, the lighter, fruitier reds, and the ports. There's also a rare prewar Georgian amber that I was quite lucky to source. And the third, ah, well, that's where the really good stuff lives, the full-bodied reds. Let's enter, shall we?"

Casper pressed his thumb to a sensor. "Biometrics," he said. There was the sound of metal gears and then a satisfying click, signaling the entrance to Valhalla was now open. He opened the outer door and several guests made their way in. The individual chambers were too small for the whole group, so they took turns. The first, largest chamber, had a small table that could seat four. "My sanctum sanctorum, if you will," said Casper with a chuckle. "Norman Mailer and I once got completely snookered in here."

William, feeling like an urban spelunker, went deeper with several of the other men. Ellie held back, unsure of her place. This seemed like a man thing. She was more curious that a facility like this existed in a New York apartment than she was about the actual wine. From deeper, she heard their voices. She couldn't make out what they were saying, but the murmur of admiration was unmistakable. After a time, William emerged. "Casper is asking for you," he said.

"For me?"

"Yes," said William.

"Why?" asked Ellie

"He wants to show you his collection, I guess. Just go."

"But I don't know anything about wine."

"Just say how wonderful everything is. Please, just go."

Ellie left the dry whites, passed through the light reds, finally reaching the third chamber, deep, dark reds. It was dimly lit, and only Casper remained, which immediately made Ellie nervous. Looking around, she saw hundreds of dusty bottles, hibernating in the quiet.

"Ellie, excellent! As the bride of our guest of honor, it falls to you to choose what we'll drink tonight." His words were muffled in the enclosed space.

"Oh, gosh. Are you sure you don't want someone else? Will knows a lot more about wine than I do," she said.

"An ingénue, perfect! I value an innocent palate—no preconceptions! But not to worry, I've made this easy. I've opened two bottles that will pair equally well with tonight's meal and poured a taste of each into these glasses. I will let you make the final decision."

Ellie looked with trepidation at the two glasses set on the small table. "I didn't know there were going to be any tests, Casper."

"Ah, but there are no wrong answers. One of these is a 1988 *Domaine de la Romanée-Conti*, one of the finest Burgundies known to man. I bought a case at auction recently for 180,000 pounds. An outrageous price, but we all have our weaknesses, wouldn't you say? The other is a 1990 *Christophe Musigny Grand Cru*, an exceptional Pinot. Can't quite recall what I paid for that one, but these were among my first significant purchases."

"Which should I try first?"

"You decide. And as I said, you can't go wrong."

Tentatively, Ellie picked up the first glass and brought it to her lips.

"No, no, take your time! Swirl the wine a bit and then raise the glass to your nose. Consider the various notes. The subtexts, if you will."

Ellie did as Casper suggested. She wasn't sure about any subtexts, but it smelled nice enough. Then she gave it a taste. "It's good," she said.

"It had better be! All right, now do the same for the other."

While this was happening, William, consumed with curiosity, made his way back into the second chamber and was looking through the glass door into the third. What the hell was going on in there? Their backs were turned to the entrance so he couldn't quite tell.

Ellie repeated the brief ritual and then tasted the second. "That's nice too," she said.

"Good good. So tell me, which shall we enjoy with dinner?"

"How about this one," said Ellie, raising the glass still in her hand.

"Ah, the *Romanée-Conti*. Excellent choice!"

Casper reached for the wine rack and pulled a bottle. "It's been waiting decades for this very moment. Here, I'll let you present the first bottle."

"Casper, I—"

The bottle was dusty. As Casper handed it to her, it slipped through her hands, smashing on the stone floor. The *Romanée-Conti's* nearly four-decade journey from France to Casper Stein's wine cellar ended as a crimson puddle slowly seeping across the floor.

DINA CAMPBELL

Across town, Dina Campbell stared at her laptop, willing the ideas to come. A weekly deadline didn't seem too onerous to an outsider, but it crept up on you like a silent cat.

Dina was a journalist, her specialty longer-form features, mostly on city culture, which the *Daily Sentinel* ran every Sunday in its expanded edition. She was expected to come up with something fresh each week. *God*, it was so much harder than people thought.

Perhaps another glass of Chardonnay.

She walked to her refrigerator, which was mostly empty. Some condiments, several boxes of wine, and some leftover Chinese takeout—the clichéd refrigerator items of any single New Yorker.

Home was a small one bedroom on the Upper West Side. Filling her glass two-thirds of the way, she returned to her desk, now occupied by her rescue cat, Ruth, named for one of her personal icons. Dina shooed her off. Why she got the thing, she still didn't know. She didn't even like cats.

Dina was working on a piece about climate-conscious food choices (vegan, basically) but knew it was journalistic piffle. It lacked *edge*. Staring out the window didn't help much either. Once, she could just make out part of the Hudson River between two other buildings. Now, she looked about twenty feet into a brick wall. Somehow a developer bought the air rights next door, and her view was now of the brick backside of a condo tower. Her apartment was rent-controlled, though, so she could never leave, even if she could afford to, which she couldn't.

The wine made her maudlin.

It wasn't supposed to be this way. Once, she'd been a rising star, a wunderkind fresh from the *Crimson*, her ticket stamped for glory. She was hired by the *Times* and sent to their Paris desk, a plum post. There, while covering other assignments, she met some Muslims, the North African ones who lived in the notorious *banlieues* neighborhoods. She painstakingly cultivated relationships with them, earning their trust, sensing it would pay off.

She saw they were a community adrift, allowed to live in France but never allowed to *be* French. France bitterly held on to its cultural self-image, and American notions of a "melting pot" were not welcome. Post-9/11, she could feel tensions rising as the police turned a sharp eye toward the Muslim populace, or in some cases, did the opposite, and allowed *banlieues* to virtually self-govern, looking the other way as they adopted Sharia law.

In the sweltering summer of 2005, things boiled over. Police, responding to a theft report, arrived to arrest several Muslim boys who may or may not have been responsible. Two of the boys tried to hide in a nearby power substation and were electrocuted. The electrocution caused a broad power outage, which, combined with the news of the boys' deaths, sparked widespread rioting. One group attacked a police station, forcing an evacuation. The subsequent occupation of the station lasted over two weeks.

The occupiers wanted someone to tell their side of the story, and, through their network, they reached out to Dina. She was invited to the station and ended up embedded there for the duration. She dictated her daily dispatches over her cell as all power to the station remained shut. It made her feel like a war correspondent.

The series, appearing under her byline, won wide notice for its compassionate portrayal of a desperate generation of young Muslims who saw no future for themselves. It scored her a Front Page Award, presented to women for achievement in journalism.

If she were giving an honest account of things, it was that moment, that exact moment, when she flew to New York and rose to the podium to accept her award, that was a personal high-water mark after which began a slow, almost imperceptible slide to her current station, writing for a tabloid from home, not even possessed of a desk in the newsroom. The *Times*, cutting back like everyone else on international coverage, let Dina go a year after the award. Americans were too insular, and frankly too *stupid*, her editor told her, to care about what happens in France or Yemen or Indonesia.

After Paris, Dina moved around the globe with the wire services, accepting diminished assignments in various posts. Her career had the patina of glamour but also made it impossible to keep relationships. She dated a series of men over the years, most from her own profession. They tended to be khaki-vested rakes, and far too impressed with themselves. There was an Al Jazeera correspondent with a fetish for mild bondage and later a CNN anchor whose amorous attentions could only be consummated while watching tapes of himself. That one had lasted a few months.

Perhaps more than anything, the pay was a source of resentment. This was not a journalistic phenomenon limited to Dina, of course. The rise of the internet also gave rise to thousands of news sources, most of them free. This led to a steady decline in compensation for the entire industry, at least relative to other professions. That there was still a constant supply of overeducated Ivy League trust-fund brats and idealistic fourth-estate groupies willing to work for next to nothing didn't help.

The worst part, for Dina, was tracking the careers of her Harvard classmates, particularly the ones she considered idiots, those eating club swells. Many had pursued investment banking or private equity and were making millions, and for what? Moving money around? Others had gone into law. She'd once respected that cadre, at least somewhat. Many had gone to law school with high ideals. But then they ended up at Skadden or Cravath or Simpson Thacher just doing the bidding of the bankers—and still making millions, although perhaps a few less than their overlords.

More than a few had houses in the Hamptons, and Dina burned with resentment that she would never be more than a weekend guest, deposited there on an overcrowded Jitney because she didn't own a car.

Dina's salary from the *Sentinel* was $90,000—to be exact, $91,250. She'd gone to *Harvard*, and here she was, on the wrong side of forty, making ninety-one thousand and two hundred and fifty goddamn dollars. Surviving in New York on that was next to impossible. Her banker classmates could take the free-market bullshit they spouted and shove it out their asses because it clearly wasn't rewarding intelligence the way it should.

Dina looked down from the brick wall and noticed her wine glass was empty. She got up to take the six steps necessary to get back to the kitchenette. Perhaps inspiration would be found there. At age forty-eight, it felt like it was all just slipping by. She needed something to rescue her from the bitterness that was becoming all-consuming.

She needed a story.

A big one.

HERE'S TO INCLUSIVITY!

O
h, my God!" cried Ellie. "I am so sorry!"

William, who had heard the crash, burst through the door to the wine cellar. "What happened?" He saw a horrified look on Ellie's face.

"It slipped," said Ellie. "It's my fault."

"Do you have any idea what these wines cost!" cried William, his face suddenly the color of the *Romanée-Conti*.

In fact, she did. "Casper, I don't know what to say."

Casper had, briefly, looked shocked but had composed himself, summoning a look of genial contentment. He was a man of means, after all, and this was merely a bottle of wine. "Not to worry, my dear," he said, touching Ellie's arm. "I have eleven more. That should get us through dinner!"

Dinner was set formally around a large table that easily fit all fourteen of them. Reflecting the season, the table was scattered with gourds and low crystal bowls of orange and red flowers. The place cards looked like autumn leaves, perhaps sugar maples, given their vibrant color. A calligrapher had carefully painted each leaf with the name of a guest. Ellie touched hers gently.

"They're spun sugar," said Missy. "Aren't they to die for?"

"Incredible," said Ellie, able to think of little else than the bottle of *Romanée-Conti* splattered all over the cold stone floor of Casper's wine cellar.

"I suppose we could all take a bite for dessert!" said Missy, laughing heartily at her own cleverness.

"So, everyone," said Casper. "In case you don't already know, William here is our new star, rising like a meteor!"

"Meteors fall, darling," said Missy.

"My wife, the language nazi. You know, William, I got an interesting call the other day from an old friend of mine, Oliver Stone. You know, the director?"

"Of course."

"It seems he wants to do a *Wall Street* sequel. This one will star George Clooney."

"That man is so handsome," cooed Cilla Fenton. "We saw him in Lake Como last year and I nearly fainted. He's even better looking in person!"

"Yes, well, Oliver had an interesting request. The two of them want to come by the company to do some research. William, I thought you might help with that."

The table reacted with a collective gasp of excitement.

"I think I could fit that in," said William, grinning.

"We take care of our winners," said Casper. "You know, I was a young buck at Salomon when Tom Wolfe came to research *Bonfire*. He sat right there at our trading desk for three days."

"Casper, you never told me that," said Missy.

"Didn't I? Well, true story."

"Were you a 'big swinging dick'?" asked Cilla, cheekily.

"I believe I'll take the fifth. But those were certainly different times. Believe it or not, we had the occasional stripper on the trading floor on someone's birthday."

"Seriously?" asked Lily.

"Absolutely true. I suspect they'd haul you off in leg irons today. William, David tells me you've joined the board at Lenox. Good for you. I served on that board for a bit myself. Wonderful school."

"So wonderful," said Missy.

"I just joined. I guess they were hard up."

The others laughed dutifully, only Ellie knowing that it wasn't in William's nature to be self-deprecating.

"I hear your annual Halloween party is fabulous," said Cilla. "I'm so jealous."

"It's our big fundraiser, yes. Ellie's been working hard on it."

Big events required immense behind-the-scenes planning, and Lenox Hill's Halloween Ball was no different. There was the selection of the caterer (everyone always had a favorite), the rounding up of silent auction items, the decorations . . . The list was endless. Ellie was on a committee of eight women who'd been making the arrangements for some months. Tizzy was on the committee too.

"Tell me, Ellie, what will you and William go as?"

"Well, last year's theme was nursery rhymes, so we were Jack and Jill, but this year it's monsters. We're thinking zombies."

"How fabulous," said Missy. "Not to change the subject, but someone told me the Gottfrieds transferred their daughter to a public school because their consultant told them she'd have a better chance at Harvard. Can you imagine?"

"The Ivies don't worship the independent schools the way they used to," said Morgan French.

"But isn't the education better?"

"I think that's beside the point now."

"You know," said his wife, Lily, "I hear some of the girls are going to these Russian math classes in Brooklyn."

"What? Why?" asked Missy.

"Well, I guess the Russians are good at math. I don't know. They're certainly good at chess. But everyone thinks *that's* their ticket to college."

"What's wrong with the math at Lenox?" asked Casper.

"Well, nothing, I suppose. But the Russians are apparently quite advanced."

"Actually," said Morgan, "it's becoming a bit of an issue. It used to be that outside tutors were used when your kid was falling behind. Now they're used to get ahead of the other kids."

"And what's wrong with that?" asked Casper.

"It's not that *I* think there's anything wrong with it, but there are those that do. Padma's not very pleased, to say the least."

"Okay, now I'm thoroughly confused. Why wouldn't she be pleased if her students are excelling?"

"The thought is that your child should not be allowed to race ahead because it might damage the others' self-esteem."

"Well, I can see that," said Cilla, looking for a way into the conversation.

"And worse," continued Morgan, "it can lead to inequitable outcomes."

"Of course it can!" bellowed Casper. "If you work harder, you get ahead."

"Certainly," said Morgan. "But the other side of the argument, if one were to make it, is that the inequities tend to fall along racial lines. Not everyone can afford outside tutors. It's a concern."

"We must do what we can for the less privileged," said Cilla. "That's what I always say."

The rest of the table agreed, making Cilla particularly pleased with herself.

"And did you all hear the latest talk?" asked Lily. "Lenox might be welcoming a transvestite into the senior class, or so I'm told. I think it's just wonderful."

Ellie saw that the mommy grapevine was doing its thing. She'd heard the same rumor from Tizzy and had asked Will about it. He hadn't known anything but mentioned that Padma had hinted at a new development. But he was sure she'd never make a decision like that without fully informing the board ahead of time.

"Fascinating. Is this true, William?" asked Casper.

"I'm afraid it's not something I can talk about."

"Oh, come. We're among friends."

"Sorry."

"Well, *I* think it's important to be inclusive," said Arthur Fenton.

"So important," agreed Cilla.

"Though, Lily, I don't think *transvestite* is a term we can use anymore," said Missy.

"Oh, really? Why not?"

"I'm not sure, but our own daughter upbraided me for using it recently."

"I think you say *cross-dresser* now," said Cilla.

"Well, good for Lenox for welcoming a cross-dresser, then," said Lily.

"Actually," said Morgan, "I don't think that's right either. That refers to a man who dresses like a woman, you know, like a drag queen. This person is transitioning."

"Good God, I'm confused."

"Well, David, what do we call this person?" asked Casper.

"The proper term, I believe, is *trans female*."

"And this is a boy who is now a girl?"

"Correct."

"But if she's in the process, as it were, and not fully transitioned, is that still correct?"

"I suppose," said Missy, "that it all depends on what she's hiding under those tartans. William, one more chance. Care to weigh in?"

"Most definitely not. This conversation terrifies me."

Everyone laughed at that, although Ellie knew it was probably literally true. She also knew he was playing coy so he didn't have to admit he had no inside knowledge.

"Well, the times, they are a-changing, aren't they?" said Casper. "And it's incumbent on us old farts to keep up."

"Is it?" asked Ellie, bringing the conversation to a temporary halt. William shot Ellie a look, shocked at her intemperance. It struck Ellie, though, that single-sex schools played an important role and that the arrival of a transitioning teenager would be disruptive. "You can't change your chromosomes," she said.

"Well, we do what we can," said Cilla. "And I, for one, applaud the board for being so open-minded."

"Yes, that must have been one lively board meeting!" said Missy. She raised her glass of *Romanée-Conti*. "I propose a toast. To inclusivity!"

"And George Clooney!" cried Cilla.

Ellie's conversational indiscretion was quickly forgotten.

CASPER'S PRIZE

After dinner, Casper suggested they all go see his latest acquisition. "Bring your port," he said.

"Oh, Casper, I'm sure people don't care!" said Missy, waving at her husband dismissively.

"Well, I'd *love* to see it," said Cilla.

"I'm sure we all would," said William.

"You know," added Missy, "Casper jokes he's made more money on his collection than on Wall Street!"

"It just might be true," said Casper, laughing.

Following the Steins, the group walked through the living room and into a study. William pulled Ellie aside before entering.

"What the hell did you do?" he said in a hushed voice.

"What?"

"The wine bottle!"

"I—it was an accident."

"Christ, El, how could you be so clumsy?"

"I don't know. It was dusty. It slipped. I feel awful. At least Casper doesn't seem too upset."

"This dinner was supposed to be about me and my future, and now all anyone will talk about is how you dropped a wine bottle that probably cost more than our X7."

"William, all I can say is that it was unintentional. I don't know what to do other than apologize. Maybe we should pay for it."

"I already offered, and he wouldn't accept." William turned and marched off to join the others. Ellie hung back for a minute to compose herself and then followed.

The study was a darker, masculine room with walls in chocolate lacquer. It looked like the paint had been applied with sponges rather than brushes. Missy called it *peinture à l'éponge*, and the other women seemed to know what that was. Apparently, it was a technique that was both time-consuming and expensive.

Despite the warm fall weather, the fireplace was stoked and burning. Its flames danced, and the wood snapped pleasingly. The bookshelves stretched high enough to require a ladder, one that moved around on a little track. The shelves were lined, mostly, with biographies and history-related nonfiction. William removed a random volume and pretended to study it. The title was *Understanding the British Empire*, by Ronald Hyam. It looked unread.

Over the mantel hung Casper's prize.

"It's a Basquiat," he said, proudly.

It was a face, or perhaps an African mask, rendered abstractly in vivid colors, mostly reds, browns, and black. Like a cartoon figure but one from a nightmare. The brush strokes were aggressive, imprecise, almost violent.

"Missy thought the colors picked up the walls of the study, so she said we had to have it," said Casper.

Ellie didn't know much about art, but knew enough to know the painting probably cost in the many tens of millions. She had to admit it was striking, if a bit angry looking. Perhaps that was the point?

"You know," continued Casper, "Basquiat sold his first painting to Deborah Harry—Blondie, remember? Two hundred dollars. If she still has it, it's worth a hundred times whatever she made selling records. They say artists of color are the best investment right now, but I just buy what I like. If it goes down in value, I can still enjoy it on my wall."

William wondered if Casper Stein had ever bought anything that had gone down in value.

The group moved closer to the prized Basquiat, leaning in and squinting their eyes ever so slightly, making sure that the Steins knew their new acquisition was properly appreciated. Casper took the opportunity to touch William by the elbow. "Might I have a word?"

GET IT DONE

Casper and William walked through the labyrinthine apartment until they reached an empty bedroom, which William thought odd. It put him on edge. Was he about to get reamed for Ellie's clumsiness?

"Casper, I am so sorry about the bottle."

"The wine? Don't give it another thought. I've already forgotten about it. Besides, we have other things to discuss."

Other things?

Casper removed two cigars from the breast pocket of his blazer and offered one to William. "Ellie hates smoking," William said.

"Well, it's just us boys, isn't it? This is the only room in which Missy allows me to indulge."

"In a bedroom?"

"We have nine, and I don't think we've ever used more than three. I doubt Missy's been in this one for over a year, so it serves its purpose."

Casper then pulled out a small box of four-inch wooden matches. He removed one and drew it slowly along the strike plate. The match flared and he brought it to the cigar, puffing a few times to draw the flame. It was a ritual he clearly enjoyed. Then he handed the matches to William, who repeated the process.

"This is a spectacular apartment, Casper," said William, to fill the silence. "You must be very happy here."

"Yes, well, it's been a good home, and it works for us, but none of the new money wants to live in a co-op anymore. Too many restrictions, and no one wants the hassle of going through a board. It's all LLCs now."

"I find that hard to believe."

"It's true enough. The layouts don't work for people either. The sequestered kitchens, the maids' quarters—it's just not how people live anymore. They want open-plan lofts downtown, in buildings with private gyms and Pilates trainers."

The conversation paused as Casper took another long draw on his cigar.

William did the same, having run out of things to say. Finally, Casper broke the silence.

"Tell me, you're close with Cy Birdwell, aren't you?" he asked.

Cy Birdwell was one of Bedrock's outside board members.

"Cy? Yes, very. We went to school together."

"Yale."

"Yes, and Andover," William added.

"Ah, I didn't realize. Good good. But you're close."

"Yes, very. Why do you ask?"

"Well, the situation's a bit awkward, and I thought, given your long relationship, you might be able to help with something, something that happens to be very relevant to you. To all of us."

"Of course," replied William, now burning with curiosity.

"As you know, we like to think of ourselves as a firm which embraces the right values. That's why we call them *Bedrock* Values. We don't shy away from doing the right thing—ever. Happily for us, doing the right thing also happens to be quite profitable."

"I came to Bedrock for those values, Casper. I had a lot of options."

"I know you did. You've always been one to stand up for what's right." By this, Casper meant William could be reliably counted on to do what was necessary to get ahead. "Which is why I need a favor," he added.

"Of course. Name it."

"We just got an RFP."

Casper let it hang there.

"We get those all the time."

"True, but some are more important than others." He paused, considering his words. "This is all strictly confidential. It will be on your desk Monday, but I wanted to bring you in the loop now."

He was in the loop!

"This one's from CalPERS."

William understood immediately.

CalPERS stood for the "California Public Employee Retirement System." It managed the retirement money for 1.5 million state employees. With close to half a trillion in assets, they were the largest pension plan in the US and one of the biggest pots of money in the world. An *RFP* was a "Request for Proposal," meaning Bedrock was being invited to compete for some portion of that half trillion.

"It's a five-billion-dollar ESG mandate," added Casper. "As you know, since ESG is part of your group's mandate, it has been an area of immense profitability for us. Hell, we practically invented it."

ESG stood for "Environmental, Social, and Governance." It was a type of investing that weighed societal factors, such as the climate crisis, when making investment decisions, rather than prioritizing potential returns alone. It was something Bedrock fully embraced, especially since the firm was able to charge higher fees for the service, sometimes as much as 40 percent higher. William's team spent much of their time reviewing companies' compliance rates with ESG "best practices," although in reality, claiming the ESG imprimatur involved little more than avoiding fossil fuel companies.

The mandate would be a huge coup for both the firm and himself. That ESG returns had lagged the market in recent quarters was beside the point. Their job was to give the market what it wanted, and what the market wanted was absolution for its sins.

"As you well know," continued Casper, "CalPERS is one of the few big pension funds that has eluded our grasp. Our institutions are both progressively minded, so I believe our values are aligned, but we've never quite crossed the finish line. I *want* this."

"What does this have to do with Cy?" asked William.

"So, here's the thing . . . the RFP. There are diversity questions."

"That should be good for us!" chimed William.

"Yes, normally, one would think."

Indeed, Bedrock had been the first Wall Street firm to have a full-time diversity, equity, and inclusion director, and they had aggressively hired African Americans and women for years. Their board had four female members, two of whom were black, and one other black male member as well. One of the women came to board meetings in a Kente cloth. They even had a Muslim gentleman who flew in from Qatar once a quarter. William heard he'd been coming to meetings wearing a keffiyeh.

"But this one has a question about our commitment to *LGBTQ*," said Casper.

"That's good, too, isn't it?"

William could think of several gay employees off the top of his head.

"The question concerns LGBTQ *board* members."

It suddenly dawned on William why they were having this clandestine conversation. "Ah, Cy . . ."

"Yes. Cy. He *is* gay, is he not? I mean, we all just assume . . ."

Cy Birdwell was the founder and CEO of Birdwell Apparel, a multibillion-dollar clothing company, and it was widely understood that he was gay. But Cy never talked about it. If he had relationships with other men, they weren't public. Nor, thought William, did Cy "act" gay (a thought for which he immediately admonished himself. Of *course* there was no one way for a gay man to act! Although Cy did dress awfully well . . .).

"Honestly," replied William, "I'm the same as you. I've known Cy since sophomore year at Andover, and I've never known him to date a woman, but I can't say I've seen him with a man either. Keeps his own counsel is how I would describe him. Wonderful guy."

"The best!" agreed Casper. "And a valued member of the board." Casper drained the last bit of port. "So, you see there's a box we need to check if we're going to win this mandate."

"You need to confirm that Cy is gay," said William.

"Yes, or at least one of those letters. I believe the RFP says LGBTQ *plus*, so there's a lot of room in there. Maybe he's just *a*sexual. That falls under *plus*, doesn't it?"

"I confess I'm a little hazy on the plus part," said William. "Maybe we could Google it."

"Yes, but regardless, since this RFP falls to your group, and since you have a long history with Cy . . ."

William swallowed. "You need *me* to confirm Cy is gay. Or . . . plus."

"Precisely."

William paused, considering the implications. He may have even gulped. "But what if Cy is staying in the closet for a reason? Some people still do that—at least, I think they do."

"Not sure why. They're the damn toast of the town these days."

"I suppose that's so," said William, careful not to say anything that could be conceived of as political.

Casper took another draw of his cigar. Exhaling, the air filled with purple smoke. "We think you're executive committee material, you know. After all, you're now running our fastest-growing department."

Careful not to let his expression change, William let the words flow through him like manna. He had assumed as much, but this was the first time the words had been spoken. And by *we*, William knew Casper meant *I*. Casper was master of all he surveyed at Bedrock. For a brief moment, William allowed himself to wonder what units in 740 might become available in a few years' time. To hell with Pilates.

There *had* to be some other way to get this done. He was about to say as much when Casper pointed his cigar at William and took a firmer tone. "But people at that level, they *get things done*, William. I want that business, and I won't let some goddamn box on some goddamn form screw things up. If they want to know who we're fucking, we're going to tell them who we're fucking. Is that understood?"

William was taken aback but made sure to not let it show. "Yes, of course."

"Get it done," said Casper Stein.

EASTER

William shut the door to his office and clicked the Zoom link on his computer. Instantly, he saw the other members of the Lenox board populate their little boxes.

"Ah, there's William. I think we're all here. We have some exciting news. Padma, the floor is yours."

"Thank you, Duncan, and thank you all for taking time out of your busy days at the last minute, especially so soon after the last meeting. You recall I hinted I may have some exciting news about our diversity efforts, and I know rumors are going around. I am delighted that I can now share that news. But before I do, let me just say I am so proud of the support this board has given me in these efforts. You are all heroes."

"Nonsense, Padma," said Duncan. "We are merely your humble servants."

"And I, yours, but I'm about to burst. As of Monday, we will be welcoming to the fold our first transgender student, Easter Riddle. Easter, who joins the senior class from Jacqueline Kennedy Onassis High School, is a transgender female and her pronouns are she/her/hers. I'd like to thank Barbara, who helped us recruit Easter—and speaking on behalf of the teachers and administrators here at Lenox, we couldn't be more thrilled."

"So overdue!" crowed Darlene Buckets. She and perhaps one or two others clapped, which came off somewhat awkwardly on Zoom.

"I'm sure everyone realizes that this is groundbreaking news for Lenox," said Duncan. "Special thanks to Barbara and of course Padma for making this happen."

So, Duncan knew, and as did Barbara Selkirk. How many others? wondered William. From the looks on their faces, none. He was curious that they would do something like this without broad board approval. There were long-cherished beliefs about the value of a single-sex education. Girls, for instance, were thought to be more confident and engaged without the distraction of boys in the classroom.

But this wasn't a boy, exactly, and he knew better than to say anything. This was a *fait accompli*, and he had no interest in self-immolating on a Monday morning Zoom call.

Padma continued, seizing on her momentum. "I will be adding an item to next quarter's board meeting: a motion to change our name to simply the Lenox School. It seems more appropriate."

Now a name change?

This was a lot to digest, thought William. Others seemed equally circumspect, to the extent he could read them. He supposed Casper (and Bob Dylan) were right: Times *were* a-changing. Who was he to question it? He was only one voice, after all, so what could he do? He remained silent, as did the others.

Except . . .

"Hi, everyone." It was Pete Richmond.

The fool! thought William. After raising concerns at the last meeting about the goblin girl, William knew Pete was on the verge of being labeled "a problem."

"I apologize, but could you remind me? Transgender female . . . Is that a girl who is now a boy, or the other way around?"

"It is a female who has transitioned from being a male," answered Padma.

"And when did . . . Easter . . . make this change?"

"Easter began her transition this summer."

"So brave," offered Darlene.

"Truly," added Padma. "And a seminal moment for our community."

"Yeah, that's something," said Pete. "I don't want to be overly focused on details, or anything, but . . . how will Easter dress, exactly? Will this require another dress code exemption?"

"Oh, no, not at all," said Padma. "She will wear the traditional tartan."

"But, under the tartan . . . does he—"

"*She*," admonished Padma.

"She . . . does *she* have, you know, uh, equipment?"

"I beg your pardon?" demanded Padma, leaning into the camera.

"I was just thinking there are locker rooms and such, so . . . isn't that . . . relevant?"

William, grateful that anyone other than he was pursuing this line of questioning, watched as Pete Richmond stood there on the edge of a metaphorical cliff, only the slightest breeze required to send him crashing to the rocks below. Padma was the image of restrained rage.

"Uh, never mind. It's great news," he said, edging back from the precipice.

Duncan Ruggles looked nonplussed by all this, but he recovered quickly. If he had a core competency in life, it was not making waves. He let the matter drop, as did the rest of the very, very successful people in their little Zoom boxes.

TRAINING DAY

"William, tell me you didn't forget," said Ellie. "I *texted* you."

"Forget what?"

"You know, the school thing. Read your texts! *Anti-racist training.* It's mandatory for parents this year."

"Oh, right." William sighed. He vaguely remembered seeing a text come across his Apple Watch, but he'd been in a meeting and didn't want to be caught looking. Later, he forgot. Now, just home from work, he wanted nothing more than a tumbler of bourbon. "Why don't you go ahead and attend for both of us?" he said. "You can tell me all about it later."

"Nooo you don't, chief. Both parents are required to go. Apparently, it's in the new enrollment contract. And you're on the board! How would it look?"

He knew she was right. That bottle of Woodford Reserve would have to wait.

They gathered in the gym where rows of folding seats had been set up in a semicircle. The parents were abuzz with the news of Easter, and more than one came up to William to congratulate him.

"Thank you," he said. "We thought it was time."

As they settled into their seats, William whispered to Ellie, "We're not expected to *speak*, are we?"

"You tell me, mister board member," said Ellie. "I've never done one of these either."

Padma Minali strode into the room with Shonda at her side. She was well turned out in her usual St. John suit, this one an elegant emerald green with a black collar and waistline. It wasn't to her taste, but after coming East she decided it might be wise to fit in with the East Side mommy aesthetic. And while she could afford Chanel on her $1.6 million salary, she didn't think it politic, so she chose St. John, a similar but more affordable designer.

"Good evening, and welcome. I'm so glad everyone could make it tonight. We're here to collectively reaffirm our school's commitment to anti-racism, and I'm just so proud of everyone in the room. In fact, let's start by giving ourselves a hand just for being here. Can we?"

She began to clap, and the parents dutifully followed suit. Padma frequently did this, made some benign comment that you couldn't disagree with and then asked everyone else for affirmative consent. It was a tactic she'd learned years before, basically training an audience to agree with her. It was remarkably effective.

"Next to me is Shonda Gomez-Brown, founder of Equivision, the renowned diversity consultant. We are proud to be partnering with Equivision in this effort. I could go on forever about how excited I am right now, but why don't I turn things over to the expert? Shonda, welcome."

"Thank you so much, Padma, and hello, everyone. Please just call me Shonda, I use she/her/hers pronouns, and I am so pleased to be your facilitator and cultural strategist tonight. And what exciting news about Easter Riddle, no?"

More clapping. William noticed a few seemed determined to clap more loudly than the others. The women, mostly.

"Before we get going, it is our shared responsibility to recognize those who came before, so I'd like for us all to acknowledge the land we occupy tonight, land which is not ours. We will observe a moment of silence and during that time I'd like you to think about the dignity of indigenous peoples and recognize both their role in providing us with the life we all enjoy today but also the injustices that were visited upon them. We recognize that our country was founded by genocide, and by acknowledging this we are providing healing to the land and recognizing a more honest history of our nation."

"The land has feelings?" whispered the man sitting just in front of them to his wife. Ellie knew them a little from school soccer games—Leslie and Bob Ellison. Their daughter and Ginny played on the team together.

"Shut up," said his wife, Leslie. "She's doing a land acknowledgment."

"A what?"

"Shut *up*."

"Here in Manhattan," Shonda continued, "we recognize the Lenape tribe, as we speak their name. *Lenape*."

There was an awkward silence. Were they supposed to repeat the name?

"*Lenape*," said a few parents. One or two practically shouted the word.

"Lenape," repeated William and Ellie, quietly, their volume perfectly matched. Neither had heard of the Lenape until that moment.

"Each of us," continued Shonda, "must consider the roles we have played in perpetuating this genocide as we continue our mutualized efforts toward decolonization. And now we will observe a moment of silence."

The room quieted, some parents looking down, as if preparing to receive a sacrament. William was tempted to steal a glance at his phone but was smart enough to understand the optics if anyone noticed.

"Thank you," said Shonda. "It's important that everyone feels free to express themselves tonight. This is a safe space, so I encourage you all to really *lean in* to the discussion. Ask questions! That sound good?"

William thought Shonda seemed preternaturally cheerful for someone referencing genocide.

"Okay, to begin, I'd like to go around the room and have everyone tell us how they identify. If you haven't done this before, I'll go first to show you how. My name is Shonda, I am a differently abled, postcolonial Indo-Caribbean American, and I was assigned female at birth."

William wondered about the "differently abled" part. Shonda had walked into the gym just fine, although she was on the heavy side. Was it a weight thing?

"Now, Padma, why don't you go?" suggested Shonda. "And I'd like to encourage everyone to stand up as they share with us."

"With pleasure," answered Padma, standing. "My name is Padma. I am a single, cisgender, Indian American. I come here by way of the rainy Northwest, and I have a serious coffee addiction!"

"Excellent," said Shonda.

A tentative hand went up from one of the patents. "Uh, cisgender?"

"I can see we're leaning in already!" Everyone laughed, perhaps a bit nervously. "*Cisgender,* which is sometimes referred to simply as *cis,* means your gender identity conforms with the biological sex you were assigned at birth."

"So, normal?" ventured Bob Ellison.

A few people gasped, and Leslie Ellison lowered her head to her hand. With every ounce of strength she could muster, Shonda forced a smile. "We don't like to use the term *normal,*" she said. "Would anyone like to tell me why?"

An enthusiastic mom raised a hand. "Because that would imply that others were *ab*normal."

"Very good. We're all here to help each other learn."

"So, gender and sex are different?" asked someone else.

"I see we have some work to do!" Shonda laughed, as if to imply she was kidding, which almost all in attendance knew she wasn't. "But that is correct.

Sex refers to your biological state. *Gender* is how you personally identify, how you feel. Your *truth*. Would someone else like to go?"

A woman in the front raised an eager hand. She was part of a same-sex couple that the school had recently all but recruited. Standing, she said, "My name is Nova. I am a genderqueer mother with androgyne tendencies. I am white and recognize my privilege and historical role in oppression. My pronouns are they/them/theirs."

"Thank you so much for that, Nova. Let's just move on from left to right, shall we?"

The next person, looking a bit flustered, said, "Oh, gee. I guess I'm white, also, and cis, was it? And I'm a mom too. Is that good?"

"Very good. There are no wrong answers here. Next parent?"

This went on for some time, moving across the rows. Parents at Lenox were, for the most part, extremely successful, and began to treat the exercise—as they did all group activities requiring their participation—as a de facto competition. The self-identity testimonies got longer and more elaborate as Shonda moved through the semicircle, particularly as white parents considered their own role, conscious or otherwise, in oppression of the *other*.

There were a number of side discussions. For instance, they learned that BIPOC did not, generally, include Asians and subcontinental Indians, which Ellie found confusing. These groups were designated as "white-adjacent."

As for the white parents—the majority of those in the room—they learned that they were supposed to be "allies." Allies were those who actively worked for social justice. They were also warned, however genially, about the shame of being mere "optical" allies. The examples given were people who dutifully posted black squares on Instagram on Juneteenth or put BLM placards in their front yards but little else. Such virtue signaling, absent of demonstrable action, was looked upon with disdain.

Ellie guessed at least half the room fell into that category.

As the parade of testimony wore on, it was the Ellisons' turn. Leslie Ellison stood, holding a Stanley water bottle with a dusty blue PBS logo. Many of the mothers walked around with these all day, sipping from them like pacifiers as they got in their ten thousand steps. Leslie gave a fairly standard answer, adding a little bit at the end acknowledging her shame that so many of her race voted for Donald Trump, even if she hadn't. Several people looked disappointed they hadn't thought of saying that.

"Well spoken, and thank you so much for sharing that." Turning to Leslie's husband, Shonda said, "And you, sir? How do you identify?"

"Bob."

"Yes, Bob, it's a pleasure to make your acquaintance. How do you identify?"

"As Bob."

"*Honey . . . ,*" said Leslie Ellison.

"Bob, is there anything else you can share?" asked Shonda.

"Like what?"

"Well, I think you've heard what others have said. Perhaps you could share something about your race?"

"Like what?"

"Well, what is it?" asked Shonda.

"I thought there were no wrong answers? I identify as Bob."

"It's not that simple," said Shonda. "Others see your race, and it affects how they think and how they interact with you."

"But you didn't ask about what others thought, you asked what *I* thought."

"Robert, *stop!*" hissed Leslie under her breath. "You're embarrassing us." She turned to Shonda. "White, we're *white.*"

"The point of this exercise," said Shonda, "is that we all have identities that are central to our lives, and certain aspects of those, skin color, for instance, we can't control or ignore. Perhaps, Bob, something else. How about your sexuality?"

"Are you seriously asking me who I like to sleep with?"

"Not necessarily. Some people don't like to sexually partner with anyone. We call these asexuals, and that's a perfectly acceptable lifestyle. There's no judgment here."

"Well, *I* necessarily think it's none of your business."

"Women, he likes women!" blurted out an exasperated Leslie. "We have children, for God's sake."

"Why don't we move on?" suggested Padma. Was she flustered or was that a flicker of annoyance?

A full twenty minutes later, the identity roundelay got to the back row and the Sandersons. It was William's turn, and as a board member, he had to keep up appearances, no matter how much he'd rather be home with that glass of Woodford. He stood.

"My name is William. I am white, a father, and cisgender. I am fortunate to have come from a privileged background, and I fully acknowledge the benefits of my upbringing, as well as the struggles of others who aren't as fortunate."

"That was excellent, William, thank you," said Shonda.

William sat, and everyone turned to Ellie. She was the last person to identify. Standing, she thought, *Well, here goes. . . .* "My name is Ellie, and—"

Just then a bell went off. During the day, it signaled a change of periods, but it was programmed into the evening.

"I'm so sorry to cut you off, Mrs. Sanderson," said Padma, "but we promised everyone we'd stop at ninety minutes, and I'm sure you'd all like to get home and have dinner. I don't know where the time went. I guess we'll just have to have another session! Next time we'll do a deep dive on what it means to be an *anti-racist.*"

They filed out with the others. Had Ellie been saved by the bell? She wasn't sure how she felt, and she hadn't been entirely sure what she was going to say. She wasn't deliberately hiding anything, but she could see it might be looked at that way. Well, that wasn't her problem.

Was it?

In the hallway, Ellie saw one of Zoey's teachers from a couple of years back. She couldn't quite remember which subject. English maybe? After a time, annual curriculum nights and teacher conferences became something of a blur. She smiled and said, "Oh, hi, Ms. Stokely, how are you?"

Ms. Stokely offered an odd expression and said nothing.

"It's Ellie Sanderson, Zoey's mom?"

Ms. Stokely's expression turned distinctly cold, the corners of her mouth turning for the floor. "Hello," she said, before spinning around and walking off.

"What did you do to piss *her* off?" asked William.

"Nothing, I don't think. How odd."

"Who was that, anyway?"

"One of Zoey's teachers from a couple of years ago," said Ellie.

"Well, you must have done something. Or not done something. She wasn't exactly friendly."

BACK IN THE GAME

Dina Campbell had just submitted her latest story, a piece on the growing friction between bikers and joggers in Central Park.

Jesus, what utterly disposable tripe.

Then, as she always did when she finished a piece, she went to the fridge for some Chardonnay. Another one, anyway. Franzia, out of the box. The little tap at the bottom made it so easy. She told herself it was late, and it would help her sleep. She was already in her pajamas—or, rather, she was *still* in her pajamas. She hadn't bothered to change out of them all day.

Dina swirled the wine in her glass, as if at a tasting. She stared at the brick wall outside her window. Not quite tired enough to crawl under her bed's down comforter, she decided to check her email one more time. She saw one from her editor, Leo Belkin. He'd probably just glanced at the biker–jogger piece and knew what shit it was. She opened it and began reading.

> A friend of mine sends his girls to Lenox Hill. It's a fancy East Side school.

Leo must think she's an idiot. *Of course* she knew what Lenox Hill was. She'd known a couple of Lenox girls at Harvard.

> Just heard they've got a new kid there who's trans. A boy, or I guess a girl now. Name is Easter Riddle. Do something on this. Something nice. 800 words. Our youth demos blow.

A puff piece, in other words. Normally, Dina would have pushed back. Leo should know she was above goddamn puff pieces. Well, she wasn't, but *still.*

The trans angle was intriguing, though. That space was white-hot, particularly with the awards people. Maybe there was more than just a single piece in this. Maybe she could get tight with the trans community the way she'd done a lifetime ago with the French Muslims.

Maybe, maybe . . . Her instincts said this might be worth it.

Dina knew, though, that she had to tread carefully. The trans community could be quite militant if you put a foot wrong. She'd already seen a couple of journalists burned at the Twitter stake for relatively mild transgressions, and God forbid you suggested that trans women shouldn't play women's rugby or whatever.

J.K. Rowling had stepped on that mine, although she had a billion dollars or so to soften the blow. Missteps like that would be career enders for the likes of Dina, who most definitely did not have a billion dollars. (In fact, right now she estimated her net worth to be approximately the same as her last pay-check, which, after federal, state, and city taxes was a shade less than $2,500.)

Not that she had any issues with the trans folks, no! She admired their bravery! She expressed this thought clearly in her head, almost as if she were being monitored for possible thought crimes.

Something came to her. What was that thing she'd noticed the other day on the Harvard Alumni Facebook page? She navigated there on her laptop and scrolled down a bit.

There it was.

Harvard was hosting a conference on trans rights for Transgender Awareness Month in November. That was a little soon, but maybe if she did this piece on the Riddle girl, she could wrangle a slot on a panel. She hadn't been to Cambridge in a while. It might be fun to drop in at the *Crimson* building on Plympton Street.

She clicked like and then, realizing that most people didn't click through to see who'd done that, added a comment for good measure.

So proud of my alma mater!

Time to dig in. She did a quick search for Lenox Hill and found that someone named Padma Minali was the head of school.

She would start there.

THE BOX

Like human resource departments everywhere, the one at Bedrock Capital had grown enormously over the years. It now occupied almost a full floor of their headquarters in the famously sleek Seagram Building, exactly twenty blocks downtown on Park from 740. Bedrock had leased progressively more floors over the years and now occupied the top twelve.

HR departments, once known simply as "Personnel," were once famous corporate backwaters, places where careers went to die. This began to change in the 1960s, when the Equal Pay Act of 1963 and the Civil Rights Act of 1964 compelled companies to focus on government compliance, which was time-consuming and paperwork driven.

More recently, "diversity, equity, and inclusion," or DEI, falling under the aegis of HR, had become an industry unto itself, requiring companies to staff up. Backwaters no longer, HR departments now had power commensurate with their growing head count.

Bedrock, which extolled its virtue as an enlightened company at every opportunity, added DEI staff by the dozen.

And so it was that a DEI issue had William riding the elevator down to the twenty-eighth floor. William made his way to the corner office, where Tanya Rose, the HR head, lorded over the department. Her door was open, but he knocked to get her attention.

"William, how nice of you to pay a visit," she said, tongue firmly in cheek. Generally, executives at William's level still made HR come to *them*.

"Always a pleasure, Tanya. I come bearing gifts." He produced a small tin of chocolate chip cookies, which he happened to know Tanya loved. "Ellie made them herself."

Which was true, if by making them, one meant taking cookies Ellie bought at the Levain Bakery out of their original box and putting them in a tin William found in the kitchen. Ellie had firmly opposed the idea. "I can actually bake cookies, you know," she'd said.

But Levain cookies were the best, and William didn't want to wait until after the weekend when Ellie had time to bake. This would be an awkward conversation at best.

Tanya opened the tin and immediately tried one, moaning in delight. "Oh, dear God, that's good. Whatever you want, the answer is yes."

William flashed his most charming smile and then waited the ritual out, taking notice of Tanya's diploma, framed on the wall. Bennington College. That was in Vermont, wasn't it? Or maybe in the Berkshires somewhere.

"So, to what do I owe the pleasure?"

"I've got a bit of a delicate situation, and I'd value your advice."

Translation: *If this goes south, I want company.*

"Go on."

"We just got an RFP, a big one, from CalPERS."

"Okay . . ."

"There's this question in there, an LGBTQ question."

"Yes, we're seeing more of those. For every nepotism case or Ivy League lax bro you guys force us to hire, we now need to find an LGBTQ applicant, or a BIPOC candidate, or we don't meet basic RFP requirements."

"Yes, well, this one is a bit different. They want to know how many LGBTQ board members we have."

"LGBTQ *plus*," admonished Tanya. "The RFP was specific."

"Plus, right." William wondered absently which one Tanya identified as. Then, a thought: "Wait, you've seen it?"

"Of course I've seen it."

"Oh. I didn't realize." *Did she actually get it before he did?* "Okay, good. I've already got my team working hard on it, and you probably know what a big priority this is for the firm."

"I'm aware. CalPERS has eluded us for years. So what's your question?"

"We have a board member that fits this category."

"That's not a question."

"Yeah, so can I just . . . check the box?"

"Sure, why not?"

"Oh, good, because we're quite confident."

"Wait, you are *confident*?"

"Yes, quite confident."

"Will you please tell me what that means?"

"Yes, well, we're all pretty sure. So, we can just check it, right?"

"So, you don't *know*."

"Well, we do know, basically, but it's not like he wears a sign around."

"But you don't know. William, I'm going to pretend I didn't hear any of this. You want to *lie* on an RFP? A company with our reputation? Not exactly *Bedrock Values*, is it?"

"Well, there *was* Stockhausen . . ."

Tanya made a face, making it clear she didn't share William's amusement. "Don't even go there," she said

When Bedrock first decided to go public, they applied to the Nasdaq exchange, but the listing questionnaire necessitated that Tanya send out her own questionnaire to all employees. Nasdaq wanted numbers on gender identities, and it was the first time anyone had seen the requirement. People weren't yet used to the new way of things.

Rob Stockhausen, then a fairly junior VP, took it on himself to go to the Nasdaq website and look up their gender definitions. It said a man was someone "assigned male at birth."

Annoyed, reasoning that his gender wasn't a conferred status decided by some goddamned doctor or whatever, he decided he wasn't a male, at least not by *Nasdaq*'s definition. He checked the "nonbinary" box, figuring it was as good as anything else. Stockhausen's answers were aggregated with all the others by a computer and sent to Nasdaq.

When Tanya found out what Stockhausen had done, she was furious, and hell-bent on firing him. First, though, she had to do some damage control with Nasdaq, so she quickly called her counterpart there. Before she could say anything, she was being congratulated for Bedrock's enlightened approach to business. They were apparently the first company to check that particular box. The listing sailed through.

Tanya found a way to terminate Stockhausen a year later when the firm managed to recruit a legitimate nonbinary applicant. Rumor had it Stockhausen was a real estate broker in Pennsylvania now, but his story lived on.

"There will be no more Stockhausens," said Tanya. "Not on my watch."

"Right, sorry. But this is different. It's not a . . . misstatement. Again, pretty sure. Odds are very strong it's the case. At worst, it would be an innocent mistake, but I doubt even that. I've known the person in question for years."

William had come to regret overstating to Casper how well he knew Cy Birdwell. While it was true they'd known each other, technically, for decades, they'd never been as close as he'd let on. Cy had been into the a cappella scene at Yale and, rumor had it, Bones. Their circles were very different. They'd say hi at the Gotham, or reunions, that sort of thing. William wasn't sure at all what Cy's circle was anymore, or even if he ever knew, which was the heart of the problem here.

Not that he had any issue with anyone's circles. Certainly not! He tried his best to appear open-minded. Circles got political, and politics was something William didn't give much thought to. The intellectual capacity was there, sure, but the work at Bedrock was demanding. Ever since he started there, he made the decision not to use much cognitive energy on anything else. His politics, to the extent he had them, had evolved into the bland middle, perhaps even center–left, a calculated position meant to offend the fewest people. That his career had led him to politically tinged sustainable investing was less driven by principle than financial opportunity mixed with the convenience of occupational virtue.

William's parents were staunch Republicans, of course. This had led to the predictable motions of rebellion as a teen. He experimented with drugs, pushed the boundaries of Grafton's dress code, and so on. He was suspended more than once from the Dunehaven Club, one time for depositing a golf cart in a pond and another for having sex one night with a date in the club pool— well, not a "date," per se, more a random local girl he'd picked up earlier at Stephen's Talkhouse. Who knew Dunehaven had security cameras?

By the time William got to Yale, it was the nineties, and the campus had turned hard left, fully embracing "political correctness" (the term predating "woke"). Campus culture had also turned on legacies, and in particular on those exhibiting the kind of privileged upbringing William had enjoyed.

Loathe to be seen in this light, and knowing what political ground Yale's fairer sex occupied, he marched against the World Trade Organization, joined Food not Bombs, at least for a while, and generally wore an antiestablishment persona on his sleeve for all to see. He made it a point to leave his Andover T-shirts at home, although he never did throw them out.

When people asked him where he went to college, he always said, "up in New Haven," giving him, he believed, the patina of cultural modesty while knowing full well people knew exactly what he meant. It never occurred to him that, to some, saying Yale in code made him sound even more elitist.

After graduating, William decided he needed a break. He used money from his trust and spent a few months chasing a girl, which involved following Phish on tour and living like a vagabond out of Kerouac. For a while, this made him feel very literary, until it didn't. Camping in tents and being around smelly, stoned people 24/7 soon grew old. Some calls were made, and

William found himself shaven, in a suit, and working as an analyst at Morgan Stanley.

He'd known, on some level, that it was always going to be this way. He told his old activist friends it would be easier to change the system from the inside. He saw them less and less over time, and eventually not at all.

The work at Morgan was mind-numbing, mostly involving spreadsheets and PowerPoint, and the hours were nightmarish. But the money was good, and he noticed that people treated him differently when he told them where he worked. Morgan Stanley was at the top of the investment banking heap.

After two years, William followed the path of least resistance, enrolling at Harvard Business School. He let his hair grow back to make sure others knew he wasn't a creature of the establishment. Then, the true prize: an associate position at Bedrock, the fastest-growing investment shop on the planet.

His hair was cut.

The one truly honest act of rebellion in William's life was to marry Ellie. She was an outsider, a thoroughly middle-class military brat, and not at all a White Anglo-Saxon Protestant. But it wasn't an act. There were any number of toothsome prospects around Dunehaven that would have enhanced both his social status and his personal balance sheet, but he chose the outsider from Anywhere, USA. He truly loved her.

His parents initially sniffed at the news, which pleased him, but they came around. It was hard not to like Ellie. He wasn't sure what he thought would happen when Ellie's parents first visited East Hampton, though. He'd brought them to Dunehaven for lunch and sat right in the middle of the beachside dining area. He was mildly disappointed when nothing did.

As for the matter that brought him this day to Tanya Rose's office, he fully supported anyone's right to be in whatever "circle" they wanted. More accurately, he just didn't care. It wasn't worth the time it took to think about. The most important thing was to navigate this dilemma with the least possible harm to his career, and that's why he needed cover.

Unfortunately, Tanya wasn't giving it.

"You *cannot* check that box," she said. "You need confirmation."

"For the sake of argument," said William, "I mean, just hypothetically, if we *did* check the box, and we were, however unlikely, *wrong*, how would CalPERS even know? The form doesn't ask *which* board members are gay, and even if it did, how could they ever confirm it? And anyone can *say* they're gay, can't they? I mean, *I* could say I was gay."

"You're not on the board."

"I know; it was just a hypothetical."

"Are you?"

"Am I what?"

"Gay. Because it would help our numbers, but I'll need to reclassify you in our records."

It didn't seem like Tanya was joking.

"*No!*"

William immediately realized his denial was a little too vehement, making it seem like the notion offended him.

"I mean, uh, I mean . . . no. You know I am married with two children, right?"

"Which would prove what?" asked Tanya.

"Just, *no*, I'm not. Can we get back to the issue, please?"

"You were the one who said you were gay."

"I did not! For God's sake, Tanya . . ."

"Just messing with you, William. You seem wound a little tight. You know we have counselors on staff. . . ."

"Back to our board member, if we may. What about privacy? Is this a HIPAA issue?" William was hoping the questionable ethics of checking the box without confirmation were less questionable than the ethics of violating someone's privacy.

"HIPAA only concerns medical records. There are no medical records involved here."

"Okay, what do you suggest I do?"

"Well, how badly do you want this business?"

"Badly."

"Okay, so he's your friend, right? Ask him, get confirmation, check the box. Or don't, but then you're not checking that box. Like I said, no more Stockhausens, not while I'm still here."

"So, the cookies . . ."

"Nice try," said Tanya. She brought another to her mouth and took a bite. "Damn, they are good, though."

William realized he'd made a terrible mistake coming here, believing HR could help him navigate this. If he'd just checked the damn box in the first place, no one would ever have known.

Five billion dollars.

He was going to have to make a date with Cy Birdwell.

THEY'VE BEEN DISAPPEARED

Y
ou remember my parents are coming this weekend," said Ellie. It was a statement more than a question.

"What?"

William was dressing for work, making final adjustments on his $400 Hermès tie. There, a perfect Windsor knot. (While most firms had long gone business casual, Bedrock still presented a traditional image. Casper thought it exhibited the requisite probity.)

"I *told* you this. It's Grandparents Day on Monday."

"Where're we going to put them?" asked William, having completely forgotten. Ellie detected a slight sigh.

"What do you mean, where're we going to put them? We'll double up the girls, like last time."

"I know, it's just that it always seems so cramped when we have guests. Christ, I can't wait to move."

"William, these aren't random houseguests, these are my parents. And they'll only be here for a couple of days. It's Grandparents Day on Monday at school, and they also want to see a show while they're here."

The Lion King, no doubt, William thought. "Is Curtis going to wear that uniform around? I mean, he's retired."

"And what if he does? He's proud of it, Will."

William planned to work this weekend. It wasn't that he disliked Ellie's parents—they were perfectly nice. It was more that they shared little in common, and he found them, well, *dull.* Conversations always seemed forced. William had little interest in hearing about the military or the prosaic happenings in whatever flyover place they were living in now, which, he vaguely recalled, was Kansas. They still lived near Fort . . . Ah, he couldn't remember.

God, and they'd probably want to talk about pickleball again. William remembered how disappointed they'd been that Dunehaven had no pickle courts. One of the most beautiful grass tennis clubs in the world, and they'd brought pickle paddles! The ridiculous *thwock-thwock-thwock* of pickleballs would not now nor ever be heard within the club's confines.

The Maddoxes had arrived in East Hampton that summer in their enormous RV. Curtis had recently retired and bought a used Winnebago. He and Ada started traveling in it a few months a year with a long list of sites to check off. William was pretty sure the world's largest ball of twine was on there somewhere. Probably Dollywood too.

Back when they still stayed at his parents' place, he recalled how the ungainly Winnebago drove up Further Lane like an enormous brown-and-beige shoebox, taking up residence in the Sandersons' driveway for an entire Memorial Day weekend. Jack and Bitsy remained polite but were privately horrified, fretting that the vehicle was fully visible from the road. Bitsy came down with the vapors and rarely ventured downstairs.

"I'm off," William said, heading for the door. "I've got a squash game and drinks after work, so I'll be a little late for dinner."

"Okay, I'll keep it warm. Oh, and remember we're also meeting with Ginny's college counselor tomorrow. You'll need to take an hour or two off."

That, I didn't forget, thought William.

Later that morning, Ellie's cell rang.

Tizzy.

She sounded breathless, which she often did when possessed of some morsel of gossip. "Did you hear about the Ellisons?"

"The Ellisons? No, what?" asked Ellie.

"They're not at Lenox anymore."

"What? Why?"

"Wendy Parker told me that the school didn't think they were a good fit, and no one's even seen either of them since. There one day, gone the next. Poof, disappeared! It's like an episode of *The Sopranos!*"

"But just like that? In the middle of a school year? Where are they going?"

"Maggie deVeaux thinks New *Jersey*. Can you imagine?"

Ellie wasn't sure why that was difficult to imagine.

"Well, you have to admit," Tizzy continued, "they weren't trying very hard. To *fit in*, I mean. That whole scene in front of Padma the other night at the anti-racist thingy. What was that about?"

"Oh, come on," said Ellie. "That can't be the *only* reason."

"It's hard to say, but Brie Summers thinks they weren't giving much, either, and the development people were getting frustrated, but you can't squeeze blood from a stone. Or is it water? Anyway, she thinks they were down to their last million."

Ellie was acutely aware that living in Manhattan and sending your kids to private school was an expensive life, one they were lucky to have. But she found the comment off-putting. A million dollars still made you a millionaire.

"I didn't know them well," she said, "but they always seemed nice. Why would they just decide to suddenly leave like that? That seems drastic."

"You're not hearing me. They were forced to walk the plank at the point of a cutlass. A figurative one, anyway. That's how it goes when you go out of your way to make waves. I'm sure they were in violation of that new parents' contract. Did you guys look at it? I hear Padma wrote it herself."

"I remember signing it and chasing Will down to sign it too. I don't think we paid much attention, though. It came with a thick packet of other materials, and besides, you *have* to sign it, right?"

"Exactly. Sign it or go somewhere else, somewhere that has its own contract that says exactly the same thing. They all force you to toe the company line or vamoose."

"There's always public . . . ," offered Ellie.

"In New York? What, are you kidding me? My Rick would have a heart attack, and so would William."

"I suppose. Will once commented how much he believed in public education. I guess not so much for Sandersons."

"Well, what did you expect when you married a certified northeastern WASP?"

"He didn't come with a handbook."

"Well look, Lenox is just so fabulous, and we're all lucky to be there. I'm sure they know what they're doing," said Tizzy.

Ellie paused. "I hope so," she said.

EXPOSURE

Head down and on her way to class, Clover Hunt, she of the goblin-core, was intercepted by Celeste Burdick, Padma's executive assistant. "Clover, if you have a minute, Ms. Minali would like to see you in her office."

"I'm supposed to get to math class."

"I'll inform Mr. Christos that you'll be a little late."

Clover thought about asking whether she was in trouble but figured she'd find out in a few minutes anyway.

Entering Padma's office, she saw Easter Riddle, the new trans girl in twelfth grade. She was already seated, along with several other adults, including Hyphen Lady. The others she didn't know.

"Okay," said Padma. "We're all here. Clover, I assume you know Easter?"

"We haven't actually met."

"Oh, well now you have. And these are her parents, Mark and Shannon Riddle."

Clover offered a hand, but Shannon bypassed it, going right in for the hug. "It's *so* great to meet you, Clover, we've heard *all* about you."

Clover stood there, stiff as a board. She wasn't a hugger.

"And this is Dina Campbell. Dina is a top reporter for the *Daily Sentinel*."

"Clover, I am so thrilled to meet you."

Thankfully, Dina Campbell was only interested in a handshake. Clover was suspicious as to the source of her newfound popularity.

"Everyone, please, sit, be comfortable," said Padma. Clover noticed that Easter looked as uncomfortable as she felt. "Dina reached out to me with an interesting idea, and I'd like her to share it with us. Clover, I did try to get your parents here, but it sounded like they were busy."

Too busy for whatever bullshit this was, she thought.

"Dina, why don't you explain," Padma suggested.

"Well, first I'd like to say it's a great pleasure to be here. I've heard so many wonderful things about Lenox Hill over the years, and I had a few Lenox friends at Harvard. Thank you for agreeing to hear me out."

Clover didn't remember agreeing to anything but was impressed how quickly Dina managed to work Harvard into the conversation.

"The *Sentinel* is very impressed with what all of you are doing here, about how you're breaking down barriers. You're setting an example the public should know about, so the *Sentinel* would like to do a piece. We heard about you, Easter, and when we reached out to Padma, we learned about you, Clover, and your own fascinating identity. There might even be a series in this, perhaps where the *Sentinel* follows both your journeys as you break barriers. What do you think?"

They all looked with anticipation at the two girls, neither of whom spoke immediately.

"Easter, honey?" said Shannon Riddle.

"I don't know . . . ," she said, in a voice that still sounded like a teenage boy's, although with the singsongy quality of someone seeking a higher register.

"We talked about this, honey, and what a wonderful opportunity this is. Dina, I want you to know that Easter's father and I are committed allies." Her shirt read Trans Rights Are Human Rights in big wavy letters.

"Absolutely," said Mark Riddle. "Easter has our full support."

Easter's parents had started an Instagram account called @SpringtimeForEaster that had made the rounds, both at school and in the LGBTQ+ crowd. It was a near daily testimonial about how excited they were as they chronicled Easter's transition. One day they filmed themselves helping Easter shop for her new clothes, the next it was the rainbow-colored cake they made for Easter's birthday. Their account was up to one hundred thousand followers. Clover heard the Riddles were dining out all over town on Easter's transition. Rumor had it Netflix had approached them about a real-time docuseries.

"And may I just add how positive it would be for the school to send out a message like this," said Padma. "We've been retooling our curriculum to reinforce the importance of gender self-realization. We call it a *culturally relevant pedagogy.*"

"And that's just one of the many reasons we feel so safe here," said Shannon.

"I'm grateful to hear that. Easter, what do you say?"

If Clover thought Easter looked horrified, she wasn't far off. It was hard enough going through the estrogen, the hormone blockers, the new school, and everything else that came with a transition without being so public about it. Not everyone wants to go full Dylan Mulvaney. She had tried repeatedly to get her parents to dial it back, but it was hard when they seemed so happy.

"Uh, I don't know. . . ."

"You don't know what?" asked her dad.

"It seems like a lot," she said, her voice tremulous.

"You'll be famous!" said her mom.

"I don't know if—I mean I think . . . I think I might be happier if I could have a lower profile?"

"Honey," said her dad. "This is a very gracious offer that's being made, but more importantly I think you know how important it is for you to set an example for your community."

"And Ms. Minali is asking this as a personal favor," added Shannon.

Easter didn't respond, hugging herself with her arms. Her mother stroked her back. "It will be fine, you'll see." Turning to Padma, she said, "You can count on our support."

"Wonderful," said Padma. "Easter, we're so proud of your decision. Clover, can we count on you as well?"

"Well, I think it would be hard to top Easter. I mean, her story is so compelling and all. I think she can carry the banner for both of us."

"Clover," said Dina. "You have my personal promise that I will treat this story with the kindness and respect you both deserve. I don't think you'll be disappointed."

"Yeah . . . I think I'm good. The thing is, my, ah, community prefers a lower profile. We all agreed at the last meeting."

"You have meetings?"

"Oh, sure."

"You know, I'd really love to learn more. Do you think I could come to one of your meetings? I would just be a fly on the wall, I promise."

"That is *certainly* an intriguing idea, Dina, but there's a strict no-outsiders policy. Our people tend to be very private. Kind of a goblin . . . core . . . thingy."

"Fascinating," said Dina.

"Perhaps you might make an exception this once, Clover?" suggested Padma.

"Hey, you know I'd love to, but I don't make the rules."

"Who does?" asked Dina.

"You know, our . . . leaders."

"Are we talking about the eco-sexuals or the goblincore?"

"Oh, well both. There's a lot of overlap, as you might expect." It occurred to Clover that she should speak the language. "It's very *intersectional*." That got understanding nods, but she really wanted this meeting to end. "Ms. Minali, is it okay if I get to math class? I don't want to fall too far behind. . . ."

Padma sighed. "Fine, but are you sure you won't reconsider?"

Hard pass, she thought.

"I think I'm good. Easter here can carry the torch." Her olive-green Crocs squeaked as she walked to the door.

Later that day, Clover ran into Easter in the hall. "Hey," said Easter.

"Oh, hey there, fellow poster child."

"Funny."

"If you say so."

"So, I was just wondering. How are you liking things, you know, here?"

"Fine, I guess. No complaints. You?"

"I don't know. The same, I guess." Easter looked suddenly downcast. "I wish I could be like you."

What, wondered Clover. A *girl*?

"What do you mean?" she asked.

"That *Sentinel* thing. I should have said no like you."

"So why didn't you?"

"It's just . . . I'm under a lot of pressure, you know?"

"From . . . your parents?"

"My parents, the school . . . everyone."

"Oh."

"I feel like everyone's watching me."

"Well, they kind of are."

"You must feel the same way."

Clover didn't, really. Or maybe she just didn't give a shit. "Yeah, I guess," she said.

"Listen, can I get your cell? Maybe we can talk sometime."

Clover had little interest in sharing stories of mutual oppression with this boy-turned-sort-of-girl but decided she was in no position to judge. And there was something sad about Easter. She hadn't had time to make friends at Lenox, and Clover had the impression she might not have any at all. Real ones, anyway.

She gave Easter her cell and they went off to their respective classes.

SO, YOU'RE GAY, RIGHT?

W illiam's squash game was rusty, and he lurched awkwardly around the court. He'd never gotten any higher than JV at Andover and later the Yale team was beyond his reach. Foreign players dominated the collegiate ranks by then. Cy Birdwell, on the other hand, had played varsity at Andover and cracked the starting nine at Yale, playing as high as seven.

They'd run into each other frequently at the Gotham Club, vowing to play sometime, but never quite getting around to it. Cy was duly surprised when William called. He agreed to play, but it wasn't much of a game, the points lasting however long Cy wanted them to last. William was in excellent physical shape but couldn't match Cy's level of skill.

"I surrender," said William, after getting thrashed 3–nil. "How about a beer?"

"Okay, but loser buys," answered Cy.

They showered just off the expansive, oak-paneled locker room. The walls were covered in plaques listing past squash and billiards champions. There were daybeds there, too, and retired members, covered in bath sheets, often napped on them, perhaps following a good steam. Generations of hangovers were dealt with in such ways.

Back in jacket and tie, William and Cy made their way down to the second-floor bar. William was hoping things were quiet, but they weren't. Post-work gatherings were in full swing, younger finance swells bellying up to the bar and older members at tables taking in the day's *Journal* or *Sentinel*.

William ordered a Harp Lager draft and Cy an Aperol spritz, something William was surprised the Gotham bartender had the ingredients to make. Grabbing a plate of the club's traditional cheddar and Ritz crackers, Will steered Cy to a booth in the room's far corner, one he'd secured while Cy was in the men's room. To say he was dreading the conversation was an understatement, and he really didn't want any eavesdroppers.

Earlier in the day, William had spotted an article in the *New York Times*.

It was in the sports section, and William thought it might be useful. The club always had copies around and he'd placed one, folded to the right page, on their table, as if some prior occupant had just left it there.

"God, I'm still sweating," William said, sitting. "You've still got game."

"Thanks. I like to stay in shape," said Cy.

William took a slug of his beer, unsure how to proceed. Perhaps some small talk. "So," he said, "how's the rag trade?"

"Oh, you know. People have to wear clothes no matter what the economy's doing."

"Still, it seems you guys really nailed the whole *athleisure* thing during Covid."

"Thanks, but as much as I'd like to say we anticipated the outbreak of a once-in-a-century global pandemic, sometimes you just get lucky."

"Well, here's to luck then, not to mention Birdwell's stock price."

They clinked glasses.

William took an extra-long sip, willing the beer to quell his anxiety.

It wasn't working.

Shit, whatever, here goes. He nodded down at the paper. "He's very brave, don't you think?"

"Who?" asked Cy.

"Da'vonte Shanks."

"What about him?"

"He came out," said William. "That's quite a thing to do, being in the NFL and all, don't you think?"

Da'vonte Shanks was a cornerback for the Cincinnati Bengals and was being widely praised for coming out in the testosterone-charged world of the NFL. The commissioner even said he wished the NFL could attract more LGBTQ athletes.

"I suppose," said Cy, looking away absently, saying nothing more.

Shit.

After that dead end, the conversation flagged and they talked about nothing in particular, and then nothing at all. Cy was always very private, which made William's agenda that much more excruciating.

Thankfully, he broke the silence. "Know what that is?" Cy was motioning toward a wildlife print on the wall. The club had an extensive collection.

"Some turkeys?" answered William.

"It's a *rafter* of turkeys. That's what a group of turkeys is called. A rafter."

"Is that so."

"Yes, did you know there are literally dozens of names for groups of species? Some are quite commonly known, like a pack of wolves or a swarm of bees, but then there are others that are obscurely entertaining, like a shiver of sharks or, my personal favorite, a parliament of owls."

"Huh," was all William could manage, frustrated with the conversation's direction.

"Why do you suppose that is?" asked Cy.

"Why do I suppose what is?"

"Why so many collective nouns for essentially the same thing? Why a murder of crows, a smack of jellyfish, or even an embarrassment of pandas when one word would suffice for all?"

If Ellie were here, she would immediately label Cy as among the curious. "An embarrassment of pandas? Seriously?"

"Yes, that's the word."

"Huh. Is this something you think about a lot?"

"No, but I was wondering about it recently, so I did a bit of research."

"And?"

"I was unable to find an answer, so it remains a delightful mystery. My theory is that it was some eighteenth-century zoologist with a sense of whimsy."

"Maybe," said William, who wondered how many straight men would use the word "whimsy" while simultaneously enjoying a drink with the word "spritz" in it.

He discreetly glanced at the clock over the bar. He was hungry and dinner was waiting at home. Time to steer the ship of this conversation around. "So," he said, "Ellie was asking about you the other day."

"Really?" Cy couldn't remember the last time he'd seen Ellie Sanderson.

"Sure. She bought some of those yoga pants of yours and said 'Hey, we just made Cy a little bit richer!'"

"Well, you can thank her for me."

"Will do. You know, we had our twentieth recently."

"Congratulations," offered Cy.

"Thanks."

Then conversation died on the vine, yet again. *Time to cross the Rubicon.* "So," said William, "seeing anyone these days?"

A look crossed Cy Birdwell's face, one William couldn't quite decipher, although it didn't strike him as a look beneficial to his cause.

"On and off," answered Cy.

Aha!

"Hey, that's great. Maybe the four of us should go out one night."

"Maybe."

"So, is it anyone I would know?"

"I doubt it."

William sighed. He would have made a terrible detective.

"Well, let me know if you guys have a free night."

"I'll do that," said Cy, sounding like he'd do anything but. "You know, this has been great, but I really need to get going. Thanks for the game. And the drink." He got up to leave.

"I'll walk out with you," said William, still determined to be the good soldier.

They left the bar, descended the grand marble staircase with the regal red carpet runner, and made their way out the revolving door onto Park Avenue, where the fall weather was still mild.

"Thanks again, Will. Enjoyed it." Cy raised his arm to hail a cab. William saw his executive committee seat slipping away.

"Uh, Cy?"

"Yes?" Cy replied, still scanning Park Avenue for a free cab.

"Can I level with you for a moment?"

"What is it?" asked Cy, lowering his arm.

"You know, Casper was just saying the other day what a valued member of the board you are."

"That's very nice of him."

"'I don't know what we'd do without Cy,' he said."

"I see. Is that really what you wanted to tell me?"

Cy was not an idiot.

"Well, not exactly, but he did say that!"

"Again, that's very nice, and it's my pleasure to serve, but I really have to go."

"Wait! It's just that we got this RFP the other day, from an account we've been chasing for years. I shouldn't say who, but it's a big one, and they're a nut we've never been able to crack. It's almost embarrassing. I mean, we're just about the biggest money manager in the world, so it's a glaring miss. Casper is beside himself to win this business."

"And what does that have to do with me?" asked Cy.

"There's just this one question on the RFP that's a little tricky. You know, they ask all sorts of things these days, and not just about performance. All sorts of things. The business is really changing, you know, and in very positive ways, if you ask me."

"William . . ."

"Okay, okay. So, this one question . . ." William swallowed, wishing he could be anywhere else on the planet but standing outside the Gotham Club with Cy Birdwell. "They want to know if any of our board members are LGBTQ plus. You wouldn't happen to know, would you? I mean, it would just be so helpful."

William could swear that, ever so briefly, Cy's eyes flashed with anger, but it was over before he could be sure. "And why are you asking *me*, William?"

"Uh, well, it's important, and you know the board pretty well. Plus, we're friends and we've known each other forever."

"The last part is true, but we've never really been friends, have we?"

"Of course we have!"

"Sorry, William, I can't help you."

Cy flagged a passing cab and was gone.

William crossed Park Avenue back to the Seagram Building and rode an empty elevator back up to his office. There, he typed the password into his computer and typed in another password to open up the CalPERS RFP.

Dinner could wait.

YALE COULD BE A REACH

We're having trouble with the essay."

"William means *Ginny* is having trouble, Ms. Collins," said Ellie.

"Of course. And please, call me Faith."

Faith Collins was Lenox Hill's longtime college counselor. Padma was also in attendance, which wasn't typical, but board members were always handled with care. This consideration pleased William.

"Yes, well, they all expect you to write about some terrific adversity you've overcome," continued William. "What's Ginny supposed to say, that she had trouble skiing the Back Bowls?"

"What William is trying to say, Faith, is that while we're proud we've been able to give our daughters a good life, it now seems like a liability we need to apologize for."

"Oh no, of course not."

This was an increasingly common source of angst, Faith knew—the challenge of growing up in a life without challenges. Most Lenox girls took for granted the kind of privilege that few in the world could even imagine. Most had second, even third, homes. Private jets were common.

"I mean look at this," said William, handing some papers over to Faith. "How are we supposed to deal with this?"

It was a printout of the Yale application. William had highlighted an essay question that read:

The lessons we take from obstacles we encounter can be fundamental to later success. Recount a time when you faced a challenge, something that really forced you out of your comfort zone. How did it affect you, and what did you learn from the experience?

Both Padma and Faith knew this was a question, in one form or another, on almost every college application. In 2023, the Supreme Court outlawed affirmative action in the famous Harvard case but left the door open a crack by allowing universities to consider candidates' "life experiences." Admissions departments could decide for themselves just what constituted the life experiences they were interested in. For many, this meant soliciting personal tales of victimization at the hands of a discriminatory culture. Affluent white applicants gainfully tried what they could, documenting every mildly unpleasant interlude in their own short lives, real or imagined.

This approach was of little use to the Sandersons.

"Our consultant says to write some nonsense about when Ginny's aunt died, but Ginny hardly knew her," said William.

Faith winced at the reference to an outside consultant. College counseling was *her* job, but increasingly parents were hiring expensive outsiders as well, ones who promised the moon and seldom delivered.

"We hear many of them are test optional now," said William. "Ginny got a . . . What was it, Ellie?"

"A 1520."

"But now, what? It doesn't matter?"

"Will, I'm sure it matters," said Ellie.

"I think I know what's going on," continued William. "Get rid of objective standards and it frees schools to pick kids just on their personal narratives. Am I wrong?"

He was not, thought Padma, but she could hardly say so, nor could she admit she was entirely in favor of the shift in policy.

"I think it's fair to say that colleges are just trying to do what we here at Lenox Hill have done, which is to make opportunities available to a wider set of applicants," she said.

"And we're all for that. We all value diversity. But I'd also like my daughter to get into Yale."

"Then you'll be pleased to know that Yale, and a few others, have reversed course on the SATs."

"Oh . . . good."

"Well, about Yale . . . ," said Faith.

Here it comes, thought Padma. She was perfectly happy to let Faith be the heavy. William Sanderson needed to be managed. Truth be told, she was kind of looking forward to it.

"We've been actively talking to the admissions people up there," continued Faith. "You should know it's going to be a tough year."

"Ellie, in case you don't speak *college counselor*, that's code for get out your checkbook and start adding zeros."

"I'm sure Padma and Faith are doing their best," said Ellie, disquieted by William's aggressive posture. It wasn't like him.

"William, Ellie, you are both highly valued members of the Lenox community, and you've been quite generous," said Padma. "I should ask, though. Is Yale officially Ginny's first choice? She hasn't shared that with us."

"It . . . will be," said William.

"Honestly," interjected Ellie, "my own view is that there are lots of places she could be happy. The Ivies aren't the only schools that offer a good education. And it seems like there's some new protest up there every week. Is that really a healthy environment?"

William looked at her as though she had two heads. "They're just being engaged citizens. It was like that when I was there too. Smart kids are like that."

Ellie did her best not to wince.

"Ginny's our daughter," she said, "and if she decides on Yale then that's what I'll support. But it's her decision, right, Will?"

He paused for just a moment. "Right," he said, finally.

"And naturally, we'll do what we can," said Padma.

"When did this process become such an ordeal?" said William. "I don't remember this from my day at all."

"It's true, things have evolved," said Padma, trying to project a warmth she decidedly didn't feel. "This can be as stressful for parents as it is for the kids. Sometimes even more so."

"Ginny's great-grandfather was class of thirty-eight. She's fourth generation."

"Yes, we know, and Ginny is a wonderful applicant. But these matters of legacy, well, they just don't carry the weight they used to."

"So, for the sake of argument, what's the number?"

Padma, of course, knew what William meant but decided to play dumb, even though she'd specifically prepared for this moment. The cynicism of the conversation carved tiny pieces out of her soul. "The number?" she asked.

"Yes, the number. What are they looking for in New Haven to make this happen?"

"Ah, I see. Well, they did suggest certain levels of support that would be warmly received."

"And they are?"

"Five million would—"

"You're kidding," said William.

"Five million will get a candidate's folder a serious second look."

"A second look? What does that even mean?"

"It's somewhat ambiguous, deliberately so, but it definitely improves one's visibility. In our experience it means that an applicant's folder will get a second read."

"How nice," said William. "Five million for an extra five minutes of their time. A million dollars a minute. New York law firms have nothing on the Yale Admissions Department!"

William now felt decidedly stupid for the apparently meaningless $10,000 gifts he'd been making annually to Yale for years, thinking he was paving the way. Last year, he'd upped it to $25,000.

"What's the *real* number?" he asked.

"Excuse me, but what happened to merit?" asked Ellie. "Shouldn't Ginny's record speak for itself? She gets straight As, she volunteers at—"

"It's more complicated than that," said Padma. "And remember, we don't have complete transparency. Yale will do what Yale will do. It's fair to say that priorities have . . . evolved."

But money still talks, thought William. He recalled how one wag called Ivy League universities "hedge funds with classrooms attached." They were nothing if not effective fundraising machines. "Which brings me back to my original question. The number. For the sake of argument, what are they actually getting these days?"

"I don't know that they like to get too specific about these things, but the number twenty million did come up. If you want to remove as much uncertainty as possible, that's the number."

"Those greedy sons of bitches."

"And usually admittance in those circumstances involves taking a gap year so the applicant doesn't get counted in the official *U.S. News* data. They call it the *Z-list*."

"William," said Ellie, "you can't possibly consider this."

"Well, there's always another way to play it, El," said William. "I think you know what I mean."

"*No*," said Ellie. "We're not going there either. This should be based on merit."

"But you just heard that it's not. I don't know why you have to be so stubborn about it."

"Is there something we should know?" asked Padma.

"It's nothing," said Ellie. "I apologize."

"Then we're back to money," said William.

"Or maybe Ginny goes somewhere else?" said Ellie. "There are lots of good schools out there. I'm hearing wonderful things about SMU, and there's Michigan, or maybe somewhere smaller like Middlebury."

"Sandersons always—"

"Go to Yale, I know, and I know you and your father had great experiences there, but . . ."

William ignored the attempt to steer the conversation in a different direction.

"There's an easier way, Ellie, and you know it."

"*No.*"

Padma wondered what William could possibly mean.

"If it's helpful," said Faith, chiming in, "the Yale pledge can be paid in installments."

"How nice of them," said William, trying, but not succeeding, to hide his contempt for the situation.

"William," said Padma. "Ginny is an excellent candidate, and we both feel she has an excellent chance at Yale. We will do everything in our power to make it happen for her. But it will need to be her first choice, and she needs to apply early."

That was all William needed to hear. "That will all happen," he said.

The meeting was concluded.

Of all the facets of her job, dealing with parents like William Sanderson was the one Padma hated the most. She had seen his type many times: Men who think things should be given to them by the simple fact of their existence. Men who drifted upward by virtue of their birth.

When Sanderson's name was floated for the board, she had done some research. His firm, Bedrock, loudly trumpeted its "values," but many on the left felt it was a cynical ploy and that their commitment was skin-deep. Sanderson dutifully parroted those values in the media, appearing frequently on Bloomberg and CNBC, but Padma's instincts told her that Sanderson's own commitment to those values was entirely situational.

quietly lobbied to keep him off the board, but Sanderson's
ollar pledge to the capital campaign secured his spot. His saving
‸, ᵤnough, was that he was a coward, or at least that was Padma's take. This
made him pliant, at least on matters that didn't concern fucking Yale.

Sandersons go to Yale.

My God, was it possible to sound any more entitled? Spending precious
political capital to get Ginny Sanderson into Yale was *not* on Padma's list of
professional priorities. The path had been cleared for the Ginnys of the world
for far too long.

The fact was that Ginny had no chance at Yale. But Sanderson was on the
board, a board she had to occasionally placate. Or act like it, anyway. As for
the half-million pledge, even he wouldn't have the nerve to welch on that
when Ginny got rejected. The optics would be bad, and optics were everything to a man like Sanderson.

Thinking about the board amused her. The board really had nothing to
do with running the school. For the most part, all she had to do was attend
quarterly meetings and tell them how well everything was going and what a
special place Lenox was and how *special* the girls were. If there were aspects
that *weren't* special—and there always were—the board really didn't want to
hear about it. People like William Sanderson didn't serve on school boards to
solve problems or do any actual work.

While, on some level, Padma found this annoying, it also served her purposes. Sanderson and the others gave her a wide latitude to run things as she
saw fit, assuming they were paying any attention at all. And Padma knew why
too. The school held the ultimate trump card, the one William Sanderson was
pushing so hard on: college recommendations.

Parents never saw the final recommendation letters. They were enormously important because they couldn't be gamed or fabricated or bought
like so much else in the college process. And at Lenox, all recommendations
had to be personally approved by *her*. She had seen to that. A simple tweak
of an adjective or two could sink an Ivy applicant. "Brilliant" became "intelli-
gent," or "outstanding" became "above average."

Padma had also tightened up the language in the parent contract, giving
her the power to banish problematic families like the Ellisons. That got approved in a single email to Duncan with the proposed contract attached. She
doubted he even opened it. No doubt the fate of the Ellisons had sent shivers
through the community.

And so, they all danced to her tune.

But her meeting with the Sandersons still stuck in her craw. Sure, board members expected preferential treatment, and they usually got it. That's the way things had worked for generations. But few tried to exploit it with Sanderson's lack of subtlety. There were others out there, others like Barbara Selkirk, who would do more than just warm a board seat and look the other way. Others who would join her in the fight.

She would bide her time. Barbara had already recommended a few names and Padma was smart, certainly smarter than Sanderson. Perhaps an opportunity would present itself to put things right. What kind of opportunity? She wasn't sure, but she'd know it when she saw it.

Sanderson had taken up enough of her time, so Padma went online to check the *Sentinel*. Padma almost never read the *Sentinel*, considering the paper to be a reckless purveyor of alt-right propaganda. But right now, it served her purposes.

And there it was, Dina's article.

A STATEMENT

Wilson Girard's position had enormous power, and he knew it. To the outside observer, this might seem like a good thing, or at least a desirable thing, and sometimes it damn well was. He was the gatekeeper to the kingdom. But it also meant everyone wanted a piece of him, a little bit of his stardust to sprinkle on their kids, their *special* kids. He'd heard that word so many times, although lately it wasn't quite distinguishing enough, so "exceptional" was becoming the more popular characterization.

Maybe it was like this for celebrities—this always having to be on the defensive. Was it like this for Tom Hanks or Taylor Swift?

No, "celebrities" weren't quite the right analogy. Wilson wasn't famous. He didn't get recognized trying to order a sandwich at a deli or have to pose for selfies with random people on the street. No, that wasn't his situation, thank goodness.

He supposed he had just the right kind of power, the kind you could wield when you wanted but also didn't infringe on your daily comings and goings.

But it wasn't all upside.

Right now, for instance, he was going through his emails, a part of his job he hated. They came and came and came, by the hundreds, an electronic fire hose he could never turn off.

Johnny is an outstanding kid and his father is . . .

Charlotte started a GoFundMe to help those poor . . .

It never ended. Each one was an ask, and they all asked the same thing.

He looked at his watch: 4:00 p.m. Damn, it would be several hours before he could go home and have a Scotch. Perhaps he'd have a belt of the bottle he kept in his desk, just a small one to tide him over.

Staring at his inbox, he fantasized about hitting Delete All, but knew the fire hose would just resume a minute later. It took little pieces out of you, the good ones, bit by bit, until all that was left was the cynic.

Most admissions directors didn't last too long, at least not at schools like Yale. Wilson figured he might make it another year or two. Maybe then he'd get around to drying out.

One email caught his attention. It was from Padma Minali, that annoyingly persistent head of school from Lenox Hill. It had a two-word subject line:

A Statement?

There was nothing in the body of the email other than a link to a *New York Sentinel* story.

He clicked it.

Friday, October 12th

ELITE GIRLS' SCHOOL BREAKS NEW GROUND

by Dina Campbell

The Lenox Hill School, the Upper East Side school for girls and long a symbol of wealth and privilege, has enrolled its first trans student, seventeen-year-old Easter Riddle . . .

Hmm, she didn't mess around, that woman. He made a note to himself to check if they'd received an application from anyone named Easter Riddle.

REAL MEN FIX THINGS

Ellie retrieved their car, the large BMW X7, out of their subterranean Third Avenue garage. One of the Upper East Side's minor inconveniences was the total absence of garages west of Lexington. The wealthy (at least those without personal drivers) were reduced to walking a few blocks to fetch their cars, not that Ellie much cared.

Wheeling her way toward the Midtown Tunnel, she thought about the beat-up Jeep Wagoneer that Curtis, her father, the military man, had held together for years with an old tool kit and the sheer willpower of a man who just knew how things worked. Not abstract things, like the financial instruments that Will and Casper and everyone else she met seemed to conjure up. *Real* things. Things you could see in front of you, things you could touch.

It wasn't that Ellie discounted what her husband and those striving men of finance did for a living. She was smart enough to know that just because you couldn't hold a product in your hands didn't mean it was without value.

But . . . *but*. There was something ineffably appealing about a man who could look at something and just *see* how it worked, and then fix it.

William had grown up in an apartment, something rendering him whatever the opposite of "handy" was. Unhandy? When William's parents had needed something fixed, they called the super, and so it was with Will. One time, when left to his own devices for a few days, Will had called Ellie, confused as to the relative identities of the washer and the dryer. In his bachelor days, he'd used his oven for storage space, never once cooking for himself.

William would not last long in the zombie apocalypse.

Ellie felt self-conscious picking up her parents in such an extravagant car, one well out of reach for most Americans. Spending six figures on a BMW wasn't her idea, but William thought it was important for their image. "I'm not going to pull up to the valet at Dunehaven in a damn 3 series," he'd said.

William was suddenly making money at levels she associated with pop stars and athletes, not middle-aged men behind desks. While Ellie wasn't privy to their exact finances, she suspected paying Yale what it wanted was not impossible. The idea horrified her.

In her quiet moments, she wondered what the point was. They were already making a good life for themselves here. They had friends and the girls seemed happy, although they were hard to get a read on sometimes. Certainly, they wanted for nothing. But William traveled frequently and put in long hours even when he was home. What was the point of all that money if you didn't have time for your family?

She pulled up to the American terminal at JFK and saw Curtis and Ada just coming to the curb.

Hugs were exchanged. It had been too long. Curtis didn't say anything about the car, but Ellie knew what he was thinking. She wondered if the old Wagoneer was still running.

When they got back to the apartment, the girls popped out of their rooms and hugged their grandparents. "Ohhh, look at you girls," said Ada. "All grown up!"

"Too quickly, Mom," said Ellie.

"Isn't that always the way?"

"Where's that husband of yours?" asked Curtis.

"Dad left about an hour ago," said Ginny.

Ellie got out her phone and texted

Where are you??? We just got back.

Had to go to the office came the response.

"It looks like he had to get some things done at the office, but I'm sure he'll be home soon. Ginny, you're in Zoey's room for a couple of days. Mom and Dad, settle in and unpack. When you're ready, it's a nice day. What would you like to do?"

"Maybe we could visit the park?" suggested Ada.

"Central Park it is. We'll all go."

"Mom, I have a lot of homework . . . ," said Ginny.

"Which I'm sure can wait a few hours because today is Saturday. Both of you, go get ready."

The leaves in Central Park had reached their full autumn palette and much of New York had turned out to enjoy them. Ellie, her parents, and the girls went where the mood took them. Ada posed for one of those corny caricature artists on Literary Walk, and then they watched a group of street performers pull off some daring gymnastics by the bandshell. Lured by the smell of roasting chestnuts, Curtis insisted on a soft pretzel. "You'll get a paunch!" objected Ada.

"Now now, baby. We're not in New York every day." Curtis was, in fact, still military trim.

They casually circled the model boat pond and then watched the smaller children climb on the bronze Alice in Wonderland statue tucked into a circlet on its north side. Ellie loved that spot and wished she could have taken the girls there when they were younger.

There were other mothers there, ones with babies and toddlers, prams and strollers parked in rows. The toddlers, the ones old enough, explored under the enormous mushroom on which Alice sat side-legged. The Mad Hatter and the White Rabbit kept her company, as they had for the better part of a century.

Watching them, Ellie felt nostalgia for a time she'd never known. Was that possible? This wasn't a place she came as a child, and it wasn't even a place she'd brought her own children. Their statue-climbing years had been else-where. But she was drawn to it. She felt pangs of envy for these women, these mothers, who seemed so grounded here. It was an easy comfort they took for granted.

After lingering a bit, they walked north and exited the park near the Met. It had been a wonderful afternoon.

That night, Curtis and Ada went to the theater, *The Lion King*, which made William, who had finally come home, privately smirk.

Sunday, they wanted to go to church and William had to Google "Baptist churches in NYC." They discovered one was just a few blocks away on Sixty-first. William, of course, went back to the office.

Early that evening the phone rang and Ellie answered it.

"Hello?"

"Mrs. Sanderson?"

"This is she."

"Hi. It's Padma Minali. I was wondering if your husband was home."

"Oh, hi, Ms. Minali. William's not home yet. Can I help with something?"

"I see. This is just a courtesy call. It's a small matter. Would you ask him to give me a call when he has a moment?"

The hair on Ellie's neck stood up. It wasn't every day that the head of school called your home in the evening, especially not on a Sunday evening. Of course, this could simply be a board matter, a scheduling issue or some dull business regarding the capital campaign. On the other hand . . .

"Can I tell him what you're calling about? Does it involve either of our daughters?"

It was Padma's turn to pause. "Well, no, but I really should speak to William first, just as a matter of protocol. Tell me, will any of the girls' grandparents be visiting with us tomorrow?"

"Yes, my parents are here and really looking forward to it."

"And we can't wait to see them. Perhaps you and William could come in with them first thing? I'd like to speak with both of you, if that's convenient."

"Both of us? And you say it doesn't involve our daughters."

"That's correct. But it's something I'd prefer to handle in person. I'll see you tomorrow."

The line disconnected, leaving Ellie with a pit in her stomach. Something needed to be "handled"? She couldn't imagine what, especially if it didn't involve the girls.

The politics at Lenox had become complicated, and somehow Ellie felt less at ease there than she used to when the girls first enrolled.

She shook the feeling off. It was probably just something Padma needed for the board.

GRANDPARENTS DAY

Most schools in America had, at some point or another, instituted an annual Grandparents Day, and Lenox Hill was no different. While the occasion helped strengthen intergenerational bonds, the quiet priority at Lenox Hill was extending their fundraising reach. Within days, grandparents would find solicitations in their mailboxes. Curtis and Ada Maddox would proudly make out a check for one hundred dollars.

The day was, as always, a precious affair, particularly in the younger grades. The girls made big welcome banners and sang rehearsed songs. They would conduct "interviews," asking their grandparents about their favorite foods and movies. Grandparents helped add decorations like painted handprints and macaroni sculptures while quietly relishing that *their* progeny were the most talented and best looking.

Interest in Grandparents Day tended to wane in the older grades as the activities evolved from the precious to the academic, and the Little Darlings evolved into surly teenagers. (Not to mention that the ranks of potential attendees tended to thin out with the passing of time.)

Curtis and Ada had not made it to a Grandparents Day since the girls were in Chicago. It wasn't that they didn't want to—they worshiped those girls—but it had never been easy getting away in the military, a place where your schedule was not yours to manage. Curtis's retirement afforded new flexibility. Physics classes or not, both were excited to follow Ginny and Zoey around and to meet their teachers.

They walked together to school that day as a family. Curtis proudly wore his uniform for the occasion. It had epaulets and was festooned with colorful bars across the chest. Together they strolled up Park Avenue, where military uniforms were not a common sight. For Ellie, it was a moment of great pride, and even the girls didn't mind so much.

Despite being two days into their trip, the Maddoxes still had the wide-eyed look of out-of-towners. "So many people here," observed Curtis as they crossed the broad avenue of Seventy-second Street with dozens of others.

Ellie glanced at William and sensed his aloofness. She also sensed he viewed her parents as something he merely tolerated. As a rule, Ellie was slow to anger, but William's attitude upset her. William's own parents, she noted, were still in East Hampton.

In truth, William wasn't thinking about Curtis and Ada so much as his annoyance at having been "summoned" by Padma. "Why didn't you just have her call me directly?" he asked Ellie as they passed the Armory. "I could have sorted out whatever this is last night."

"I told you, she was quite insistent about meeting in person. I didn't feel like I was in a position to push back."

William grumbled something unintelligible and looked at his watch.

At school, Curtis and Ada decided to divide and conquer, with Ada following Ginny and Curtis Zoey. They would switch later.

First period was social studies, and the discussion today was about America's time in Afghanistan, or rather its "occupation," as Ms. Raynor, the teacher, put it. "It was all based on the naive, even imperialist, assumption by the Bush administration that we should use our power to remake other societies in our own image. Our time there was marked by subjugation and violence. Yes, Clover."

"I see Zoey's granddad is in the army. Maybe we should see what he has to say."

Ms. Raynor seemed visibly uncomfortable at the presence of a military uniform in her classroom. "I don't know if . . ."

"Mr. Maddox, did you ever go to Afghanistan?" asked Clover.

Curtis hesitated. He was reluctant to be drawn in, but he didn't want to give the impression he was ashamed of his service, not in front of these girls, and certainly not in front of Zoey. "Well, I should mention I'm retired and only wear my uniform for special occasions, and this certainly counts! As for Afghanistan, yes, I did. I served our country there twice."

"Did you fight? Did you ever shoot a gun?" asked Coco French.

For the countless men through the ages who'd seen the violence of war up close, from Antietam to the Somme to Guadalcanal, the experience was a deeply personal one. It was never shared frivolously, and seldom with an audience of fifteen-year-old girls.

"To tell you the truth, it seems like a long time ago now. . . ."

Ms. Raynor stepped in. "I'm not sure Mr. Maddox—"

"Actually, it's Colonel," said Zoey.

"That's quite all right, Zoey," said Curtis. "I—"

"Did you ever *kill* anyone?"

"Coco!" cried Ms. Raynor.

"It's okay. Kids are curious, and that's okay. Coco—is that your name? Let me just say I was proud to serve and leave it there."

Curtis's phone buzzed with a new text. He didn't get many, so he snuck a look. Reading it, he then stood up. "My apologies. I'll be back in a few minutes."

MEET THE PARENTS

Earlier, Ellie and William had been met by Celeste Burdick at the front entrance after goodbyes had been said.

"Mr. and Mrs. Sanderson, good morning."

"Celeste, how are you?" asked Ellie.

In her capacity on various committees, Ellie had dealt with Celeste on many occasions, and they had developed a warm relationship. She found her to be caring and professional. Once in a while, Ellie dropped homemade banana bread off at her desk just to be nice.

"I thought I would walk you back to Padma's office myself."

"That's thoughtful of you."

"How are the girls getting along this year? I have a soft spot for them, you know."

"Just fine. They love it here. We all do, of course."

"That's so good to hear. I confess I let Zoey hit my candy jar now and then."

"Ah, so we have you to thank for the dental bills!"

"Oh, I'll stop it if you like."

"Just kidding, Celeste."

"All right, here we are. Padma is waiting for you inside."

They went in and Celeste closed the door gently behind them.

"Mr. and Mrs. Sanderson, good morning," said Padma. "Thank you for coming in on such short notice."

Ellie noted they were not on a first name basis this morning.

"I confess my curiosity as to the agenda," said a brusque William.

Ellie was embarrassed by his abruptness. No small talk this morning.

"So, what did the girls do?"

"Will, I told you it didn't—"

"This doesn't involve your girls," said Padma. "This concerns the other evening."

"What other evening?" asked William.

"The night of the anti-racist training. I gather you, Mrs. Sanderson, said hello to Ms. Stokely."

"Yes, I remember. She's so nice."

"There was just one problem," said Padma." "That wasn't Ms. Stokely. That was Ms. Mooney."

"Oh . . . how stupid of me," said Ellie, trying now to remember what the real Ms. Stokely looked like. "I apologize. I hadn't seen either in some time."

"And that's all you have to add?" asked Padma.

"I'm . . . sorry?"

William interjected. "Padma, respectfully, am I to understand that I up-ended my schedule just so you could tell me my wife called a teacher by the wrong name?"

Padma ignored him.

"I'm happy to apologize to Ms. Mooney in person if she's offended," said Ellie.

"Suffice it to say, she is. And an in-person apology might be difficult as she declined to come to school today, nor is she likely to tomorrow."

"All because I confused her name?"

Padma had a different look about her. William didn't notice, but Ellie did. She was a predator circling her prey.

"Ms. Stokely was *also* upset when she heard what happened and she, too, may not come in tomorrow. Mrs. Sanderson, is it really necessary for me to spell this out for you?"

"Wait," said William, "I want to make sure I understand this. These teachers can't bear to come to work because Ellie confused their names? That strikes me as a bit of an overreaction, wouldn't you say?"

"Ms. Minali," said Ellie. "I'm afraid I'm confused. I feel stupid, but it was an innocent mistake."

"Innocent . . . That's an interesting characterization. Both Ms. Stokely and Ms. Mooney are African American, and you confused the two. I'm guessing you can see why that might be a problem, particularly in light of the fact you and Mr. Sanderson had literally just walked out of anti-racist training."

Ellie now fully understood the situation, innocent mistake or not, as did William. "Oh, Christ," he said.

"Ms. Minali," said Ellie ". . . *Padma*. I'm not a racist. You know that."

"Of course she isn't!" bellowed William.

"Well, none of us thinks we are, do we?" said Padma. "And yet here we are. For a board member's wife to set an example like this is quite problematic for the school, regardless of good intentions. It has also been brought to our attention that neither of you posted any supportive social media content in the aftermath of George Floyd."

"I'm sorry?" said Ellie.

"I don't even use any of those things. My firm doesn't allow it!" cried William.

Bedrock had a full social media ban on their employees, other than LinkedIn. The narrative was something they would control.

"I'm curious. What do you both think I should do about this?"

Both Sandersons were a little shocked at the tone Padma had taken. Deference had left the building.

William spoke first. "What you should *do* about it? If this woman is really so upset, have Ellie apologize and be done with it. Seriously, Padma, who's in charge here?"

"William, *please*," said Ellie.

"When a teacher chooses to boycott this school, it's more serious than that," said Padma.

"Boycott?" said William. "Are we being a bit hyperbolic here?"

"I don't believe so. You should know that in light of this, and what Ms. Mooney believes has been a pattern of systemic racism here at Lenox, she tells me she will be issuing a series of demands."

"Demands? Demands about what?"

"Demands regarding basic racial equity. Eight pages of them, in fact."

"Wait," said William. "How did we get from a mistaken name to eight pages of demands?"

"As I said, it isn't just about the names, but that appears to be the catalyst."

"Respectfully, Padma, aren't you the school's leader? If there's any truth to this, if there really *is* racism here at Lenox, why haven't you done anything about it?"

Padma stiffened. "A leader can only do so much in a given amount of time, and there's a *lot* of work to be done here."

"This is ridiculous," said William. "Just put an end to it. The demands, I mean."

"I suppose I could do that, but others are talking about signing the document as well. How would that look?"

"Others? What others?"

"Teachers and other employees."

"How many?"

"It's hard to say, but it's gathering momentum. You know how these things can go."

"No, actually, I don't."

"Well, the next thing I'd expect is the media."

"The *media*? Why would you say that?" William was beginning to see the ramifications, the "bigger picture."

"The signatories will be looking for exposure. Exposure gives them leverage."

"Padma, you need to get on top of this. Does the rest of the board know?"

"Not yet. Duncan is my next call. But I wanted to give you and Mrs. Sanderson the courtesy of knowing first, given your unique exposure. . . ."

"Our exposure? Are we somehow named in these demands?"

"You are."

"Fuck . . . *fuck*!"

"Mr. Sanderson, please."

"I apologize for William," said Ellie, still trying to keep the peace. "He's under a lot of pressure at work."

"Of course," said Padma.

"My work has nothing to do with this. Ellie, we need to talk for a moment. Padma, I'm sorry to be so short with you, but this is all a bit of a surprise. Is there anything else I need to know?"

"Not at present."

"Can you please send me those demands?"

"I'm not sure it's a completed document. But I will certainly send a copy to the entire board when I have it."

"Would you mind if Ellie and I stepped outside for just a moment?"

"Of course."

William led Ellie outside, past Celeste's post, and into the empty hallway. "We need to get ahead of this. I'm exposed."

"Oh, just you?"

"You know what I mean. *Work*."

"I will call Ms. Mooney right now and apologize."

"What? Jesus, you don't get this, do you? We're about to be crucified."

"Well, I don't know what else to do!"

"Yes, you do. We can diffuse this thing right now, at least where you and I are concerned. You know what I'm talking about."

She did.

"Will, you *know* I don't want to do that. It feels *cheap*."

"The word I'd use is *honest*. You have nothing to be ashamed of."

"*Ashamed*? Of course I'm not ashamed. Why would you even suggest that!"

"Yeah . . . sorry. You know what I mean."

"William, I understand your frustration, but I don't want to do it. What I *am* going to do is go back in there and offer a pound of flesh to keep the peace. Maybe I'll even grovel. You know, after what happened to the Ellisons, I took the time to read the parents' contract. You need to look at it. It is so broadly written that the school can basically toss any family at any time if they decide you're not a *good fit*."

"Which is exactly why I'm suggesting what I'm suggesting. Insurance."

"No. You and I are going back in there right now to make nice."

Ellie went back in. William, dreading the idea of prostrating himself to Padma, held back for a moment and quickly typed a text. Then he followed Ellie back into the office.

"Ms. Minali. I apologize if we took the wrong tone. Right, William?"

". . . right. It was quite wrong of us."

"I think you know this was an innocent mistake, but we fully understand the sensitivities involved," said Ellie.

"We certainly do," said William.

"The point is, we value this school and its staff. What can we do to make this right?"

Padma leaned back, enjoying the moment, letting the Sandersons squirm for a little longer. But the fact was, she had set things in motion and she was going to let it play out. Screw the Sandersons.

She'd been standing nearby, that night, when Ellie Sanderson confused the names. She'd gone over to Diane Mooney as soon as the Sandersons left. While mildly annoyed, Diane didn't seem too put out. This frustrated Padma. Blithely mistaking one person of color for another—*they all look alike!*—was textbook racism. You didn't have to read Kendi or Robin DiAngelo to know that. This was the *exact sort* of behavior that would be expunged on her watch. That the behavior had come from the wife of a board member was doubly problematic, but she knew it might also be convenient. Taking down a board member would leave no doubt in anyone's mind who was in control.

Padma counseled Diane Mooney to take a few days off. When she politely resisted, saying exams were coming up, Padma pressed the issue. "You've been through a lot. We'll cover for you here." Padma would teach those classes herself if she had to. She placed a reassuring hand on Diane's arm, who saw she had little choice in the matter.

On the screen in front of her, Padma had a list of demands, demands that she herself had drawn up and would give to Diane. Others would join, and the media would quietly be alerted. Dina Campbell would be of use. Perhaps other schools would join. They would make Ellie Sanderson the face of this, and by extension, her husband.

That Padma was potentially unleashing chaos, a chaos anyone would be hard-pressed to control, didn't matter. Chaos was always the necessary precondition for change. And Padma was nothing if not confident she could make whatever ensued work to her benefit.

"Here's what I will propose," she began.

Just then, there was a knock at the door and an unfamiliar face peeked in.

"Oh, sorry, we didn't realize we were interrupting. We were asked to come here?"

"I'm afraid you've been misinformed," said Padma. "Was my assistant not outside?"

Celeste, as it happened, had briefly abandoned her post to use the facilities.

"Dad?" said Ellie, who then stared daggers at William.

"Padma, I don't think you've met Ellie's parents," said William, smiling broadly. He got up and opened the door further to make both Maddoxes visible. "Curt and Ada Maddox, meet our head of school, Padma Minali. She does such a wonderful job here."

If Padma had words, they weren't forming in a mouth that now hung fully open. She struggled to process what she could plainly see.

Shit was mostly what she thought.

Rendering her speechless wasn't Curt Maddox's uniform, as problematic as that was. Rather, it was the thing that anti-racist training taught them all to understand, that none of us are individuals so much as members of categories, or identities, and those identities drew clear lines between oppressors and oppressed.

Curtis and Ada Maddox, the two kindly grandparents standing in her office, in-laws of the odious William Sanderson, were undeniably among the oppressed.

Which, she immediately realized, meant the same for Ellie Sanderson.

Fuck!

That disagreement the Sandersons had in the meeting with Faith Collins suddenly made sense.

Padma smiled stiffly through the pleasantries, and then everyone left—that bastard Sanderson was still grinning as he walked out the door.

Padma stared at her list of demands. It included many long-needed strides for equity such as abolishing AP classes, which her BIPOC students were not qualifying for in sufficient numbers, as well as hiring permanent DEI staff.

She sighed, knowing she would have to find another way. She hit her intercom.

"Celeste, are you out there?"

"Yes, ma'am."

"Cancel my call with Duncan Ruggles."

She moved the file to a folder and saved it to Dropbox, perhaps to be utilized on another day. Then she called Diane Mooney and told her to come back to school.

MY NEW BLACK FRIEND

Houston come you didn't tell me? I'm hurt!" exclaimed Tizzy, fetching Ellie once again from the waiting lounge at the Mayflower. Ellie had just returned from dropping Curtis and Ada at JFK.

"Tell you what?"

"That you were African American, of course!"

"How come you never told me you were white?"

Tizzy made some sort of exasperated noise. "But isn't it . . . ?" She was about to say "obvious" but decided against it. "You shouldn't hide it, you know, you should celebrate it! I want you to know that Rick and I gave money to Black Lives Matter."

"Tizzy, I don't care, and I don't want to be celebrated because of my race. I don't think it should be an advantage, and I don't think it should be a disadvantage. I don't think it should mean *anything.*"

That's why she'd pushed back against parading her parents into Padma's office, not to mention using Ginny's mixed ethnicity to game the college admissions process.

"And for what it's worth, I'm half white."

"Oh, I see. So how do you identify, then?" Tizzy was trying to decide if she was half disappointed.

"Do I need to identify as something?"

"No, I suppose not."

Ellie sensed Tizzy's confusion, and as much as she was tempted to let her stew in it, she relented.

"Okay, so here's the story. My real mother, who was white, died shortly after I was born. I never knew her. My father got remarried to Ada a year later. Ada raised me as her own, and I call her mom, because she is."

Tizzy leaned in and appeared to be examining Ellie. "Yes, I can see it."

"Oh, for God's sake, Tizzy." Ellie realized that Tizzy was trying to "see" the black in her.

The revelation of Ellie's identity had spread like wildfire in the forty-eight hours since Grandparents Day, and Tizzy had been beside herself with excitement. She had a black friend! No, she had a *Black* friend, with a capital *B*, just like in the *New York Times*.

Ellie certainly *looked* white, thought Tizzy. She supposed with mixed race situations it just happened that way sometimes. Like Derek Jeter or Meghan Markle. But now that she *knew*, she could kind of tell! She'd always thought Ellie's looks were "exotic," a word Ellie would have hated if she'd known Tizzy was thinking it.

She quickly moved past the part where Ellie was merely half black.

"I just don't understand why you would keep this a secret."

"I wasn't keeping it a secret. It's just not something I care about, and until I moved here, it never came up. Do you care about being white?"

"Yes, I do, because I feel terrible about it." They were in the dining room now and Tizzy was picking at her arugula salad. "I mean the privilege and all, and what we did to your people. Ugh, it's simply more than I can bear sometimes."

"Oh, for God's sake stop. You didn't do anything to *my people*."

"Well, some Addison of yore probably did."

"Can we please talk about something else?"

"Yes, because I have news! Are you sitting down? Yes, of course you are, I meant figuratively, of course. I got a call from Cynthia Powers, the head of admissions last night. Are you ready for this? You're in!"

"What? I don't understand."

"There's nothing to understand! You're in, or at least you will be at the next meeting."

"Really?"

"Really."

"William will be thrilled."

"But not you?"

"Oh, of course. I'm thrilled too. But I thought this was supposed to take much longer. What about the whole gestation thing?"

"Well, it usually takes longer, but I don't know, you must have impressed the committee."

Ellie was skeptical. "So, this has nothing to do with what we were just talking about."

"Of course not! Why would you think such a thing? You totally deserve this! Oh, speak of the devil. Here comes Cynthia."

A rail-thin woman with hair expensively tousled just *so* was walking their way with two other women in tow. No, thought Ellie, she was *gliding*.

"There she is! Ellie Sanderson! We are *sooo* thrilled that you're considering joining our little club."

"Thank you, and it would be an honor."

"Ellie Sanderson, meet Julie Redfield and Samantha Marsh."

Julie and Samantha enthusiastically thrust out their hands. "We're so excited to meet you," one said.

"Jules is on the House Committee and Sam's on Social."

"Yes, it's *very* busy around here," said Samantha. "Maybe we can borrow you after you're done and show you the sights. Tiz, would that be okay?"

"Of course."

"You know," said Cynthia, "we just can't wait to get you involved." She spoke very fast with animated hands. "Tiz says you're on the Monster Mash committee at Lenox with her. Maybe we can get you on a committee here! There's just so much to do, you know. We all agreed we need more people like you around this stuffy old place."

"I'm sorry?"

Cynthia Powers's hands arrested themselves and her face went blank, ever so briefly. But she hadn't climbed to the heights of running the admissions committee of the Mayflower Club without possessing a certain social dexterity, and she quickly recovered. Her hands came to life again and one gave Ellie a playful slap on the arm. "Well, new members with fresh ideas, of course! Anyway, we just can't *wait* to get to know you better. Make sure Tiz treats you right and whatever you do, be sure to try the aspic!"

Cynthia laughed as she and the others glided away, leaving Ellie to wonder what aspic was.

BIRTH OF A GOBLIN

Later that week, as school let out, Zoey found herself walking out beside Clover Hunt. "Hey," she said, tentatively.

"Well, hey back!" said Clover.

"How have you been?"

"I'd have to say just great, Zoey."

She wasn't sure why, but Zoey was beginning to think there was more to Clover than the counterculture vagabond she appeared to be. She decided to do something bold, at least by her modest standards of boldness. "Hey, uh, lots of the girls go to this place EJ's after school. I was wondering if maybe you wanted to go."

EJ's Luncheonette, a diner on Third Avenue, had been an East Side fixture for decades and was a popular after-school hangout.

"Together? Like a date?"

"Yeah, no! I mean, I just thought you might like to hang out."

"I'm just messing with you, Z. Can I call you that?"

"Sure, I guess."

No one had ever given Zoey a nickname that wasn't derogatory before.

"Okay, then. Sounds like a plan."

They walked the few blocks and found EJ's already crowded. Zoey was bummed to see Coco, already holding court in a large booth. They made their way to the far side, as far from Coco as they could get, and ordered two milkshakes, Zoey chocolate and Clover matcha green tea.

"So, *you're* very brave," said Clover.

"What do you mean?"

"Being seen with the weirdo."

"Is that what you are? A weirdo?"

"Well, of course I am, can't you tell? I'm weird, dammit."

"Were you always . . . What do you call it again?"

"*Goblincore*. What, the diversity dream team didn't fully prep you for the weird kid? I'm on the spectrum, you know. I was held back in first grade."

"They might have said something."

"I'm sure they did," said Clover, laughing.

"So, have you been this . . . way . . . for long?"

"Is eight months long?"

"No, I don't suppose. What got you into it? I mean, if I can ask."

The waitress arrived with their milkshakes. They had pleasing spirals of whipped cream on top.

"Let me answer that with a story," said Clover. "At St. Michael's, my old school, there was this boy named Julian. He was a serious prick, if you know what I mean."

"I guess," said Zoey, who really didn't.

"He was a bully. Used to terrorize kids and get away with it. His dad was somebody important, and all the kids were too afraid to say anything because they knew if they did it would just get worse. He was verbally abusive, and he'd post horrible things online about people. Anonymously, of course, on Yik Yak, but everyone knew who it was. Then he went after a friend of mine, spray-painting the word *slut* on her locker. I mean, other than being an awful thing to do, that's so *after-school special*, am I right?"

"What's an after-school special?" asked Zoey.

"Oh, these stupid movies they used to have. A bunch of clichés, just like Julian. No one ever accused him of having an original thought. Fucking meathead."

"Why did he do it?"

"Because he kept chasing my friend around and couldn't take polite noes for an answer. She finally told him to fuck off."

All this was very exotic territory for Zoey, whose experience with boys had been mostly confined to those awkward interschool dances that she finally got the nerve to start attending. This strange girl sitting across from her was so oddly self-assured. Not at all what she expected and *definitely* among the curious.

The diversity people had told everyone to handle Clover with "sensitivity," which suggested to Zoey that Clover's self-esteem might not be fully intact, but that didn't seem to be the case at all. And behind the theatrical presence, she seemed very pretty, with a delicate bone structure and auburn hair of a thickness all but required to make the nest effect work.

Having passed the age by which all girls become acutely sensitized to their appearance, Zoey knew she would never grow into a great beauty. But she'd come across a phrase in a book they were reading for French: *jolie laide*. It was meant to describe women who, while possessed of traits not considered classically beautiful, perhaps even homely, were beautiful still. Those traits worked together in such a way as to *make* her beautiful. Sarah Jessica Parker was the example people always used. There were aspects of Zoey's appearance, the *parts*, that when she considered herself in the mirror, made her self-conscious—a slightly crooked nose, oversized lips, and eyes that were too close together. But she decided she could be *jolie laide*.

"So what happened?" she asked.

"Well, I knew it was Julian, of course, but just to be sure, I snuck a look in his backpack, and sure enough, there was a can of red spray paint stuck inside one of his shin guards. Like I said, a dumb fuck. Not even smart enough to ditch the evidence. Anyway, I confronted him in the hallway, and he said some not-very-nice things about my friend and about me. Horrible things."

"What did you do?" asked Zoey.

"I took a swing at him."

"No!"

"Yes," said Clover.

"You actually hit a boy?"

"Right in the damn jaw." Clover held up a fist to underscore her point.

"And what did he do?"

"He hit me back, of course," said Clover. "And then it just turned into a brawl. A teacher broke us up and we were both hauled off to the principal's office."

"Well, *he* must have gotten in the most trouble," said Zoey. "I mean, he's the boy!"

"You'd think that, wouldn't you? I got suspended, and he didn't."

"C'mon!" objected Zoey. "I don't get it."

"It probably didn't help when I lit up a cigarette in the headmaster's office."

"Are you serious? Wait, you smoke?"

"Once in a while. I don't even like it, but it's fun to watch how it sends some adults over the edge. I mean, you can light a joint in a crowded elevator in this town and no one bats an eyelash, but light a cigarette? Off with your head!"

"So that got you suspended?"

"Z, there's more to the tale. Julian told them that I punched him first, which was entirely true, but there was something else, something I only found later. A week or two earlier, our friend Julian had come out as a poly-sexual."

"What's that?" asked Zoey.

"I didn't know either. I had to look it up. It means someone who likes to get it on with any of the other genders."

"You mean he was a bisexual?"

"Bisexual? No, he's—*where* have you been? Did you completely sleep through diversity training? There must be a hundred genders, at least at last count. *Demi-boy*, that's my personal favorite. It means, *less than a complete boy*, which is how I personally choose to view Julian."

"Okay, so he's a poly-whatever," said Zoey. "What does that have to do with it?"

"Everything," answered Clover.

"I don't understand."

"Once Julian declared himself as anything other than straight, he was untouchable. He had blanket immunity."

"What? Why?"

"Because that's how things work now, Z! Seriously, have you been paying any attention at all?"

"I guess?"

"Schools now keep careful count of not just their BIPOCs but also their nonbinaries, their LGBTQ *pluses*. I looked into it. There's this out-fit called the NAIS. National-something-something-something. I read all about them on *Undercover Mothers*. Anyway, they certify all the private schools and they require diversity reports, or you don't get accredited. That dumbass Julian suddenly had a cloak of protection around him, but poor white, cis me? Totally expendable. After hitting him in the jaw, it was suggested to my parents that I might no longer be a *good fit* at St. Michael's. That's their way of telling you to beat it, you know? You're not a *good fit*. I hated that place anyway."

"But Julian . . . was he . . . ?"

"Actually a polysexual? Oh, hell no. I mean, the asshole was fat and barely fifteen. He wasn't getting it on with anything but his right hand. But *claiming* to be might have been the one clever thing he's ever done in his life. So clever that . . ." Clover seemed to consider Zoey for a moment. "Are we under a cone of silence here?"

"What's that?"

"That means the conversation goes no further."

"Oh, yes, of course."

"I decided to borrow the idea."

"That's when you started . . . dressing like this?"

"Well, I had to find a new school, and my parents were *not* down with public, so I had to figure out how to get in. There're not a lot of openings in tenth grade. So I decided to kill several birds with one stone. Three, in fact. Bird number one is, get into a good school. I knew adopting a ridiculous persona could seal the deal. Schools eat this shit up. Colleges will too."

"But, goblincore? Is that even a real thing?"

"Oh, yeah. Google it."

"I'm still confused. It's not about race. . . . Is it even a gender thing?"

"Excellent question, young Skywalker. While the *plus* in *LGBTQ plus* has been expanding at lightspeed it doesn't yet include mere lifestyle choices. Not yet, anyway. You still need a gender angle. I thought, briefly, about going with polysexual myself, which would have been easy since I like boys and I could just pretend all the other genders were on my radar. But I didn't want to borrow from that dumbass Julian. That's when I discovered a connection between the goblincore and eco-sexuals."

"What are those? They didn't exactly tell us."

"Eco-sexuals are people engaged in amorous relationships with nature. Trees and waterfalls and flower beds and such. And yes, it's also a thing."

"Wait, you don't actually—"

"Don't be ridiculous."

"But that's what you're claiming to be?"

"I see you're catching on," said Clover.

"Oh," said Zoey, taking all this in. It had been a long time since a conversation had so fully captured her attention.

"It gets me firmly under the *plus* umbrella. "*Goblincore-slash-eco-sexual*. It's an immunity twofer!"

Clover giggled at her own joke.

"What do your parents think of this?"

"They were profoundly unhappy, at least at first. But I reassured them that I don't, in fact, have carnal knowledge of trees, and that calmed them down a bit, plus I always get straight As, which helps. The whole St. Michael's business was tough on them, but then getting into Lenox calmed them down *a lot*. So now they just kind of look the other way and hope that I grow out of it, which I conveniently will do after this gets me into college. I'm thinking Princeton."

"I just . . ."

"What?"

"I just don't know what I'm supposed to think right now."

"Think whatever you like. Obviously, I'm used to it."

"What about the other birds?" asked Zoey.

"What?"

"You said you were killing three birds with one stone."

"Oh, right. I found out you guys had a dress code, and I had no interest in dressing like some kind of Scottish zombie-girl. The goblincore, conveniently, dress quite comfortably, and a lot of my wardrobe happens to be earth tones. As an added bonus, I got to change my name."

"Why, what's your real name?"

"Amy. Can you think of anything more boring? It's like Pam or Jane or something."

"I think it's nice," said Zoey.

"Then you are welcome to it."

Zoey couldn't help but giggle, and not for the first time that day. This strange girl was making her laugh, and it felt good.

"And the third?"

"The third what?"

"Bird!"

"Oh. Well, that would be my immunity, of course. The school won't bother me, and neither will simpleton bitches like Coco French."

"I *hate* her," said Zoey.

"If I were a better person, I'd say something like, 'People like Coco aren't worth the time to hate,' but they totally are."

"You know she has this club, or group, or whatever you want to call it. They call themselves the *BB Girls*. Supposedly, it stands for *Blonde Bitches*. Some of the others call them the *blondterage*."

"And what do they do?" asked Clover.

"I don't even know. Walk around in a pack? Plus, everyone knows they cheat on all the tests together. . . . Can I ask you something?"

"Sure," said Clover.

"Does this make you feel . . . I mean being someone you're not, do you feel . . ."

"Do I feel like a big fat liar?"

"Well, yeah."

"I look at it this way," she said. "I didn't make these rules. I don't even know who did. People like Hyphen Lady, I guess. Do I think they're a joke? Of course I do! But no one can call me out for playing by them. . . . Oh, don't look now."

"What?"

"Her highness is walking over here."

TALKING SHIT

"Oh, God," said Zoey, not daring to turn and look. "She has a couple of henchmen with her. Or would it be hench-wenches? Yeah, I like that. Henchwenches."

"Maybe we shouldn't have come."

"If you like it here, don't let someone like Coco French chase you off."

"Well hello, Doughy!" crowed Coco, suddenly looming over the booth. Two of her BB Girls, Millie Hicks and Jennifer Mann, flanked her.

"Hi, Coco," said Zoey, avoiding eye contact.

"So, are we making new friends today or just practicing a little horticulture? Hobbies are *so* important."

Zoey slumped in her chair, looking like she wanted to teleport herself elsewhere. Clover, for her part, sucked her milkshake through her straw, making a deliberately loud slurping sound.

"No, wait," said Coco. "I think it's feeding time at the zoo. Or perhaps just a little bird watching. Something could fly in and start nesting, after all."

"You know, Coco—" said Clover.

"Oh, look, the vegetation speaks!"

Clover slurped again, then said, "I have a problem."

"This is supposed to be news?" Coco said, voice dripping with her trademark sarcastic resonance.

"You know what my problem is?"

"Woodpeckers?" cracked Coco, laughing hysterically.

"Good one," said Clover, unfazed. "No, my problem is clichés. You know what those are, right? They are boring things, overused things, things that lack original thought. Did you know people can be clichés? For example, a person who comes walking over here like some pathetic female Draco Malfoy knockoff, complete with stereo toadies, looking to demean others for no other reason than to bolster their own pathetic sense of self-worth. Now, *that's* a cliché."

Coco's unnaturally blue eyes, the result of tinted contacts, flashed with rage. Where did this walking bush get off talking shit to *her*? That was not the order of things! That was not . . . "Well, at least I don't, I don't . . . ," she sputtered.

"You don't *what*, Coco?" asked Clover, glaring directly at her.

Coco seemed to be groping for just the right comeback, or perhaps *any* comeback, but it was eluding her. "Smell!" she said, finally.

"Oh, that is *dev*astating. And it took so much thought! Careful, or you'll burn through your last few brain cells. I mean, you must be down to so few you could give them each a name."

Coco made some kind of guttural cry. Knowing she had to seize back the upper hand, she searched her brain, opened her mouth a gaping centimeter, and came up empty. Out of ideas, she grabbed what was left of Clover's milkshake. It looked, at first, like she was going to dump it on Clover, but she turned instead and dumped it on Zoey's head. "Oops, sorry, Doughy!" she said. "It slipped!"

By this point, most of EJ's had gone quiet, focused on the drama in booth seven. Some of the students started laughing. Others gasped.

Clover stood up, clearly ready to throw Coco a right hook.

"No, d-don't!" said Zoey.

"See you around," said Coco, before exiting EJ's with her sidekicks.

Zoey had never felt so humiliated. Clover could see her fighting the tears that were welling up in her eyes, and the gaze of everyone at EJ's was upon them. "Let's get you out of here," said Clover, throwing some cash on the table. The two of them made their way outside where, thankfully, Coco and her cronies were no longer around.

"Oh God, I can't walk all the way home like this," said Zoey, still fighting off the tears. "People will see."

"Where do you live?"

"Sixty-fourth and Park."

"I'm calling an Uber."

BUBBLEGUM IS GOOD FOR THE SOUL

They went straight to Zoey's room. Zoey didn't know if her mother or Ginny were home, but she didn't want to run into either of them if they were.

Like most adolescent girls' bedrooms, the decor in Zoey's could never quite keep up with her chronological age. Hers represented her persona perhaps two years earlier, when she was going through a regrettable boy-band stage. The walls were covered with posters and cutout pictures of K-pop bands, plus Taylor Swift and others. There was even a life-size cardboard cutout of Harry Styles.

"Really, Z? That doesn't scare you in the middle of the night?" asked Clover.

"Oh, uh, no, I guess not. I don't really follow him much anymore."

Embarrassed, Zoey was grateful that Clover didn't pursue the line of questioning further. She ran into her bathroom, rinsed her hair under the tap, and emerged wearing sweats. "I'll be right back," she said, leaving the room with the still-wet school uniform. She went behind the kitchen and threw her uniform in the wash. Then she darted back to her room, shut the door, and sat on the bed with Clover. Only then did she allow the tears to come.

"That's it, get it done," said Clover. She rubbed Zoey's arm sympathetically.

"School tomorrow is . . . I can't even . . ." Zoey sobbed.

"There is no school tomorrow, dummy. It's Saturday."

"Oh, right."

"Do you have a Bluetooth speaker?" Clover asked.

"Over there on the shelf . . . Why?"

"No questions, just give me the name," said Clover, examining her phone.

Zoey did, and the speaker came alive with a song.

Yummy yummy yummy I got love in my tummy

"What is that?" asked Zoey, still sniffling.

"It's called bubblegum music," answered Clover. "It's good for the soul."

"You're crazy."

"It's from, like, a thousand years ago. I stumbled on it, and you could say I'm going through a phase. It's totally cheesy, but you can't listen to it and not be in a good mood. It's scientifically proven to be impossible."

Ooo love to hold ya!
Ooo love to kiss ya!

Zoey managed a laugh and blew her nose. It *was* kind of catchy.

Just then, the bedroom door opened and Ginny entered. Zoey quickly wiped her face in her sleeve. "Zo', can I borrow your . . . Oh, I thought you were alone. And *what* is that music?"

Ooey little Chewy!
Don't know what you're doin' to me!

"It's called bubblegum," answered Zoey.

"It's so . . . *treacly*," declared Ginny.

"Stop trying out your dumb words on me," said Zoey. "The SATs are over."

"But yours aren't. Just trying to help you out, baby sister. So who's this?"

"Clover, this is my sister, Ginny," said Zoey in a deliberate monotone. "She's a dumb senior."

"Hey," said Clover.

"Ah, you're our new nature-loving schoolmate," said Ginny.

"Yup, that's me. I see you've been prepped."

"To each his own, I say. Nice to meet you."

"So, you're a senior? Do you know Hats Down Thug?"

Hats Down Thug, or just HDT, was a white rapper in Ginny's grade at Grafton. He had over a hundred thousand downloads on Spotify, making him somewhat of a local celebrity. HDT's real name was Asher Chatfield.

"I know him," answered Ginny. "Sometimes we hang out."

"Cool," said Clover. "I love his stuff."

"Well, your tastes are certainly *eclectic*."

"Stop!" said Zoey. "And what did you want, anyway?"

"Just your black sweater. Mine's at the dry cleaner."

"Why?"

"I'm going out later."

"Where?"

"None of your business. Sweater."

"Second drawer," said Zoey. "But don't stretch it out!"

"Wouldn't dream of it, baby sister. . . ." Ginny located the sweater and left.

"She seems cool," said Clover.

"I guess. I don't know," said Zoey.

"Well, at a minimum she's cool-adjacent."

Zoey just grumbled.

"Listen," continued Clover, "I am so sorry about what happened. It's all my fault."

"No, it's not."

"It totally is. She was going to dump that shake on me, but she's not stupid. She knew what would happen. Remember the new rules. So you should blame me."

"I blame *her*."

"She's a little shit, for sure, but the world is full of Cocos, and they're all cowards. Every one of them. You just have to punch back harder than they punch you."

"I'm afraid I'm not much of a puncher. But that was amazing . . . that stuff you said."

"I find it useful to have a strong insult game. But again, this is on me. I'm pretty sure she only came over because she saw you talking to me. And it's probably not over. She's pissed now."

"Well so am I!" Zoey protested.

"Z, you're too nice to play this game, and you don't even have an entourage to back you up like Coco."

"I have you," ventured Zoey.

This seemed to surprise Clover. Her plan had been to get through the balance of high school at Lenox with as few entanglements as possible, get into a good college, and then do her thing. She already had friends. But *plans are what everyone has until they get punched in the face*. Clover didn't know who'd said that, probably a boxer. She liked the quote and never forgot it. Smiling genuinely, she said, "Yes, yes, you do."

The conversation flagged for a moment, neither girl having come to school looking to make a new friend that day. "Have you met that other new girl?" asked Zoey. "The trans one? She's in my sister's grade."

"The famous Easter Riddle? Of course. I met her at the LGBTQ plus Jamboree."

"There was an LGBTQ plus Jamboree?"

"Yes, but it was totally beat. The Gs wouldn't talk to the Ts and we pluses just hung out in the corner all night."

"Really?"

"Gosh, you're gullible, but I guess there could have been, considering. Yes, I met her briefly in Padma's office with some idiot reporter. If I were you, I wouldn't go within ten miles of Easter Riddle. Tell your sister too."

"Why?" asked Zoey. "My mother always says I should have an open mind."

"And you should, but that doesn't mean you should be crazy either."

"What do you mean?"

"You have so much to learn, Padawan. The trans are at the absolute freakin' top of the oppression ladder. They are untouchable. If there were an oppression Olympics, Easter would totally kick my ass. So, steer clear, because she's as dangerous as she wants to be. It's a total immunity situation."

"But maybe she's nice."

"Maybe, but do you want to be the one who finds out otherwise? Besides, don't feel sorry for her. At every school people are tripping over everyone else to be friends with the trans kids—you know, be *allies*. It shows what an inclusive person you are."

"Really?"

"Yeah, *plus* most of the trans are influencers on TikTok and Insta. I mean, you can't get any hotter. They're totally on fire."

"That seems so cynical," said Zoey.

"Just telling you how it is. Like I said, I didn't make the rules."

"But what about eco-sexuals?"

"Oh, we're just weird. No one wants to talk to us, thank God."

"What about that reporter?"

"Yeah, no thanks."

Zoey flopped to a prone position on her bed and buried her head in its countless pillows. Clover reached for her phone in the manner of all adolescents who found themselves with a spare nanosecond.

There was a knock at the door.

"Go away, Ginny!"

The door opened. "It's your mother."

"God, is there no privacy around here?" said Zoey.

"I heard voices. I didn't realize we had a guest."

"Hello, Mrs. Sanderson. I'm Clover Hunt." Standing, she extended a hand.

"Oh, how nice to meet you."

As she got up, a pack of cigarettes fell out of Clover's pocket, which took Ellie aback. She didn't think kids smoked anymore, particularly kids from around here. But Zoey didn't bring many people home, so Ellie didn't say anything. It wasn't that she didn't have friends, but the process of making them didn't come as naturally to her as it did to Ginny. Making friends was Ginny's superpower. So Ellie was pleased to see Zoey making progress on that front, even if the friend did have a twig in her hair. Was that some new trend?

She decided to let the cigarettes slide. "Are you at Lenox Hill?" she asked.

"I am. I just transferred from St. Michael's."

"How nice, and welcome! Can I get you girls anything?

"No, Mom. We're good. Can you please go away?"

"Okay, I get when I'm not wanted. Hey, what is that music, anyway?"

"Mom!"

"Okay, you two enjoy yourselves."

"Nice meeting you, Mrs. Sanderson," said Clover as the door shut.

"Jeez, someone sure is polite," observed Zoey.

"I find it expedient to have parents like me," said Clover. "And they are *so* easy to impress. Nice greeting, good handshake, and you're in."

Clover was scrolling through her phone. "God, have you ever looked at her Insta?"

"My *mother's*? I don't think she has one."

"No, dummy. Coco's."

"Oh. I don't know. I guess."

"It's puke-worthy, a photo diary of the good life. Expensive meals, trips, etc. This is exhibit A for inducing eating disorders."

"I think she wants to be an influencer," said Zoey.

Clover stuck a finger down her throat and made a gagging noise.

"I'd rather not talk about Coco, if that's okay," said Zoey.

"It sure as hell is, but I should get going."

"Oh, don't. Hang a little longer. I could make some hot chocolate."

"You know, as much fun as that sounds, I need to beat it. There's this symposium tonight at the 92nd Street Y on varieties of tree bark and, you know, I have to keep up appearances."

"That's a joke, right?"

"You're catching on, Z."

"C'mon, you just got here. You could put on some more bubblegum."

Clover let out a theatrical sigh. "All right, fine, but I'm going to insist on that hot chocolate."

Zoey smiled. "I'll be right back," she said, rushing out the door.

She returned minutes later with two mugs.

"Marshmallows," said Clover. "Nice."

JESUS, MOHAMMED, AND
BUDDHA WALK INTO A BAR

L ooking for something to talk about, Zoey said, "So, are your parents going to the Monster Mash?"

"What's that?"

"It's the school's big annual fundraiser. All the parents get dressed up."

"I don't know. Not sure my parents are into the whole benefit scene, or Halloween, for that matter."

Zoey, on the other hand, adored Halloween. Uncomfortable in her own skin, she loved dressing in costume. Unfortunately, she'd aged out of trick-or-treating.

"Do you do anything for it?"

"Every day is Halloween for me, or hadn't you noticed?"

"Oh, right," said Zoey, giggling.

"Actually, despite appearances, I'm not into it. Some of my old friends like to go to the parade in the Village, but I might have to come down with a fungus that day."

"Huh?"

"Yeah, well, you never know what sort of things we eco-sexuals can pick up."

"Gross," said Zoey.

Clover glanced at her phone. "Funny you should bring up Halloween. A friend named Rhonda from St. Michael's is texting me about it."

"Why?"

"She's looking for ideas. They do this thing every year where you have to go in groups of three dressed thematically, and it had to relate to something we were studying. Like math, say. You could go as three functions."

"How would *that* look?" asked Zoey.

"I don't know, you had to get creative. But every year all the girls would have meltdowns about who was partnering with who. Three is a *very* political number."

"So why is she reaching out?"

"She's looking for ideas. Say, maybe we can put our heads together. I hated going to the thing, but I don't mind brainstorming. What do you think? They take all the same classes as us."

"Sure." Zoey was quietly thrilled her new friend wanted her help. "We could try Ginny, too, if she hasn't left. She's very clever." Zoey texted her, despite being in the next room. "She says she'll help. The three of us should be able to come up with something."

"Okay, I'll make a group chat with Rhonda. What's Ginny's number?"

The girls went to work, letting their imaginations, and their thumbs, roam. The texts came in rapid fire.

How about Washington, Jefferson, and Madison?

BORING!

Gin, can we just come to ur room?

NO! TAKING A BATH

Big plans?

Shut up

Okay think

A PROTON, NEUTRON, AND ELECTRON?

Promising

SINE, COSINE, AND TANGENT

Idk. What would they wear?

DECLENSIONS? SUBJUNCTIVE, INFINITIVE, AND IMPERATIVE

Again . . .

JUST RIFFING HERE

Federalists, democrats, and whigs!

NOT BD

A banana, apple, and strawberry

WHAT CLASS IS THAT?

Bio?

LAME

Maybe they cud b isms. You know, like racism, sexism, and anti-

SEMITISM

Ooo, woke points!

How about the father, the son, and the holy ghost

TOO TRIGGERING

I think we could trigger better than that

HMM, WHAT R THE WORST THINGS WE CUD BE?

Jeffrey Dahmer, Jack the ripper, and . . . some other guy

TED BUNDY

Yeah

A colonist, a native, and a slave

Omg

A TRANS MAN, A TRANS WOMAN, AND A GENDER FLUID

I thought those were GOOD things these days

THEY R, BUT NOT IF ITS PEEPS LIKE US,
STUPID

I don't think I could pull off the clothes,
anyway

**Maybe . . . Stalin, Hitler, and
Mussolini-a trio of fascists!**

Stalin was a communist

WHATEVER

**How abt a cheerful feminist, a
menstruating man, and a unicorn**

????

3 things that don't exist!

Ur bad

OK, LAST BAD ONE: JESUS, MOHAMMED,
AND BUDDHA

I don't have time 2b someone's fatwa

Are fatwas still a thing?

SALMAN RUSHDIE GOT TOTALLY FATWA'D!

Oh right

Their creative juices finally exhausted, they broke the chat.

A few minutes later, Ginny walked in wearing a bathrobe. "I just got a weird text from someone at school."

"What do you mean?" asked Zoey.

"It says, 'Who's Rhonda?' How would she know about Rhonda? That's your friend's name, right?"

"It is," answered Clover, who picked up her phone and started to work it. "Rhonda posted the thread to her Insta. It looks like it's getting a lot of comments."

"That should help her, right?" asked Zoey.

The others didn't answer.

"Right?"

Clover then did something she almost never did. She made an actual phone call.

"Rhonda. You need to take down that post—*now*!"

DON'T MAKE WAVES

Y ou're home early," said Ellie. It was six o'clock, at least two hours before William's usual arrival.

"Can't stay, unfortunately. I have a dinner, just stopping off for a
quick change and shower." He took off his jacket and slung it over a hallway
chair.

"Oh, I was about to make something."

Ellie followed William as he progressed through the changing closet to
their bedroom. "You know, there are studies that say that families that eat
together produce smarter children."

"Ours seem pretty smart."

"Still, it would be nice if you could join us for dinner more."

William decided not to engage. Looking toward the door, he cocked his
head. "What is that I'm hearing?" he asked.

"Music. Zoey has a new friend over. Isn't that nice?"

"Sure."

"It doesn't come easily to her, you know."

"Mm," muttered William, still stripping.

"Say, have you heard anything about the Ellisons?" asked Ellie.

"What am I supposed to hear about the Ellisons?"

"Apparently, they're gone."

"What do you mean, gone?" he asked, pulling off his undershirt. "Gone
where?"

"They withdrew their girl from Lenox and nobody's heard from them.
Calls are going unreturned. It's like they've *disappeared*. Do you know anything about it, any talk from the board?"

"I don't know a thing," answered William.

"Tizzy says they were counseled out."

"What? Why?"

"She says it was because of their attitude," said Ellie.

"Well, Bob wasn't exactly playing along at that training session. I'm not totally surprised."

"You don't think he was making a reasonable point? *I* do."

"Whether he was making a reasonable point or not is beside the point."

"And why is that?" asked Ellie, furrowed brow suggesting a touch of challenge.

"You just don't make waves at a place like Lenox. Everyone knows that. It's a stupid thing to do and Bob Ellison should have known better." William entered the shower while Ellie lurked just outside. "Honestly, I never cared for Bob much anyway. Always seemed a little Trump-y, you know? I hear he never even got vaxxed."

"Are we really still talking about that?"

"It's just, you know, a pattern. He doesn't play ball."

"I heard something else today," said Ellie, still hanging outside the shower. "Jen Crenshaw told me she heard from someone else that Yale will only take two kids from Lenox this year."

"And who did she hear *that* from?"

"She didn't say, but she seemed to think it was true."

"That doesn't seem right," said William. "Our relationship with Yale has been improving, and I'm sure I would have heard something."

"I guess," said Ellie.

"How is Ginny's application coming? The EA deadline is, what, next week?"

"She doesn't exactly share with me, but I'll ask."

"And the essay? Did she finally settle on a topic?"

"She said something about leaving her comfort zone."

"Would you hand me a towel?" William asked. "And which comfort zone is that?" he continued. "Her whole life is a comfort zone."

"Yes, and I worry about that sometimes."

"It's better than the alternative," said William, emerging from the shower.

"Anyway, I don't know any specifics. She won't let me see anything, but honestly, this is something she needs to do on her own, don't you think?"

"Hell, no. Do you think any of the other kids are doing applications on their own?"

"I wouldn't know."

"Well, let me help you out here—they're not."

EXITING THE COMFORT ZONE

Ginny left 580 just before sundown and turned uptown, still thinking about Halloween. Halloween played out a bit differently in a place like Manhattan. There weren't any neighborhoods where kids could just wander from house to house, ringing doorbells, and the apartment buildings wouldn't allow nonresident trick-or-treaters without an invitation.

Her first year in New York, Ginny had been a little too old to trick-or-treat, but she got invited to a friend's towering condo tower on First Avenue, and it was too ripe an opportunity to pass up. The building was thirty stories high with seven or eight apartments on every floor. They scored so much candy they periodically had to stash some in the stairwell.

This year, Ginny and most of her friends planned to go to the parade in Greenwich Village. Team Pride knew how to put on a show.

Tonight, though, she had other plans. Not wanting to stand out, she wore all black, Zoey's sweater, and a pair of jeans. The smell of weed was in the air, but that was more or less a constant in New York now, an accepted part of the landscape. Ginny didn't care for it, but there wasn't much to be done.

She passed the architectural monstrosity otherwise known as Hunter College, a looming block of Soviet-style brutalist concrete that cast right-angled shadows across Park Avenue's genteel apartment buildings. It was a commuter college, so students had left for the day, and things were quiet. Past Hunter, she approached the steps into the subway at Sixty-eighth Street, right by Shakespeare & Co., her favorite bookstore. Descending, the air was pungent with the smell of urine, another fact of life in the big city.

Riding the subways didn't intimidate Ginny, even as their crime-ridden reputation had scared off many of her friends. It was simply the easiest way to get around, so that's what she did. But she wasn't stupid about it. You didn't stand by the track's edge, not anymore, and it was best not to make eye contact with anyone but at the same time not obliviously disappear into your phone. There were more than a few people living out their psychoses down here.

After waiting a few minutes, she boarded the uptown 6 and found a seat. It was the usual New York melting pot. One guy was dressed as the Joker with his evil grin. Was he celebrating Halloween early? Possibly, but more likely he just liked to dress that way. Across from her was a homeless person, prone, feet bare, occupying at least four seats in the crowded car. He'd brought a shopping cart, festooned with various rags, bottles, and bits of this and that. One took all these things in stride.

Her father said the city hadn't been like this when he was young, but she could only take his word for it. Like most kids, Ginny knew the world she was growing up in and couldn't imagine anything else. It was your own personal normal and you embraced it. In fact, Ginny loved the city. She felt a sense of propriety about it, despite her relative newcomer status. It was *her* city.

The train made its way north, passing under Yorkville, and finally reaching Harlem. At 125th Street, she ascended the stairs and emerged onto the busy thoroughfare. It was often considered Harlem's main artery and was bustling with shops and people, even at this hour, nearly eight o'clock.

Heading west, Ginny crossed Park Avenue. This was a different Park Avenue from the Sandersons'. The commuter trains out of Grand Central were elevated here, having emerged a few blocks south on Ninety-sixth Street from a giant subterranean maw. Not coincidentally, and certainly unknown to Ginny, Ninety-sixth was also where the northernmost "dilatory domiciles," those tony addresses that made the *Social Register*, made their stand.

The overhead tracks were a sinister presence, blocking out the sky and casting a permanent shadow during daylight hours. By now it was dark, though, and a train thundered overhead.

Walking on, Ginny crossed over Malcolm X Boulevard and, just before reaching the famed Apollo Theater, turned right on Adam Clayton Powell, another of Harlem's major arteries. A few blocks farther, she turned left.

Harlem had undergone something of a renaissance in recent years. Real estate money had flowed in like a green river, as row upon row of dilapidated brownstones caught the covetous eyes of developers. White people, many political progressives who loved the optics, moved in like settlers. Bill Clinton famously chose Harlem for his post-presidential offices, although he rarely visited after the fanfare died down.

These new residents were sometimes called "urban pioneers," a term black residents, particularly those whose families had been there for generations, found wildly offensive. There was occasional pushback, but block after block yielded to inevitable gentrification.

The dimly lit side street on which Ginny found herself was no such block. It was a throwback to a more forsaken time, one of crack dealers and urban blight, one where some areas were barely distinguishable from 1945 Dresden.

Following the instructions she'd been given, Ginny found a vacant lot strewn with loose rubble and garbage. She pushed back a bit of the torn fencing and walked in. As she did, the thumping sounds emerging from the building on the far side of the lot suggested she'd found the right place. There was an open door there, one revealing nothing but darkness.

She'd found her destination.

Reaching the threshold, Ginny paused, allowing her eyes to adjust. The walls were flaked with ancient paint like some molting reptile. The repetitive, pounding noise made its way from the floors above.

There was a person there, on a stool, wearing a hoodie, his features indiscernible beneath it.

"Password," he said.

"Payday," answered Ginny.

"Ten dollars."

Ginny produced a ten-dollar bill, which she'd been told to bring. (She couldn't remember the last time she'd used cash for anything.)

"Upstairs," said the person.

As Ginny made her way up, the pounding got louder and louder.

CASA RICA

Casa Rica was a recent addition to the Manhattan private club scene. It had acquired a beautiful beaux arts townhouse in the East Sixties and renovated it from top to bottom. Despite offering little besides food and drink, it commanded a $300,000 initiation fee, many times that of other nearby private clubs.

It was one of several new clubs that had sprouted up in recent years to solve a market problem: The old-line outfits like the Gotham couldn't keep up with the ranks of newly minted wealthy, nor did they care to. (That the Gothams and Mayflowers cast a dismissive eye in their direction bothered the nouveau crowd, but only a little. Archaic racquet sports or 11:00 a.m. watercress sandwiches weren't the amenities they were looking for.)

Casa Rica's roster of members filled quickly and included an impressive array of celebrities, media barons, and finance moguls.

William had heard of Casa Rica, everyone had. He looked vaguely down on the place, an all-but-required attitude of someone as long-clubbable as he. He'd never been, though, and the hype made him intensely curious.

He approached an impeccably manicured woman behind the reception desk and was greeted with an indefinable European accent.

"Good evening, and welcome to Casa Rica. May I have the name of your host?"

"Casper Stein," answered William.

"Yes, of course. You are expected, Mr. Sanderson. Mr. Stein is already on premises. You may find him in the Havana Room on the second floor. There is an elevator just to the right, or you may take the stairs, as you wish. I will take your coat."

"Thank you," said William, handing over his Burberry. Heading up the curved staircase, he admired the decor. All warm earth tones with subdued accent lighting. It was a place, he thought, of shared confidences. The contemporary art collection, widely talked about, was cleverly juxtaposed with more traditional furnishings. And while he was far from an expert, it was easy to identify the joyful Keith Haring that greeted him on the second-floor landing. A few steps farther on he spotted a closed door with the words Havana Room painted in an elegant script.

Entering, he was met by a wall of smoke.

The cigar room, of course. There were a handful of members there, enjoying smokes in oxblood-red leather lounge chairs. On one side was a glass door that led to a walk-in humidor.

"Ah, William. There you are." Casper was sitting in the corner, deep in conversation with another man whom William immediately recognized as the mayor. He walked over as the two men rose. "You know Mayor Reynolds, I assume."

"We've never had the pleasure."

"Please, call me Tom. It's always a delightful occasionality to meet a constituent, particularly a friend of Casper's."

Like most politicians, the mayor was a vigorous handshaker. He also, famously, had an approach to the English language that was, well, his own.

"The mayor likes it here because of the privacy," said Casper.

This surprised William. Tom Reynolds, an effusive and well-dressed black man in his fifties, seemed to be photographed almost nightly emerging from benefits or fashionable restaurants. It was also only two weeks until Election Day, so it was curious to see him anywhere other than a public event this late in the game. This no doubt had something to do with how much money Bedrock's executives contributed to the mayor's PAC. Regardless, he seemed a likable man and William was happy to vote for him over the dour Republican whose name William couldn't quite place just then.

"Yes, it's nice not to have a camera pointed in your face all the time," said the mayor.

"Well, Tom, if you'd excuse us, William here and I need to chat."

It wasn't lost on William that Casper could dismiss the mayor of New York. A net worth of $8 billion let you do that.

"No problem, I should be departing anyway." The mayor turned to William and said, "So nice acquainting with you, William, and I trust you'll keep our little secret." He nodded at his cigar and winked.

"Of course," answered William, a little bewildered.

After the mayor left, William said, "He doesn't want anyone to know he smokes?"

"Smoking isn't a good look for politicians these days, unless it's cannabis. But there's also the fact he likes Cubans."

"Are those still illegal?" asked William.

"They are. Trump, that impetuous dolt, reinstituted the ban. But you'll find more than a thousand of them behind that glass door over there."

"His secret's safe with me," said William.

"We all need our little vices, don't we?" said Casper, puffing. "Sit," he said. William took the mayor's chair. "He's a good man, the mayor, and quite pleased with the returns we've given him on the city's pension plan."

Another long puff. Casper appeared to be contemplating something.

"Not the brightest fellow, thinks he can run for the Oval, which will never happen. But he's someone we can work with. That's all you can really ask."

William wondered just how large Casper's donations to Reynolds were. It would be a matter of public record, but then he decided he didn't care enough to look it up. William had made a generous donation himself, at Casper's urging.

"Anyway, I took the liberty of picking something out for you." Casper motioned to a nearby waiter, who brought over a silver tray. It contained a single cigar on a small cushion, along with a cigar cutter and some five-inch wooden matches. The cigar was very dark in color, almost a deep chocolate, and had a red-and-gold band.

"It's a Gurkha Black Dragon, from Honduras. Very hard to come by and not for beginners. I'm sure you'll enjoy it."

The waiter held the tray under William to catch the small slice he extracted from the end. Then William dragged a match slowly along the striker until it flared in a satisfying fashion. He held it an inch or so below the cigar's open end, allowing the heat to travel up and catch the wrapper. He then made a series of exaggerated puffs to draw the flame. William didn't partake often, but he understood the ritual. The cigar was strong and bitter, and he knew the aftertaste would be with him in the morning. "It's wonderful," he said.

"Good man. Rolled on a virgin's thigh, or so goes the legend. Tell me, can you stay for a bite to eat? Would I be intruding on Sanderson dinner plans?"

"Oh, no, not at all."

Casper knew his invitation would not be spurned. "Excellent. When we're done with these, we'll go upstairs to the dining room. After that, we'll visit the bar and we can talk a little shop. They make a sublime pisco sour."

Dinner was served slow and late in the Latin tradition, with a number of courses on small plates. William was burning with curiosity as to the evening's real agenda, but he knew he couldn't force it. It would come.

His phone vibrated in his pocket. He couldn't answer it here, and he doubted he could even expose the screen to see who it was. He decided to sneak a discreet look beneath table level.

Unknown Caller.

He hit the decline button. A few minutes later, his phone vibrated again. *Dammit.*

He snuck another look and saw it was Ellie this time. He thought about shutting off vibrate, but he wasn't sure he could pull that off without being indiscreet. He shoved the phone into his pocket and vowed to keep it there.

"So, how are things going on the Lenox board?" asked Casper.

"Oh, just fine. There've only been a couple of meetings."

"Such a wonderful school. Harper loved it there."

"I hear she's a great kid," said William. "Where is she now?"

"Wharton undergrad."

"Good for her. Harper, that's an interesting name. Is it a family name?"

"No, Missy loved *To Kill a Mockingbird*. She's very concerned about social justice, you know."

"Very commendable," said William.

"We all need to play our part, don't we? Although Harper herself informs us that *Mockingbird* has fallen out of favor. Something about white saviors. She says she might have to change her name."

"Oh," William muttered, sensing dangerous waters and not knowing what else to say.

After the final course—the tarte tropézienne for Casper and an incredible crema catalana for William—the two colleagues repaired downstairs to the bar. Casper led them to a discreet corner table where drinks were already waiting, Casper having placed orders ahead from the dining room.

William's phone made its presence known yet again. Curse the damn thing! He left it in his pocket.

"So," began Casper, "you may have suspected there was more to this evening than good company."

"No, not at all," replied William. "You're so kind to bring me here. What a spectacular dinner."

"Yes, Chef Urvano was an incredible find. I'm told they discovered him in a six-top restaurant on some back street in Valencia."

"Wow," said William, desperately hoping Casper would get to the point.

"Anyway, this evening is about congratulations. It happens I got a call earlier today from Jasmine Wu."

"The California state treasurer?"

"The same."

"We got the business!" cried William, trying, and failing, to keep his voice down. "I mean, did we?" he asked, now more quietly.

"We did. All I can say is, *well done.*" Casper offered his glass in a toast and they clinked pisco sours. "I'm quite sure the executive committee will be welcoming a new member soon."

"Whatever I can do to help the company, Casper. You know that."

They both took a deep drink. For William, this was a heady moment, fueled by the several rounds of alcohol. The wine pairings, the pisco sour, and now the news. . . . William's head swam with glorious thoughts of his future. He was entering rarified air, a place of private jets and personal profiles in Forbes, a place where you no longer updated your LinkedIn profile, you deleted it altogether.

Casper grinned and noted the slightly glazed look that overcame William. He knew full well his head was tripping the light fantastic.

"You know, Jasmine fancies herself a bit of a golfer," said Casper.

"Sorry, what?"

Casper chuckled. "Do you need a minute?"

William gathered himself, realizing he must look like an idiot.

"No, I'm good. Just pleased about the news."

"Anyway, Jasmine. She's a golfer, and she's not half bad. I played with her at Bel-Air once and I think she shot an eighty. The point is, she's coming East next week. I know this is very short notice, but can we put a little outing together for her at Dunehaven? Just a few foursomes. We need to deepen our relationship."

"Certainly." William was on Dunehaven's board and, in truth, relished playing host at his highly exclusive club.

The golf course at Dunehaven was a famed links design by the ocean. It was regularly rated in the world's top fifty courses, and both men knew the business utility of hosting outings there. Casper, who was Jewish, wasn't a member, nor was he likely to be. It's not that the Dunehaven members were prejudiced—the days of anti-Semitism as an official policy were long past. The force of tradition, though, and the need to accommodate legacies had preserved Dunehaven as a redoubt of understated WASPiness. Perhaps more relevant, in Casper's case, was that high-profile billionaires were still viewed as *arriviste*. Perhaps if Casper were *less* successful, he'd be somebody you could put up.

Casper belonged to the Scuttle Hole Golf Club in nearby Bridgehampton, another excellent course, and a club where his two-ton Maybach earned admiring looks rather than withering contempt.

"Wonderful," said Casper, appearing to ponder his pisco sour. Then: "So I guess you sorted that business with Cy."

The corners of William's mouth turned down, almost imperceptibly. "Yes. All sorted."

"Was it an issue?"

"No, not at all."

"Good man," said Casper. "Let's be sure to have Cy to the outing as well. We'll put him in the foursome with Jasmine. Put our best foot forward and all."

A club employee approached the table. "Excuse me for interrupting, but there's a phone call for Mr. Sanderson at the front desk. I'm told it's an urgent matter."

William's high was about to thoroughly crash.

THE HOSPITAL

Ellie was in full-fledged panic mode. All they'd said was that Ginny was there, at the hospital, and because she was underage a parent should come.

"What happened??" Ellie cried.

"I'm sorry, I don't have that information right now," said the person.

"What do you mean you don't have it? She's *there*, isn't she?"

"Yes, ma'am, but I'm just going off a form they gave me."

"Can you go and see?"

"I'm sorry, ma'am. I can't be leaving my desk. Best to just come here yourself."

Ellie's mind raced. Why hadn't Ginny called herself? Was she badly hurt? In the Uber, Ellie checked Find My Friends on her iPhone. Ginny's phone was pinging in Harlem but not at the hospital. What was Ginny doing in Harlem, and why was her phone pinging somewhere other than the hospital?

Worst-case scenarios swirled like fast-moving full-fledged nightmares in Ellie's head. Had she been attacked? Were drugs involved? Oh, God, was it fentanyl? Ginny was a smart girl and would never knowingly take something like that. . . . Would she? No, Ellie didn't think so. But someone could have slipped something in her drink!

Oh God oh God oh God. Let her be okay.

Ellie bolted out of the Uber and ran through the doors of Metropolitan Hospital, Harlem's primary health facility. "I'm looking for Ginny Sanderson," she spouted, nearly out of breath. "I'm her mother."

The woman behind the desk cast Ellie a disdainful look. This was a busy place, and just who was this expensively dressed lady coming in here and demanding immediate attention? She thought about telling her to sit and cool her heels, but probably best to get her out of the way. She clicked a few keys on her computer. "Through those doors, down the hall on the left."

Ellie raced down the hall, passing a series of treatment bays. *Where is my daughter?*

Ginny was sitting there, on the edge of an exam table, holding her arm. Zoey's sweater was bloody and torn. There was a bandage on her forehead. "Oh, honey!" cried Ellie. She ran in and gave Ginny a hug. "What happened?"

"I'm fine, Mom. It's no big deal."

"No *big deal*? I get a call from a hospital in another neighborhood that you've been admitted, they won't tell me why, and it's no big deal?"

"It's nothing. Just a scratch. Do we have to do this?"

"You're kidding, right? What are you doing up here, and where's your phone?"

"I lost it."

"You lost it?"

"Yeah, sorry."

"Why don't you tell me what happened."

"I came up here for something," said Ginny.

"Something? *What* something?"

"It was kind of a party. A rap-off."

"A what?"

"A rap-off. They do it every Friday. It's all extemporaneous. Rappers given a subject like, say, *prison*, and they have to come up with a rap about it. It's kind of like improv. Crowd response chooses the winner. It's actually pretty cool."

"And you thought to come up here without even telling me."

"I wasn't sure you'd approve."

"You *think*?"

"It was for a good cause. My essay!"

"What essay?"

"For Yale. You know, about getting out of my comfort zone."

"For the love of God, Ginny!"

"I did some research. They eat this kind of stuff up. You know, multiculturalism and all."

Ellie realized this was probably true. "How did you even know about it?"

"My friend Asher, he's one of the rappers. Goes by Hats Down Thug. He's killing it."

"And just how do you know a rapper?"

"He's at Grafton, Mom. I see him all the time."

"A rapper from Grafton?"

"*Mom*."

Ellie sighed. "So, again, what *happened*?"

Just then, a doctor entered the bay.

"Hello," she said. "I'm Doctor Patel. Are you Virginia's mother?"

"Yes," answered Ellie. "How is she?"

"She's going to be fine, but I'd suggest some rest at home. She suffered a mild concussion as well as a nasty scratch that may have come from an old nail from the sounds of it. We gave her a tetanus shot as a precaution."

"Is there anything else we need to do?"

"Here's a prescription for some antibiotics and make sure to change the dressing every day for a week. Other than that, get her home and let her rest. Ah, here's the nurse with her discharge papers."

As they left the building, a town car pulled up to the emergency entrance. William got out.

"What happened?" he said.

"Get back in the car. Ginny, get in." Turning to William, her mouth a tight line, she said, "Where the fuck have you been?"

William couldn't remember the last time he'd heard Ellie swear.

YOU'RE TOUCHING ME!

They rode downtown from the hospital in silence. Casper had lent William his car and driver, but William didn't want to have a discussion in front of Casper's driver. The conversation could wait until the privacy of their apartment.

While Casper's driver didn't concern Ellie at all, she was content to let Ginny stew a bit, and she could use the time to let her nerves settle now that she knew Ginny wasn't seriously hurt. She'd been going on adrenaline and was suddenly exhausted.

In the light of the apartment foyer, Ellie said, "Oh, honey, your eye."

Ginny went to a nearby mirror. "Oh, that's just great." She had developed a dark, purplish ring around her right eye, which had started to swell.

"Will someone please tell me just what the hell is going on?" implored William.

"Well," said Ellie, "if you ever answered your phone, you might actually know!"

"I was with Casper. It was important."

"Oh, well, if it was important."

"Will you two please stop?" said Ginny.

Zoey emerged from her bedroom to see what the commotion was about. If Ginny was in trouble, she wanted a front-row seat.

"My sweater!" she cried. It looked like a write-off.

"Yeah, sorry about that," said Ginny.

"Back in your room!" thundered William, and Zoey reluctantly complied, slow-walking so she could glean as much information as possible. "We're going in the den, and then I want to know exactly what's going on."

"She's not seriously hurt," said Ellie. "Did you maybe want to ask about that?"

"I assumed as much when I first saw her, although I didn't notice that shiner." He turned and walked toward the den. Ellie was tempted not to follow but knew the conversation needed to happen.

"I'll be there in a moment," she said. She went into the kitchen to retrieve an ice pack from the refrigerator to give to Ginny. "Here," she said. "Press this against your eye. Let's go talk to your father. There's a lot *I* want to know too."

They made their way to the den.

"All right, then. What are your injuries?" asked William.

"A scratch and a bump on the head," answered Ginny. "And I guess now a stupid black eye."

"She has a mild concussion and also received a tetanus shot for the scratch, which might have come from a rusty nail," said Ellie.

"And where did all this happen?"

Ginny recounted the story of why she went to Harlem and the rap-off, putting a heavy emphasis on research for her Yale essay. "Everyone's always saying we need to leave our comfort zones," she said.

"Hmm," said William. "That's not the craziest angle I've ever heard."

"William!" cried Ellie.

"I'm just saying."

"*Enough*. Ginny, how did you end up at the hospital?"

"Was it those rapper people?" asked William. "I've heard they can be quite violent."

"Those *rapper people*? That is so racist," said Ginny.

"William," said Ellie. "You need to stop speaking."

William complied.

"No, it wasn't *rapper people*," said Ginny. "It was crowded, a lot of people were drunk—and no, *I* wasn't. . . . It was just a stupid argument with some girls. I think they were from Brearley."

Brearley was another private school on the Upper East Side, and a rival of Lenox's.

"And a guy too. Dillon something. He's a wrestler at Grafton. I used to see him at dances and stuff and apparently he's a douche now."

"What were they arguing with you about?" asked Ellie.

"Just stupid stuff."

"*What* stupid stuff?"

"Really stupid stuff. Trust me, Mom. Just girls being bitchy, plus this idiot Dillon. But then he started getting really obnoxious. He kept moving forward, getting in my space and then yelling, 'You're touching me, you're touching me!' He even called me the c-word, if you can believe that. So I said, 'Dillon, *dude*, chill out,' and he just loses it. I have no idea why. He shoves me, so I shove him back."

Of course you did, thought Ellie. She hardly blamed her.

"Then I think one of them actually tries to take a swing at me, and I trip over something getting out of the way. That's when I hit my head and I guess got this scratch too. I'm not sure because I guess maybe I blacked out for a second. Next thing I know, Asher Chatfield is putting me into a car and taking me to the emergency room. He had his dad's driver there. Dad, I tried calling you from Asher's phone, but maybe you didn't recognize the number."

"Why didn't I see him at the hospital?" asked Ellie.

"He had to perform. I told him I was fine and to beat it."

"Is this Victor Chatfield's son?" asked William.

"I dunno," said Ginny. "But he's a rapper. Hats Down Thug. He kills."

"Why was he helping you?" asked Ellie. "We'll need to thank his parents."

"I know him, Mom. Like I said, he goes to Grafton. I really didn't want to go to the hospital, but he said I had to, and it was kind of sweet. I was going to walk out after he left, but then some pushy nurse said I needed to be looked at."

"And your phone?" asked Ellie.

"I dunno. It must have been knocked out of my hand when I fell. Look, this is all no big deal. Can we end the interrogation now?"

"Just go to your room and get some rest," said Ellie. "And you're grounded until school on Monday."

"And you're paying for a new phone, young lady!" added William.

"Whatever, Dad, just don't ever call me that again. Are you ninety years old?"

Ginny then went to her room, not because she thought any of this was fair but because she wanted the conversation to end. After she left, William said, "She seems okay."

"Well thank God it wasn't worse. It's just like her to go and do something like this. I'm surprised we've managed to keep her alive this long. And why *weren't* you answering your phone?"

"I was at Casa Rica with Casper. You're not supposed to just whip out your phone at the table."

"William. Listen to me. Family first. When you get repeated calls, maybe you should stop what you're doing and find out why."

"Fine, but it's not like I was at the gym. I was with Casper. And we got CalPERS, by the way. That's what he wanted to tell me."

"I don't care."

"You'll care when you see my bonus."

"William, seriously? Your daughter went *by herself* to Harlem to an underground rap party, ends up in the hospital, and you're talking about money?"

"I'm going to bed," he said.

"You do that."

WE HAVE A BIT OF AN ISSUE

It was Monday, and Padma greeted the girls as they arrived, as she did every day. She saw that Diane Mooney was back.

She retreated to her office and read some emails, worked for a bit on next year's budget, and then checked on how the Monster Mash was coming along. The week began in a familiar routine.

She could hardly know it wouldn't finish that way.

An hour or so later, she pushed her laptop away and allowed her thoughts to drift to her current *bête noire*: the Sandersons.

Ellie Sanderson was African American? She hadn't seen *that* coming. She'd since learned that Ellie was biracial, but the distinction hardly mattered. *Obama* was biracial. She couldn't make the Sandersons the straw man on an issue of racial justice.

But there was always a plan B—it just hadn't fully revealed itself. In front of her, though, on her desk, was enough to chip away at the problem.

She read the student complaints one more time, as well as the comments from Shonda. She also read the article in the *Sentinel* again.

Yes, she could work with this.

Zoey was in fourth-period math when Padma strode into the classroom. She appeared to scan the room, and much to Zoey's horror, Padma's eyes settled on her.

"Miss Sanderson, would you come with me please?"

"Now?"

"Yes, now."

"Should I leave my books?" Zoey asked.

"You can bring them."

Zoey stood and scooped up her books, including Zinn's *A People's History of the United States*. Padma held the door open. Zoey avoided the gaze of her classmates, although she felt their eyeballs boring into her as they tracked her exit with white-hot interest.

In the history of education, no child has ever been yanked from a class and taken to an administrator's office for something good. It went without saying that this was a first for both Sanderson girls. When they arrived at Padma's spacious office, Zoey was surprised to see Ginny already there. They exchanged concerned looks.

"Sit," said Padma.

They complied, taking seats in matching university chairs, the kind with spindles and the school logo on the top rail. Padma pondered them for a few moments, which just made the girls even more nervous.

"I need to talk to both of you about a serious matter, but first, Virginia."

No one ever called Ginny "Virginia."

"Imagine my surprise," continued Padma, "when I opened the paper over the weekend." She produced a hardcopy of the *Sentinel* and thrust it across the desk. It was open to an interior page and a relatively small item. The headline read

UNDERGROUND RAP PARTY RAIDED

Of course, Ginny had heard about the raid over the weekend, and seen the *Sentinel*. The raid must have happened after she left. She gathered nothing much came of it, a few misdemeanor arrests for trespassing, disturbing the peace, and that sort of thing. In New York, misdemeanors carried less weight than parking tickets. She almost wished she'd been there when it happened. Getting arrested would have been perfect for her essay. How outside-the-comfort-zone would *that* be? She imagined her father coming to bail her out at the precinct. The thought might have made her smile, if it weren't for the fact she was sitting across from a glaring Padma.

"Apparently," continued Padma, "there were drugs at this party. But what caught my attention was that the article mentions there were a number of underage private school children in attendance. You can see, I'm sure, why this aspect of the story makes it of interest to a paper like the *Sentinel*. And imagine my further surprise when the article mentioned Lenox Hill. I've had to field calls from the school's board already."

Specifically, Barbara Selkirk had called Duncan Ruggles over the weekend. Duncan had then placed a call to Padma, politely suggesting she look into the matter. Shonda had noticed too.

"Is there anything you'd like to tell me about this?"

Someone must have told Padma she was there, Ginny thought. She couldn't imagine who, but there were a lot of kids there, so it could have been anyone.

"No, not really," said Ginny.

"But you were there," said Padma.

For Zoey, sitting quietly, the events of Friday night were becoming clear. She couldn't decide whether to be titillated by her sister's getting the third degree or nervous over her own presence in the Head's office.

Ginny decided that there was no use denying her presence at the party, Padma obviously knew. And besides, she hadn't done anything wrong. "Not for long," she said. "I left early, and no, I didn't drink or do any drugs. I *don't* do drugs."

"And why did you go to this party?"

"I like rap music."

"You say you left early."

"I did."

"And why was that? Does this have something to do with your eye?"

Ginny's shiner had achieved a deeper eggplant shade over the weekend. Concealer helped, but not much.

"I got a slight injury, as you can see. It's nothing. I tripped and fell. It looks worse than it is."

"You . . . fell."

How much did they know? She was telling the truth but perhaps not the entire truth.

"Yes, I fell."

"And then what?"

"A friend said I should go to the hospital and get it looked at. I said it was nothing, but he insisted."

"And that would be Mr. Chatfield, correct?"

Who was telling her all this?

"Yes, he was very nice."

"He was also one of the people arrested," said Padma.

Ginny was aware. She and Asher had texted over the weekend (Ginny from her MacBook; her phone was probably for sale on craigslist by now). Asher, having spent an entire night in jail, was quite pleased with the turn of events. The arrest added to his street cred and his Insta was lighting up.

"Look, let's get to it," said Padma. "This goes beyond the party. There seems to be a pattern here, and we have an issue."

Pattern?

Padma's intercom came to life. "Ms. Minali, Ms. Gomez-Brown is here."

"Good. Would you send her in please?"

Crap, thought Ginny. Whatever this was, it was heading south.

THERE'VE BEEN COMPLAINTS

Shonda, I appreciate your joining us," said Padma. "We've been discussing the events of the weekend. Before we get to the main issue at hand, I understand there was some ground you wanted to cover."

"Yes, thank you, Padma. Girls, there have been complaints."

"About what?" asked Ginny.

"Virginia, you are the one who attended the event, correct?"

"Yes."

"Why don't you tell us what you were doing at a rap party?"

Shonda was profoundly bothered by these rich white girls feeling like they could wander into a historically and culturally neighborhood of color like they were going to an amusement park.

"I like rap," answered Ginny. "And besides, I was being multicultural. Isn't that what you always tell us, embrace multiculturalism?"

Shonda looked angry. "I'd suggest you tread carefully, Ms. Sanderson. You are in no position to be questioning me or anyone else. Now, why don't you tell us how your *multicultural field trip* ended up with you getting hurt. I understand there was an altercation."

Hyphen Lady was fishing, but why? Ginny had nothing to hide. She would err on the side of truth.

Shonda, in fact, had heard through the DEI network that there might have been a fight, and she strongly suspected Ginny was involved. It would explain the eye.

"I wouldn't exactly call it an altercation," said Ginny.

"So you *were* involved."

"I'm not sure what happened to me is what you heard about. I mean, it was a couple of shoves. Maybe there was a fight later?"

"We don't condone violence of any sort," said Shonda.

"Well, I don't either, Ms. Gomez-Brown, but I got shoved first, so I shoved back. What do you want me to do?"

"Who shoved you?"

Ginny paused. She didn't want to name names, even if they *were* complete dicks. "I don't really know. It was noisy and dark. Like I said, it really wasn't anything."

Shonda glared at her.

"And why would they shove you?"

"Shonda," interjected Padma, "perhaps we should get to what we brought the girls here to speak about."

Shonda raised her hand dismissively, an act of disrespect that surprised both Padma and the girls. "I'm getting to that," she said. "I think this is all connected."

"All *what*?" asked Ginny.

"Just answer the question. Why were you in a fight?"

"I don't know," said Ginny. "It was stupid stuff."

"Stupid stuff, like social media?"

It suddenly dawned on Ginny where this was going. For her part, Zoey still had no idea. Two years and a lot of savvy separated the two sisters.

"They called me some things I didn't appreciate."

"Like what?"

"Oh, groovy things like racist and transphobic, and some other stuff, I think," said Ginny. "I don't respond well to that."

"And why would they do that?" asked Shonda.

"You'd have to ask them."

"Did they have a point?"

"A point about what?"

"Have you done anything to offend anyone lately?"

"No."

"Are you sure?"

"I'm *not* a racist. Or a transphobe."

"No one thinks they are, do they? And yet the things we do . . ."

"I'm sorry, what things?"

Shonda ignored her. "You have been very busy online lately, haven't you?" She made a point of looking at each girl when she said it.

"We're teenagers, so . . ."

Ginny couldn't help but say it with a slight eye roll, which only further infuriated Shonda.

"There were some posts, I gather, from earlier that night, posts that upset some people," said Shonda.

"Upset who?" asked Ginny.

"*Whom*," said Padma. She was still an educator.

"Upset *whom*," said Ginny.

"Those people at the party you were fighting with, for starters, but students here, as well."

"We're talking about the Halloween costumes here, right? That's what has everybody bent? Seriously? I'd like to know who."

"We'll get to that," said Shonda. "The important thing to consider is how you—*both* of you—made others feel."

"How about how *we* feel?"

"And how do you feel?"

"Right now, really annoyed to be missing AP Physics to be called a racist."

"No one here called you a racist."

"It kind of sounded like you did."

"Miss Sanderson," said Padma, "you are skating perilously close to the line."

"Okay, sorry. Maybe you could just say what upset them exactly."

"It doesn't matter," said Shonda. "What matters is that they *are* upset, and *you girls* are what upset them. You two had a text conversation about Halloween costumes that was posted online where you apparently managed to be racist, fascist, transphobic, and religiously offensive all at once. That's quite an accomplishment. Needless to say, we take these matters *very* seriously."

"So, we're back to us being racists?"

"It's not so much that you—and your sister—are racists, at least not consciously. But your own view of yourself might not comport with your effect on others. You are aware, in addition to students of color, we now have a trans girl with us."

"Really? When did that happen?"

Ginny couldn't help herself. Easter Riddle was all anyone was talking about. Shonda looked as though a vein in her forehead might burst.

"*Careful*, Miss Sanderson," said Padma.

"Ms. Minali, Ms. Gomez-Brown. We were talking about things that would be offensive to wear, things we specifically *wouldn't* wear. We aren't racist, transphobic, or . . . the other things you said."

Shonda waved a hand dismissively. "Whether you think you are or not hardly matters. It's how you are perceived through the lens of others. It's their emotional truth, and we have to respect it. You were using oppressed *others* as fodder for your jokes, which is unacceptable. *Un-ac-cep-ta-ble.* Some of our students feel violated and victimized. Several of them were brought to tears."

"Tears? Seriously? Who?"

"Why, so you can bully them further?"

"Now we're bullies too?"

"Effectively, yes. And the who of it is irrelevant. As two children of privilege, you need to be more sensitive to the cultural realities of the less fortunate."

"I should tell you girls I'm tempted to suspend you both," said Padma.

Zoey, for her part, was beginning to panic and decided to jump in. "We'd be happy to apologize to anyone who was offended, Ms. Gomez-Brown. We really didn't mean anything bad."

Ginny wanted to object to her sister's proposal but decided, uncharacteristically, to demur. As a senior with college admissions pending, she was in a particularly delicate situation. The two grown women across from her could make things difficult, should they choose. Reluctantly, it was time to suck it up. She tried her best to look contrite.

"Yes," said Ginny. "Upon reflection, we'd like to apologize. We meant no harm, but with your valuable guidance, we now understand what we did was thoughtless."

Shonda smiled. She knew damn well when someone was bullshitting her, but she'd made them say the words. That was always the first step. One day, they would *believe* the words.

"Girls," said Padma, "you've both been outstanding students and good citizens of this school, until this incident. I think with some simple apologies we can all move past this. There are two girls in particular you should talk to, and I should caution you that it had best be done with sincerity."

What Ginny wanted to say was, *Who are the dumb bitch snowflakes that ratted us out?* Instead, what came out was, "To who—*whom*—do we apologize?"

Padma told them.

"Shit," said Ginny, under her breath.

She also wondered why only two of them were called into Padma's office instead of three.

After the girls left, Padma was lost in thought. As much as she had longed to use the information to rid herself of the Sandersons, she couldn't risk the fallout getting to Clover Hunt. She had fought too hard to expand Lenox Hill's vision of diversity to let something like this affect one of her prize recruits. She could already see the cover of next quarter's *Lenox Leaders*, the alumni magazine, with two of their three Prep for Prep scholarship girls, an Asian

Westinghouse winner, and Clover, right in the middle. Maybe she'd throw in a legacy to keep the wolves at bay.

Easter she would save for next quarter and her very own cover shot.

"Shonda, you have a copy of these posts, right?"

"No."

"But you read them?

"No, I haven't seen them."

"But you said some fairly specific things about them. . . ."

"All you have to do is hear what's being said, the reactions people are having, and you will learn all you need to know, because *that's* the reality. There is an emotional correctness, no matter what the texts say."

"So, you don't know what they actually said?"

"I see the hurt they caused. That's all that matters."

Padma paused for a long moment and then replied, "So true."

SORRY NOT SORRY

Classes broke for lunch shortly after their meeting with Padma and Hyphen Lady.

"C'mon," said Ginny, "let's get this over with before I become physically ill."

Ginny and Zoey entered the dining hall. Nearly every head turned in unison, like at a tennis match. Ginny didn't care much but Zoey wanted to melt into a wall.

The dining tables at Lenox were all round, someone having decided that rectangular tables resulted in power imbalances. No one sat at the head of a table here!

They scanned the room for their would-be accusers.

"There," said Ginny, spotting one of the two girls, neither of whom she'd ever met. "Where's the other one? They're both in your grade, right?"

"Over there," said Zoey. "On the other side."

"Let's do the bitch first," directed Ginny.

They walked over to find Coco French holding court, defying the table's geometry. "Oh, look who it is," she said. "The Sanderson sisters. Nice shiner your sis has there, Doughy. Very goth."

"Yeah," said Ginny. "Keen observation. We need to talk to you for a minute."

"Well, I'm pretty busy," she said. The other girls laughed.

"Look," said Ginny. "We need to talk because Ms. Minali says we need to talk."

"Well, then, go right ahead. What could this possibly be about?"

There were five other girls at the table, and the conversation had their rapt attention. "I mean privately," said Ginny.

"No, I don't think so," said Coco, poking at her salad.

It was horrifying for Ginny to have to debase herself in front of one tenth grader, let alone six. "Still, we should step aside."

"Maybe if you tell me what this is about? What do the Sanderson sisters want? Doughy, cat got your tongue?"

Zoey turned a deep shade of crimson while Ginny bit her lip. "It's about the other night, and her name is *Zoey*."

"Hmm, which other night is that?"

"The texts. You know damn well what I'm talking about."

"Oh, *that* other night. *So* traumatic. But I don't feel we can talk about this without Jemma. I'm not the only victim, you know."

Jemma, Zoey's black classmate who'd been humiliated during the privilege walk, was the other student who had officially complained. "She's terribly injured, you know. I'm surprised she even made it to school today. I see her eating over there, though. Let's go see her and you can tell us both what you have to say."

Coco rose out of her seat. "Girls, don't let them clear my salad."

Jemma, who had always seemed painfully shy, was eating alone, absently poking at some mac 'n cheese. Zoey could relate.

"Jemma!" said Coco. "Look who I brought over. Apparently the Sandersons have something to say to us." Coco sat down, putting an arm around Jemma's shoulder, which visibly stiffened. "Okay, now what is it?"

"We wanted to"—Ginny took a deep breath—"apologize."

"For what?"

"For the other night."

"I'm sorry," said Coco. "Which other night was that again?"

"We were just talking about it. Don't be a bitch."

"Language! And I just want to make sure Jemma is up to speed."

"The night we texted . . . a bunch. Of stuff. We understand some of it was found to be offensive, by you two specifically, so if you were offended, we apologize."

"Hmm," said Coco. "That sounded pretty lame to me. The old, 'I'm sorry if you were offended' bit. Seriously, that's the playbook you're going with? What do you think, Jemma?"

Jemma had been silent up until that moment. "I don't know," she said, barely audible.

"The poor girl can hardly speak, she's so hurt," said Coco, rubbing Jemma's shoulders up and down. Zoey couldn't recall ever seeing Coco talk to Jemma before. "I mean, those were some *horrible* things you two said."

You *two*. Three of them had participated in the conversation, and it was Clover's friend Rhonda who had put the whole thing on Instagram. Surely Ms. Minali knew about Clover's involvement! But it looked as though Clover's role in this was officially being whitewashed.

"Coco," said Zoey. "We are truly sorry. Now can we just let this go, please?"

"Well, I suppose *I* can, and Jemma too—Jemma, we're good, right?" Jemma nodded, almost imperceptibly. Turning back to Ginny and Zoey, Coco said, "Maybe I'll be a good girl and tell Padma you apologized, you know, if I don't have anything better to do. But you two cast quite a wide net, didn't you? I mean, we had natives and slaves and fascists—am I leaving anything out? Oh, wait, right. Almost forgot. You made fun of the *trans* too. Those poor misunderstood people. And this is sort of a pattern with you, isn't it?"

"I have no idea what you're talking about," said Ginny.

"Is that right? Well, I'm not trans, so it's not for me to be offended, but if I were, gosh, I just hope nothing bad comes of this."

"C'mon, Zoey," said Ginny. "We've apologized, now let's go."

Outside the dining hall, Ginny said, "What a complete bitch. I'm sorry you have to be in the same grade with her."

"Tell me about it. I think her father is on the board with Dad."

"Of course he is."

Just then, Clover found them. "Hey, you guys. I am so sorry. I feel very guilty right now."

"Yeah," said Ginny. "How come you didn't get to attend our little inquisition in Padma's office?"

"Oh, I met with her, and Hyphen Lady too. Just now. They asked me if I knew anything about the posts. I said yes. Then they suggested that maybe it was you guys who did most of the texting. They hadn't even seen them! I said, no, I was fully doing it, too, which didn't seem to be the answer they wanted. They also asked me about the rap party, but I told them I wasn't there. Then they had me wait outside while they talked. When I went back in, Padma told me to be mindful of what I say in the future and that I could go. She also said my apology was accepted. I didn't even say sorry!"

"That's it?" said Ginny.

"That's it," said Clover.

"Immunity," said Zoey. "You were right!"

"Yeah, but suddenly I feel like crap."

"What are you talking about?" asked Ginny.

"Clover says that her chosen identity of an eco-sexual member of the goblincore gives her a free pass from stuff," said Zoey.

"So, wait. You're not actually into that scene?"

"I mean, who's to say, really—wait, there's a scene? I wasn't informed. Do we have good parties?"

Ginny burst out laughing. "Fucking brilliant."

"Then how come right now I feel like crawling into a hole?"

"Don't worry about it," said Ginny. "Maybe this is over, anyway. And besides, our dad's on the board. That's got to be good for something."

Coco had, in fact, approached Easter Riddle, just as she'd approached Jemma, to make sure she knew she should be offended, but couldn't convince her to get involved. It had been hard enough to convince Jemma. But, as she scanned Instagram, seeing yet another post from Easter Riddle's parents, another approach came to mind.

She'd been talking to the wrong people.

She sneaked off to the new yoga studio to use her phone. No one would be there during lunch.

EASTER IS A SENSITIVE GIRL

That afternoon, Celeste informed Padma that Shannon and Mark Riddle were on the line.

"Padma Minali."

"I thought you said we were safe at Lenox, or were those just words?" bellowed Mark Riddle, dispensing with formalities.

"I'm sorry," said Padma. "You have me at a loss."

"Two of your students, the daughters of a board member, no less, were *mocking* the trans community on social media. Is this something you find acceptable?"

Padma sighed. The Sandersons. Again. "You're referring to the texts."

"They discussed the idea of dressing up as trans people for Halloween! Can you imagine how that made Easter feel? We had a lot of choices, you know. And we still do."

Padma thought she'd put this to bed, making sure that Clover Hunt wasn't collateral damage. Now she wished she'd bothered to read the texts. She should probably make a point of it.

"We only recently became aware of the situation, and yes, there were some complaints, although not from your daughter. I hope Easter's not upset."

"Well, of course she's upset!" said Shannon. "Wouldn't you be if someone mocked your gender preference? Easter is very sensitive."

"I completely understand. On behalf of the school, I apologize. I will make sure the Sanderson girls formally apologize to Easter. I will talk to her as well."

"Save your apologies, because it's worse than that," said Shannon. "The other night Ginny Sanderson attacked a trans girl, one from another school. Easter does *not* feel safe!"

"What? I know nothing about this."

"How is it we know, and you don't? You run this school!"

"Whom did she attack?"

"Someone like Easter from another school."

"Another trans girl?"

"Yes."

"And where did this happen?"

"At a party in Harlem. Did you know about *that*?"

It seems Ginny Sanderson had not told the full truth. "Yes, we're aware."

"And this, after we gave you our full cooperation for the *Sentinel* piece!" barked Shannon.

"And we remain very appreciative. Believe me when I say I'm on your side. I just need to gather a few facts before I take any action."

"*Facts*." Shannon practically spit the word into the phone. "At this point, what do those matter? The damage is done."

"I'll make sure Easter meets with our counselor," said Padma.

"Sure, wonderful, but how can she come to school with Ginny Sanderson walking around? She's in danger!"

"I assure you we will take all steps necessary to make sure no violence occurs in this school."

"Not good enough," said Mark. "We're considering pulling Easter out for a couple of days and then we'll see where things stand. Lenox may not be the best place for her."

"Please, Mr. Riddle. We are an inclusive school and will do whatever it takes to make this a safe place for your daughter. Sometimes change rattles some cages, but we are committed to it. I think you will see that. And I will get to the bottom of this, you have my word."

"Well, we'll see, won't we? You should know Dina Campbell is very interested in this."

"Mr. Riddle . . . Mark. And Shannon. Might you give me a couple of days to sort through this before we further involve the media?"

"Too late."

"You've already spoken to Dina?"

"Yes, we thought it best. You should also know we have sought legal representation."

"What? Why?"

"We're keeping our options open."

This was not going well. Padma knew none of this would please the board, and there'd be no getting around reporting it to them if she couldn't manage the situation.

Fundamentally, she was entirely in sync with the Riddles but only when *she* was controlling the narrative. This caught her by surprise. She needed to put a cap on the damage and repurpose this situation to her needs, not those of the two crazy parents fulminating on her phone. Padma swallowed her pride for a moment.

"Thank you so much for bringing this to my attention, but this all seems a bit precipitous. May I suggest the following? With your permission, I will look into all this immediately and then get back to you very soon. We will handle things, I promise. In the meantime, Easter is excused from any classes and can meet with Ms. Kirby, our school counselor, if she wishes. Does this meet with your satisfaction, at least for the moment?"

"Hold on." Padma was out on hold. "*Fine,*" said Shannon, finally. Then the line went dead.

Padma wrestled with the situation. She could *not* afford to lose Easter. She had to make sure the Riddles were happy.

But how?

Did Ginny Sanderson really attack a trans girl? That would be plan B, wrapped in a bow. But before she could do anything, she needed more facts.

She had an idea.

COCO DISHES

"Celeste, would you pull Coco French from class and ask her to come to my office, please?"

Coco might not have answers, but she was a responsible girl and, as class president, was plugged into student life in a way no teacher could ever be. She was also a bit of a suck-up, which might prove convenient.

Moments later, Coco appeared at Padma's door, looking apprehensive.

"Close the door. Please sit."

Coco did, assuming a bolt-upright posture.

"Don't worry, you're not in trouble. I just want to ask you a few questions, then you can get back to class."

"Of course, Ms. Minali."

"Those texts that the Sanderson girls were sending around, the ones you quite properly brought to our attention. . . . Do you still have them?"

"I don't know, I might. They weren't the kind of thing I ever wanted to see again. So painful . . ."

"I understand, but would you mind checking?"

"Do I have permission to take out my phone?"

Lenox had a strict no-cell-phone policy during school hours. "Yes, of course."

Coco fished out her iPhone. Padma marveled at how quickly her thumbs navigated the device. "Yes, here they are." Coco handed the iPhone to Padma.

"Is there a way to print something from your phone?"

"Yes, if you have a wireless printer here, I could connect to it."

Padma hit the intercom. "Celeste, is our printer wireless?"

"Yes, it is. Can I help with something?"

"Just ask her which one I should connect to," said Coco.

"HP Officejet Pro," came the answer.

"Found it," said Coco. "Printing now."

"Celeste, would you please bring that in after it prints?"

"Of course."

Padma took her hand off the intercom.

"There's something else I'd like to ask you about . . . in confidence."

"Yes, Ms. Minali. You can totally trust me."

"There was an event the other night, a rap party."

"Oh, sure. The one in Harlem where all those people got arrested. Everyone knows about that."

"Were you there, by any chance?"

"Oh, no! That's not something that would interest me, although I do find rap to be a relevant form of cultural expression."

"Sure, sure. It appears that Ginny Sanderson was there, and something happened. A fight. I'm sure you noticed her black eye today. Has she apologized to you, by the way?"

"Yes, Ms. Minali."

"Good. Anyway, the black eye. Do you happen to know how she got it? I know you weren't there, but I thought maybe you'd heard something."

"I may have, but I hate to pass along gossip. I'd feel like a snitch."

You had no problem snitching about those texts, thought Padma. But right now, that was beside the point. Coco was proving useful.

"I understand, but there are bigger issues at play here, ones that involve the safety of this school and its students. Let's just say I absolve you of any part in this."

Coco had friends everywhere, not just at Lenox. She knew exactly what went down in Harlem, and she knew it wasn't much. But Coco was savvy to the crosswinds of modern culture, the media, and socials.

"I may know something," she said.

"Would you please share that with me now?"

"Well, okay, as long as you understand I'm reluctant to say anything."

"Noted," said Padma, becoming exasperated. "Now, Coco, please, if you would."

"Ginny was there, and a bunch of kids from other schools too. I guess some of them had seen those texts because they made the rounds, plus the article in the *Sentinel* came out that day, so it was all anyone was talking about."

"Just so we're clear, you mean the article about Easter."

"Yes."

"Go on."

"Some of them were upset, you know, about the texts. One of the kids there was someone from Grafton who's decided to transition. She used to go by Dillon, but now she's Violet."

"Wait, Grafton has a transitioning student? When did this happen?"

"After she heard about Easter. I guess she'd been thinking about it for a while."

"I don't understand. When did she begin her transition?"

"When she read about Easter."

"You mean, in the *Sentinel*?"

"Yes."

"The article that came out Friday."

"Yes."

"You're telling me Dillon—Violet—announced her transition on Friday?"

"To some friends, yes."

"It's only Monday. How do you know this?"

Coco's expression, however briefly, suggested that was a stupid question.

"Never mind," said Padma, considering the information.

"Anyway," continued Coco, "from what I hear, she was upset about the texts but *also* upset because the *Sentinel* article could have been about *her* if only she'd decided to transition sooner. The trans can be very competitive, you know."

"So what happened then?"

"Well, when Violet and some of the others found out Ginny was at the party, they didn't feel safe—I mean, who could blame them? So they told Ginny. They asked her to leave, and I guess she refused. There was a fight."

"So would you say that Ginny *attacked* Violet?"

"Well, I wasn't there, so I really couldn't say."

"But what have you heard?"

"There was a lot of confusion, and Ginny . . . Well, you know how she can be."

Indeed, Padma did. The girl was headstrong.

Celeste came in with the printout.

"Thank you, Celeste. Coco, thank you for your assistance. You may return to class."

"Always happy to help, Ms. Minali."

Padma read through the texts after Coco left. Ginny was right, they were talking about costumes that would be offensive to wear, but that hardly excused the matter. Ginny and Zoey had used serious issues like the trans movement as fodder for humor, and that crossed a line.

Clover Hunt's involvement was problematic but easily dismissed. Clover was a unique case who had no doubt suffered all too much oppression in her own life. It wouldn't do to subject her to more, and besides, she had clearly been roped into this by the Sanderson girls. *They* were at the center of it all, ground zero for hate at the Lenox School.

There would be a price to pay.

SYLVIA HAFFRED

It didn't take long for Padma to meet the Riddles' lawyer. The next day, before Celeste could warn her, the door to her office swung open, and a woman with a helmet of auburn hair and a smartly cut blazer walked in, immediately establishing a proprietary air. Easter and her parents trailed in her wake like ducklings.

"Padma Minali? I'm Sylvia Haffred."

She thrust out a hand, which Padma reluctantly took. She knew exactly who Sylvia Haffred was and, as it happened, grudgingly admired her work. This admiration, though, was secondary to her consternation at Haffred's unannounced presence in her office.

"Forgive my confusion, did we have an appointment?" asked Padma.

Haffred ignored the question and sat down. The Riddles followed suit, taking the couch. Easter's left arm was bandaged and in a sling. Padma, noticing: "Easter, what happened?"

"I, uh—"

Haffred interrupted before Easter could say anything else. "This is a beautiful school," she said. "I went to Stuyvesant, myself. The Lenox School for Girls wasn't teeming with Jews in my day."

That was true, Padma knew. "Things have changed," she said.

Haffred stared for a moment. "Have they?"

Padma bristled at the implication. She, Padma, was the very embodiment of that change! But she let it go. Best to find out what the agenda was here.

"As you may know," continued Haffred, "I like to champion those who lack a voice."

And yourself, thought Padma. Haffred did good work, but it was dangerous to stand between her and a camera. And the assumed familiarity with her career was thoroughly annoying. Not everyone on the planet knew who Sylvia Haffred was, even if Padma did.

"Most recently, I have taken up the cause of the trans community. Last year, you likely remember I represented a Yale trans athlete in her efforts to compete in women's ice hockey. We successfully petitioned the NCAA to change its rules."

Padma had followed the case. The feminist community was split on the issue of trans athletes. Younger, progressive feminists were all-in, while more traditional feminists often objected to the idea of more muscular ex-men taking women's spots on teams. Haffred had thrown in with the more progressive crowd, as had Padma. In fact, Easter had just gone out for the Lenox field hockey team. But their comity on the issue still didn't make it a good thing that Haffred was sitting on the other side of her desk with the school's sole trans student. Padma sat quietly and listened, hoping Haffred would get to the point.

"I want to be straight with you at the outset," said Haffred. "We've been in touch with the media, so you can expect some attention."

"Are you suggesting we have something to hide? As an institution, we've been quite progressive on this issue. In fact, just last week—"

"The Dina Campbell article, I know. I've spoken to her at length. That was a PR piece. Your so-called inclusiveness is a sham."

"Excuse me, but Mark, Shannon, we spoke at some length just yesterday. I thought we agreed that I would have some time to investigate this matter."

"That was before," said Mark.

"Before what?"

"Before Easter got hurt."

"What happened? Easter, honey, are you all right?"

Easter just looked at the floor, not saying anything.

"You know," said Haffred. "There's a name for what you do here. It's called *transwashing.*"

"Trans—I'm sorry, you have me at a loss, but it's clear you've come here with a grievance, so perhaps you could share it with me. Is this about the party?"

"This is about what kind of environment you seem to be fostering here, Ms. Minali."

"I assure you, the Lenox School fully embraces inclusion and encourages social action."

"Funny, then, that your students publicly mocked the trans community online and then one went on to assault a member of that community. Is that what you call inclusive, Ms. Minali? My client is traumatized, both mentally and physically, and no longer feels safe at your school. The question is, what are you going to do about it?"

Padma was momentarily speechless. She looked at Easter. "Easter, honey, what happened to you? Are you hurt?"

"*Yes*, she's hurt. I think you can plainly see that."

Was Easter involved with the fight at the rap party? It was time to find out what cards Haffred was playing with. "Could you elaborate, please?"

"Gladly."

Haffred launched into a diatribe about the Halloween texts.

"We know about the texts, and we are dealing with it," said Padma.

"And do you know that when my client confronted one of them about it, she was *attacked*. Specifically by Ginny Sanderson."

"I'm sorry, was Easter at the rap party?"

"No, I'm referring to my other client, Violet Skinner."

"They are *both* your clients?"

"They are."

"So, if she wasn't there, why is Easter's arm in a sling? Easter, will you please tell me in your own words what happened?"

"She's too traumatized to talk," said Haffred.

"Okay, then I'll ask you. Why is Easter's arm in a sling?"

"She cut herself, Padma!" broke in Shannon, raising her voice. "Easter is very sensitive, and all this is just too much."

"I'm sure, Ms. Minali," said Haffred, "you've heard of cutting as a form of traumatic self-mutilation."

"I have, and I'm going to ask that our nurse take a look at that."

"Absolutely not," said Haffred.

Padma was reasonably certain she was being played, but she also realized there might be an opportunity here, one that would please certain parties. Barbara Selkirk, for one. Barbara was an increasingly important presence on the board and wanted, like Padma, for Lenox to adopt a higher profile in the fight for social justice.

Sylvia Haffred was a grifter, Padma knew. A shameless opportunist, posing as a progressive, fishing for settlements. And the Riddles were little better. They would post something about Easter's alleged injury and probably even manage to leverage it into sponsorships.

But no matter. Padma realized she might have leverage of her own. Two could play this game. Change was made possible by just such moments. Education, the "three Rs," and so forth, was important, but it was useless if the world wasn't a level playing field.

The Sandersons wouldn't be happy, but they were a vestige of another time. Padma quietly seethed at the mere thought of William Sanderson. The sheer audacity, to think his daughter was entitled to go to Yale simply because she was his daughter . . .

She hit her intercom. "Celeste? Would you mind coming back in? I'm going to need to email the upper school faculty. There's a change of plan for tomorrow. Sylvia, thank you so much for bringing the full import of this situation to my attention. I assure you, Lenox stands with the trans community."

"That is so good to hear," said Haffred. "I'm sure you'll do the right thing." Haffred marched out, the Riddles trailing in a tight clump of three behind her.

A statement. Wasn't that what Wilson Girard said? She hadn't heard anything from him after sending the *Sentinel* article. Probably too busy slurping up rice pudding.

As she sat there, spinning a pen in her fingers, plan B took shape.

"I have Dina Campbell for you on line one?" said Celeste over the intercom.

"I'll take it."

SUSPENDED

That evening, the landline rang at the Sandersons' apartment. The caller ID read: Lenox Hill School.

At this hour?

"This is Ellie Sanderson."

"Mrs. Sanderson, hi, it's Padma Minali."

"Ms. Minali, is everything okay?"

"Oh, yes, of course. Is Mr. Sanderson home? Perhaps I could speak with both of you."

Ellie was immediately wary. "Is this about us again, or one of our daughters?"

"The latter, but there's nothing to worry about. This is a courtesy call more than anything. Perhaps you could get Mr. Sanderson and put me on speaker?"

Ellie had a bad feeling. A nighttime call about her girls? She retrieved William from the study. "Okay, we're both here."

"Hello, Padma," said William. "Burning the midnight oil?"

"A head of school's job has no hours, I'm afraid."

"What can we do for you this evening?"

"This is just a courtesy call, really, and there's nothing to worry about, but your girls have been caught up in something. Ginny in particular."

"Is this about the other night?" asked Ellie.

"Yes . . . in part."

"Go on," said William.

"It's nothing, really. Just a bit of a misunderstanding, but you know how these things can get blown out of proportion."

"No, we don't," said Ellie. "What things?"

"Ellie, please. Let Padma speak."

Padma continued. "It seems the other night, before the party, they were texting things—silly things, really, about Halloween costumes, and the texts got around somehow. They were meant to be harmless, I'm sure, but some people were . . . Well, let's just say their feelings were hurt."

Ellie bristled. "Their feelings were hurt? By what? Who were these texts about?"

"Not any specific people, exactly. But as I said, feelings were hurt."

"And why would hurt feelings be something the head of school takes a personal interest in? That seems a little under your pay grade."

"Ellie, please," said William. "I'm sure this is nothing."

"Well, I suppose I wouldn't ordinarily, but your husband is on the board, so I just thought you should know. As a courtesy. It's best to nip these things in the bud."

"That seems wise," said William.

"We had your daughters apologize to some of the girls here at school who were upset, and I'd hoped that would be the end of it."

"And?"

"Well, there was a bit more to it, and that's where the party comes in."

"Yes," said William. "We're aware she went."

"Of course we're aware," said Ellie. "We picked her up at the *hospital*."

"Oh, yes. I did see her eye."

"She's fine," said William. "Please continue."

"Apparently, your daughter was approached by some girls who weren't happy about the texts."

"Yes, there were three of them, and a boy, and they attacked her," said Ellie. "Did you know that? This could have been much worse. She thinks they were from Brearley. And a boy from Grafton."

"It's possible that's not the entire story," said Padma.

"And how is that?"

"I've been in touch with June Freeman, the head of school at Brearley, and the other girls claim Ginny attacked *them*."

Ellie wasn't taking this. "Oh, so she gave herself that black eye?"

"I don't really know about that, but the fact is, we have the word of one versus the word of three."

"And it's your position that Ginny, all one hundred and thirty-five pounds of her, beat up three girls and a boy."

"Well, I didn't say *beat up*, exactly. I said *attacked*. The others say she was the aggressor."

"Even though it was they who first approached Ginny."

"We're doing our best here to get all the facts, Mrs. Sanderson. That's the most important thing. But I should mention that the boy, as you call him, is a bit of a sensitive case."

"And what does *that* mean?"

"Padma, please hang on just a moment." William hit the hold button. "Ellie, please. I'm sure this will all sort out."

"Is that what you think, William? That our daughter is being accused of assault and it will all just *sort out*?"

"Padma's on our side, and I'll remind you, we *need* her on our side."

"Oh, right. *Yale*."

"I'm putting her back on."

"Hi, Padma, sorry about that. You mentioned something about a sensitive case?"

"Yes, well, you know how these things can be, and I just want to do everything I can to nip things in the bud."

"Yes, you keep saying that," said Ellie, earning a glare from William.

"The boy, as you said, was not a boy. Her name is Violet Skinner."

"I don't understand," said Ellie. "He goes to Grafton."

"It is true that *she* goes to Grafton. You see, Violet recently transitioned."

"What? When?"

"I don't know all the facts, Mrs. Sanderson." That was true, thought Padma. She didn't know *all* the facts even if she did know that Violet's transition began on Friday. "But the timing isn't relevant. She has chosen to identify as female, so that's what she is. The NAIS guidelines are very clear on this, and we must honor her choice."

"Padma," said Ellie, "according to my daughter, *Violet* Skinner is a Grafton wrestler and outweighs her by forty pounds."

"She was a wrestler?" chirped William. "I used to wrestle, at least until I discovered squash."

"William, for God's sake."

"Violet's background isn't really the issue here either. We must respect the decisions she's made, just as we do for our own trans student, Easter Riddle, who, I will add, is quite concerned for her *own* safety right now, as are her parents."

"*Her* safety?" barked Ellie. "Safety from what, our daughter? Are you kidding?"

"Do I think Ginny would attack Easter? No, Mrs. Sanderson, of course not. At least, I don't think so. But we can't deny Easter her feelings. Easter's lived experience is quite different from ours, and I've seen firsthand how this has upset her. But this is more about a climate of hostility."

"I don't even know what you're saying right now," said Ellie.

"Well, as I said, we're still gathering the facts, and there's one more aspect of this that is of concern. Apparently, Ginny also called Violet something problematic. She referred to her as *Dillon*, and also as *dude*."

"And?"

"It may have been what caused things to escalate. Ginny's being accused of both misgendering and deadnaming."

"I'm sorry, what, and what?" asked William.

"Misgendering. I think that one is self-explanatory. And she also used Violet's deadname."

"Her deadname."

"Yes, Dillon, her name before transitioning. This may all sound silly to you, but words have meaning, and they can hurt."

"This is lunacy," said Ellie.

"Yes, well, I appreciate and value your view, of course. But just for safety's sake, I'm going to ask that your girls stay home tomorrow."

"Excuse me, what? Why?" Ellie was leaning over, mouth practically eating the phone.

"It's just precautionary, for everyone's safety. It's a sensitive time right now, and I want to give this twenty-four hours to cool off. And, as William is on the board, I want to make sure none of this touches him either."

"Why would this touch *me*?" asked William.

"I'm sure it *wouldn't*, at least I can't imagine it would. But I find it always pays to manage for every contingency."

"Yes, that seems wise," said William.

"So, we'll let the rest of the girls talk it through tomorrow and that should be that."

"What do you mean, talk it through?" asked Ellie.

Padma immediately wished she hadn't mentioned that part.

"Just talk," she said. "Nothing serious. It's important for our students to express themselves. We can't let anything simmer."

Ellie hit the mute button and glared at her husband. "This is bad."

"It's not ideal, I'll admit, but it will all blow over in a couple of days. Everyone will move on to something else. Plus, I'm on the board. She's not going to screw me."

"She's screwing you right now, you just don't see it."

Ellie took the call off mute.

"Ms. Minali, getting back to the genesis of this, what did our girls actually *say* in the texts?"

There was a brief pause as Padma considered how to answer. "As I said, silly things about Halloween. Apologies were made, and we're just trying to move past that part."

"Well, good," said William. "That seems best."

"It's been nice chatting," said Padma, "but I'd better get back to it."

"Okay, well thank you so much for the call, and thank you for handling this," he said.

"My pleasure." Padma hung up the phone.

William looked at Ellie. "There, see? Board membership has its advantages. I doubt others would have gotten a courtesy call like that."

Ellie glared at him. "You know, sometimes I think you're a complete idiot. Our girls were just suspended and you're crowing about your position on the board?"

"Suspended? They weren't suspended."

"Oh, really? Is that what you think? That they're just getting a day off? I *do not* trust that woman. I think we need representation."

"A lawyer? Don't be ridiculous. What kind of message would that send? We can't be seen as adversarial."

An exasperated Ellie marched out and headed straight for Ginny's room. She was going to get answers.

"Hey, how about some privacy?" cried Ginny. Ellie had not obliged with her usual courtesy knock.

"Okay, let's see those texts. Now."

"What texts?"

"The ones that you and your sister are suspended over tomorrow. Did you know that?"

"I wasn't suspended. Padma made us give stupid apologies to a couple of girls and that was that."

"Oh, really? Did you just get off the phone with her? Because I did. She told us *both* of you are to stay home tomorrow. It seems that in addition to the texts, people are saying you attacked a trans girl at that party."

"*What?* That's bullshit!"

"The texts, *now.*"

Although the texts had been deleted on Clover's end, they were still on Ginny's MacBook, which she retrieved. Ellie took a few moments and read them. "What am I missing?" she asked.

"Nothing. That's it."

"But this is harmless."

"No kidding!" said Ginny. "People are crazy."

"Send these to the printer in the den."

"Okay, whatever."

"They also seem to be upset about how you addressed this person you had the fight with."

"Who, that douchebag Dillon?"

"Yes. He's apparently not Dillon anymore."

"What do you mean?"

"He goes by Violet and he's transitioning, or at least plans to or something. Who knows? He's like Easter. They say you misgendered him. Or her."

"Well, how was I supposed to know? Was there a memo? This is bullshit!"

"I'm just telling you how *they* see it. The Riddles say it makes Easter feel unsafe."

Ginny's face screwed up and she let out something like a primal scream. Then she spun on her heels and marched to her bathroom, slamming and locking the door.

"What the hell is going on?" said William, drawn in by the noise.

"Just your daughter, being perfectly reasonable."

William decided the best course of action was to retreat to his study.

A DAY OF HONEST DISCUSSION

The next morning, as Clover entered the Lenox courtyard, there was a buzz. It was more than the usual arrival-time chatter. "What's going on?" she asked a nearby classmate.

"No classes today," came the answer. "Upper and middle schools only."

"Why?"

"I don't know."

"So, can I go home?"

"No, I think there's something else."

Filing into the school lobby, they were met by Ms. Minali. "Everyone make their way to the auditorium, please. We're having a town hall."

"What about?" asked Clover.

"Just go on in and find a seat, please."

Clover went in and sat down, deliberately choosing a seat near the back in case she chose to nod off, which she considered a high probability. Up on the stage, there was a giant screen that read:

A DAY OF HONEST DISCUSSION

Hyphen Lady was up there, plus two empty chairs. Clover's bullshit meter was suddenly on high alert. Coco and the rest of the BB Girls were seated nearby and looked excited. She could hear Coco say, "This is going to be so fucking good. There should be popcorn."

What the hell was going on?

Looking around again, Clover noticed Easter Riddle's parents standing in the back, cameras out. They were probably posting to Instagram, where they were becoming semi-famous, along with Easter. Dina Campbell, the reporter, was with them too. They seemed attached at the hip.

Once everyone was seated, Padma took the stage behind a lectern.

"Okay, girls, quiet down," she said. "I am joined by Shonda Gomez-Brown, whom you all know. At this time, I would like to ask two of our seniors to the stage: Kiara Thomas and Easter Riddle."

The students applauded enthusiastically. Kiara was president of Students for Equity, and Easter, well she was Easter, emerging trans poster child.

Hyphen Lady took to the podium first. She shushed the students, who largely ignored her. Then she tried just standing there, silently, until they got the point. When the room finally quieted, she let the silence hang there for a moment, as if to underscore the seriousness of the moment.

"As many of you know, there were some recent incidents, ones that were a gross violation of our community standards, and ones that involved our own. Jokes were made online, highly unfortunate ones, that were tinged with racism, transphobia, and other offensive content."

Clover sat bolt upright. *Oh, shit,* she thought. She swiveled to scan the room for Ginny and Zoey but didn't see them anywhere.

More words came out of Hyphen Lady's mouth, all part of the usual narrative, one she'd heard a hundred times by now. Clover suspected there might be a handful of others who knew what crap it was, but it hardly mattered. This was the regime talking, and the penalties for stepping out of line were severe. Thank goodness for immunity.

Hyphen Lady's tone got progressively angrier, and Clover imagined her as one of those unintelligible adults in a Peanuts special. Systemic racism. *Wah.* Privilege. *Wah Wah.* Oppression of the other. *Wah Wah Wah.* The narrative was being molded to fit recent events in a strategy used countless times before. Most, Clover knew, would accept it as congregants listening to the gospel.

Her head began to throb, and she raised her hands to her temples, pressing hard to make it stop. This was all her fault!

Kiara was invited to the mic. She was *terribly* offended by events, felt unsafe, and all but named Ginny and Zoey. She didn't have to—everyone knew. The rivers of social media moved swiftly indeed.

Kiara sat and Hyphen Lady said, "But recent events have been hurtful to more than our students of color. As we welcome our next schoolmate, I'd like to remind everyone that personal expression is the highest value there is. Easter, would you come up?"

The students applauded. At first, though, Easter didn't move, seemingly glued to her seat.

"Easter?" said Hyphen Lady. "We'd love to hear what you have to say. Give us your truth."

The applause now organized itself, finding a cadence, as the students lent their encouragement. They were a single organism now, shaped by countless fingers hitting countless "likes," and one that agreed overwhelmingly with the decision to bring trans students into Lenox. "We love you Easter!" someone shouted. Then the chanting started. *"Ea-ster! Ea-ster! Ea-ster!"*

Easter rose from her chair.

Clover thought she looked ridiculous, her heavy legs stretching below a tartan skirt. She also looked shaky, unsteady on her feet. Was it an act? And why was her arm in a sling? Turning her head, Clover saw Easter's parents, faces aglow, filming the whole thing. She wanted to punch both of them in the face.

Easter got to the mic and stood there, staring, as the chanting died down and the auditorium grew silent. Still, she said nothing. The silence then stretched uncomfortably, and Easter continued to stare. Whatever it was, Clover no longer sensed it was an act. Easter did not want to be there.

"Uh, hello," she said. People clapped again as Easter stared fixedly into space, focused on something, or nothing. Her energy didn't match the energy the room had given her. She was sweating, something accentuated by the bright stage lights. Silence fell again. A seat shifted, a cough echoed.

Padma, who had a handheld mic, said, "Easter, please tell us what you're feeling."

Easter's gaze broke and her eyes darted about. "I feel . . . I feel . . ."

Even from the back row, Clover could identify a panic attack. Perhaps Easter really was offended by events or maybe she didn't like public speaking. Or maybe she suspected, as did Clover, that she was a pawn in a larger game.

Easter's mouth moved, as if to form words, but none came. Padma rose and crossed the stage, trying to raise a reassuring hand to Easter's back. Before she could, Easter turned and walked off the stage. It would be more accurate to say she *fled*.

Just then, the whooshing sound of pneumatic brakes caused Clover to turn and look back. In the rear of the auditorium there was a lone window to the courtyard and the street beyond. A large bus had pulled up, and people were getting off. People with signs. Was Dina Campbell smiling?

Oh, shit.

Clover discreetly slid her phone from her pocket and started texting.

Ellie's cell buzzed. It was Tizzy. "El, sweetie, do you know what's going on down at school?"

Ellie assumed Tizzy was fishing for gossip about the girls, so her guard was up. "I'm not sure . . . Why, what's going on?"

"I don't know, exactly. I was hoping you knew more than I did. But I got a cryptic text from Chrissie. I think there's some kind school-wide meeting going on. I'm not sure what it's about, but I think your girls are involved somehow. Have you heard from either of them?"

"They're actually home sick today."

"Oh, are they okay?"

"They're fine. I'm sure they'll be back tomorrow."

"Oh, good. I . . . Wait, I just got another text. Something about protesters."

"*Protesters?* About what?"

"I don't know. The girls aren't supposed to use their phones at school so I'm just getting bits and pieces. I wish I could tell you more."

Just then, Ginny and Zoey emerged simultaneously from their rooms, both staring down at their phones.

"Uh, Tizzy, I have to go." She punched out of the call.

Zoey held up her phone. There was a text from Clover, also addressed to Ginny.

> SOS!!! Big meeting here. Hanging u guys out to
> dry!! Protesters outside. WTF?

"We need to get up there!" cried Ginny.

"No! You two are not going anywhere. I'll find out what's going on, but I'm calling your father first."

"Jesus, look at this!" said Ginny, again holding up her newly acquired phone. It was a short video of some protesters shouting something Ellie couldn't make out. There were maybe a couple of dozen in all, and they were clearly standing outside Lenox Hill. It was an eccentric group in various states of undress. They had signs.

"Where are you seeing this?"

"On X," said Ginny, thumbs a blur on her phone's tiny keyboard. "But it's popping up on Insta now too."

Ellie punched William's entry on her phone. It went to voicemail. She called his office number. His assistant answered. "Teresa, it's Ellie. I need William."

"I'm sorry, Mrs. Sanderson, but he was asked into an executive committee meeting, and I can't disturb him. Can I have him return your call when he's out?"

"No, this is an emergency. Please get him."

"Mrs. Sanderson—"

"*Teresa.*"

"All right. I'm going to put you on hold."

A minute or two went by. "Mom, what the hell is going on?" asked Ginny.

"They're finding your father." Ellie decided to retreat to the den for some privacy.

She heard the line come back. "Mrs. Sanderson? I have your husband."

"Please tell me this is good," he said.

"Will, there's some kind of protest at school, and I think it's about the girls."

"What girls?"

"*Our* girls."

"What on earth are you talking about?"

"I don't know exactly, but Tizzy called and—"

"Oh, Tizzy. Well, then."

Ellie's breathing grew rapid. "Also, the girls are getting messages, I don't know, exactly, but I think the school is using them as scapegoats, and I'm just really panicked right now."

"Scapegoats? Over what?"

"The damn texts!"

"What, the Halloween stuff?"

"Yes!! And maybe the trans kid, I don't know."

"Oh, come on, El. We both know that was a big nothing burger."

"Oh, my God, sometimes you can be so naive!"

"Calm down. It sounds like you're hyperventilating."

"Don't tell me to calm down! This is Ginny and Zoey we're talking about."

"They might be reacting to that article in the *Sentinel*. It barely mentioned the school, but Lenox hates publicity. At least that kind."

"And Ginny was gone before the police got there, so it shouldn't matter. I'm *telling* you we don't know the whole story."

"Okay, okay. Look, I'm on the goddamn board, I trust Padma. They're not going to do anything to our girls. Something just got lost in the translation here."

"Oh, right. Mr. Big Stuff on the board. Believe what you want, but I'm going to school now, and I think you should come. Did I mention there are *protesters?*"

"Correct me if I'm wrong, but our girls are home today, right?"

"Yes."

"So, nothing's going to happen to them. They're perfectly safe and they've done nothing wrong. If it makes you feel any better, I'll call Padma later and find out what's going on."

"I think you should come with me now, Will."

"Ellie, do you have any idea what you pulled me out of, apparently for nothing? I was asked to present to an Executive Committee meeting. I look like a fucking idiot right now. I have to get back in there."

If she'd been on a landline, she would have slammed down the receiver. As it was, she had to settle for a resolute jab to the side of her phone to disconnect her husband.

Then she grabbed her coat.

GOOD LITTLE SOLDIERS

Clover's head was on a swivel. There was the villainous Coco to one side, so excited she could hardly contain herself. In the back, Dina Campbell was making for the exit, sensing the story was moving outside. Mr. and Mrs. Riddle rushed up the side aisle, probably on their way backstage to find Easter. No doubt they would publicly document whatever was going on with her.

Up on the stage, Kiara Thomas looked, what? Disappointed? Annoyed? Her brow furrowed and her mouth turned down at the corners. Yes, Clover decided, it was annoyance, but why? She had a hunch: There was a changing of the guard here, one that didn't favor Kiara. Critical race theory, anti-racism, all those culture-changing movements given birth in the Summer of George were taking a back seat to a new cultural wave, the transgender movement. The BIPOC were being upstaged by the gender-fluid.

It was almost hard to keep track, things were moving so fast, but Clover was a keen observer of the cultural firmament. Indeed, she had deliberately placed herself squarely in the middle of it, even if her chosen persona was little more than a construct. (She quietly suspected the same was true of many of the other "plus" people.)

Padma and Hyphen Lady told everyone to stay seated. From outside, someone chanted into a bullhorn. It was loud enough to be heard in the auditorium, although the chants were a bit difficult to make out. One thing was clear, though.

Sylvia Haffred had arrived.

Padma should have known better!

She had invited Haffred to come to the town hall, to see for herself how Lenox was not the school she imagined. But Haffred was nowhere to be found in the audience, opting instead to make trouble outside. The woman was an opportunist, no doubt sniffing a settlement on behalf of the Riddles. Lenox's $210 million endowment made a tempting target. That the rap party and the texting both happened outside of school property would be beside the point. Haffred never went to court. She was a shakedown specialist who knew how to leverage the media. That her target was a private school unaccustomed to transparency or scrutiny was a bonus.

Standing on the stage, Padma did her best not to let her anger show. The girls were buzzing and she considered her options. Her ability to control events was rapidly evaporating. The only question was how to play this. If she kept the girls where they were, it might look as though she were impeding the Movement. If she excused them, who knew what might happen outside? She could be blamed if things went south. Either play entailed risk.

Padma had a quick sidebar with Shonda. Shonda's view was that they should continue inside with the program as planned. This didn't surprise Padma. Shonda had made her bones—and her burgeoning bank account—on matters of race. Neither she, nor anyone else, had seen the sudden tidal wave of the trans movement coming. It wasn't so much they had a problem with it—of course not!—it was more that professional pivots were never easy. There was also the fact that Shonda herself was Hispanic, part of the greater BIPOC, and not trans, so she wasn't a natural spokesperson.

Padma's phone buzzed with a text, and she took a discreet look. It was from Barbara Selkirk.

I have been observing.

Was Barbara *there*? The woman moved like a ghost.

Activists arriving outside. Fluid situation. Chaos
= opportunity. Advise dismissal.

Padma had been the one who had quietly engineered Barbara's appointment to the board, and she trusted her implicitly. The Lucius Trust, which Barbara ran, was an organization known to few but had well-funded tentacles everywhere, particularly in education. Behind the scenes, they were powerful advocates for educational reform. Their agenda was something known as "culturally relevant pedagogy." These were words that meant nothing to outsiders, intentionally so.

Private girls' schools were their top priority and Padma had been advancing the cause at Lenox. *Private*, because change could be affected more rapidly than through the sclerotic public school system. And *girls*, because of their malleability, the teenage ones in particular. Far more than boys, they were pack animals and highly susceptible to social activation. This made them good little soldiers, and none more so than the white ones. They had been highly supportive of the "#Blackat" movement that was so influential during the Summer of George, and later in the struggle for Palestine. How quickly they became allies. Padma sometimes marveled at how easy they were to manipulate.

Instill guilt. Appeal to virtue. Activate. Repeat.

The safe thing to do was keep the girls inside, but activism was an essential part of the learning process, of the *pedagogy*. What Barbara really wanted was clear: let the girls go outside, let them become part of the solution.

Padma and Barbara were both drawn to chaos, believing that chaos paved the way for social change. But she had to make sure that chaos didn't sweep her away as well.

She raised her microphone. "Girls, in light of events, we're going to dismiss everyone early."

A cheer went up. Padma decided to find Dina Campbell to make sure this got spun in a favorable direction. She'd specifically invited Dina along with Haffred, and at least Dina had come inside. Before she could exit the stage, though, Shannon and Mark Riddle emerged from the stage wings, walking—no, *marching*—directly toward her. Padma quickly turned off her mic.

"*Where is Easter?*" asked Shannon, finger pointing like a dagger.

HEY, HO!

Clover filed outside with the rest. A few girls filtered off, but most stayed. It wasn't every day your school got protested.

A large bus was parked directly in front of the courtyard and a second one was just pulling up. Who were these people and why were they here? Was it related to their aborted "Day of Honest Discussion"?

Some of them were carrying signs. One read:

RESIST THE CIS-TEM!

Another was a picture of a rainbow-colored fist. Many of the protesters were dressed flamboyantly, and some hardly at all.

Things started to fit for Clover. Someone had been tipped off about the recent events at Lenox. This was a trans-rights demonstration. Clover, seeing Dina Campbell already interviewing two participants, was pretty sure she knew who did the tipping. But who told *her*? Dina had been inside. . . . Had she been invited?

There was a small placard face-out in the windshield of the first bus. It read *NYSUT*. She didn't know what that was, but a quick Google search revealed it stood for "New York State United Teachers."

A teachers' union was staging a trans rally? This was curious. Lenox, being private, was nonunionized.

As the second bus unloaded, many of her schoolmates seamlessly joined the protest. One of Coco's posse called out to Clover. "Well, aren't you joining? I would think this was right up your alley. Aren't you a . . . something?"

"Yes, I'm a proud something." Clover raised a half-hearted fist in mock solidarity.

This presented an awkward situation. While Clover had no interest in the gathering insanity, her chosen persona suggested otherwise. At least the focus was no longer on Ginny and Zoey, or so it seemed.

A well-groomed woman in a striking blazer seemed to be orchestrating events. Blazer Lady, Clover immediately dubbed her. She was a marked contrast to the rest and looked familiar to Clover, but she couldn't place her. Some of the others were setting up a microphone on the sidewalk directly in front of the school.

Just when Clover was thinking she should slip away, she felt a tap on her shoulder.

"Mrs. Sanderson!"

"Hello, Clover. Can you please tell me what's going on?"

"We were having a town hall but then these people came. Mrs. Sanderson—"

Ellie cut her off. "How does this involve my daughters?"

"During the meeting, Ginny and Zoey, well, no one was using their *names*, exactly, but they were basically getting called fascists by Hyphen Lady."

"Hyphen Lady?"

"The diversity person. Shonda something-something. She was here and then Easter the new trans girl got up to talk I guess about how oppressed and offended she was but then had some kind of nervous breakdown on stage and ran off and then these people pulled up in buses and Padma told us all we could leave and now I don't know what's going to happen, but this is a really weird day. I texted Ginny and Zoey. I *really* don't think they should come down here."

"Clover, what am I missing here? Is this still about those texts?"

"I . . . guess? Can I just say how sorry I am about that?"

"You didn't do anything wrong. Who are all these people?"

"I don't know. I thought this was a race thing, but then it turned into a trans thing."

"Jesus, is that Sylvia Haffred?"

Someone tested the mic. "Check check." It worked, but Haffred held back, waiting, chatting earnestly with Dina Campbell, who was taking notes.

"Who is that other woman?" asked Ellie. "Is she someone from school?"

"Her name is Dina Campbell, and no. She's a reporter. She's the one who did the story on Easter."

Haffred and the activists stood around, oddly, doing very little. Just why became apparent moments later as a local news van—*Pulse of the City!*—turned onto the block. Suddenly, the group became animated and began chanting. It was as though someone had thrown a switch.

Hey, ho, hey, ho!

The binary world has got to go!

Haffred strode up to the mic. She said nothing for some minutes, allowing time for the news crew to set up their cameras as the chanting continued. A dozen or so protesters squeezed behind her, fists pumping while Haffred affected a posture of grave concern. After a minute or two, cameras safely rolling, she motioned for silence.

"My friends. Behind me is the Lenox Hill School for Girls, a bastion of privilege that costs sixty-five thousand dollars a year, well beyond the reach of ordinary Americans. Here is an institution, more than any, that should be upholding American principles of basic decency, but no. I'm here to testify that they have fallen woefully short. The Lenox School pretends to acknowledge the trans community, but it's an act. One of their own, Easter Riddle, is currently transitioning, and she has been harassed by two fellow students and has even come to physical harm. The Lenox School has allowed this atmosphere of hate to fester.

"We all must ask why such things are tolerated. Could it be because the two girls in question have a father on the board? Do these events have the stench of special treatment?"

Ellie snapped to attention, her face a fixed mask of astonishment. "Oh, my God," she finally whispered.

"This is total bullshit," said Clover.

"I can't be here," said Ellie, turning and leaving.

Clover was taken aback by Haffred's audacity, but she clearly wasn't an idiot. Haffred recognized that all ingredients were prepped and lined up to make a media-friendly stew: a transitioning girl, an elite school, allegations of a cover-up. . . .

"I'm here today," Haffred continued, "to announce that my office will be conducting an investigation into these events, and we will leave no stone unturned."

Just then, Shannon and Mark Riddle appeared next to Haffred. "Please welcome Shannon and Mark Riddle, parents of the brave Easter, the sole trans presence at Lenox Hill. Perhaps they would like to say a word about what has happened here."

Haffred moved aside to allow the Riddles to step up to the mic. Instead,

Mark Riddle pulled Haffred aside, looking concerned. A few words were exchanged. Mark Riddle then took the mic.

"Please, has anyone here seen Easter? We can't find her and we're very concerned."

Can't find her? wondered Clover. She'd been in the auditorium not fifteen minutes before.

"She's in distress," Mark continued. "It's not like her to walk off, but she hasn't felt safe here. Not at all."

Coco French spoke up. "She just posted something!"

"May I see that please?" said Mark, reaching out his hand.

Coco walked closer and handed over her phone. Mark peered at the screen and then showed it to Shannon and Haffred. Haffred then pulled the mic close to her mouth. "Everyone, please listen. Easter Riddle is missing and it is urgent that we find her."

THE DAILY SENTINEL

Thursday, October 25

FEARS OVER MISSING STUDENT

by Dina Campbell

A demonstration outside the prestigious Lenox School for Girls turned chaotic yesterday after a student was reported missing and later posted a troubling message to Instagram.

The student, Easter Riddle, is Lenox Hill's first trans female and was profiled in this paper only last week. A series of troubling events regarding the school's allegedly inclusive environment culminated in a town hall where Easter was to speak. Appearing in distress, she fled from the podium and has not been seen since.

The disappearance coincided with the arrival of activists as well as prominent attorney Sylvia Haffred, who called on the community to find Easter.

Haffred represents the Riddle family and has launched an investigation into the events. According to Haffred, Easter was bullied by two other students and the school's practices have been called into question. The *Sentinel* can exclusively report that legal action against the school is being contemplated.

Easter's Instagram message was posted not long after she disappeared from school property. It was a blurry selfie in which she appeared to be in tears. She added the caption, "I can't go on like this. I'm so sorry."

The message has led many to fear for Easter's safety, and a widespread search is underway. Mayor Reynolds has pledged to use city resources to aid in the effort. Easter's parents, appearing later with the mayor, announced a GoFundMe to defray private expenses. As of this writing, the campaign had collected over $70,000. Lena Dunham and Ellen DeGeneres have each reportedly contributed $10,000 to the effort.

A candlelight vigil is planned by the National Transgender Advocacy Coalition tonight outside the school.

Those with any information are encouraged to call the authorities.

The article was accompanied by the picture from Easter's Instagram as well as another shot in her Lenox school uniform. *Have you seen this girl?* read the caption.

TRANSPHOBES LIVE HERE!

Padma made the decision to cancel classes for the rest of the week. Working with the Riddles, she encouraged the girls to form search groups to look for Easter. They speculated she might gravitate to places she knew. That was assuming she was still . . . Well, no one quite wanted to say it.

Several groups were assigned to Central Park, Washington Square Park, and other favorite hangouts of Easter's gleaned from her parents, her socials, and the head of Lenox's LGBTQ+ Allyship Committee, who knew Easter as well as anyone at Lenox. Others combed the alleys and underpasses frequented by LGBT runaways. These groups were accompanied by volunteer parents.

The Riddles posted shots of themselves, putting on brave faces while handing out flyers with Easter's image in Tompkins Square Park, the IRT stations up and down Lexington Avenue, and the High Line.

The next morning, Ellie decided to go for an early run around the Central Park Reservoir to clear her head. She left the girls still sleeping, which was good because she hadn't been able to dissuade them from doomscrolling on social media the night before. The things they saw kept them up late. Ellie convinced them to stop only after Zoey, in tears, showed her an anonymous threat of assault.

Down in the lobby, Pablo, the doorman, said, "They got here real early, Mrs. Sanderson."

"Who?"

"That lot." He pointed outside the door.

A handful of protesters. Maybe ten or so.

"They spray-painted the building about half an hour ago. I called the police, but they said they can't spare the manpower to track down graffiti artists. I said I'm looking right at them! So they asked if I knew which one did it. When I didn't, they said maybe they'd send someone by later. I'm not holding my breath."

"How did they find us?"

"I sure don't know, Mrs. Sanderson."

In the coldly efficient manner of social media, it hadn't taken long to identify who the alleged bullies were, not that the word "alleged" appeared in any tweets. News of the rap party spread, as well, and how Ginny Sanderson had attacked a trans girl. Neither did it take long for the Sandersons' address to be shared, along with pictures of the family. Ellie would learn they had been "doxxed," a word with which she was previously unfamiliar.

Still, she wasn't going to be a prisoner in her own building. She ran out the door but was quickly recognized by the protesters.

Glancing left, she saw the spray-painted message, scrawled along the limestone base of the building.

TRANSPHOBES LIVE HERE

"Hey!" one protester yelled. "That's the mother!"

This was bad. Adrenaline-fueled, Ellie shot off for the park. Maybe they'd be gone by the time she got back.

An hour later, they weren't. In fact, it appeared their ranks had doubled. Rather than run by, though, she decided she might try to talk to them. Perhaps calm reason would work.

"Good morning," she said.

"It's the mother!" yelled one woman. She immediately took out her cell and began filming Ellie.

"Yes, I am the mother. My daughters have done nothing wrong, but I understand you have a different view. I fully respect your right to protest, but I hope you also respect that there are other people who live in this building, so perhaps you could protest quietly and not do any more property damage."

There, that was reasonable.

In response, one brandished a bullhorn and began shrieking. "We will not be silenced! Genocide is being committed on the trans people! Stop the genocide! Stop the genocide!"

They began to advance on Ellie, who didn't move. Her father fought in the hot sands of Afghanistan, so she wasn't going to let this pink-haired rabble intimidate her. She made one last attempt to be reasonable. "Please, I'm only asking—"

One of them, a girl wearing an NYU Theater T-shirt, advanced far enough that she bumped into Ellie. "You're touching me!" the girl yelled. "Stop touching me! You are violating my space!"

"You are the one touching *me*!" cried Ellie.

"Ow!!" the girl cried, grabbing her elbow. "You're hurting me!"

Ellie was shocked at how performative this was. Pablo suddenly appeared and got between Ellie and the shrieking girl. "Mrs. Sanderson, I think you should come inside."

She heeded Pablo's advice, and they retreated inside.

"Thank you, Pablo," said Ellie.

"Of course, Mrs. Sanderson. My two cents? Don't talk to these people. Don't make eye contact. They're not all there, if you know what I mean."

"I think I'm starting to realize that. I'm so sorry about all this. I hope they don't cause you any more trouble."

"Oh, don't worry about me. I love my job, but sometimes it can get a little monotonous, you know what I mean? Not today!"

Ellie rode the elevator up to seven and found William dressing for work.

"I suppose you saw what's going on outside," he said. "I heard the bullhorn."

"Yes, and one of them practically accused me of assault for just standing there. Do you understand the problem now?"

William, for the first time, looked concerned, but he was loathe to say as much. "Those people will move on to the next thing. Maybe they'll glue themselves to a Hockney or something."

"I just tried speaking to them and they're crazy. You shouldn't go out there. Why don't you call in sick?"

"Look, I can't focus on this right now, all right? This weekend is too important."

"What, the golf?"

"*Yes*, the golf."

"Cancel it."

"Cancel it? What, and let those assholes downstairs win?"

"Will, our daughters are freaked out right now. Are we even going to talk to anyone about this?"

"I'll call Padma and maybe Duncan Ruggles when I get to the office. We'll sort it out." He pulled back a curtain and looked down. "They don't *look* dangerous, anyway."

"We don't know what they're capable of. Do you know they graffitied the building?"

"Seriously? I'm calling the police."

"Don't bother, Pablo already tried. They're not interested. And I strongly suggest you walk out the service entrance."

"I am not skulking out of my own building."

"Do what you want, but I won't be here when you get back. I'm getting the girls out of here. We'll go to East Hampton today. It'll be safe out there."

"So, you're taking the car?"

"*Yes*, I'm taking the car."

William realized he was coming across as a bit too cavalier. "Okay, I can take a town car or the Jitney out tomorrow." He put his hands on Ellie's shoulders. "Sweetheart, I know this is difficult, but it will sort out, I promise."

"You need to get proactive," said Ellie, gritting her teeth.

"I will. But now I have to go."

He gave her a quick kiss. Before William could get out the door, though, his cell rang. It was Clifton Morris, president of the 580 board.

"Hello, Clifton. What can I do for you?"

"William, sorry to bother you so early, but I've been getting complaints. Those people outside that you apparently have something to do with are upsetting the other tenants. Do you know they're shouting at everyone who comes and goes, calling them names and so forth? They called Libby Colgate a fascist! She just turned ninety! We can't have this. The Southworths are worried enough that they're canceling their dinner party tonight!"

William made a mental note that the Southworths hadn't invited them.

"I'm sorry about all this, Clifton. These people are lunatics with nothing better to do with their time. I'll pay for the cleanup. And take care of Pablo. Has the building followed up with the police? I understand Pablo called. . . ."

"Of course we have. Imagine our surprise that they don't appear interested in rushing to a graffiti incident on Park Avenue!"

"Clifton, you should know that Ellie and the girls are leaving shortly to go out east, and I'm joining them tomorrow. Maybe when they see we've left, they'll lose interest. I'm not sure what else I can do."

"Well, all I know is our residents are upset and you all are apparently the cause. There must be something you can do. Issue a statement or something."

"What kind of statement?"

"I don't know—something!"

"This will blow over soon, Clifton. I promise."

But Clifton Morris was no longer on the phone.

Downstairs, just inside the entrance, William paused, taking in the scruffy band of protesters. Most looked quite young, maybe even high schoolers. It confirmed his view that they shouldn't be taken seriously. The idea of letting this clown car of stupid kids muscle the building around grated on him. He walked outside.

"You all need to leave!" he shouted above the din.

"It's Sanderson!" one yelled. He walked directly toward William, who made it a point not to yield ground.

There was something in his hand, William thought. What was it?

"The blood of our sisters and brothers is on your hands!"

The person heaved something toward William. A bottle. What flew out was red and sticky.

Paint? Jesus, *blood*?

"You freaks!" screamed William, looking down at his suit. "It's a Brioni!"

As William retreated to go back upstairs and change, one of the protesters hit Send.

Later that morning, Ellie snuck out the building's maintenance entrance. She'd borrowed a Grafton baseball cap from Ginny and pulled it low on her face. She couldn't think straight, so she stopped at a Starbucks and ordered a venti herbal tea.

She glanced at her phone. Three texts from Tizzy, expressing concern.

Ellie decided that Tizzy wanted to inject herself in the drama and so she ignored them.

She retrieved their car from the Third Avenue garage. The girls, fearful of the rabble outside, waited in the mailroom until Ellie texted them to come out the side.

They would hole up for a few days, walk on the beach, order out for food. Maybe Will was right, maybe this would blow over. She almost wished he wasn't coming out. She could use some alone time, or at least some non-Will time. Thankfully, his parents had just left for Europe. They had their own house now, but it wasn't far from Jack and Bitsy's. She had no bandwith at the moment for her in-laws.

YOU CALLED THEM *WHAT?*

Wearing a fresh suit, William exited this time through the service entrance. He peeked around the corner and saw that the crowd continued to grow. He walked south toward Midtown.

Ten minutes later he reached his office and took the elevator up. "Mr. Stein asked to see you," said his assistant, Angela.

"What, now?"

"So I gather. He's in his office."

William threw his leather Buccio messenger bag on his desk and made his way to Casper's corner office, the one with the northwest view. Tanya Rose from HR was there, as was Meredith Singer, the head of Bedrock's PR department. What the hell?

"Have you seen this?" said Casper, skipping the pleasantries. He tossed a copy of the *Sentinel* across his desk. William skimmed it and words jumped out.

> Search ... trans ... Lenox ... harassment ...

"Obviously," he said, "you've heard my daughters are caught up in this, but it's all bullshit."

"Perhaps you should keep reading," said Tanya, stone-faced.

> The alleged harassment, the *Sentinel* can report, involves the daughters of a prominent Wall Street executive who also serves on Lenox Hill's board ...

"Oh, hell."

"That's one way to put it," said Tanya.

"Needless to say," said Casper, "this firm does not need to be associated with a situation like this. The entire matter conflicts with our stated values."

"Additionally," said Meredith, "your name, not to mention this *firm's*, are all over social media. We are being crucified out there. I'm surprised they're not outside our building."

"Yes, I noticed that rabble outside 580 this morning, William. We don't need that here."

"You don't have to tell *me* that," said William. "One of them actually threw blood or something on me when I was walking out. I had to go back and change."

"Dear God," said Casper. "This is turning into a circus."

"I'm worried this could affect our ESG score," said Tanya. "As a firm that actively promotes ESG standards, we can hardly afford to take a hit by those same standards."

"For something my daughters did, or rather *didn't* do?"

"The scorekeepers are keeping an eye on socials now. And as for your daughters' actions, whatever happened is hardly relevant at this point. Narratives are being woven, and we need to get out ahead of them. It may even be too late."

"William," said Casper, "you are a loyal and valued member of this firm, but this needs to go away."

"It will. This will blow over in a couple of days," he said, for perhaps the tenth time in the last two days.

"Perhaps, perhaps not," said Meredith. "What if this girl turns up dead? Have you really thought this through?"

"And Sylvia Haffred's involved," said Casper. "Vultures always sniff out the deepest pockets. I'm telling you, we're exposed. Also, we've got Jasmine Wu coming. The last thing we need is for CalPERS to get cold feet. They're a bellwether. *Everybody* watches CalPERS."

William sighed. "What do you suggest?"

"You need to disappear until this dies down," said Meredith, "at the very least until the girl turns up. If she's alive, maybe this dies down. We play it by ear. If it turns out she's dead, there's no telling how crazy this gets. We'll have to go outside for help, probably Teneo. I'll put them on notice. And you'll have to issue a statement. Here's a draft." She got up and handed William a document, which he examined.

"You want me to say *this*?"

"Only if the girl turns up dead. If she's just hanging out somewhere smoking joints with friends, maybe it can be avoided."

"Wow, I don't know. . . ."

"William," said Casper, "I'm sure Meredith is right, and the girl's just run off for a few days. Let's not fixate on things that may not happen. We'll get through this. But I hope you understand that my job is to protect this firm, so I have to consider all the contingencies. In the meantime, we'll still need you for golf but after that we don't want you anywhere near where this reporter, Campbell can find you . . . or Sylvia Haffred or those nutjob protesters. Think of it as a few vacation days. Understand?"

"Yes," said William, now staring blankly down on Park Avenue. He stuffed the statement into his suit jacket.

"I can't imagine it will be more than a week. Now, you should leave this building and get yourself out to Long Island."

"Oh, crap," said Meredith, looking at her phone.

"What?" asked Casper.

Looking up at William, she said, "You actually called them freaks?"

"They threw blood on me! Wait, what are you looking at?"

"And you said something about your suit? Brioni?"

"Shit," said Casper.

"I was upset."

"Was it actual blood, or just red paint?" asked Meredith.

"It wasn't paint, I can tell you that," said William, who had begun to speak rapidly. "As to where or what the blood came from, I don't know, and I suspect my dry cleaner doesn't test for DNA. *What* are you looking at?"

"The *Sentinel* online. There's video. Dina Campbell posted it. That woman has been busy. I'm worried Jasmine Wu could see this. In fact, she probably will."

She handed her phone to William, who watched the video for himself. Casper watched over his shoulder.

"Jesus! How could you be so stupid?"

Casper began to pace, something he did when fretting and thinking at the same time. "Perhaps she won't, at least not right away. She's traveling today, and it's a Friday. Maybe this gets lost in the wash over the weekend."

"Maybe," said Meredith, "but I'd plan otherwise."

"Well, we can't very well cancel the outing. How would that look?"

"Agreed. The optics would be terrible. In any case, we'll get a few hours with Jasmine to downplay this. If she hasn't seen it, we should make her aware and spin it our way. Because eventually she *will* see it."

"Agreed. If there's a silver lining, I suppose the outing is well-timed. William, I'd tell you to disappear for it but unfortunately you're the goddamn host. After the golf, you'll hide for a while until this thing is behind us. And *pray* someone finds that goddamned kid!"

DINA GETS A TIP

Dina Campbell sensed this was finally her moment. She congratulated herself on her foresight—for *knowing* there would be a bigger story. It was called journalistic instinct, and she had it. Was it luck that Easter Riddle pulled a disappearing act? Maybe. But it was her instincts that put her in position to take advantage of the situation.

The *Sentinel*, which normally just gave her a Sunday column, was encouraging her to run with it. Daily pieces. They were out ahead of the other papers and needed to stay there. Those bastards at the *Times*, the ones who had fired her years earlier, had even grown interested. They considered LGBTQ+ coverage to be in their wheelhouse and had a full complement of staffers on it—but there was no way Dina would let them outhustle her.

As it happened, luck, perhaps the residue of instinct, was about to smile on Dina Campbell again.

Her cell rang. It was a Harvard friend named Delia Price. Delia had gone on to business school, made lots of money as a banker, and then quit when she married a colleague who made even more. Back in the day, Delia had been a campus radical but then decided that she liked the aesthetic of being poor more than the actual reality of being poor. Later, she quietly ditched the aesthetic part too.

But at the same time—and this is the part that really triggered Dina—she still fancied herself the same activist who'd once occupied buildings and burned George W. Bush in effigy. Today, her activism consisted of deeply held convictions on Facebook and Instagram. Dina resented everything about Delia but not enough to turn down one or two invitations to her house in the Hamptons over the years.

It was an *amazing* house.

"Delia, how have you been?"

"Peachy!"

"The kids?"

"All good. Teddy has his eye on Andover."

"How nice. I'm sure he'll get in."

"James and his brothers went there, and he's on the board, but you never know these days."

"I suppose not."

It would be difficult to overstate Dina's lack of interest in the scholastic fate of Teddy Price. Dina recalled the kid was a little shit.

"Listen," said Delia. "I've been following your work lately—so impressive! There's something I thought I would pass along. Perhaps it could be . . . useful."

"Oh?" Dina couldn't imagine how anything Delia knew would be useful.

"You recall that James and I are members of Dunehaven, out on the island."

"I've been there with you. I stayed with you for the summer lawn party."

"Oh, right, of course. Well, you know how James loves his golf, right? Well, he went to make a tee time for tomorrow morning and was told the course was booked for an outing. A *corporate* outing."

"Okay . . ."

"Well, he was *annoyed*, of course. They're not supposed to book outings on weekends, it's against the rules! So, James asked who'd booked it and the pro shop said it was sponsored by William Sanderson. William is on the board, so apparently the rules don't apply to him!"

"Just to be clear, you're talking about William Sanderson who's also on the board of Lenox Hill."

"Who called trans people freaks, yes. And whose daughter bullied that trans girl. Poor thing!"

"Interesting."

"I thought you might think so. Imagine, in the middle of all this with the girl missing and all, running off to play golf. Anyway, I've got to scoot!"

"Okay, thanks for calling, Delia."

Dina hadn't given much thought to William Sanderson other than to post the video she was sent from outside his apartment. Until that moment, her focus had been on his daughters and the presumed role they'd played in Easter's disappearance. But now she wondered if this wasn't a rich vein.

Rich.

She chuckled at her own thought-pun. William Sanderson certainly was rich, which made him a less-than-sympathetic player in this drama. Dina wondered if the Sanderson girls were getting special treatment at Lenox. William Sanderson was no doubt a large contributor, all board members at schools like Lenox were, although Padma Minali didn't strike Dina as someone who put up with the old-boy bullshit.

She flipped open her MacBook and Googled Sanderson. His background was totally establishment. Someone born to money who managed to make even more of it. No surprises there. Then she Googled Bedrock. Their landing page featured an attractive rainbow of employees. The lead About Us paragraph cheered Bedrock's commitment to diversity. After that, sustainable investment practices. By appearances, this was a very progressive company, about which Delia would normally approve.

But they employed people like William Sanderson.

Perhaps their progressivism was merely a cloak they wore, and underneath they were just greedy little capitalists like everyone else.

Did the actions of Sanderson's daughters put Bedrock in an uncomfortable situation? It seemed a stretch. But Sanderson had given her a gift, a single word wrapped in a bow:

Freaks.

She pondered the new information, courtesy of her annoying classmate, no doubt calling from her twelve-thousand-square-foot house. What awards had *she* ever won? Not a goddamned one.

Whatever.

She wouldn't look a gift horse in the mouth. Obviously, Delia had a grudge against Sanderson, but what of it? That was none of Dina's business.

An idea formed, a wicked one. As a journalist, sometimes you had to give circumstances a tiny little nudge. Oh, it was officially frowned upon by the mandarins at Columbia Journalism School, but everyone quietly did it.

She would make a call.

But first she would bang out tomorrow's column. Sunday's, she suspected, would be even better.

EASTWARD HO!

The next morning, Dina boarded the Hampton Jitney, getting off in the village of East Hampton. From there, she caught an Uber to a public beach parking lot just adjacent to the Dunehaven Club.

She was stiff after the seemingly endless drive in traffic—it was bad enough on the Long Island Expressway, but got truly punishing once they reached the South Fork. Leaving her shoes behind next to a bike rack, she walked down to the sand. The looming mansions, set slightly back from the dunes, stoked her resentment for the people who could afford to live in them, the hedge funders and celebrities and private-equity partners. The money changers. The oligarchs.

She hardly noticed the glorious fall day and the waves that rolled in gracefully from an outside sand bar. There were whirling flocks of seagulls above the water and several surfers in wetsuits below making the best of it.

Turning west after the dunes, she walked a hundred yards or so until she reached Dunehaven's lifeguard stand. From there, through a path between two dunes, she could easily see the club's outdoor pavilion, which occupied the space between the clubhouse and the beach. It was where, at this time of the day, most of the members could be found having lunch. She took a couple of discreet photos and waited.

Sylvia Haffred brushed a few hairs from her blazer. She'd been told by a consultant once to avoid wearing patterns on camera, and she was on camera a lot, so this led to a closet full of solid colors. She favored the bold ones, because that's what she was, a bold woman. That, and she would always stand out in a crowd.

Right now, Sylvia was a bit cranky. She wasn't used to riding buses, particularly not with this noisy lot, but she kept busy, working her phone. She had made a point of sitting all the way in the front. She couldn't be sure, but there might be activities happening in the back that she didn't care to see up close. Her passengers were nothing if not rambunctious.

The ride from the East Village to East Hampton was torturous. Traffic, as always, was bad. It was a Saturday, so most Hamptonites had come the previous day, but there were countless day-trippers, schlepping east to beaches or wineries.

Near Southampton, the relentless monotony of the LIE yielded to the two-lane nightmare of the Sunrise Highway, the Hamptons' only east–west artery. *Why do people choose to come here*, Sylvia wondered.

She knew well enough. The estate sections were uniquely beautiful, with their perfect green lawns, weedless, sweeping from magnificent houses to distant hedges. The beaches were wide and endless. And there was something about the light. Artists noticed it first, over a century ago, when they established a colony near the Shinnecock Reservation in Southampton. The famed American impressionist, William Merritt Chase, had been their informal leader. No one could explain it, but the light was perfect for their lazy days of painting *en plein air*.

Sylvia herself had a place in Westhampton. Westhampton was the Hamptons' somewhat weak sister, reputationally (assuming you didn't count Hampton Bays, which nobody did). Perhaps a juicy settlement out of the Easter Riddle affair could allow her to upgrade further east. She spent a few minutes on her Zillow app, checking out the market.

Finally, the two chartered buses reached East Hampton. They passed the shady pond in the village center with its weeping willows and proud swans. Could it look any more English? Then they turned into the monied precincts of the estate section, where starter homes ran $8 or $9 million. After nearly four hours, the restless passengers spied their destination. A whoop went up from the back as the hedge rows gave way to a more open view of a golf course, and, on the far side of it, Dunehaven.

DUNEHAVEN

This was the day they would lock down the CalPERS account.

Jim Hansen, who ran the new crypto department and was along for the outing, pulled William aside in the locker room.

"So, we're finally bagging the elephant," he said quietly in case there were eavesdroppers in nearby rows.

"Nothing's done till it's done. You know that."

"It's all but there, at least that's what I hear. Just don't chop it out there. What are you playing to these days. An eight?"

"Six," replied William.

"Look at you. Will Sanderson, elephant slayer. What's our fee gonna look like?"

"Eighty bips."

By this, William meant eighty basis points, Wall Street vernacular for 0.80 percent.

"So that's"—Jim looked at the ceiling while doing some quick math in his head—"forty mil a year. Not bad! Color me jealous, my friend."

"We're all on the same team, Jim."

Neither man believed this, but protocol required the words to be spoken.

"You bet," said Jim.

The men walked outside to find Jasmine Wu on the practice putting green. Cy Birdwell was there too. "This is a beautiful club you have here, William," she said.

"Thank you. We plan to host the Walker Cup in a few years."

"That should boost your ranking even higher."

Dunehaven's golf course was currently ranked by *Golf Digest* as the thirty-sixth finest in America. The facility also boasted grass tennis courts and a grand century-old clubhouse overlooking the ocean.

"Your honor, Cy," said William, as they reached the eighth tee sometime later. He had planned to innocently "forget" to invite Cy, claiming to Casper that Cy was sick, but it turned out Casper had already issued the invitation himself.

The hole was a beautiful par 4, its fairway running like an emerald-green stripe between two parallel dunes by the ocean. Cy striped the ball down the middle. Cy was a natural golfer too. A four handicap. This annoyed William.

So far, Jasmine hadn't brought up Easter Riddle, or trans people, or anything else other than small talk and golf. She must not have seen that morning's *Sentinel*, or if she had, she wasn't saying. Casper had gone to the Candy Kitchen in Bridgehampton first thing to get a physical copy, which he always preferred. The headline was a single word:

FREAKS!

And there, right on the front page, was William, suit covered in blood-red splotches, face filled with rage. There was a secondary article entirely about his suit, the Brioni, pointing out that it cost $3,000. There were small photos of various men's stores like Paul Stuart and Turnbull & Asser, helpfully pointing out other places where $3,000 suits might be acquired.

Casper had promptly called William's cell. There were no opening pleasantries. "Do you know you're on the cover of the goddamned *Sentinel*?"

He did. Friends had been texting all morning, mostly in the form of good-natured ribbing.

"You just had to call them freaks. Are you an idiot? Everybody has a camera now."

"What was I supposed to say? Thank you?"

"How about next time you run in the other direction! Jesus, this is bad. I doubt Jasmine Wu reads the *Sentinel*, but she'll find out soon enough. Let's just try to get through today. I'll try some preemptive damage control when we get out there. I'll wait a few holes and bring the matter up casually. So be prepared. In the meantime, Tanya is redrafting your statement in light of this. She'll send it to you shortly."

"Nice ball," said Jasmine, watching Cy's drive sail far out between the dunes. She then drove her own ball solidly up the middle. She wasn't long, but she hit it straight with a consistency William found elusive. William's own ball bounded into the rough but remained playable, while Casper topped his drive once again.

As they walked down the fairway, Jasmine said, "Cy, I just wanted to say how much I've looked forward to meeting you. My girls and I adore your clothes."

"Thank you. I noticed you're wearing one of our performance shirts."

"I don't wear anything else, at least on the course!"

"You're very kind. My shareholders thank you."

"You know, I was thinking," said Jasmine. "We're having a conference next month about the importance of diversity in the investment management industry. It's out on the Coast, and I know you must be very busy, but I was thinking you would make a wonderful speaker. I could still fit you into the schedule."

"I'm flattered, but I'm not sure why you'd want *me*. As you know, it's not my industry, and I'm not sure what I could add to the subject."

"Oh, don't sell yourself short! I'm sure you could be very compelling. And you're on Bedrock's board. I think that your perspective, in particular, would be valuable."

Cy seemed bewildered. "There must be other people."

"Not enough, if you ask me, and that's the shame of it, isn't it? Did I mention the conference will be at Pebble, and that we might be able to sneak a few people onto Cypress?"

"You suddenly make a compelling argument."

"What are you two conspiring about?" asked a concerned William, catching up after playing his ball from the rough.

"Just getting to know your people better, William. I'm hoping to entice Cy out West to a little conference we're having."

"And she's quite persuasive," said Cy.

The hair on the back of William's neck stood up. "Oh? What's it on?"

"Fore!" came a shout.

Casper's third shot came bounding through them, another ground ball, causing them to scatter. "Damn!" he yelled, eyeing his 3-wood, which he suspected as the true culprit. Before William could pursue the conversation any further, Casper had caught up and they played the hole out.

For his part, Casper decided it was almost time to have the "conversation." If Jasmine was aware of William's travails, she still hadn't let on. Casper suspected she wasn't.

The next hole, the ninth, had been the scene of an infamous incident some years back, one that had entered golf lore. William told the story any time he had guests, as did most other Dunehaven members. As they stood on the tee, he began the tale.

"As you can see, this is a blind par three, which is quite unusual."

A dune cut diagonally across their view, blocking the entire green from sight. The clubhouse could be spied just beyond.

"You can just spy the tip of the flagstick peeking over the dune. Anyway, a few years back, we were having the Dunehaven Bowl, our annual member-guest, and one of the matches came to this tee box. All four players hit their shots and then walked around the dune to see the results. There were three balls on the green, but the fourth, belonging to a guest, was nowhere in sight. They searched for it, combing the surrounding bunkers and nearby dune grass, but to no avail.

"Just before they were about to run afoul of the time-limit rule, the guest, over in a patch of dune grass, yells *found it!* and then he plays his shot. They continue on, that is, until the first putt was holed by one of the members. Reaching down for his ball, imagine his confusion when he found two! The other ball was the guest's actual tee shot. He'd scored a hole in one but never thought to look in the hole."

"Oh, c'mon. That sounds like an urban legend," said Jasmine.

"No, true story."

"What happened then?"

"Well, they could have played on, the penalty for cheating being a loss of hole in match play, but the member who'd brought the cheating guest was so mortified that he left the grounds immediately, dragging his guest with him. The fellow was permanently banned, and the member didn't show his face for a while."

"All right, then the *first* place I'm looking is in the hole," said Casper.

They each played their tee shots, watching their balls sail over the dune and hoping for the best. As they began walking, Casper said, "Jasmine, there's a small something I wanted to bring to your attention. Just a little fly in the ointment."

"Oh?"

But before he could answer, the clubhouse came fully into view, and they heard a commotion. This was odd, as the Dunehaven Club was nothing if not a harbor of subdued behavior.

"Sounds like some excitement," said Cy.

Was that . . . a bullhorn?

THE PEACOCKS HAVE LANDED

Drag Queen Story Hours had, by all accounts, modest roots. They had started in San Francisco about a decade before. A local activist, who self-identified as queer, took her young son to a children's library event. She enjoyed it but found it, in her estimation, "heteronormative." She imagined something different, an event that might be more inclusive and affirming to local LGBTQ families. Instead of nice, middle-aged ladies with library science degrees reading books, why not drag queens?

It was there, at the Harvey Milk Memorial Library, that Drag Queen Story Hours were born. A 501(c)(3) was formed and the idea spread quickly, with chapters opening in thirty-five cities across the country. The New York chapter became particularly active. Dina had done a story on them a year or so back.

It would have been easy enough for Sylvia to rally some of the activists who'd protested outside Lenox Hill on Wednesday, but today she wanted something more, something . . . splashier. It made for better copy. And so, Sylvia tapped into the city drag community, notably the Story Hour crowd.

Sylvia was well connected, so normally, this would have been a straightforward matter, a mere phone call or two. But this was more involved: Drag queens often needed time to prepare their elaborate outfits, and few ever rose before 10:00 a.m.

There was quite a bit of scrambling, and a fair bit of complaining. One or two grumbled that the trans community was sucking all the air out of the room, although drag queens were, themselves, increasingly made up of the transgender. Ru Paul's Drag Race had let trans women compete for several years now. It still rankled among a few of the old-time queens, though, who were simply gay men who liked to dress in women's clothes.

Haffred was no amateur, though, when it came to navigating the complex and shifting politics of the LGBTQ+ crowd, and she'd pulled off the outing in less than twenty-four hours. The holdouts were persuaded by the opportunity to take their street theater to a new audience, particularly *this* audience. It was too delicious to pass up. There would be no children's stories this time.

It hadn't hurt that Barbara Selkirk, an old acquaintance, had provided generous funding from the Lucius Trust. Each of the participants would be paid $400 plus meals, although Sylvia suspected most would have done it for free.

Sylvia pondered Barbara's motivations. Clearly, despite the expensive outfits, Barbara's personal politics were quite radical. That much Sylvia understood. It seemed odd, though, that she would secretly try to undermine both Lenox Hill, a progressive school, and Bedrock Capital, a progressive company on the forefront of the ESG movement. She had the sense that Barbara didn't think they were progressive *enough*. Indeed, Bedrock had been accused, from some leftist quarters, of "greenwashing," a relatively new term. Similar to Shonda Gomez-Brown's "optical allies," greenwashing described companies whose commitment to environmental causes was merely skin deep. Sylvia supposed that by stirring the waters, Barbara thought she might achieve her goals faster.

Of course, Sylvia didn't really care one way or another about Bedrock or Barbara Selkirk. Her priorities were green, too, but more of the pecuniary kind. She'd long found that allying with progressive causes was highly rewarding. There were the settlements but also the pockets of funding from the NGOs and others. They were a deep well that never seemed to run dry.

Sylvia smiled to herself. While she had initially focused on the school, Bedrock's pockets were far deeper, and no one would have much sympathy for them, particularly after William Sanderson had made this all so easy.

She looked again at the *Sentinel*. She'd made sure to pass it around the bus, stoking the flames.

Bringing a case against Bedrock was an easy call, at least from a public relations standpoint. Legally, she was on shakier grounds. Bringing suits against employers for actions taken by their employees while not at work was a precedent she and a number of her legal peers were very interested in advancing. As yet, though, it was an innovation not fully realized.

Of course, it might not matter. It was possible, no, *likely*, that Bedrock would settle just to avoid the publicity. The brand was everything to these people.

But . . . there was always the chance they would call her bluff.

It was a high-stakes game.

Sylvia hadn't yet decided whether to bring action against Lenox Hill. They had a sizable endowment, at least for a small private school, but it was nothing like Bedrock's billions and trillions. Barbara had informed her, though, that Lenox had a decent amount of liability coverage.

That step would require further thought.

The convoy drove past the members-only sign out front and pulled up on the circle in front of the club's main entrance. Forty-two drag queens poured out of the two buses.

There was Tiffany Diamond, dressed like Madonna in her Material Girl days, and Trinity Chu, who channeled a Liza Minelli cabaret look, complete with cane and bowler. Velvet Angel had feathery wings so large he took up two seats.

And still they came.

Adoré Milano wore an antebellum dress of pink, which likewise had proved a problem on the bus as it was impossible to sit in it. He rode the whole way out in his tighty-whities, stowing the hooped skirt in the luggage compartment.

Sister Jade had white face paint, neon green hair, and three-inch spangled eyelashes. The outfit was made complete by a live boa constrictor draped around his neck. China del Rio, opting for a more minimalist look, wore a gold lamé thong and a sports bra.

Rosie Wild, who was fully zaftig, came in elaborate sadomasochistic regalia, all leather and spikes with a strapped ball in his mouth. Some of the others had complained this was not an S&M space, but Rosie, removing his ball, accused them of not being inclusive and the others quickly relented, taking solace in the fact that Rosie kept the ball in his mouth the whole ride out.

The bus drivers, who hadn't managed to lose their bewildered looks all morning, opened the cargo hatches and the drags retrieved dozens of signs.

As much as she wanted to stretch her legs, Sylvia remained in the first bus. She had friends at Dunehaven and quite enjoyed being invited there. She had only come along to make sure things went smoothly, which is to say not smoothly at all. She sent a quick text to Dina Campbell:

The peacocks have landed.

SO UNATTRACTIVE

The Dunehaven Club posted a single staffer in its reception area. Velvet Angel laughed when he asked "of whom" the party was a guest. "We're America's guest, sweetie."

The small army of queens streamed by the poor man, ignoring his objections, and walked through the quiet clubhouse. Sylvia had told them that they would find everyone out back, having lunch, so that's where they went. Out the other side, they descended, almost cabaret-like and in step, down two sets of stairs to the pavilion.

Dina Campbell, walking into the pavilion from the beach side, went completely unnoticed. At that particular moment, a passel of Kardashians might have entered unnoticed.

As Emily Post was silent on the matter of mass drag queen intrusions, most of the members were rendered mute. Was this some sort of odd club event they'd missed on the calendar?

Emmet Hendrey knew otherwise. The club president, he rose to confront the first descending queen, Velvet Angel. The group didn't have a leader, but if they did, it would have been Velvet. She had the best outfit.

"Excuse me, but what is this?" Emmet demanded, summoning his huffiest voice.

Putting her hands on either side of Emmet's face, Velvet kissed him squarely on the lips. "It's a protest, darling. Now be a good boy and go back to your cheeseburger. Love the madras shorts, by the way. Fierce."

Too shocked to respond, Emmet decided to summon the local *gendarmes*. Cell phones were strictly forbidden, even in the event of unscheduled drag queen outbursts, so he scurried inside his cabana where he wouldn't be seen.

Tiffany Diamond handed Velvet a bullhorn. "Well, *hiiii*, everyone! It's so nice to be here. Aren't you all just so beautiful. I know we're all going to be the best of friends! Oh, and by the way, this is a protest. We are here to stop trans genocide!"

"Stop what?" asked John McNulty to his lunch partner, Mark Grand.

"Some kind of genocide, I think he said."

Velvet turned to his fellow queens. "Wave your signs, girls!"

They did. The signs, printed up for the occasion by Haffred's staff, said things like, "Bedrock Harbors Transphobes!," "Bedrock Values = Fascism," and "Hey, Bedrock, Where's Easter?"

"Bedrock. Doesn't Sanderson work there?" someone asked.

In truth, few of the queens had ever heard of Bedrock Capital, but Haffred told them about the "incident," and that William Sanderson worked there. That was all they needed to know. And while many drag queens were not technically "trans," they decided to be allies today.

"That's right, Bedrock Capital supports transphobia!" the queens hissed as one.

Hisssssssssss!

"Now, sit back and enjoy the show!"

They wound through the aisles, conga-style, carrying their signs. "*Boo, hiss, Bedrock is cis!*" they chanted.

"What does that even mean?" asked John McNulty.

"I have no idea," said Mark Grand.

"Is it some sort of pejorative?"

"I doubt it's a compliment."

They had marched through to the beach side, the side where Dina Campbell was filming. Angel, still holding the bullhorn, said, "We find you guilty of hosting a transphobic company and supporting genocide. Shame! Shame!"

"Shame!" repeated the other forty-one.

Then they laid down their signs and dispersed through the crowd. It was time for free-form expression.

Trinity Chu, a former gymnast at NYU, discovered that the pavilion's support poles could be repurposed as stripper poles. This made Velvet envious, as his elaborate costume limited his range of movement. Others vogued and catwalked, some focusing their drag queen arts on specific tables.

Millicent Eastwick, a third-generation member and well into her seventies, had been enjoying a light salad Niçoise with friends when China del Rio decided they needed to be entertained. He thrust the hairy business-side of his thong into the group and began to twerk.

"*So* unattractive!" Millicent exclaimed.

"It would be one thing if you could pull off a thong, dear, but, honestly!" said one of the others.

China sniffed with indignation. He reached over, grabbed a handful of someone's lobster salad, and smeared it over his bare chest, writhing with the kind of ecstasy some can only get while smearing other people's expensive food on their bodies.

"That's local lobster!" cried one member. Hamptonites were very proud of their lobster, many plucked right from the Great Peconic Bay.

"*So* wasteful," said Millicent, just at the moment China spun into a RuPaul-worthy death drop, leg extended, at Millicent's feet.

The pavilion then descended into something resembling the late Roman Empire with writhing bodies and orgiastic groans. This was a bit more performative than Drag Queen Story Hours, but they had been encouraged to be fully expressive.

Sylvia Haffred, watching via a FaceTime from Dina, grinned from ear to ear. She was getting her money's worth. This was *good*.

It was just about then that William's foursome made its way around the dune to the nearby ninth green.

"Whaaat the hell?"

Understandably, the sight of dozens of drag queens dancing around one's club took a moment to process. It occurred to William that it was possible he was connected, somehow, to this tableau of debauchery. What they were doing at Dunehaven, though, was a mystery, and one he was not inclined to solve just now.

"Interesting club you have here, William," said Jasmine, smiling, perhaps impishly. "More inclusive than I imagined."

William couldn't tell if she was being serious or not. Either way, no reason to risk getting closer to whatever this was. "Why don't we move on to the tenth?" The tenth hole was on the other side of the clubhouse, safely out of view.

"You know," said Cy, "curiosity has the best of me. I'll catch up with you guys on the tee." Cy headed toward the commotion.

Shit, thought William. "Okay, let's move on." William led them away, concerned that Jasmine was looking over her shoulder, rubbernecking.

Cy strolled over to the pavilion, where he was immediately greeted by Rosie Wild. "Hello," said Cy.

"Mmffft!" said Rosie. It was difficult to speak with a ball in your mouth.

"What's this all about?"

"*Mmpphf mmfft!*"

"I'm afraid that doesn't clear it up for me."

Rosie then pointed to some discarded signs, which Cy went over to examine.

A few minutes later, two officers from the East Hampton Village Police Department arrived, responding to Emmet Hendrey's 911 call. Used to dealing with DUIs and illegal share houses, a spontaneous outburst of drag queens was a new one for them.

"They are trespassing!" cried Emmet. "Arrest them!"

Sergeant Vincent Gallo tried to suppress a smile. He was not, nor would he ever be, a member of the Dunehaven Club. And while he had no animosity toward it or its members, the summer community did get on his nerves sometimes. Things were so much calmer during the winter months. Another week or two and all these people would be gone.

"Sir, I'm guessing you've never visited our town jail."

"Of course not!"

"Well, I'm thinking we could fit maybe four of your friends here, depending on whether they were wearing wings."

"But they are trespassing!"

"So, you're confirming that none of these people are guests."

"I assume that was rhetorical, sergeant," huffed Emmet.

It was true that the sergeant was being a wiseass. He was rather enjoying this.

"All right, all right," he said, still suppressing a grin. "Do they have a leader?"

"That one, I suppose." Emmet pointed at Angel, who just then was pretending to fly around the pavilion, head back and arms wide.

"You, with the wings! Over here."

Angel flitted over to the sergeant. "Ooh, a man in uniform!"

"And what is your name?"

"Velvet, sweetie. Velvet Angel."

"Do you have some sort of identification?"

She pointed to a tattoo on her arm. Sure enough, it said "Velvet Angel."

"I was thinking more along the lines of a driver's license."

"I don't drive."

Officer Gallo sighed. "Okay, why, may I ask, are you disturbing lunch for these fine people?"

Listening to the convoluted explanation, something about Bedrock Capital and a missing girl in the city, Officer Gallo knew right away this was above his pay grade, which was to say he wanted no ownership of it. He called his captain, who, recognizing the same thing, immediately called the Suffolk County Police Commissioner, who, in turn, called the DA, Andy Sullivan, who was reached on the eighth hole of Bethpage Black. This all happened in less time than it took Millicent Eastwick to finish her salad Niçoise.

"Oh my God," said Sullivan to the Commissioner. "We don't want to be within a hundred miles of this. Tell the officer to politely ask them to leave and then get the hell out of there."

This command was sent rapidly back down the chain. Officer Gallo was only too happy to comply.

Dina texted Haffred that she had what she needed and Haffred gave word for the queens to retreat back to the bus. They would stop by Citarella for their per diem lunches. China hoped they had some of that lobster salad. What dripped into his mouth from his greasy fingers was rather delicious.

Out on the back nine, William thought he had successfully steered the golf game away from the protest, but Cy came out and opened his big mouth. The Easter Riddle story hadn't yet received much play outside New York, and Jasmine hadn't known any of it after all. She immediately started peppering them with questions.

"How is Bedrock connected to the disappearance of this girl?"

"We *aren't*," said Casper.

"Then why did I just see a small army of drag queens who, according to Cy, feel otherwise?"

Casper sighed. "One of William's daughters had a disagreement with some *other* trans girl before Easter Riddle disappeared. People are suggesting the two things are connected."

"I'm confused. William, your daughter is trans as well?"

"What? No!"

This earned a glare from Jasmine Wu. William lowered his voice. "I mean no. She's—" William was about to say "normal" when he remembered that painful evening at Lenox.

Casper decided to intervene. "William's daughter had a disagreement with an unrelated trans girl. It was a harmless thing, by all accounts. Teenagers being teenagers. But people suggested that the recounting of it somehow upset Easter Riddle."

"This is ridiculously hard to follow. William, how is any of this your fault?"

"Well, it's *not*, obviously!"

"William is on the board of their school," said Casper. "People are suggesting William has put pressure on the school and that his daughter is getting favorable treatment."

"And is she?"

"No!" cried William. "If anything, she's being persecuted. They actually suspended her. For her own safety, if you can believe that."

"I see. So why is the trans community upset with Bedrock?"

"It's ridiculous," said Casper. "It's this Sylvia Haffred, whipping up a lot of nonsense. We're the deep pockets."

"*She's* involved?"

"She has inserted herself into this situation, yes."

"That woman is trouble."

"We know."

"What is she saying, exactly?"

"That we're harboring a *transphobe*."

"Just because of something his daughter did?" Jasmine asked, pointing at William with her driver.

"Well, there was one other thing. It's silly, really."

"Define *silly*."

"William was assaulted outside his apartment by some activists yesterday. They threw blood on him."

"Oh, how awful. But what am I missing here? How is that his fault?"

"It isn't, of course. But he got upset. . . ."

"I *was* upset," said William.

"Who wouldn't be?"

". . . and he said some things. . . ."

"What things?"

"He called them . . . freaks."

"So, William, question. Were any of these protesters members of the trans community?"

"I don't know. I didn't stop to ask. I had blood all over me."

"They may have been," said Casper. "At least, that's how it's being portrayed in the press. An act of transphobia."

"This has hit the press?"

"Well, yes, somewhat. It's tabloid garbage."

"And for the record," said William, "I have no issues with the trans community."

Jasmine took a moment to stripe another tee shot down the middle. She picked up her tee and said, "Casper, I'd like to think I'm a fair person, and it sounds like you guys are getting a raw deal, but you should know that treatment of the LGBTQ community is an important aspect in ESG scoring."

"This is all just a damn shakedown!"

"It sounds like it, especially if Haffred is involved. I'm not unsympathetic to your situation, but there are the optics to consider. We have a large LGBTQ community in California, as I'm sure you know, and we can't afford to be seen as unsupportive. They are very well funded and very well organized. The trans, in particular. This could affect you, and our ability to invest in you. Bottom line is that you need to fix this."

Casper sensed his prize slipping away. "We will. You have my word. William is going to issue a statement. Isn't that right, William?"

"Uh, right," said William. "Of course."

After the round, they enjoyed drinks on a patio overlooking the ocean. They all tried "Southsides," a minty cocktail native to Long Island clubs. William broke his usual rule of never having more than two. Halfway through his third, Emmet Hendrey approached the group. "William, a word?"

William got up and followed Emmet indoors to a quiet lounge.

"Listen, Will. I've spoken with some of the other board members and we all agree. You need to hold off having any more outings. And maybe try to be scarce for a couple of weeks."

"You're blaming me for this?"

"Well, is there someone else you'd like to suggest? We're going to be all over the news, and you *know* how we hate publicity."

"I know, I know. Listen, I had no idea."

"Just so you know, one or two of the others brought up the idea of a suspension."

"Who? Hutchins? Was it Hutchins?"

"That doesn't matter. I pointed out that we signed off on this, letting you skirt the rules by having an outing on a Saturday. But to have it end up like this . . . My God, one of those . . . *people* rubbed his ass on Martha Symington!"

Emmet walked off, leaving William to down the rest of his Southside in a single gulp.

THE NEW YORK SENTINEL

Sunday, October 28

MISSING GIRL PROTESTS SPREAD TO ELITE CLUB

by Dina Campbell

In one of several protests concerning the disappearance of Easter Riddle, diners at the exclusive Dunehaven Club in East Hampton were greeted with the unusual sight of dozens of colorfully attired female impersonators staging a protest at their club yesterday . . .

She was back. She was goddamned *back*. Dina walked briskly over to the newsstand on Broadway and Seventy-second. Her story was on the cover of the Sunday edition, and she wanted a hard copy for herself. It hadn't hurt that she'd supplied a number of salacious photographs to accompany her reporting. The one they'd chosen for the cover featured Velvet Angel and Sister Jade leaning over and kissing Millicent Eastwick's cheeks from each side. Millicent was recoiling in horror, although it was unclear if what unsettled her was the kisses or the live snake inches from her face. In fairness, probably both.

The headline read:

LADIES WHO LUNCH!

Overlaid on the main photo was a smaller shot of Easter, which was tagged with "The Search Continues."

Dina had video, too, of course. That turned out to be gold. Had she not been legally obligated to give it to the *Sentinel*, she could have sold it for thousands. But the *Sentinel* was pushing it hard on their website and generating huge traffic. From there, it migrated to social media, and from there the world.

The drag queens had been the perfect clickbait to catapult the Easter story onto the national stage, and Dina was right in the middle. It was *her* story, and it had legs. Who cares if the connection between Easter and Bedrock Capital, not to mention the Dunehaven Club, was tenuous, at best. CNN and Fox had both invited her to appear in prime time tonight! The story played to both sides of the political divide, although for admittedly different reasons.

It was time to work on a piece for tomorrow, but first she needed to book a last-minute hair stylist.

Still at his house in Bridgehampton, an angry Casper called William's cell. "I just got a courtesy call from the mayor. Do you know what's happening tomorrow? Sylvia *goddamn* Haffred is staging a press conference outside our office. Also, this *goddamn Sentinel* reporter called and asked if I had any comments about the disappearance of the trans kid."

"What did you say?"

"What do you think I said? Bedrock Capital is not involved with this, and we hoped they would find the *goddamn* kid *goddamn* safe and sound. The mayor will cover for us, I've seen to that, but he'll only go so far. The election is around the corner and if that girl, or boy—that *student*—turns up dead, the calculus for him will change. We would become the evil corporation in an instant. I also told him we sent one hundred thousand dollars to the parents' GoFundMe. What they're going to do with that money, I have no idea. What a shitshow."

MONDAY

Ellie read what was on the piece of paper again. She'd found it in Will's jacket. Surely, she hadn't read it right.

She had.

Her stomach twisted and a dizzying wave of nausea came over her. She ran to the bathroom and heaved into the toilet. She had to confront William, but she let her stomach settle first, resting her face against the cool porcelain.

After a few minutes, she found William in the study.

"Outside," she said. The girls were around, somewhere, and she wanted to shield them from this.

"I'm in the middle of something."

She held up the sheet of paper. "Outside, *now*."

William complied, and they went out by the pool.

"What is this?" she demanded.

"El—"

"No, just stop talking and listen, because you know what this is? A betrayal—of your *family*."

"I think that's a little dramatic, don't you?"

"You're putting your job above your own family. Hell yes, it's a betrayal. *God*, you're being a complete weasel."

"My *job* pays for everything in this family!"

"At what cost? Throwing our daughters under the bus? Apologizing for things that aren't true? Oh wait, sorry. You did call them freaks, didn't you?"

"A moment of weakness, I'll admit. Listen, El, if I don't release this statement, we'll lose CalPERS, and I'm liable to lose my job. Is that something you could deal with?"

"You mean, could *you* deal with it? I don't come from—" Ellie motioned around her—"*this*, and I'm doing my best to fit in, but the price is suddenly getting very high." She waved the sheet of paper. "You cannot release this statement."

"Look, I get why you're upset. I do. But everyone will forget about this by next week."

"Stop saying that!"

"Well, it's true. The tabloids are all excited now, but tomorrow or the next day some celebrity will overdose or get divorced or something and it's on to the next thing."

"You are completely clueless," said Ellie.

William's phone buzzed. A moment later, so did Ellie's.

"Shit," he said.

Their fight was temporarily suspended as they each stared down at the same news flash from the *Sentinel*.

BODY THOUGHT TO BE
THAT OF MISSING TEEN FOUND

PRESSING FOR ANSWERS

The mayor hastily summoned a press conference on the steps of City Hall. When she heard about it, Sylvia Haffred postponed her own presser at Bedrock's offices and hustled down to City Hall. No one asked her, nor did anyone stop her when she took a place behind the mayor, squarely in camera view.

"I can confirm that earlier today our divers pulled a body from the East River," said Mayor Reynolds, his voice mournful.

He was as dapper as ever in a slim-fitting royal-blue suit with purple tie and matching handkerchief. He continued with his usual rhetorical flair. "At this time, we are endeavoring greatly to identify the deceased, but the remains are not in an idealistic condition."

The questions came in a torrent.

"Do you believe this is the body of Easter Riddle?"

"We believe it quite likely, yes, as the decedent's age and size are a match, and the body was found in the water in approximation with Easter's school."

"What about the body's gender?"

"That is a very complicated . . . That is to say, I don't have that particular information in front of me, but I'll be sure to get back to you."

"Was it a male body, Mr. Mayor?"

"As I indicated, I will offer some clarity as appropriate. My administration is the most transparent in our great city's history."

"Were there any identifiable articles of clothing?"

"There were not. The body was found stripped of clothing, in a naked state, as it were."

"Easter Riddle has only been missing for a few days. How could her body be difficult to identify?"

"This is a matter of some delicacy. The body appears to have encountered some marine life."

"Do you mean it was eaten?"

"That's a very harsh word, and a bit overstated. Can we please respect the family here? I don't think we need to be too graphic."

"Mr. Mayor. What marine life is present in the New York Harbor that could do something like that?"

"Well, as you know, we have made significant strides to clean our waterways, and those efforts have borne fruit. Unfortunately, that, along with rising sea temperatures, has brought predatious creatures into the area. This is a good time to remind everyone that the climate crisis affects us all. I would refer anyone to my newly formed task force on climate for additional information."

Sylvia Haffred, sensing the press conference veering off track, stepped forward and, wedging herself between NYPD brass, stood shoulder to shoulder with the mayor, who appeared taken aback. He did his best to salvage the situation. "Uh, our good friend Sylvia Haffred is going to say a few words." Haffred all but grabbed the mic.

"I'm here to tell you there will be hell to pay," she said. "The parties responsible for this will be held to account."

The press, happy to have avoided a lecture on climate change, was even happier the presser had been redirected to more salacious matters. Haffred was immediately bombarded with questions.

"Will Easter's parents be identifying the body?"

"Yes, I will personally be escorting them to the city morgue later today. This is a horrible task that no parent should ever have to face."

"Do you plan to bring any suits?"

"It is under serious consideration, yes."

"Sylvia! Sylvia!"

"Yes, in the back."

The reporter was looking at his phone. *"It appears William Sanderson has just issued a statement. Do you care to comment?"*

"All my focus has been on the search and on Easter's parents in this tragic situation. Perhaps you could read it to us."

Haffred, being a lawyer, would not normally prompt a response when she didn't know what was coming back at her—but what could Sanderson possibly say? It couldn't hurt her, and it might help.

The reporter read the statement from his phone.

"That certainly sounds like culpability to me," said Haffred.

"Will you be bringing an action against Sanderson?"

In a bolt of inspiration, the way forward came to her.

"Perhaps the real question we should be asking is why a company like Bedrock Capital, a company that trumpets its progressive values, would employ a blatant transphobe like Sanderson. All their advertising and their out-facing content tout inclusive values. They repeatedly highlight the LGBTQ plus community. Their legal documents, their prospectuses, annual reports, and so on, reinforce this message, but their actions say something quite different, don't they? Are investors being sold a bill of goods? There's a word for what Bedrock does, you know. It's called *transwashing*, and we won't let them get away with it."

This was it, this was the play!

By employing the likes of Sanderson, Bedrock was defrauding investors with false representation. Sanderson's inclusion of Bedrock in his apology played entirely into her hands. Perhaps Sanderson was vile, or perhaps he simply had a bad day—it didn't matter either way. Sanderson was small beer next to the company he worked for. Who knows, maybe Haffred would name him in the suit just for the sport of it. It might be worth another million or two, particularly if this body turned out to be Easter's. But the number she would get out of Bedrock would be much larger. They would settle quickly just to make this go away. The Riddles were about to become very rich people—even after paying Haffred her 35 percent.

Sylvia's mind drifted briefly to those listings in the Hamptons, only now she imagined herself on coveted land south of the highway.

"Do you plan to sue Bedrock?"

"All I can say is, stay tuned. But if I were Casper Stein, watching this from his expensive office in the Seagram Building, I would be very concerned. And now, if you'll excuse me, I need to be with my clients in this terrible hour."

Haffred left the podium, leaving a visibly annoyed Mayor Reynolds in her wake.

"Mayor Reynolds, do you agree? Do you *believe Bedrock is liable?"*

"Uh, that is a quite intricate question you pose. Bedrock has been a valued partner in this community, but we will have to consider the various multifaceted angles that Ms. Haffred has raised. Thank you very much, and we'll keep you appraised of any further details. Please pray for Easter."

The mayor practically ran into a waiting car.

Casper Stein looked for the nearest item on his otherwise pristine desk. It was a photograph, encased in Lucite, of his foursome the previous spring at Augusta. Bill Gates had been in his group. He hurled it at the TV monitor, leaving a small crack. "Fucking Sanderson!" he yelled, at no one in particular. "And he can fucking forget about Clooney!"

The email from Jasmine Wu would come later that day, informing him that the State of California's decision was "on hold."

MEANWHILE, BACK IN THE HAMPTONS

Ellie was on the back porch, sipping tea, trying, and failing, to calm her nerves. Ginny ran out. She was crying.

"Honey, what's wrong?"

"Have you *seen* this?" Ginny thrust her phone out.

"What?"

"Just hit play."

It was a clip of the reporter reading William's statement.

> I unequivocally support the LGBTQ+ community, including those identifying as trans. Neither my daughters' actions nor my own represent our family's values, nor those of Bedrock Capital, my employer. I am deeply regretful if my actions or those of my daughters caused harm or offense. I offer the trans community in general and the Riddle family in particular my sincerest apologies in this difficult time.
> —William Sanderson

Ellie boiled over with frustration. "When was this?"

"A few minutes ago. My phone is blowing up. *Everyone* is seeing this."

"Is your father here?"

"He said he was going to hit balls."

"You're kidding."

"I can't believe he said those things!"

"I have to go find him. You girls don't budge, do you hear me? Order out if you're hungry."

Ellie rose and left the house, spitting pebbles as she raced out of the driveway, her hands practically strangling the wheel.

The club was less than a mile away. Sure enough, there was Will, hitting balls on the driving range. He had decided that "being scarce" did not include using the range on a Monday.

"What are you doing here?" he said. "Is something wrong?"

"Is something wrong? Jesus, Will, our world is melting down and you're hitting golf balls! How's your swing? Everything good?"

"Would you keep your voice down? There are members around. People will talk."

"Are you listening to yourself right now? People are already talking. You are the reason the entire drag community came to lunch, and your little episode in front of our building is everywhere. And now, *this!*"

Ellie thrust her phone at William, who recoiled.

"El, the rules! You can't have that out here."

"Oh, is that right? Hey, everyone! Member with a cell phone here!"

Ellie waved her iPhone around comically. It was an October Monday, so there were only two or three others on the large range. They looked up, perplexed by the raised voices.

"*Would you stop that!*" barked William. "I'm in enough hot water around here as it is." William grabbed for the phone, which fell into one of his divots. Picking it up, he retreated to a nearby area of bushes, walking behind them to examine the video. He emerged and handed the phone back to Ellie. Then he grabbed his clubs.

"You just had to go and do it, didn't you?" pressed Ellie.

"El, everyone will know it's just a pro forma thing, something I had to do. For Christ sake, who doesn't have to apologize for something these days?"

"But you mentioned *Ginny* and *Zoey*, Will. You threw them under the bus without even telling them."

"They'll understand. And it will—"

"If you're about to say, *blow over*, I will fucking take that nine iron and hit you in the head!"

William picked up his bag and slung it over his shoulder.

"What are you doing?"

"I'm going back to the city. I need to make sure things are copacetic at work."

"You're only going to make things worse."

"I can't be out here hiding like some sort of coward."

"William, you *are* a coward."

"We obviously don't see this the same way. I did what I had to do. For us."

"For us. Sure, tell yourself that. I'm not sure the girls will ever forgive you. I'm not sure *I* will. But by all means, go make sure you're still getting promoted."

William started to walk off to the parking lot. "I'll call you later when you've decided to calm down."

"Don't bother!"

DAMAGE CONTROL

This was not going to be a fun meeting.

Normally, the trio summoned to Casper's office might have taken a moment to admire the Rothko hanging on the wall, but right now the boss was furious. He had one of those rubber stress balls filled with beans, and he was squeezing it hard enough that the veins on the back of his hand bulged noticeably. The Lucite-encased picture from Augusta was still on the floor, and no one was sure if they should pick it up.

Present were Tanya Rose, the HR head; Elton Tribble, chief in-house counsel; and Meredith Singer, head of PR. They all waited for Casper to speak.

"A decade ago, those clowns who started Occupy rallied half the country against us, all because some MIT quant jockeys couldn't figure out how to structure a damn mortgage product. Now . . . Christ, just how exposed are we on this?"

Elton, the lawyer, knew the question was probably his to answer. "Legally or reputationally?"

"Both."

"From a strictly legal perspective, we are in a strong position on two fronts. First, there's the issue of standing. We checked, and the Riddles are not Bedrock shareholders, nor do they own any of our funds, but Haffred will likely have them buy a nominal amount of something and then backfill the suit with other claimants to make it a class action. They will say they've been duped into buying an investment that they otherwise wouldn't have bought. Their real problem is demonstrating harm, because to sue, there has to be a financial loss."

"If the Riddles, as lead plaintiffs, can't demonstrate harm, this gets tossed, correct?" asked Meredith. "We win."

"Hah!" yelped Casper, knowing better.

"Yes, but it would potentially take months to reach that outcome. Time is not our friend here, which I'll get to."

"What's the second thing?" asked Tanya.

"It centers around a single question. Are we, as a company, responsible for the private actions of one of our employees? Additionally, Sanderson, the employee in question, has done nothing to break the law, and anything else he *did* do had nothing to do with Bedrock. But—"

"But we made him put out that statement with our name in it. Meredith, that was *your* goddamn idea."

"We needed to get ahead—"

"Elton is doing the damn talking now!"

Meredith sank in her chair.

"Elton?"

"Well, yes, this point should also work to our favor, but I'd be lying if I said it was as solid as it might have been a few years ago. There are cases out there working their way through appellate courts where litigants are trying to hold companies liable for their employees' private actions. It's preposterous, of course, but one of the cases is in front of the Ninth Circuit, and they're notoriously flakey. It's anyone's guess what they'll do. Right now, there's nothing to stop the Riddle family from suing us, although, as I said, Sanderson never did anything illegal. His—and his daughters'—actions are protected speech. Based on current case law, we should prevail in court, but that may be beside the point."

"No shit," said Casper.

"Which brings me to another issue, that of double standards. The issues Haffred raises here are a reach, at least legally, but they may be valid in the court of public opinion, which is why I said time is not our friend. The wheels of justice grind slowly, and the longer this is out there, the worse it is for us. The protests could get worse. Perhaps Meredith should address that area."

"In a minute," said Casper. "Have you reviewed our documents?"

"Yes. As a firm, we have trumpeted our values with some . . . vigor, and one of those values is inclusiveness. This includes members of the so-named trans community. They feature prominently in our PR. Our website's homepage features a photo of an ambiguously gendered person. Beyond that, there is exposure in more formal legal documents such as our various prospectuses. Again, it would be difficult to find us at fault because any plaintiff would have to prove we knew of Sanderson's personal views before all this, which would be impossible. But I doubt that will deter Sylvia Haffred. The problem we face is that while we will likely prevail in court, it would be a Pyrrhic victory. The publicity would not be favorable to us, but that's not my area."

"We're already taking on the goddamn chin, and our stock is down five points!" bellowed Casper.

"Six," said Tanya, peering at her phone.

"And it's only been a day or two," said Elton. "A trial would drag out the exposure for months, potentially."

"And what if that body in the morgue is Easter Riddle?"

"Legally, it doesn't change the situation, at least not theoretically, but you never know how a jury might react to that. There's already a great deal of sympathy for the family."

"This is insane," said Casper.

"And there's one more thing I feel I have to mention." Elton paused, looking hesitant.

"Well, *what*?"

"If William Sanderson remains in our employ, we will no longer be able to plead ignorance."

"Explain."

"What I mean is that we can credibly claim, now, that we never knew of Sanderson's—shall we call them inclinations? We only came to realize his true nature in the last few days. Going forward, that claim will lose credibility."

"Meaning . . ."

"Meaning, practically speaking, from this point forward we can be said to possess full knowledge of said inclinations. Thus, our exposure increases every day he remains at our company."

"And this is all because of a single word."

"He called them freaks," said Tanya. "A few years ago, he might have gotten a pass, but now . . ."

"And it's all over social media," said Meredith. "People are using him to make memes. 'It's a Brioni' is getting a lot of play."

"What the hell is a me—" At that moment, the rubber stress ball reached the end of its useful life and burst in Casper's hand, little beans spilling all over his desk. He threw the depleted bag across the room. "We are getting muscled by a shakedown artist and a bunch of fairies!"

"We don't use that word anymore, Casper," said Tanya.

"Actually, we never did," added Meredith. "And technically, they are *trans*, not gay."

"I don't give a shit!"

He turned his glare to Meredith. "I'm not forgetting for a moment that you are partially responsible for this, but what's your take?"

Meredith swallowed. "At this point, it's safe to say we have a PR crisis, and whether it's fair or not is beside the point, as Elton suggested. We find ourselves open to accusations of hypocrisy. In a crisis where there's perceived culpability, the first step is to come clean."

"Be specific. You're talking about throwing Sanderson under the bus."

"Well, in so many words. We need to demonstrate remorse, not merely claim it. Words are only the start. Our actions must reflect those words, and it all must be consistent with our stated values. Then, we need to do whatever needs to be done to make this go away quickly."

"Jesus, it's like I'm talking to a cloud! You mean we start writing checks. Elton, what's it going to take to make Sylvia Haffred go away?"

"I should point out that she hasn't filed anything yet, but I would say it is imminent. But specific numbers? That's premature, but certainly millions."

"*And*, if I may," interjected Tanya, "we will need to do something for the trans community."

The money, in the scheme of things, was irrelevant. Bedrock was awash in it, and he himself a billionaire. But the *company*, that was everything. When he'd left Davenport Trumbull, an elite investment bank, to start Bedrock on a shoestring, everyone said he was crazy. Now, just look. Davenport Trumbull was long gone, and Bedrock was bigger than Davenport had ever been. He did that! Casper Stein!

The throne was his, and he looked down over everyone else.

But now, he stared down the barrel of the progressive social media mob, the very crowd he'd been playing to these past years. His own daughter was giving him crap! Meredith explained that #Bedrock was trending, whatever that meant, along with #ItsaBrioni.

Casper knew that things that took decades to build could be destroyed overnight in the glare of the mob. Didn't these people know he shared their values? He'd never voted for a Republican in his life!

But what to do about Sanderson. Casper was leaning toward feeding him to the wolves, but Sanderson did run Bedrock's most profitable division. And was there a chance that firing him so quickly would make them look guiltier? This was a decision that couldn't be made lightly.

Just then Casper's administrative assistant peeked in the door.

"Mr. Stein?"

"We're busy, Jane."

"Cy Birdwell is on the line."

"Tell him I'll call him back."

"He's quite insistent that he speak with you now."

"Jesus Christ, fine." To the others, he said, "Give me just one moment." He picked up the phone. "Cy! How are you?" he said, forcing his tone to something more genial.

"Oh, well that's an interesting question, Casper. How am I? Let's see, I'm fucking *pissed* is how I am."

"What's wrong?"

"What's wrong is that your pal Jasmine Wu just sent me the schedule for her little diversity conference I'm supposed to speak at."

"Okay . . . that sounds like a good thing."

"Oh, does it? Does that sound like a good thing, Casper? Do you know what my topic is? The importance of an LGBTQ presence in the investment business. I called her up and it seems she thinks I'm gay! I said, 'Gee, I'm flattered, I guess, but I'm not gay.' Do you know why she thinks I'm gay? Because your people told her!"

Fucking Sanderson!

"So, you're . . ."

"What, straight? Yes! I should have put two and two together after a strange night I had with Sanderson at the Gotham. This is all about CalPERS!"

Strange? Could Sanderson have made a pass at Cy to test the waters? For a moment, Casper thought: *loyalty, impressive.* But the moment was fleeting. Sanderson was still the cause of all this.

Jasmine would have known that Bedrock—*Sanderson*—had checked the LGBTQ box. But how, Casper wondered, did she know Cy was the designated person? The RFP didn't ask for a name. Casper assumed William was somehow responsible for the leak as well.

In fact, he wasn't. Sometime after Tanya Rose met with William, she saw the final RFP and that William had checked the box. That could only mean he'd cleared it with Cy Birdwell. At an internal HR meeting about best practices, Tanya reviewed the incident with her senior staff, emphasizing the need for transparency in their diversity efforts.

Although Tanya never mentioned Cy's name, everyone in the meeting knew who they were talking about. Wando Perez, a recent transfer from Bedrock's LA office, was gay and very plugged into the gay community on the Coast. They were all fans of Birdwell's clothes. He mentioned to one of his friends that Cy Birdwell was finally "out." That person mentioned it to someone else, who mentioned it to someone else, and, well, it didn't take long until it reached the ears of Jasmine Wu, who thought Cy would be perfect for their upcoming conference.

Not that any of that would have mattered at this point.

Casper was thoroughly confused. Cy Birdwell was a closeted *hetero*sexual? He pleaded with him. "There must be some misunderstanding here, my friend. We can fix this."

"We can start with my resignation from your board. There, that opens a spot for you to find an actual gay person."

"Cy, please, I—"

The line went dead.

"Fuck!" He slammed the phone down. "Sanderson's a dead man!"

How many other things had Sanderson lied about? On top of that, he had no control over himself *or* his family.

Jane was at the door again. "I'm sorry to interrupt, but William Sanderson is here. I told him you were in a meeting."

Casper smiled wickedly. "No, that's fine. We're done here. Send him in."

Birdwell Apparel's headquarters were in Tribeca in a converted warehouse with twelve-foot ceilings. Its original use was for the storage of tea and coffee imports, and later it became a Wall Street printer. Eventually the internet made the physical printing of financial documents unnecessary, so the building sat unoccupied until Cy Birdwell decided it had the perfect amount of edginess for his growing clothing empire.

From his office there, Cy typed a hasty email to Jasmine, backing out of the conference. He banged at the keys in anger. Given his prominent place in the fashion industry, he'd long found the misperception over his sexuality professionally convenient. In reality, he was a full-blooded heterosexual who'd managed, for years, to keep his personal life and his taste for much younger women to himself. It just wasn't anyone's business.

But this whole conference thing was a bridge too far, and it was forcing his hand. Does one "come out" as a heterosexual?

He'd have to think on that.

YOU HAVE A FUTURE IN PATHOLOGY

The New York City morgue was tucked away in the Kips Bay neighborhood of Manhattan. Haffred had never been, and she didn't particularly want to be there now, but it was important to support the Riddles. Or at least to be seen supporting the Riddles.

They were met in the lobby by the city's chief medical examiner, Dennis Rizzo.

"I'm sorry we couldn't meet under better circumstances," he said. "I'm praying for you. In fact, I think the whole city is."

"Thank you. Let's get this over with," said Shannon.

Haffred was surprised at her tone, almost dismissive. Still, who was she to judge how people should behave in such horrific circumstances?

"Of course," said Rizzo. "If you would follow me."

He led them through a series of drab institutional hallways, finally reaching a door that read Examination Room. Opening it brought a rush of cool air. It smelled strongly of chemicals.

There were several long metal tables, but only one appeared to support a body. There was another man there, too, in a lab coat.

"This is Jay Osterman, our top pathologist," said Rizzo.

"Hello," said Osterman. "I have the body ready for viewing whenever you're ready. Please, take your time."

"We're ready," said Mark Riddle.

"Very well. Who will be identifying the remains today?"

"We both will," said Mark.

"Certainly. This way please. I should prepare you for this. The remains are not . . . in ideal shape. You may find this difficult."

"Just show us, please."

They walked over to the table with the ominous lump underneath a sheet. Haffred held back at a respectful distance, masking her intense interest.

"Are you ready?" Osterman asked.

"Go ahead," said Mark.

Osterman pulled up the sheet, allowing the Riddles to see the body's head and shoulders.

Haffred stole a glance, and it was a gruesome sight. The body appeared greenish black, and there was a chunk missing from one shoulder. She was no expert, but that didn't look like a body that had only been in the water for a few days.

"That's not Easter," said Mark.

"That must be a great relief," said Rizzo.

"Yes," Mark replied.

"I'll just wait out in the hall. Come out whenever you're ready."

Rizzo exited, and the Riddles followed. Haffred held back for a moment and watched Osterman cover the body back up.

"Dr. Osterman, may I ask a question?"

"Of course." Haffred got the impression he didn't get many visitors.

"That body . . . I mean, I don't know about these things, but it looked in pretty bad shape."

"You noticed. Perhaps you have a future in pathology."

She ignored his tone. "What I'm getting at is, is it possible for a body to look like that after only a few days, even if it's been in the water?"

"Zero chance. I told Rizzo, and tried to tell the mayor's office, too, but they didn't seem to be interested. I've only been doing this for thirty years, so what do I know? John Doe here is at least a month old. I guess they just wanted to be sure, with all the publicity and all."

Interesting, thought Haffred.

The announcement around the body had only increased public interest. Why would Reynolds do that if he knew the body wasn't Easter's? Was the mayor part of the game? Then it occurred to her that the election was only a few days away and Reynolds was probably benefiting politically from his demonstrative show of concern around Easter's disappearance.

Perhaps Sylvia had underestimated the mayor.

Another thing gnawed at her. The Riddles had seemed oddly detached, as if they were just going through the motions. Had they been clued in about the body too? Why would they go along with the charade?

Haffred didn't like the feeling that there was a game going on here and she didn't know the rules. And was part of her disappointed that the body wasn't Easter's? A tragic end would have multiplied the settlement ten times. . . .

Haffred's internal monologue was going places she did her best to suppress.

The thoughts were inchoate, swimming around, but still lurked there like sharks, just below the surface.

In any case, the publicity surrounding the body had already proved useful. Easter Riddle was a national story now. Perhaps that was the angle everyone was playing here.

"Thank you, doctor," she said, heading for the swinging doors.

She found the Riddles already out on the street. Mark was holding his phone in front of his face and talking into it. Who the hell was he talking to? Haffred feared the Riddles were becoming difficult to control.

"I'm here outside the city morgue with Shannon. We are just so, so relieved. The body . . ."

Mark suddenly choked up.

"The body we just saw was not Easter. Our baby's still out there, somewhere. Easter, if you're seeing this, please come home. We miss you terribly. Your mother and I . . . We're just so proud of you and everything you've accomplished. Know that *everyone* is thinking about you."

He hit stop. Glancing toward Shannon, he said, "What hashtags should I use?"

PRINCETON WASN'T A WASTE

The next morning, when the doors opened at the Daniel Patrick Moynihan Courthouse in lower Manhattan, a paralegal working for Sylvia Haffred was already waiting. She went directly to the clerk's office and filed a suit with the famed Southern District of New York:

Shannon and Mark Riddle et al. v. Bedrock Capital Corporation

As soon as it was in the system, she texted Haffred confirmation.

Where Bedrock was concerned, Haffred didn't anticipate any more action to be necessary, at least on the legal front. She'd never argued in an actual courtroom before and wouldn't this time either. In her view, the best lawyers achieved their goals without ever seeing the inside of a courthouse.

Haffred summoned her driver to take her uptown. "Lenox Hill," she said. The S-Class Mercedes insulated her from the sounds of the city, giving her time to think through what she would say. This time, she was expected.

Haffred marched through the front gate and across the courtyard, where a receptionist checked her ID. Reaching Padma's office, she saw she was not alone. Someone else was with her, a silver-haired man in a lightweight gray suit, and Celeste, the assistant.

"Hello again, Ms. Haffred. Allow me to introduce Bennet Smith from Davis Polk. They act as general counsel to the school. I thought it best to have him here. I have also asked Celeste to sit in and take notes. I wouldn't want there to be any misunderstandings."

The venerable Davis Polk, founded in 1849, was the go-to law firm for New York private schools. With silver hair and a Gotham Club bow tie, Bennet looked every bit the old-world lawyer.

"It's a pleasure to meet you, Ms. Haffred," he said, offering his hand and bowing his head ever so slightly.

Haffred gave his hand a perfunctory pump and took a seat. "Likewise, but you can stand down, Slick, at least for now. I haven't decided whether to bring action against Lenox."

This surprised Team Lenox. "Well," said Bennet, "that is tentatively welcome news—not that my client did anything wrong to begin with."

"Right. Well, I don't deal in right and wrong. I deal in actionable or not."

"And this is most certainly not actionable."

"That's what you think, is it, Bennet?"

"It certainly is. You would never prevail in court. The student in question was barely here a week. There's no basis for a suit."

"Don't get out much, do you, Bennet?"

"I beg your pardon?"

"I mean, in the real world."

"I don't follow."

"If I sue, we won't go to court. You will settle."

"And why on earth would we do that?"

Haffred leaned back in her chair. "Do you like classical music, Bennet?"

Bennet's bushy eyebrows climbed up his forehead. "I'm sorry, what?"

"Do you like classical music?"

"I've been known to attend the New York Philharmonic," Bennet said, confused.

"Me too. I like Tchaikovsky, in particular. Very literal, not hard to tell where he's coming from."

Bennet gave a slight smile. "At the moment, I fear, the same cannot be said of you."

"Take the *1812 Overture*," Haffred said, ignoring him. "The beginning is real quiet, just some French horns. It's very peaceful, almost calming."

"Yes, I recall it."

"But you just know what's coming, don't you? The music builds and builds and then it's the entire thunderous orchestra, at full volume, with kettle drums blasting like cannons and cymbals crashing like explosions. You are fully engulfed in the mayhem of battle."

"May I assume this is a metaphor of some sort?"

"Bennet, that Harvard education wasn't wasted after all."

"Princeton."

"You know, when I'm trying to score easy points with sarcasm, it's best not to go out of your way to help me."

Bennet grimaced. "Could we, perhaps, bring the metaphor home?"

"Certainly. If I choose to sue, something that is still very much on the table, and you don't settle quickly—and I mean quickly—I will take this to the streets and social media. What you've seen so far are but the French horns, a gentle foreshadowing of the mayhem to come. Oh, you might prevail in court, but you will never let it get that far. Your board won't allow the reputational damage, plus I assume Davis Polk isn't helping out of the goodness of its heart. What do partners charge these days? Couple of thousand an hour?"

Bennet didn't bite.

"Your board will be screaming to settle like they had kidney stones the size of ping-pong balls."

Bennet cleared his throat. "May we assume, that should you demur, it would not be out of a sense of personal charity?"

"So cynical, Bennet! But it happens there might be a way or two we could help each other. This morning I filed a class action against Bedrock Capital for three hundred million dollars. It might just be that *they* are the true villains in this sordid tale and, as such, could be the sole focus of our litigation. *Could* be."

"And what a coincidence that they are also the deep pockets in this symphony," said Bennet.

"What a coincidence, indeed."

"And the price of your munificence toward my client?"

"My *possible* munificence."

"As you say."

"For starters, and I mean *starters*, I want you to drop William Sanderson from your board and issue a public statement, *tomorrow*, that the school could not abide by his actions. You can add some boilerplate about the Riddle family. Thoughts and prayers, yada yada."

"You want us to bolster your case against Bedrock."

"Very perceptive. I see why you make the big bucks. I will consider it a down payment. I'm not sure why you'd want that asshole on your board, anyway."

"A down payment? What else is there?"

"We can get into that later. Sanderson first."

"We'll have to talk this over."

"Yes, of course you will. You have until the end of the day, after which I may not feel as charitable. I understand you have a robust liability policy, and it just might prove too tempting."

Haffred got up and left.

Bennet spoke first.

"At the risk of belaboring the point, neither the school, nor you, have done anything wrong, and what's happening here is tantamount to blackmail."

"And yet we're going to do what she asks," said Padma.

Bennet considered this. "If that's your intention, you'll need to run it by the board. It's not as if you can fire one of them on your own."

"Of course. In fact, let's ring Duncan right now. I'd like you on the call."

Padma knew the board always did her bidding, but it would be impolitic to not at least give them the appearance of control. "Celeste, please get Duncan Ruggles on the line."

Padma explained the situation to Duncan, who pushed back, however gently. "Sanderson has been very loyal to this school, and he's pledged half a million to the capital campaign!"

"Yes, it's safe to say we won't see that, but it's better than the alternative."

"Is it?"

Bennet responded. "Our alternative is a legal battle, one, as your lawyer, I am delighted to fight. In fact, I don't doubt we would win. But it would be an expensive win, fee-wise. We could also settle, and insurance would cover it, but your rates would rise substantially. Either way involves reputational risk. There would be publicity."

"And how do you put a price on our reputation?" offered Padma.

"I see. What about the girls?" asked Duncan.

"What girls?" asked Padma.

"*Sanderson's* girls, of course."

"Oh, well I suppose we'll have to counsel them out. I don't think the other girls will feel safe with them here."

"This all feels like . . . weakness."

"But what choice do we really have, Duncan? We have to protect the institution. That is our first obligation."

There was an audible sigh over the phone. "I tend to think you're right. When do we have to do this?"

"She insists on knowing today," said Bennet.

"I suppose I should call Sanderson first," said Duncan. "As a courtesy."

"It's the right thing to do," said Padma.

"Absolutely," said Bennet.

A LITTLE DAY DRINKING

William sat alone at 580 Park. He'd been there since the day before, since coming back from the office. The shades were down and most of the lights were off.

He was quite drunk.

He looked at his watch.

Ten thirty.

You can't drink all day if you don't start early, he reasoned. Was that a country song? If it wasn't, it should be.

It was a funny feeling, being drunk in the morning. Quite pleasant, really.

He tried to remember the last time.

Hmm.

Could it have been as long ago as college? Yes, that was probably it. Maybe that away game at Princeton senior year when they all went tailgating at the eating clubs. One of the Cottage guys threw up in the bushes. Ha! Pussy couldn't hold his liquor. . . . And there was a girl he'd been chasing. . . . What was her name again? She had a ponytail and one of those Fair Isle sweaters they all wore. . . .

Damn, he couldn't come up with it.

Then he tried to remember the last time he'd gotten drunk *alone* in the daytime, and he was pretty sure this was his virgin run. He resolved to change, to do better. From now on, he'd get drunk alone in the middle of the day *lots*. It was highly underrated.

There was an almost sepulchral silence in the empty apartment as he sipped his Woodford. He looked around the den. Had that bird print always been there? He'd never noticed it before.

What an asshole Casper was. *I have to protect the institution*, he'd said. And then that other asshole Duncan Ruggles called and thanked him for his service on the board.

"I've been there for two meetings," William said.

"Yes, well, thank you nonetheless."

And then he delivered those apparently magic words: *I've got to protect the institution.*

William Sanderson was now officially toxic to institutions.

And for what? A single word?

A single *accurate* word, he thought. Why should saying something that was true get you in trouble?

His self-pity only grew when he considered what they'd likely be saying about him later at the Gotham. They'd all be getting schadenboners, those pricks.

William loved that word, "schadenboners." Who told him that one again? Fucking genius. It would come to him later.

Then there was the email from his broker informing him that the co-op board at 895 Park had turned him down. At least William hadn't told many people that he was planning on moving. Maybe word of this particular indignity wouldn't get out.

Nature called and he went to the bathroom. He decided to piss in the sink because, why not? It was kind of like a urinal if you thought about it.

His cell rang.

Ellie.

He sent it to voicemail.

Almost before he pressed the side button, a text from Ellie filled his lock screen.

Where ARE you?

He walked to the bar, put the phone in the ice bucket, and placed the lid back on.

Problem solved.

He refilled his lead-glass tumbler and returned to the leather club chair. How come he'd never noticed how comfortable it was?

Maybe he could just do this every day. Maybe he'd be a successful drunk, one of those functioning alcoholics he'd always heard about. He tried to think of some precedents. Hemingway was a drunk, right? Except William had never tried writing fiction. Monthly client letters were the extent of his compositional efforts.

Hmm, who else?

Ulysses Grant! Legendary drunk! Lincoln said he'd rather have a drunk Grant than anyone else sober. Maybe politics was the answer? William delighted in this idea for a few moments until he considered how his recent travails might play in the New York market. Probably not great.

Fuck 'em.

Artist! He could be an artist! Weren't they *all* drunks? Hell, Jackson Pollack was pissed out of his mind when he wrapped his Oldsmobile around a tree right there in East Hampton. And how hard could painting all those swiggles and swirls be?

Yeah, that's what he'd do.

Satisfied, a plan in place, William decided he could close his eyes, just for a minute or two.

It really was a comfortable chair.

A HAUNTING IN STARBUCKS

It was day 6 of Ellie and the girls' self-imposed exile in East Hampton.

Ellie sat on the back porch, watching Ginny and Zoey play cornhole. Apparently, they were stir-crazy enough to get off their phones and go outside.

She hadn't seen them play together like that for years, not since they lived outside of Chicago and the girls made forts, played zoo, and dug holes in that small lawn.

Had they been right to move to New York? It was what she thought she'd wanted, but now Manhattan seemed like a test they were failing. If it hadn't been for Will's career path they'd still be in Winnetka, where everything seemed simpler.

But no, she couldn't blame Will, or Bedrock, or anything else.

She'd finally reached William the previous evening, and the conversation had not gone well. She wanted to be conciliatory after the way things had been left, but William was clearly blind drunk. He was going off about Casper and Duncan Ruggles and how the world was ganging up on him. It was all about him, which seemed to be the way of it these last few years.

A disgusted Ellie hung up the phone before William had a chance to go into the details of his current situation.

She decided to get out of the house, if only for a few minutes. "Girls, I'm going to Starbucks," she shouted. "Text me if you want anything!"

She ordered her usual venti herbal tea, waiting for its calming effects. Thoughts, all negative, competed for her attention.

There was William. His cavalier attitude was something she couldn't understand, and the more she thought about it, the angrier she got. He was prioritizing his job over his family, and for a time she'd accepted this as a temporary restacking of priorities. But time passed and nothing changed. Will was hard for Ellie to understand, even after all these years.

There had always been this passivity, the way he avoided confrontation, and it gnawed at her. "It will all work out" could have been his motto, and the funny thing was, it usually did. He floated with the current, especially when the current almost always floated in a direction that suited his ambition. It was a character trait she never fully appreciated in the early days of her marriage.

Thinking back, it occurred to her that William probably just assumed she'd come around to his marriage proposal. The idea that she'd been yet another pleasant inevitability in Will's life frustrated her. Lately, though, even Will's studied insouciance had left him, his moods growing more erratic.

Mostly, she worried for the girls. How would they come back from this? She would jump in front of a bus for them, but what if the bus was a thousand social media posts? How do you jump in front of that? This was an incomprehensible storm, almost Kafkaesque, and somehow Ginny and Zoey were at the center of it.

They would leave the nest soon, the girls. It seemed like just yesterday they'd clamored for American Girl accessories and Butterfinger McFlurries at McDonald's. Now, they were facing down the worst of what the adult world had to offer. Zoey, in particular, wasn't ready for this.

Outside, she saw a child walk by dressed as a cowboy.

Halloween.

She'd almost forgotten.

The big party was tonight, the Monster Mash. She and William had paid for tickets, ordered costumes, and she'd been part of the planning—but they weren't going, of course. With the hysteria around Easter Riddle, she wondered if it was still even on. . . .

"Hello, Ellie."

Looking up, she saw a ghost, right there in Starbucks.

"Bob?"

"In the flesh."

It was Bob Ellison, he of the *disappeared* Ellisons. He was sitting just a couple of tables away. She'd been so wrapped up in her thoughts she hadn't noticed. "How nice to see you."

"And you."

"I should have asked—*Bob*, is that still how you're identifying?"

Bob chuckled. "You seem surprised to see me."

"No, I—sorry, it's just that I heard you guys had moved."

"We did. New Jersey. We found a nice parochial school out there that would take us on short notice. The nuns run the place with an iron fist."

"Oh, good. I'm happy for you."

"Moving is a pain in the butt, but it's good for us."

"What brings you to East Hampton?"

"I'm heading out to Montauk. Some friends have a place there and they lent it to us to decompress for a few days, I guess. The kids won't start at school until Monday. Leslie's already out there and I just stopped in for some caffeine."

Ellie paused. What do you say to a ghost?

"Bob, I'm really sorry about what happened to you guys."

"Don't be. It's for the best. I'm only surprised they didn't parade us around in dunce caps and confessional signs. But I've heard about what's been going on since we left, obviously, and what we went through was nothing compared to what you're dealing with. I hope you're doing okay."

She wasn't, not in the least, but she wasn't about to say as much.

Would she become a ghost herself?

"Thanks, Bob. I'll admit it's no fun, but we'll get through it."

Bob seemed to consider this. His voice modulated into a minor key. "I'm not sure you will."

Ellie was taken aback. "Excuse me?"

"Sorry, you've probably noticed I sometimes speak first and think second. It's just . . . It's funny running into you like this. I'd been thinking about reaching out."

"About what?"

"About what's happening."

"Oh."

"Yes, I had some thoughts."

"That's nice, Bob, it really is, but I'm not sure what's to be done about it."

Bob rose from his seat and walked over to Ellie's table. "May I?"

Ellie wasn't in the mood for company, but she *was* curious about what Bob had on his mind. To say she had increasing doubts about the Lenox Hill School for Girls was an understatement, and all she got from her usual circle was a Greek chorus of praise.

It's such a special place.

Bob, no doubt, had a different take.

"Sure," she said.

He sat down.

ALL THE LOVELY PEOPLE

There's no reason for you to know this, but before I went into advertising, I was a high school teacher. I taught history, a subject I still love. I did my PhD thesis on social and political movements, particularly the ugly ones. The French Revolution, Iran in seventy-nine, the Nazis, those sorts of things."

"And why were you drawn to those?"

"That's an interesting question. I guess they all represent a form of mass psychosis, and I find it fascinating that we never seem to learn from them."

"Okay . . ."

"There are patterns," Bob continued. "History repeats." He sipped his coffee. "Let me put it this way. Evil doesn't just happen. It's *allowed* to happen, often by the seemingly well-intentioned people who might otherwise be in a position to stop it."

"I don't understand," said Ellie.

"The social dynamics of these movements may seem differentiated and complex, but they're really not. There are only, ever, three groups at play: the true believers, the cowards, and the sleepwalkers. That's what I call them, anyway."

Ellie wasn't sure where this was going but she didn't have the psychic space right now for a history lesson. "Bob, I have a lot on my plate right now."

"Please, Ellie, I feel like I ran into you for a reason. I mean, what were the odds? I have no right to ask, but will you indulge me for a moment?"

"Well, sure—I haven't finished my tea, so . . ."

"I guess I'm glad it's a venti, then. Okay, my little speech. First, the true believers. They're the ones pushing change, and they are first and foremost revolutionaries. They don't eat or sleep and they're one hundred percent committed to the cause. They're especially effective at exerting control over institutions, something that gives them maximum cultural leverage. The media, for instance, and educational institutions.

"The interesting thing is that they are rarely anything close to a majority of the population. More like a tiny minority. But they are highly focused on their goals, and willing to cut ethical and legal corners to achieve them. *Padma* is a true believer, with her 'anti-racism.' The first victim of totalitarianism is always the dictionary."

"She wears very awfully nice clothes for a revolutionary," said Ellie, trying to lighten the mood.

"Revolutionaries almost always come from the privileged. Friedrich Engels was a wealthy man."

"I see."

"Then there are the sleepwalkers. They're the biggest group. These are the people too caught up in their daily lives to question what's going on. You can look around this very coffee shop and see them, because they're everywhere, noses buried in TikTok or Candy Crush. They don't pay much attention to the revolution because no one's come for *them* yet, but come they will. Just ask the Jews in the late thirties."

"And the cowards?"

"The cowards, now they may be the most interesting group. These are people of importance, people with money and power. People that run things. They know, to one degree or another, the threat posed by the true believers, but they find it expedient to work with them because they are doing just fine, thank you. At least, until they aren't. Think of the German industrialists. They all understood Hitler was a maniac, but they were making a fortune rearming the country. And where would it get them to stand in Hitler's way? What good to raise your hand and question things when no one else was? You might lose everything."

"Bob, are you suggesting we're in the middle of a revolution?"

"Aren't we?"

He could see the quizzical look on Ellie's face.

"It's important to understand something. For true believers, the revolution is a permanent state, even after they've succeeded in seizing power. That's why the goalposts always move. There will always be a 'next' movement, something else to march for. They also understand that schools are fulcrums for social change, which is why they've been very clever to gain control of them. It's part of the Long March, that's what they call it. As I said, Padma is one of them. Oh, she may disguise her agenda when parents are around with soothing talk about *excellence* at Lenox, but it's all a lie."

"And the cowards?" asked Ellie. "Who are they?"

"They're the ones I save my deepest contempt for. Sorry, I don't mean to be so blunt, but . . . Well, I do, I guess. The cowards are the ones who could *do* something, but they sit on their hands, thinking they can keep living their pleasant lives in perpetuity, just like the monied classes in Germany or Iran or France thought before them. They believe the cost of speaking out is too high, and it often *is* high. In Germany in 1936 or Iran in 1979, speaking out might have cost you your fortune or your freedom. In 1787 France, you might have lost your head. But today, what are the stakes? Your children might not get into Harvard? Is that really all it takes to dissolve the spines of our rich and powerful?"

"Are we talking about school boards here, Bob?"

"Among other things, yes."

"You do know that Will is on the Lenox board, right?"

Ellie did not yet know that William had been "thanked for his service."

"I do," said Bob.

"And you think my husband is one of your cowards."

"I don't know, he just got there, right? Perhaps he'll be the one to raise his hand and say *stop*."

Unlikely, thought Ellie. It was clear Bob suspected the same without saying it.

"You know," he continued, "the funny thing is, they are very nice people, the cowards. You can even say they are good at being nice, like it's a practiced skill. If you sat next to one at a dinner party, you'd think, *What a lovely person*. But these same lovely people do nothing while the very principles that allowed Western civilization to thrive, principles from the Enlightenment like reason and objective truth and natural law, are being destroyed on their watch by petty tyrants like Padma Minali."

"I don't know, Bob. That all seems . . . a bit extreme."

"Does it?"

"Maybe a bit."

"I'd be very happy if you were right. You'd think private schools like Lenox Hill would be resistant to it, but they're even worse than the public schools. It's because they've *got* you. Sign the contract, be good little parents, or Chelsea doesn't see the inside of a quad in Cambridge or New Haven."

Ellie was well past that point, of course. She was on the verge of losing all the things that every tough decision had pointed her toward, the home she'd made and the *belonging*. Her eyes suddenly prickled with tears, which she tried to hide. "You know . . . my daughters didn't even *do* anything."

Bob reached across the table and placed his hand on Ellie's. "I know. But it doesn't matter, does it? Your daughters, Will, even you, have been objectified, turned into symbols. All the facts in the world don't matter now."

"Bob, why are you telling me all this?"

Bob took a sip of his coffee while he considered how to answer.

"Someone once said, people go mad quickly, and in herds, and recover slowly, one by one. We're in the *going mad* part. I fear you guys haven't even begun to see what will happen. These people are vicious, and now you're in their sights."

"Bob, we're already all over social media, they're outside our apartment with megaphones, they're calling us fascists and transphobes—what else do you *think* might happen?"

Bob paused.

"Violence," he said, finally.

Ellie thought about the protesters in front of 580. Were they capable of that? They did throw blood at Will. God, Easter Riddle was out there some-where. What if she . . . Ellie didn't think so, but she couldn't be sure.

"It's good you left the city. I'd stay out here for a bit," Bob said.

Ellie began to rise. "I should get back."

Bob also rose from his chair. "I wish you the best, I really do. Oh, and I would get yourselves out of Lenox, too, assuming you don't get shown the exit first like us. Nothing good is happening there."

"We've put a lot of time into that school, Bob. Maybe Will can make a difference."

Even as she said it, she didn't believe it.

"And the girls have to get into . . . Which Ivy is it?"

Ellie didn't answer but gave Bob a hurt look.

"I'm sorry, that wasn't called for. Hey, I know we never knew each other that well other than the sidelines of soccer games, but I've always sensed you were a good person, so I was worried. Then I saw you here. I'll get out of your hair."

"Nice to see you, Bob, and thanks for the talk, but I'm sure this will work out."

It wasn't until the door closed behind Bob that she realized she sounded just like Will.

EMBRACING THE OTHER

Right about the time Ellie was leaving Starbucks, things were busy back in Manhattan.

Most schools are content to hold their annual fundraisers in the school gym. For the Lenox Hill School's annual Halloween Ball, this wouldn't do, not when asking $1,000 a ticket. Lenox moved the party around each year, touring Manhattan's tonier event spaces. Last year, it had been the Rainbow Room in Rockefeller Center, and the year before the Mandarin Oriental.

This year, the chosen venue was Cipriani, a landmark space in the Italian Renaissance style with marbled floors and columns, a soaring ceiling, and immense chandeliers. Improbably, it had once been the main branch of the Bowery Savings Bank, back when bank branches were built like timeless monuments to fiscal probity.

With Easter missing, the decision as to whether to hold the event at all was one that required discussion. They concluded the best way to deal with it was to have Duncan say a few words and then have a moment of silence. All agreed this would be appropriate, as would the half million dollars they expected to raise.

Inside, the event planning staff and the party committee were hard at work converting the cavernous space into a spooky wonderland. There was an immense cobweb in one corner with a six-foot spider. A witch on a broomstick was suspended between billowy cotton clouds. Was a witch a monster? They weren't sure but went with it anyway. Someone tested the fog machine, which worked perfectly.

Tizzy was running about, making sure everything was just so. At the moment, she was busy setting up the silent auction tables, a huge annual money maker. There were dozens of items, including a private jet rental, rounds at various Hamptons golf courses, a home-catered meal from Chef Jean-Georges—and a walk-on part in Martin Scorsese's next movie.

Tizzy was thinking about bidding on that one.

The event's "sub-theme" theme was Embracing the Other.

Normally, there wasn't a sub-theme. This development came about be-cause of a ninth-grade girl named Tabitha Burke. The word "monster" of-fended her, although she wasn't entirely sure why. She decided to research the etymology. It turned out that "monster" came from the French word *monstre*, which meant "evil omen." These omens, in medieval days, were the unfor-tunate children born with birth defects such as hare lips or hermaphroditic parts.

Aha!

The moment Thomas Edison discovered the correct filament to light a bulb had nothing on Tabitha Burke. "Monster" was both ableist *and* trans-phobic! Never in her fifteen years had she felt so validated. Breathless, she contacted Shonda Gomez-Brown with her concerns. Shonda wasted no time in calling Padma.

Committees were formed, meetings were held. Duncan Ruggles was brought in. Padma sided firmly with Shonda, that they should find some other theme for the event. This precipitated discussions as to what the theme might be, but every suggestion met with thorny issues. Someone liked Su-perheroes, but then someone else pointed out that nearly every superhero was white. Someone else suggested Celebrities, but then another committee member said this could open the door for a Donald Trump costume.

This went on for some time until Duncan asked what the party planning committee's thoughts were on the matter. It turns out no one had thought to ask them. Tizzy immediately melted down over the idea of a new theme.

"All the decorations have been ordered, most of the parents have their costumes, the invitations have been printed—we can't change it!"

Thus, it was decided they had to find some way to make monsters cultur-ally digestible. More meetings were held, and various sub-themes discussed and argued over: Why Can't We Be Friends? and Don't Judge a Book by Its Cover were pondered and their potential meanings dissected, until they settled on Embracing the Other.

Shonda came up with that one. She explained that the process of "other-ing" turned fellow humans into abstract entities that could then be treated as less than human—monsters, even. By "embracing" the "other," they were implicitly rejecting this judgmental, dehumanizing labeling.

To underscore the sentiment, a famous scene from the movie-monster canon was recreated in papier mâché. A design and fabrication studio in Brooklyn was hastily engaged to get it done, producing a life-size Franken-stein's monster, kneeling with a little girl, helping her pick flowers. There it was, on a platform in the center of the vast space, surrounded by a bar facing in all directions. There was grass and fresh daisies and the girl, smiling beatifically, conveying all the innocence of a child not yet sullied by the hate-inducing prejudices of grown-ups.

She could see that Frankenstein was no monster at all.

The point would be lost on no one.

"Perfect," said Tizzy, who'd come over to make sure the pickle-green napkins that matched the monster and the petal-pink napkins that matched the girl's hair bow were alternated and fanned out just so.

A GATHERING OF MONSTERS

They were all there.

There were the classics, like Wolfman and the Mummy, Franken-stein, of course, and a few of his brides. There was Godzilla, whose tail kept knocking into people's ankles, and Stephen King's Pennywise.

Lenox parents threw themselves into the spirit of the event, as they did every year. No one would be outdone!

Morgan French thought he was very clever coming as the Creature from the Black Lagoon but soon discovered that the rubber suit was unbearably hot, and the mask made it impossible to eat or drink. Ten minutes into the party, sweat dripping over his face, he ditched the headpiece and made for the multitiered sushi bar.

Padma Minali had just finished her remarks, something about the importance of . . . Well, in truth, few heard her. It was almost impossible to get everyone in the vast space to quiet, and the further you got from the stage, the more the conversations continued.

Jake just got a commitment letter from the Brown lacrosse coach . . .

I hear the chicken pot pie at the Waverly just isn't up to snuff anymore . . .

They say they're sticking it out for the kids, but I hear they think it's too expensive to get a divorce . . .

The effect was a white noise of society chatter.

Presently, it was Mayor Reynolds's turn to speak. Someone finally thought to turn off the fog machine as it was working almost too well, and it had gotten difficult to see.

The mayor, not in costume and dressed in his traditional closely tailored suit, had arrived with his usual entourage and security. He'd jumped at the chance to come. Knowing there were many existing and potential donors in the audience, the mayor had reached out to Casper Stein about making an appearance. Casper had called Duncan Ruggles, who was only too happy to oblige.

But there was another reason.

The LGBTQ+ community was a growing political force, particularly here in New York. A flash internal poll done by his people the day before showed Reynolds's numbers on the rise, buoyed by his leadership in the search for Easter Riddle. He was pleased to see Dina Campbell here. Her reporting had been excellent, and she would capture the moment.

As the mayor stepped to the mic, the chatter continued, and he was having none of it. He used a technique he'd learned from his old friend Joe Lieberman, the late senator from Connecticut, who himself had learned the technique from earlier politicians. He put his mouth to the microphone, almost swallowing it, and let out a long "Shhhhhhhhh . . . ," loud at first, but then fading slowly.

The din quickly died. It worked every time.

"It's so great to see everyone tonight. Normally I'd start by saying I've never seen such a good-looking crowd, but . . ."

The crowd laughed, the bonhomie of the evening established. He went on to say a few words about Easter and how much he deeply, deeply cared about diversity. Monster heads everywhere nodded in agreement. He called for a moment of silence, which was observed.

"And now, I'd like to ask Lenox Hill's board chair, Duncan Ruggles, to join me in making an important announcement."

Duncan was dressed as Count Dracula, one of at least half a dozen.

"Nice outfit!" someone yelled.

"Thank you, that's very kind. And to the other Princes of the Night, I have been assured the bar is serving Bloody Mary's and there will be no garlic in tonight's entree!"

More laughter. Duncan's wife had thought of that one.

"Turning a bit more serious, tonight is a night to celebrate, but I think, as I'm sure we all do, that a bit of temperance is called for. One of our own, Easter Riddle, is still out there, somewhere, missing. I'd like to call up to the stage Easter's parents, Mark and Shannon, along with Sylvia Haffred, who has been by their side since the beginning."

Like the mayor, neither the Riddles nor Haffred were in costume. That would have been unseemly. Nor would they stay for long, lest they be perceived as enjoying the evening.

Duncan continued. "We debated whether tonight's party was appropriate, given the circumstances, but after a great deal of thought, we decided that maybe this event was happening at exactly the *right* time, that we could leverage it for the good of not just the Lenox Hill School, but for the community. With that, we have, as Mayor Reynolds mentioned, an important announcement to make. I'd like to invite Sylvia to the microphone to share the details."

Off in the wings, Dina Campbell took out her phone and started recording. In the old days, a journalist would have used a pencil and notepad, but the phone always caught a complete record, and there could be no disputing it.

Dina wasn't sure why she was here, but Haffred told her she would be making an announcement and that Dina would be on the official guest list, no costume required.

This was all curious, but Dina would follow the story wherever it led.

At a minimum, she mused, there was a piece here about how all the filthy rich East Siders partied away while one of their own students was probably lying dead in a ditch somewhere. The school wouldn't like it, but what the fuck ever.

She considered potential titles. Perhaps just "Monstrous!"

Simple, to the point.

The story would practically write itself.

"Thank you, Duncan, and it's so wonderful to be here tonight as you celebrate Lenox Hill. Such a *special* school, don't you think?"

She paused, which was her way of indicating that everyone was expected to clap, which they dutifully did, led by Duncan. But there was a sense of confusion, mixed with curiosity. Hadn't Sylvia Haffred been threatening to sue the school? Word had gotten around.

She continued. "But Lenox is part of a broader community, is it not? And that community is suffering today, suffering because one of its own is somewhere out there, alone, and possibly hurt, and we cannot forget her. Whatever happens, Easter Riddle is a hero and an example for us all."

More clapping, louder this time. Virtually no one in attendance had ever met Easter, and while most probably did care about Easter's fate, *all* knew it was important to be seen caring deeply.

"Tonight, we'd like to announce the launch of the Easter Riddle Foundation, which will dedicate itself to the emotional wellness of the entire trans community."

As the audience responded one more time, more loudly, Mark and Shannon Riddle pressed their hands over their hearts, as if to say, "We love you too."

Mayor Reynolds, leaning into the mic, said, "And the City of New York will donate the first two hundred and fifty thousand dollars to this very worthy cause!"

A cheer went up from the monsters. *What a mayor!*

"Furthermore, I am pleased to add," said Duncan, "that we have agreed to donate tonight's proceeds to the effort, as well as an additional five hundred thousand dollars. Everyone, give yourselves a hand!"

Wait, what?

That caught everyone by surprise. Their $1,000 tickets were now going to some trans "emotional wellness" fund? But, gathered together like that, each knew better than to express these thoughts out loud. They clapped, if a hair less enthusiastically.

The idea for the foundation, and Lenox Hill's participation, had come about that afternoon. There had been an intense negotiation between Sylvia and Bennet Smith. They were debating the remaining price of Haffred's "munificence." Duncan and Padma were there, and Celeste took notes.

Padma was completely sympathetic to the plight of the trans community, and she took pains to say so several times. She thought this was self-evident enough when she went out of her way to recruit Easter. But things don't always work out in the linear fashion one imagines, so right now she had to make sure that Lenox, and by extension she, was not the focus of the trans community's ire. Already her reputation as a progressive reformer was taking a beating on social media. It also wouldn't do to go through the expense of engaging in a protracted legal battle. Padma had plans, and most of them involved money. Full rides for all BIPOC students, for instance.

"I don't care that you care about the trans community. Bully for you," said Haffred. "I care that you demonstrate it."

As the talks progressed, it was clearer than ever that Haffred wanted to point her guns at Bedrock, but, also, she would leverage the concessions from Lenox to aid her in that effort.

"Whatever we agree to," said Bennet, "Lenox can't be seen in any way as overtly helping you with Bedrock. There must be complete separation. Casper Stein is one of the school's biggest benefactors."

"I getcha, Harvard boy."

"Princeton."

When Haffred proposed the idea of a foundation in Easter's name, Bennet was open to the idea but had reservations. "Doesn't it make it seem like this poor child is already deceased? What if, God willing, she turns up?"

Haffred pointed out that foundations were often named after the living.

"I don't understand, then. You could just start a foundation anytime," Bennet pointed out. "You don't need us for that."

"Well, I may not need you, but I *want* you. In fact, I insist. The final condition is that we want all of the proceeds from the Monster Mash, plus say, another half million, to go to the foundation. An even million. And I want you to announce it at your party tonight."

"What? Why would we do that? This is starting to sound like a settlement!"

"The better question is why would *we* do that when we could go for so much more if we filed the suit. But that's not your concern. Your focus should be on how this is less than a settlement, and on how much goodwill you will create. Of course, we can always litigate, in which case we can talk about how Lenox Hill tolerated the harassment of its sole transgender student, protected those who made her feel unsafe, and all at the behest of the transphobe it harbored on its board, who, not coincidentally, was about to donate a lot of money. How does that sound?"

"Other than Sanderson's bequest, which Lenox will no longer accept, none of that is true!" cried Duncan.

"Prove it."

"This is a ruse. You are bluffing."

"Try me. Oh, and on top of all that, should Easter come back to us, she will no longer be attending your school. I gather you were quite anxious that she return. I wonder why."

"Why is this foundation so important to you?" asked Bennet.

"Again, not germane to our discussion. Let's just say it would be a nice thing to do. For the community."

The truth was, for Haffred, having the school as a partner rather than an adversary was an opportunity to create goodwill with the public. This was why she wanted Dina Campbell to come to the Monster Mash. The warm feelings generated tonight would help her in the court of public opinion as she went after the real prize, Bedrock.

She saw no reason to mention she would also install herself as a paid director of the foundation.

"The eyes of New York are on your nice little school right now. Think of it as an opportunity to be on the right side of history. Or not."

"This seems preposterous," said Duncan.

"Does it? I suppose that depends on one's perspective."

In the end, Team Lenox was left with little choice. All parties came to the Monster Mash with varying degrees of contentment. They did their best not to allow nagging doubts about the fate of Easter Riddle, the titular focus of tonight's attention, to overly weigh on matters. Things had to move forward.

"And now," said Duncan, "if we can have your attention for just a bit longer, I'd like to ask Shannon and Mark Riddle to say a few words."

The Riddles came to the mic. Mark Riddle wrapped two hands around the mic stand, looking like he needed it for support. It appeared he wanted to speak but was choked up. Shannon rubbed his back for reassurance.

"We love you guys!" yelled a Wookiee.

"We love you too," said Mark, gathering himself. "You know, we're new at Lenox Hill, so we haven't had the chance to meet many of you yet, but can I just say . . . can I just say . . . the outpouring of love and support has just been so overwhelming. Truly, we feel it, and I'm sure, wherever she is tonight, our dearest Easter feels it too. Shannon and I—"

There was a small commotion from somewhere in the crowd. Mark couldn't make it out.

"Shannon and I sincerely—"

"LIARS!!!"

It came from the back. The entire gathering of monsters turned as one. It was a woman, dressed in a zombie costume with tattered clothing and incredibly realistic bruising. Those on the stage squinted to see beyond the lights.

The zombie woman was making her way forward, limping through the residual fog that clung to the floor.

Wait. Was that . . . *was that?*

It couldn't be.

And as she approached, a few began to realize it wasn't a costume at all.

EARLIER THAT DAY (THE GIRLS BOLT)

Ellie got back in her car to drive home, only realizing how unsettled her strange encounter with Bob Ellison had left her when she nearly ran a light. She pulled over to gather herself when her cell buzzed.

Tizzy.

She strongly suspected Tizzy just wanted to put herself in the middle of a drama, and she was reluctant to oblige her. But part of her also wanted information, and Tizzy usually had it.

She picked up but not before putting the car back in gear. She wanted to get home.

"Tiz."

"Oh, El, honey, how are you? I've been so worried."

"I've been better. We've been holed up out east."

"Is *that* where you are."

Ellie could hear noise in the background. "Yes, where are you?"

"I'm helping with setup for the party."

"Oh, right."

"It seems like people are going all out with the costumes, despite everything. I feel so bad you won't be here."

"Don't."

"Listen, you want me to come out there and keep you company for a couple of days? After the party, I mean."

"Thanks, but I'm hoping the girls can get back to school in a day or two. Maybe Easter will turn up safe and things will quiet down."

"Oh, honey."

"Oh, honey, what?"

"You didn't see the statement? It was emailed to everyone. I should tell you that it may throw a wrench in the works at the Mayflower. I mean, they *know* none of this is your fault, but they don't like publicity."

"Tizzy, *what* statement?"

"The school put one out—about Will."

"What? What did it say?"

"Well, it was pretty similar to the one Bedrock put out. Don't read it."

"How could they do this! We have been so supportive of that place."

"You have. And it's just not right, especially after what they did to Will."

"What are you talking about?"

"Sweetie, you don't know? Haven't you talked to Will? Isn't he with you?"

"No. Will and I are—Tiz, can you *please* just tell me what you're talking about?"

Just then, Ellie pulled into her driveway. The garage door was open. They kept a second car in there, a Ford Bronco, mostly for getting around in the summer.

It was gone.

The girls were under strict instructions not to go anywhere.

"Tiz, I have to go."

"But—"

Ellie disconnected the phone.

"Girls!" Ellie ran through the house, shouting their names. They were not on the property. She tried calling on her phone, but neither picked up. She quickly group-texted both.

A reply came from Zoey moments later.

> I'm with Ginny. We had to take the Bronco. It's
> important, I promise. Please don't worry.

ROAD TRIP!

That same morning, Clover had been sitting in her first-period class, Poetry as Protest, when she felt her phone buzz in her pocket. She discreetly removed it and glanced at the text. It wasn't from any of her contacts. But . . . holy shit.

> Hey. This is Easter. What r u doing?

Clover immediately excused herself to go to the bathroom. She checked to make sure it was empty and then went into an empty stall. She texted back:

> **What do u mean what am I doing? What are YOU doing?**
> **Where r u?**

> I really need to talk to someone. Can u talk?

And then, a moment later:

> Please, don't tell anyone.

Clover remembered giving Easter her cell, but she didn't recall getting hers, which meant the texter was unidentified by her phone. This could be an ill-considered prank, maybe by Coco or one of her goons.

There was one way to find out. Clover dialed the number.

"Hi," said Easter.

"Oh, my God, are you all right?"

"I don't know. I guess."

Her voice sounded tremulous and far away.

"Do you know the *whole* fucking world is looking for you right now?"

"I didn't mean for any of this to happen! I just needed to be by myself."

"Easter, listen to me. You need to come back."

"I can't . . . my parents . . ."

"I'm sure they'll understand."

"No, trust me, they won't."

"What? Why?"

"They . . . You wouldn't understand."

"Try me."

There was a pause. Clover thought maybe the connection had died. "Easter?"

"Listen," said Easter. "Can you come? Here, I mean."

"Sure, where are you? Somewhere in the city?"

"Not exactly."

"Okay, where?"

"Middletown, Connecticut."

"What the hell?"

"I know."

"Okay, sure. I don't have a car, but I'll figure something out. Text me the address."

"Thank you."

Clover hung up. The first person she thought to reach out to was her new friend Zoey. They were rich, maybe she got a car for her Sweet Sixteen or something.

"I don't have a license," said Zoey.

"Do you know how to drive anyway?"

"Not really. Wait, Ginny has a license. Maybe she can drive. Is it okay if I tell her?"

"I suppose. But no one else! I wasn't supposed to tell anyone at all."

Ginny, as it happened, readily agreed. She had become bored out of her mind after nearly a week in off-season East Hampton, and this sounded like an adventure. They would drive to the city, pick up Clover, and then head to Middletown. Their mother inadvertently helped with the plan when she went to the village. As soon as she was gone, they found the key in the kitchen, in the blue ceramic bowl she'd made in fourth grade, and made off with the Bronco.

Back in the city, Clover slipped quietly out of Lenox Hill as soon as Zoey texted they were near. It wasn't difficult as things were a little crazy, the whole school having been transformed into a "find Easter Riddle" project. She contemplated calling the police, but something told her not to. She remembered thinking, back when she'd met Easter in the hallway, that she didn't need a messed up trans person in her life, and the thought made her feel guilty. Easter sounded . . . off. Maybe what she needed was a friend.

Or three.

Ginny and Zoey picked her up on an agreed-upon corner, Eighty-first and Lexington, and they shot out of Manhattan and over the RFK bridge.

"Where exactly is Middletown, anyway?" asked Clover.

"It's in the middle of Connecticut. Your friend didn't exactly pick a convenient place to hide."

"I'm sure when Easter ran away," said Zoey, riding shotgun, "the first thing she thought was 'Let me pick somewhere inconvenient for when I ask someone to come get me.'"

Ignoring her, Ginny said, "I was going to program the address into Waze, but then I remembered we'd better keep our phones off. I had to write down the directions. Can you imagine that?"

"Can't you turn off tracking?" asked Clover.

"I don't know, and I don't want to figure it out now."

Clover then Bluetooth'd her phone to the car to control the music. *Her parents didn't track her phone.*

The music blared.

Sugar, oh honey honey!

"Oh, you're not," said Ginny.

You are my candy girl
And you got me wanting you!

"Don't change it!" said Zoey. "Bubblegum is exactly what we need right now."

"Bubblegum is what the *world* needs right now," added Clover.

Ginny reluctantly went along. It was kind of catchy if she were being honest.

"So," she said, "let me get this straight. Easter makes one phone call from the wild and it's to a girl two grades below her? Do you even know her?"

"We met once," said Clover. "I think she views me as a fellow misfit and that we bonded over it. I don't think she has a lot of real friends."

"Color me shocked."

"Hey, that's not nice," said Zoey.

"You know what's not nice? She and her trans mafia getting me, you, and our whole family in deep shit."

"I don't think she had anything to do with it."

Eventually, they passed New Haven. Ginny could see Yale's graceful spires in the distance. She still hadn't gotten around to finishing her application.

They turned north, toward Hartford.

"Okay, so what exactly is the plan?" asked Ginny.

"I don't have one," said Clover. "In fact, she's only expecting me."

"You didn't tell her?"

"Not exactly. Maybe I just go in first and tell her then?"

"You know we're going to have to bring this dude back. Or at least call someone and wait for them to come."

"She's a girl," said Zoey.

"She's a boy, pretending to be a girl. But let's shelve the whole woke discussion for now, shall we?"

"Let's talk to her," said Clover. "Figure out what's going on. I think she's in a very bad place. But I agree, we're either going to have to take her back or at least call someone."

"And why is she in Middletown, Connecticut, again?"

"She didn't say."

"And you didn't think to ask?"

"I did but decided not to. If you'd heard her, she sounded pretty fragile. I figured we'd find out anyway."

Sometime later, they pulled off I-91 into a bucolic area of the state. The leaves up here were hitting their peak. A sign said "Middletown 3 Miles."

"Okay, we're getting close." They pulled alongside the Connecticut River and then into downtown Middletown. Its Main Street was lined with coffee houses and bookshops. They came to another sign that said "Wesleyan University, Founded 1831."

"So this is where Wesleyan is," said Ginny.

"Are you applying?" asked Clover.

"Not my flavor of smoothie."

Just past campus, they came to a leafy road called Ludlow Street.

"Okay, this is it," said Ginny. "Look for number one-thirty-one."

They spotted a packed-earth driveway and turned in, coming to a small Victorian house that looked like it had seen better days. An old Subaru Forester with a "Coexist" bumper sticker was parked in front. It was half covered in leaves.

"Stop the car here," said Clover. "She said she's in the back. I should go alone. I'll come get you after I tell her you're here."

Clover walked around the house. In the back, there was a tiny cottage, almost more of a shed. She walked up and knocked. And then Easter Riddle, the most famous missing person in America, was there, standing in the doorway. She was dressed in sweats and a hoodie and looked terrible.

"Hey," said Clover.

"Hey."

"How's your arm?"

The sling Easter had had on the day she disappeared was gone, but there were still bandages.

"It's fine."

"So, what is this place?"

"It's my parents'."

Gone was the singsongy voice from school. She sounded like a boy, not a boy trying to sound like a girl.

Clover took in the space. It was a single room, perhaps once used as an office. It was very spare, with a couple of chairs, a barren desk, and a pullout bed where Easter had been sleeping.

"And you've been here the whole time?"

"Yes."

"Listen, Easter. I had to get a ride here, so I came with Zoey Sanderson and her older sister from school, Ginny."

"Shit, really? What did I say!"

"It's okay, I promise. There was no other way I could get here. We needed a driver and Ginny has a license. Maybe you know Ginny, she's in your class. You can trust them, and we haven't told anyone else, I promise."

Easter appeared to consider this but didn't say anything.

"Can I go get them?" asked Clover.

Easter seemed defeated. "Okay," she said, shrugging her shoulders.

Clover ran out and returned moments later with the others. Zoey, not sure what to do, gave Easter an awkward hug. Ginny demurred. "Hi, I'm Ginny, the chauffeur," she said. "We're in the same class."

"Well, thanks, I guess," said Easter.

"Now can you tell us what the hell is going on?"

"Ginny, can you take it easy?" implored Zoey.

"Everyone in New York has lost their minds, you and I have been suspended, and I just drove a car we swiped from our mom four hours to get here. I think some answers would be appropriate."

Easter stood there, arms wrapped around herself. "I get it. I'm sorry. I didn't know what to do or who to talk to."

"Whose house is this, anyway?" asked Ginny. "Tell me we're not breaking and entering."

"It's her parents'," answered Clover.

"What?"

"My dad used to teach at Wesleyan before we moved to the city," said Easter. "Sociology. They were going to sell this place, but the market is soft or something."

"And they haven't figured out you are up here?"

"Oh, they know," said Easter. "They're the ones who told me to stay."

HOT POCKETS MAKE
EVERYTHING BETTER

I'm sorry, but *what* did you just say?" asked Ginny, staring in disbelief.

"My parents know."

"What the fuck? I mean, what the *actual* fuck."

Easter's eyes welled with tears.

"Maybe we should all just sit down for a minute and let Easter tell the whole story," suggested Clover. It looked like Easter was on the verge of a breakdown. Ginny remained standing, not as gifted in the ways of empathy.

Easter began.

"That day at school, when they wanted me to speak, I just couldn't. I felt like a specimen in a zoo. I had to get away, anywhere but there. So I went to my locker, grabbed a hoodie, and just walked out the door. Those protesters showed up around then, so no one really noticed. I didn't know where to go, and I couldn't just go home. I needed to be alone, so I thought about this place."

"How did you get here?" asked Zoey.

"I hitchhiked."

"You *hitchhiked*?" cried Ginny. "That I need to hear about."

"I couldn't Uber because it's on my parents' account and they'd know right away where I'd gone. I turned off my phone, too, so they couldn't track me."

"We did the same thing," said Zoey.

"You are aware that no one has hitchhiked in this country in, like, a hundred years," observed Ginny.

"I know, and I didn't know if it would work. I had a little bit of cash, so I used it to take a taxi to the Bronx because who's going to pick up a hitchhiker in Manhattan? It took a while, but I got my first ride from this trucker on a 95 access road, a spot where you had to stop at a light. He was nice. That got me all the way to New Haven. A couple of more rides got me to the edge of Middletown. I think maybe they're lonely, the truckers, you know? Anyway, I just walked the rest. I know where my parents hide the key."

"So, what have you been doing this whole time?" asked Clover.

"Mostly nothing. Stared at the walls, thought about stuff, or just sat outside looking at the leaves. For a couple of days, anyway."

"Well, at least you picked a scenic time of the year to make everyone hysterical," said Ginny, helpfully.

"Ginny!" barked Zoey. "How are we even sisters? Easter, I apologize for her."

"It's okay. I really didn't know any of this would happen, and I didn't know that everyone was looking for me because I was too scared to turn my phone back on. I mean, I guess I figured my parents were, but honestly, I didn't care about that."

"What did you eat?" asked Clover.

"There were some crackers in the house. I'd spread some mustard on them. I was out of money so I couldn't get anything in town."

"Ew," said Zoey.

"And what happened after a couple of days?" asked Ginny. She'd started to get suspicious.

"That was when my dad showed up. He guessed I might be here."

"He must have been so relieved!" said Zoey.

"Relieved? I'm not sure that's how I'd put it."

"Does this all have something to do with your transition?" asked Ginny. "Were they against it or something?"

"Against it? You must be the only person who doesn't know about their socials. They are fucking cheerleaders."

"So, help us out here," said Ginny. "Was it people at school? Hey, be whatever you want as far as I'm concerned."

"Yeah, just look at *me*," said Clover, sporting a twig with some dried berries in her hair.

"No, you were all very welcoming to the zoo animal."

"Okay, let's stop with the twenty questions. What's going on?" asked Ginny.

"Look, I feel, I feel . . . just lost, okay? I don't know who I am or what I'm supposed to be, even though everyone else seems to. I wasn't even one hundred percent sure I wanted to transition. But when my parents found out I was thinking about it, they were excited and encouraged me. So did my teachers at my old school. It seemed like everyone wanted me to do this, calling me brave and everything. I was miserable and depressed all the time, so I thought, why not? Maybe I'll like life better as a girl. I'd never been comfortable in my own skin anyway. Then my parents began documenting the whole thing on Instagram. My mom would take me shopping for dresses and, boom! Posted! My dad takes me to the clinic for hormone therapy? Boom, posted! The *likes* and follows kept pouring in. It was starting to freak me out, but I didn't want to spoil things. They seemed so proud of me."

"You didn't want to do that article, did you?" asked Clover.

"I should have said no, like you, but I didn't have the guts. Everyone wanted it so bad. My parents couldn't wait to see the *Sentinel* every day, checking to see if the article was up online and everything. After it came out, I felt like the whole world was staring at me, calling me things like *trailblazer* and *hero*, and I really didn't feel like one, you know?"

"Why did you switch schools?" asked Zoey.

"My parents decided I needed a change of scenery. A chance to reinvent myself. But really, it was about money. Lenox offered me a full scholarship. My parents aren't rich. Also, I think they liked the idea of hanging around other people who are."

"Hey," said Ginny. "We're dancing around the central issue here. Your parents have known where you were for, what, four days now? And yet they're still crawling around Manhattan with everybody else looking for you."

"I know. After my dad left, I'd turn on my phone sometimes to see what was going on, but just for a minute. There's no TV here and I was afraid someone else could track me somehow. At least, they can on TV . . . But I saw what was going on, that they found that body and everything. I fantasized it was me and about what people would say at my funeral and how sorry my parents would be. . . ."

Ginny groaned. "Okay, so that's grim, but again, why didn't he bring you back?"

"He got really mad at me, and he said he couldn't just tell everyone I'd been hanging out at our Connecticut house, that I'd embarrass him and Mom, especially after he'd set up that GoFundMe and people started donating. He went and bought me some food and then told me to stay here and keep my phone off until he thought of a way to bring me back. He worries about all of us losing face, I think. He's working on an alternate story, that maybe I was kidnapped or something and then I'd escape. He told me to move out of the main house and hole up in here just in case anyone came around."

"Meanwhile, their GoFundMe keeps growing," said Ginny.

"And their socials keep going viral," added Clover.

"They just posted again," said Zoey, daring to turn her phone back on for a moment. "It's a picture with the mayor."

"I fucking hate them," said Easter.

"I'm beginning to see your point," said Ginny.

"So, what are we going to do?" asked Zoey.

"I don't know about you guys, but I'm hungry," said Clover. "I haven't eaten all day."

"I still have some Hot Pockets that my dad got. They're in that bag," said Easter. "There's a microwave over in that corner."

Clover rifled through the bag. "Pepperoni, yes!"

Ginny and Zoey followed. "I swear to God," said Clover, mouth full of Hot Pocket exactly one minute later. "If I was on death row, this would be my last meal."

"You're not having any?" asked Zoey, looking at Easter.

"I'm not hungry."

"When was the last time you ate?" asked Ginny.

"I don't know. A couple of days ago maybe."

"Jesus. Will you please have a bite. You look like shit."

Ginny handed her a Hot Pocket and Easter took a tentative bite. Then Ginny filled a glass with water and gave it to her as well. Easter took some sips.

"Hot Pockets will make it all better," said Clover. "Hot Pockets make *everything* better."

Easter stood up suddenly and ran to the bathroom. She heaved violently into the toilet.

"I stand corrected," said Clover.

"I haven't been able to keep anything down," said Easter, emerging a few moments later.

"Look, we need to figure this out," said Ginny. "Obviously, you can't stay here. You're not doing great."

"We're worried about you," said Zoey.

"I'm just going to say it," said Ginny. "We need to take you back."

"I can't! My parents will just start lying about everything and everyone will be talking about me. I have about ten messages on my phone from that reporter."

"Dina Campbell again?" asked Clover.

"Yeah, her. You saw. My parents and her were plotting to make it a whole series. I saw her in the back of the room when Ms. Minali wanted me to speak. It's lucky I didn't puke right there."

"Yeah, she's been going to town on this," observed Clover.

"But listen, Easter," said Ginny. "You can't just stay here. It will just get worse. And you can't go along with some scheme about you being kidnapped. That will blow up in your face. Why don't we just get in the car and drive back. I'm sure people will understand you were under a lot of pressure."

Easter didn't say anything, not right away. Her eyes got teary again. "My parents won't," she said.

"Well, they can suck it, right?"

Easter laughed slightly at that.

"Well they *can*, right? I mean, maybe you should just call them out."

Easter gave a wan smile. "Maybe I should."

"Tell them you're not taking their shit anymore. It's your life, am I right?"

"It's my life."

"It's your fucking life!" repeated Ginny, with vigor.

"It's my fucking life!"

Suddenly there was the unmistakable sound of a car pulling into the driveway.

"Who the hell is that?" said Ginny.

Zoey ran to the window. "It's Mom!"

IT'S NICE TO SEE YOU, MRS. SANDERSON

No!" cried Easter, darting into the bathroom. The girls could hear the lock turn.

Outside, they could see Ellie walking around the main house. She knocked on one of the doors and then peered through a window.

"She's gonna come to the back next, you know," said Zoey. "She saw the Bronco."

"So what's the plan here?" asked Clover.

"I have no fucking idea," said Ginny. "How did she even find us? Zoey, did you leave your phone on?"

"No!"

"Well, she's coming this way."

They watched as their mother approached the door.

"Oh, screw it," said Ginny. She opened the door. "Hi, Mom."

"Oh, thank goodness," said Ellie, hugging Ginny. "I thought you'd been carjacked or something."

"In East Hampton?"

"Well, with everything going on . . ."

"How did you find us?"

"The Bronco is so old it has LoJack. Amazingly, it still works. Now, do you want to tell me right now what the hell you girls are doing in Middletown, Connecticut? Oh, and I see you have company."

"Hi, Mrs. Sanderson," said Clover, ever cheerful. "It's nice to see you."

"Do your parents know where you are, Clover?"

"They think I'm at school."

"So, no. Okay, answers, now! For starters, whose house is this?"

Ginny and Zoey looked at each other, each hoping the other would speak first. Ginny relented. "Mom, Clover got a text, and she reached out to Zoey, and I was the only one who knew how to drive."

"This was just a little excursion? Is that what you're telling me?"

"Well, no. We thought you'd understand, given everything."

"Understand what?"

The girls exchanged looks again. And then Ginny nodded toward the bathroom door.

"What?" said Ellie. "Is there someone in there?"

Ellie walked toward it, turned the knob, and discovered the door locked. "What are you girls playing at? Is someone in there?" She knocked on the door several times, but no one answered.

Something outside caught Clover's eye. "Uh, guys, I think she crawled out the window."

"*Who?*" cried Ellie.

They went to the door, which was still open, and spotted a figure darting across the small yard.

"I think she's going for her parents' car!" said Clover.

"Oh, boy," said Zoey. "Not good."

"For the last time, what is going on?"

"Mom, we can't let her go. She's not doing well."

"*Who?*"

"Easter."

"*That's* Easter Riddle?"

"Yes."

"And you came up here to look for her?"

"To get her, yes!"

"But—"

"She's getting in the car!" said Zoey.

"What am I missing here?"

"Mom, not now. We need to get to her. C'mon!"

The girls ran out, followed by a bewildered Ellie. Easter was trying to start her parents' Subaru, but the engine wasn't turning over. The girls caught up, but Easter had locked the doors. "Go away!" she cried through the glass.

"Easter, stop," said Clover. "Let's just talk. This is crazy."

The ancient Subaru suddenly came to life and Easter threw it into drive. The fallen leaves blew off the hood as she raced out the dirt driveway.

IT MIGHT JUST REALLY HURT

We have to follow her," cried Zoey. "Mom, let's go!"

The four of them piled into the X7 and Ellie drove. They quickly got the Subaru in their sights.

"What about the Bronco?" asked Ellie. "We could be following this kid all the way to New York."

"Mom," said Zoey. "That's not important right now. Just keep up with her."

They reached Wesleyan's leafy campus, but Easter wasn't stopping.

"Do you want to tell me why she's here?" asked Ellie.

"That's her parents' house from when they lived here. She's been hiding there the whole time. Her parents know."

"You've *got* to be kidding me."

"Not kidding, we'll tell you the rest later. Keep up!"

Now they were downtown, and Easter, after pausing briefly, blew through two lights.

"This is getting dangerous. Jesus, Ginny, call the police." Ellie silently chided herself for not doing it right away.

Before Ginny got out her phone, they reached an arching steel bridge spanning the Connecticut River. A sign said:

ARRIGONI BRIDGE—BUILT 1936

"Where on earth is this kid going?" asked Ellie.

"She's slowing down!" said Zoey.

Easter pulled to a stop at the bridge's center and jumped out. There was a small pedestrian lane with a protective railing on the bridge's outside edge. Easter crossed the lane and climbed over the railing.

"Holy shit," said Ginny.

Easter was now standing on a metal ledge, perhaps four inches wide.

Ellie pulled her car to a stop just behind the Subaru as traffic continued to flow by in the other lane. Some people honked.

"Oh, my God," cried Ellie. "We have to stop her."

Clover was the first out of the car, running to the spot where Easter climbed over. The others followed.

"Stay back!" shouted Easter over the traffic. Her eyes were wide, and she appeared to be crying. Other cars were now stopping, and a few people got out to see what was going on.

"Easter, please, climb back over," said Clover. "We'll take you back."

"What, to my wonderful parents, who wanted me to stay hidden up here? No, I don't think so." She was shouting through the tears now. "There's nothing for me back there!"

"We'll figure something out! How about you come back over and we'll talk about it."

"It's just better this way," said Easter.

Ginny started climbing over the railing herself. "Ginny, what the hell are you doing?!" screamed Ellie.

"I got this!" she hollered back.

She was over it now and inching toward Easter. Her feet were bigger than the ledge and she was holding on to the railing as she went.

"I'm with your mom," said Easter. "What the hell are you doing?"

"Just coming to have a little chat."

"I don't want to chat. Just leave me alone!"

"Well, this wasn't my first choice of things to do today either."

"Don't come any closer!"

"Okay, you're the boss." Ginny stopped about four feet from Easter. For a few moments, they just stood there. Ginny took a look down.

"So, this is the way you want to go, is it? Wouldn't pills be easier? That way seems less violent, but not much drama, I guess. Is that what you're going for here, drama?"

"What? Shut up!"

Ginny gazed down again at the Connecticut River flowing beneath them. It looked like a sixty-foot drop, give or take. "I don't know, Easter, I'm not sure that's enough to kill you. It might just really hurt."

Easter didn't respond, although she did steal a glance below.

"Unless, that is, you do a header. That might do the trick. Might be tough to get it just right, though. You could end up a vegetable, which would kind of suck. Or maybe in a wheelchair."

"Ginny!" cried Zoey, horrified.

Easter remained silent.

"So, what's the strategy, then?" asked Ginny. "A graceful swan dive or just a plain old jump? Personally, I'd go with the swan dive if you're planning on checking out, but you'll need to pull your arms in at the last second to get them out of the way. Full cranial impact, you know?"

"You are horrible!" yelled Easter.

"Is that the best you can do, girly boy?"

"Fuck you!"

"Okay whatever you say, but can I just ask? How long are we going to be here? Personally, I'd rather be back home in New York instead of standing on a ledge with psycho girl. Frankly, this is a little scary."

"Then go back!"

"Ginny, stop it!" yelled Zoey.

Ellie put a hand on Zoey and shook her head.

"Look," said Ginny. "All I know is, if you do this, they win. They'll say you didn't have the guts to face your problems. Is that what you want?"

Easter looked tentatively in Ginny's direction. Police sirens could now be heard in the distance.

"Well, *is it*?"

Traffic had now stopped on the bridge in both directions and it was oddly quiet. A gentle breeze came off the river.

"It's your life, Easter. Fuck all those other people."

Easter appeared to consider this.

"So, what do you say? I think that water's probably really dirty anyway. I think I see some garbage down there." Ginny inched closer and held out a hand, which Easter examined.

"And what's *your* plan here?" said Easter. "Just gonna toss me back over the railing with your free hand? Have you considered the physics of this?"

"Well, no. I was going for empathy."

"Well, you suck at it."

"She really does," said Zoey.

"You people are going to annoy me to death before I can jump. *Fine*."

Easter turned to climb back up, but as she did, she slipped. Ginny thrust out an arm and they locked hands. Unfortunately, Easter outweighed her by a good thirty pounds and pulled her right off the ledge.

The two of them fell silently toward the river.

THE RESCUE

Oh my God! Ginny!"

Ellie looked around frantically. There were police sirens, but they still sounded hundreds of yards off, likely having trouble navigating the developing gridlock.

She made a snap decision, the kind that only a parent can make. She tossed her cell phone to Zoey and tore off her shoes.

"Mom, what are you doing?!"

Ellie then climbed the railing . . . and jumped.

In the seemingly endless drop, she remembered once seeing videos of high divers; they'd always enter the water feet first, toes pointed. As she plummeted downward, she did her best to achieve this position. Despite this, the impact, when it came, seemed painful and violent, and she knifed deep into the murky water. When her momentum finally stopped, she struggled back to the surface, eyes wide with fear and adrenaline.

"GINNY!" she screamed.

At first, she couldn't see her anywhere, so she made some frantic strokes downstream. Still fully clothed, swimming was difficult. Then—there!— something floating along, perhaps thirty or forty yards ahead. She swam toward it.

It was Easter, who appeared unconscious. Ellie took one more look around for Ginny and didn't see her anywhere. Had she been able to articulate a complete thought at that moment, it might have been, "I would prefer to save my daughter than the person who caused this mess," but her brain was only capable of stabbing, binary bits of expression. *This* was the available option.

Save the person she could.

Save Easter.

If she could.

Ellie closed the remaining yards and put an arm around Easter. She began a powerful sidestroke, memories returning of a long-ago lifesaving class at one of the bases. Which base was it again? Fort Carson maybe? Or Fort Riley?

And why was she trying to remember that? What a ridiculous thing to take up brain space when you're trying to rescue someone else's kid and you don't even know where your own daughter is. *The brain works in funny ways under stress,* she thought. Then she chastised herself for *that* thought.

Focus.

One stroke at a time.

Easter outweighed Ellie by a fair amount, so she labored. Exhaustion was quickly winning its death match against adrenaline.

Luckily, the current seemed to push them closer to the side of the river. A few more strokes and she would make it. There was a grassy bank that looked accessible.

A minute later she was there.

She hauled Easter halfway out of the water. It was all she could manage, her chest heaving for breath. She wanted nothing more than to collapse but Easter didn't look like she was breathing, so Ellie began compressions.

1–2–3...

Almost immediately, water burst out of Easter's mouth, and she began breathing. "That hurt," Easter said, gasping.

"Save it," said Ellie, refocusing.

Ginny.

Where was Ginny?

She stood up, despite her exhaustion, and scanned the river. She couldn't see anything, but there was faint screaming, coming from back on the bridge. It was Zoey and Clover. They were pointing at something, pointing downriver.

But what?

Perhaps a hundred yards farther was an old railroad bridge. Was that it? Ellie looked beneath at where its rusty piers descended into the river. There, clinging to one, was Ginny. A small power boat was already making its way toward her.

All three of them were going to make it.

They had survived the fall from Arrigoni Bridge.

LOVE HURTS

An ambulance transported Ellie, Ginny, and Easter to nearby Middlesex Hospital. Ellie felt like she'd gone ten rounds with Mike Tyson, but the medic confirmed that nothing seemed broken. She'd sprained an ankle hitting the water. She'd be bruised and battered for a few days but that was about it.

Ginny broke two fingers, which the medic splinted, and Easter had a dislocated shoulder. Easter yelped as the medic reset it with an audible pop.

"You are all very lucky people," said the medic.

"Hey, there are two girls with us still on the bridge. One is my other daughter. They're with two cars we came in but neither of the girls can drive."

"I've already been in touch with Middletown police," said the medic. "They are transporting the girls and the cars to the hospital."

"Thank you."

The police, along with Clover and Zoey, were already at the hospital when they arrived. "Mom! Are you guys all right?" Zoey cried.

"I think so, honey. Maybe just a little beat up."

"Mrs. Sanderson, can I just say? That was so badass," said Clover.

"Let's just be thankful everyone's all right."

A doctor greeted them in the reception area and confirmed with the medic that there were no life-threatening injuries. "But we should examine you further, just to be sure. We'll get you to rooms as soon as something is available. It shouldn't be long."

"Thanks, doc," said one of the officers. "While they're waiting, I'm going to ask them a few questions."

"Certainly."

They sat, still cold and wet. Easter wrapped herself in a blanket while Ellie and Ginny shared one. Ellie didn't want to let her go.

"You guys have had a rough day."

"Yes" was all Ellie said.

"Before I forget, here are your car keys. We left the cars outside."

"Thank you, officer."

"Okay, then. Let's start with your names. Ma'am?"

"I'm Elenore Sanderson, this is my daughter Virginia." She looked at Easter. "And this is—"

"Richard Riddle," said Easter.

The others all turned at that and Easter shot them a look. The officer was taking notes.

"Are you guys all local?"

"No, we're from the city," said Ellie.

"Boston or New York?"

"New York."

"Now, can I ask what happened?"

They explained what happened at the bridge, leaving out Easter's backstory. Ellie wanted a moment to talk to Easter first.

"Are you having suicidal thoughts right now?" asked the officer.

"No," said Easter. "I'm fine."

"That's good. I'm required to ask." The officer looked at Ellie and Ginny. He seemed kind. "That was a brave thing you both did, or maybe stupid, I don't know."

They didn't respond, still processing the day's events.

"Listen, Richard," the officer continued. "Given the circumstances, the state requires us to have you talk to a psychiatrist. There's one here at the hospital, and she'll just want to ask you a few questions. Would that be all right?"

"Okay, I guess" said Easter, looking into space.

"Good. Well, I have to call a couple of things in. You all just sit tight. I'm sure a nurse or doctor will be right out." He walked out to his cruiser.

Ellie turned to Easter. "East—or Richard, or whatever. We need to let people know you're all right."

"My parents already know."

"Yes, I understand. But no one else does, and they're all still looking for you."

"God, this is going to be so embarrassing. Can we just go back? I need to figure out what I'm going to do."

"Hey," said Clover. "Your parents just posted something."

"They're always posting something."

"This is a video."

They all gathered around Zoey's phone. Mark Riddle began:

It has now been one week since our beloved Easter has gone missing. Our hearts grow more desperate with each passing day. Please, if you have any information that can help us, call the hotline. Your privacy will be protected. We just want our girl back.

Then Shannon spoke.

We also wanted to thank all of you out there who have been so supportive with your time and your money.

Then Mark again.

We're off now to personally thank the wonderful people at Easter's school, Lenox Hill. They have been so supportive. We'll update you again soon. And remember, the genocide of the trans community cannot be ignored any longer.

"Easter, I don't think I like your parents very much," said Zoey.
Easter started to say something, but instead managed a laugh.
"They must be going to the party," said Ellie.
"What party?"
"The big fundraiser. It's Halloween."
"God, I almost forgot," said Clover.
The doctor who had greeted them appeared down the hall. It looked like he was coming back.
"I think we're about to be admitted," said Ellie.
"I want to go," said Easter.
"I don't think we can just run out of here."
"Mom, none of us want to be here," said Ginny.
"Don't you think Easter should be checked out first?"
"I'm fine," said Easter.
"You don't look fine."
In fact, all three of them, the bridge divers, were starting to bruise significantly from the impact. Their clothes were in tatters and their still-damp hair hung limply.
"Watch." Easter stood up and did a few jumping jacks. "Like I said, fine."

"Gin?"

"Sore as hell, but I'll be okay."

Ellie looked down the hall. The doctor had been waylaid by a nurse, but it looked like they were finishing up.

"I've got some Advil in the car. Girls, we are getting out of here."

THE DEVILS ARE HERE

Ellie drove Zoey, Clover, and Easter in the X7 while Ginny followed in the Bronco. They decided the Riddles could deal with their damn Subaru, so they left it at the hospital.

The girls were still shivering, so Ellie turned the heat up on high.

"Mom, you're really starting to bruise," said Zoey.

Ellie glanced in the rearview mirror. It was true, her face suddenly looked horrific, the impact of the dive finally showing up.

They drove down mostly in silence, exhausted, each left to their own thoughts. Ellie's were particularly dark. Her girls, she knew, would not likely see the inside of the Lenox Hill School again. Where could they go now? She wasn't even sure what the public school was in their district. And William . . . She wasn't sure she knew the person her husband was anymore, this bluntly striving man who wilted in the face of adversity.

She thought of her father, a man who had been on the receiving end of enemy fire, who had watched friends next to him die, who handled himself with grace. "Grace" was not a word that came to anyone's mind when thinking of Will.

Marriage was a funny thing, Ellie thought. It was the most important decision anyone made in their lifetimes, but most of us make it when we are youthful fools. Who's to say someone you know for six months or a year in your twenties is someone you will still want to be with, every day, decades later? A certain amount of it seemed like luck: People change, and may not change in ways amenable to the other.

Had Will changed, or had he always been this . . . this hollow man of ambition? Perhaps she hadn't noticed the changes because they came in little pieces over many years, like a species evolving.

She searched for clues in their shared past. She had always been sober and cautious in her decision-making when she was younger, hadn't she? Or had she wanted the things that Will represented just a little too much and not acknowledged it, even to herself?

She had no answers, nor did she have regrets. How could she? She had Ginny and Zoey, two very different girls, yet both brave and wonderful girls. She wondered, idly, if Will was still sitting in the apartment getting plastered. She tried and failed to care.

The exits on the Merritt Parkway passed without notice. She drove in a trance.

A sign said "New York City 35 Miles."

New York. The place that was supposed to be more than one of life's stops, the place that would be her home. Well, that was blown up now, too, wasn't it?

Ellie wanted so badly to cry but couldn't let herself, not in front of the girls. She had to be strong for them. Instead, she let anger replace despair. Anger at Will, but also the others. Padma, but all those sycophants too. The people who would do nothing, about *anything*, lest they offend. And the Riddles. There were no words for what they were doing.

She had to figure out what came next.

They crossed over the RFK Bridge and back into Manhattan and its canyons. It was dark now, and somehow foreboding, past the time when little kids trick-or-treated. The night belonged to the adults, and the creatures of this Halloween night were everywhere, making their way through the dimly lit streets. They were febrile and laughing, reveling in their temporary anonymity. The city was touched by madness, Ellie thought. The Big Apple was Gotham tonight.

"Hell is empty and all the devils are here," said Clover, seemingly reading Ellie's thoughts.

"I think you may be right."

"That's *The Tempest*," said Zoey. "We just read it."

"It seemed appropriate," said Clover.

Her dark reverie broken, Ellie said, "Easter—or Richard . . . Actually, what would you like to be called?"

"I don't care."

"Okay, I'll stick with Easter for now. We have to make a decision and I want to know your thoughts. Do you want me to take you home?"

"No."

"I know how tough this must be. . . ."

"*No.*"

"Okay, then where? People have to know you're all right."

Easter thought the situation through, and the more she did, the angrier she got. Very quickly, that anger turned into something that had been entirely missing from her life: resolve.

"Then let's show them," she said, finally. "Let's go to the party."

"The Lenox party?"

"Yes. My parents will be there."

"Stick it to the man!" cried Clover.

Ellie was good with any comeuppance the Riddles might receive, although showing up at the Monster Mash seemed like an insane idea.

She stewed on it for a minute. What the school was doing to them, her *family*, was unforgivable. She realized that even if Ginny and Zoey *could* stay, she would never allow it. They would never spend another day at Lenox Hill.

Her phone buzzed. She didn't recognize the number and didn't answer it. Then a text appeared:

> Mrs Sanderson, this is Celeste from school.
> Can we talk? Important.

The phone buzzed again and Ellie picked up.

"Celeste."

"Mrs. Sanderson, I'm so sorry to bother you, it's just that some things have been happening here, things I don't like."

"Go on."

Ellie listened in silence as Celeste told her everything. That William had been tossed from the board and that her own girls would be asked to leave the school entirely. That the Sandersons were a sacrificial lamb to avoid a large lawsuit.

"Celeste, thank you for calling. I know this was a risk."

"It's the least I could do. I feel so awful. You've always been very nice to me, and I do love the girls."

Ellie hung up and anger turned to rage. The Sandersons would damn well leave the school on *her* terms, not theirs. These sniveling cowards!

She would take Easter to the party. She *was* on the damn committee, after all. Whatever happened, happened.

"We're going," she said.

Clover squealed. "Tonight, we summon the Furies!" She and Zoey high-fived.

Ellie called Ginny and told her where they were going.

"That is totally badass," said Ginny.

"You should just go home, and I'll drop Zoey and Clover off too."

"Are you kidding?" said Ginny.

"What she said!" cried Zoey.

"Clover, I can drop you—"

"Not a chance," came the answer.

"Mrs. Sanderson," said Easter, "I don't know how long my parents will be at the party. We should hurry."

"Okay, it looks like I've been outvoted. We're all going to the party."

SUMMONING THE FURIES

New Yorkers are a different breed. Celebrities feel the city's gravity because it's one of the few places on earth they can feel anonymous, where they aren't pestered for autographs and selfies by random strangers. For locals, a studied indifference to their surroundings is practically an art form, a point of pride.

John Lennon had once chosen New York as his home precisely because people left him alone, at least until an out-of-towner shot him.

Above all, strange was normal in Manhattan, an accepted part of the landscape.

Walking toward Cipriani on East Forty-second from a nearby garage, the girls didn't merit a second look. With three of them sporting deep bruises and tattered clothes and Ellie limping on her sprained ankle, they were, *obviously*, a zombie family. It was Halloween, but it could have been a random Tuesday.

They paused outside Cipriani's main entrance.

"Clover? Ellie asked. "Do you have a cigarette?"

"Mom!" cried Zoey.

Clover smiled, understanding, and retrieved a Camel, handing it to Ellie. "Your mom's just being badass, like your sister said."

"Oh."

"Do you have a light?" asked Ellie.

Clover produced a small Bic lighter and helped Ellie light up. Ellie's hands were visibly shaking. "Disgusting," she said, coughing once or twice. "Clover, don't get hooked on these."

"Don't worry. I kind of hate them."

"Easter, are you sure you're ready for this?"

"One hundred percent."

"I think it's best if I go in first, just in case."

"Just in case what?" asked Ginny.

"Just in case . . . I don't know. It just seems like I should, and we're doing what I say. Easter, you follow me. Ginny, Zoey, you can come after her or wait out here. Up to you."

"Wait out here? You're kidding, right?" said Ginny. Zoey seemed to agree.

"All right. Let's go."

Ellie opened the door and walked into a vestibule with a registration table against the back wall. She realized she didn't have a plan and probably should have asked Easter exactly what she had in mind. A big public spectacle? There would be little pulling back from that, socially speaking, but to say she didn't care was an understatement.

It was time to pull back the curtain.

The event was well underway, but the reception table was still manned for stragglers. One of the mothers sat there, dressed like Cat Woman, looking bored. Was Cat Woman a monster? Ellie knew the woman slightly.

"Hi there," said Cat Woman. "Great costume! *So* Walking Dead." It was clear she didn't recognize Ellie. "Oh, I'm afraid there's no smoking inside."

Ellie glared at the woman and then blew some smoke in her direction, willing herself not to cough. The woman decided she wouldn't push the issue. She didn't do confrontation. "Name, please?"

The table had name tags for the guests, and a few remained. Ellie noted that neither hers nor Will's were among them. They were already being disappeared. This didn't surprise her, but it bothered her all the same. She grabbed an unused card and a Sharpie and scrawled her name on it. "Sanderson," she said, practically holding the card in the woman's face. Then she slapped it on to her ripped blouse.

"Oh . . . my God," said the woman, finally recognizing Ellie. Her mouth formed a little O.

Ellie ignored her and walked into the event space where, for a moment, she took in its vast splendor. The committee had outdone itself.

Words from the stage echoed:

"We're new to Lenox Hill."

The Riddles . . .

"Truly, we feel the love."

. . . up there with them all. Duncan, the Mayor, Sylvia Haffred . . . Padma . . .

"I'm sure, wherever she is tonight, I'm sure Easter feels the love too. Shannon and I—"

Ellie didn't have to summon the rage. It burst from her without thought, coming from a place she didn't know existed. She had summoned the Furies.

"LIARS!!!"

The Riddles stared out, and even the distant back-of-the-room chatter fell silent as everyone turned to see the source of the commotion.

Ellie found herself limping toward the stage. "My God, that's Ellie Sanderson," she heard someone say. "Is that a cigarette?" said someone else. A few hands flew to flutter over delicate noses. The presence of a cigarette, in polite company, was almost as shocking as the appearance of Ellie herself.

Word of the Fall of the Sandersons had spread swiftly over the last twenty-four hours, and there was little sympathy for the plight of William. A thinly disguised *schadenfreude* was the common reaction, just as William had predicted.

But there was still some sympathy for Ellie and the girls.

Right now, though, sympathy was trumped by curiosity. Ellie Sanderson, she of the fallen Sandersons, looking just terrible—but maybe that was a costume? . . . but what was she supposed to be?—was parting the room like the Red Sea. Something interesting was happening, something you could tell others later you witnessed yourself.

But what?

"Ellie?" said Duncan, into the microphone.

Tizzy emerged from the crowd and approached her. "Ellie, hon, are you okay? What happened? I think we need to get you some help." She touched Ellie's elbow.

"No!" growled Ellie.

Tizzy had never heard this tone from Ellie. It was low and commanding.

"I think she's been drinking," said someone.

"Excuse me," said Mark Riddle, still on the stage, squinting. "I don't know what's happening down there, but we're here tonight for Easter."

"LIAR!!!"

It was someone else, in the back. The monsters turned to see who, and they saw that it was *Easter*, making her way into the main room. Ginny and Zoey followed.

"Oh, crap," whispered Haffred to herself, seeing her dreams of East Hampton go up in smoke. At almost precisely the same moment, Duncan realized he could have saved the school a million dollars if the damned girl had shown up ten minutes earlier. Dina Campbell, on the other hand, couldn't believe her luck.

No one at Cipriani, perhaps, was as shocked as Mark and Shannon Riddle. "Easter!" cried Mark. "My God!"

"My baby!" screamed Shannon, running down from the stage. Mark was on her heels. They needed to get Easter out of the room as quickly as possible.

"Stay away from me! Frauds!!"

"What did she say?" asked someone in the crowd.

"She said you're frauds, all of you!" replied Ellie in a calm but strident voice as she advanced on the stage. The last of the fog swirled around her feet.

The mayor, stepping away from the mic, leaned toward Duncan. "This woman does not look well. What's going on here?"

"Her family's been a problem for us," Duncan replied.

Meanwhile, Shannon Riddle, speaking to Easter in a stage whisper, said, "Baby, you've been hurt. We've got to get you to a hospital."

Directing her response out to the crowd, Easter yelled, "They knew, they knew all along!!"

"Sweetheart," said Mark. "You've been through a lot, and we will find out who did this to you, but right now we need to get you to a hospital where a doctor can look at you."

"Did Ellie Sanderson do this to you?" asked Shannon, raising her voice.

Ellie was getting near the stage. With fire in her eyes, she summoned the military bearing she'd spent half her life around: "You! *All* of you—are cowards!"

She raised a hand to point. One of the security detail, who was on the stage and trying to assess the threat, squinted to make Ellie out through the stage spotlights. She appeared deranged. As Ellie's arm rose, he thought he saw a glint, which was, in fact, Ellie's rather large wedding ring.

"Gun! Gun!"

He and the others leapt into action. Two of them tackled the mayor, shielding him with their bodies. The others gang-tackled Ellie. The rest of the crowd, hearing the word "gun," had the following thoughts in the space of perhaps a second:

1. Ellie Sanderson had been through a lot;
2. Did she have something to do with Easter's disappearance?
3. She looked crazy, possibly drunk; and
4. Mass shootings were kind of a thing these days.

By second number two, they ran for the exits. The Wolfmen, Draculas, and Godzillas, fueled by Tito's and Glenfiddich, lurched and stumbled for the nearest escape. The fog had made the floor slick, and many slipped and fell. The Wookiee, having trouble seeing through his hairy mask, crashed into the bar, which, in turn, knocked over the papier mâché Frankenstein. He crashed down on the little girl with the flowers, crushing her.

Ellie was quickly subdued and handcuffed, despite there being no sign of a gun. They stood her up, and she looked around, concerned for the girls. There they were, toward the back, together. Ellie looked at Ginny and mouthed the word "go." Ginny gave a look back that said, *Mom, I've got this.*

Ellie had never been prouder of her girls.

Just before the security detail rushed Ellie out, she had a moment to take in the unfolding chaos, with everyone running over each other for the exits.

Not very brave monsters, she thought. *Not brave at all!*

This made her laugh, and the more she thought about it, and her day, the more and more she laughed, hysterically, almost bringing herself to tears.

The officers, now guiding her out and reading her rights, wondered if they should be heading to Bellevue.

WHO'S IN CHARGE HERE?

Ginny called William and told him what had happened, or tried to, anyway. Not much of the story computed for William, especially since he was still quite inebriated. But he got the fact that Ellie was under arrest and being taken to the Seventh Precinct.

"What's she charged with?"

"I don't know. An assassination attempt?"

"A—what? What the hell are you talking about? And aren't you all supposed to be in East Hampton?"

"Dad, it's a long story. Can you just meet us there?"

William splashed cold water on his face and, for the first time in three days, left the apartment. He Ubered to the station after Googling its location. He found all three girls, side by side on a scuffed and dirty-looking wooden bench.

"Who are you?" he asked Clover.

"Dad, this is Clover," Zoey said. "She goes to school with us. She's been with us all day."

"Nice to meet you, Mr. Sanderson." Clover thrust out her hand. Confused, William shook it limply.

"Can someone please tell me what's going on?"

Ginny began to recount the day's events.

"Wait, Easter Riddle is alive?"

"That's what I'm telling you. We went to get her."

"Where?"

"Middletown, Connecticut."

"Middle—never mind. I need to speak to someone in charge here."

"The news is out," said Clover, who'd been scanning her phone. "Dina Campbell just posted something on the *Sentinel* website and it's lighting up."

William grabbed her phone. The other girls immediately got out theirs.

BREAKING

EASTER RIDDLE FOUND!

FINANCIER'S WIFE INVOLVED!

MAYOR'S LIFE THREATENED!

The *Sentinel* can exclusively report that Easter Riddle, the trans student who disappeared from the renowned Lenox Hill School for Girls last week, has been found, having walked into the school's fall charity gala where Mayor Reynolds was addressing the audience. She appeared injured, with tattered clothes, and in a state of confusion.

Arriving with her was the parent of two other students, identified as Elenore Sanderson. In a rapid series of events witnessed by this reporter, Sanderson, who appeared deranged and was speaking unintelligibly, charged toward the mayor, possibly brandishing a gun. She was immediately tackled and arrested by officers in the mayor's security detail. The mayor was rushed from the scene and is unhurt.

Elenore Sanderson is the wife of top Bedrock Capital financier William Sanderson, who himself was in the news days ago for threatening comments made to trans activists who had been protesting his possible role in Easter's disappearance. Mrs. Sanderson's role in that disappearance and her motives for attacking the mayor remain unclear, but some are questioning whether it may have been a case of abduction.

DEVELOPING . . .

"Whaaat the hell?"

"Dad, this is all bullshit," said Ginny.

William walked over to the main desk. "Excuse me, I need to speak to whomever is in charge."

The desk sergeant glowered down from his perch, which was deliberately set higher than the floor.

"Oh, do you."

"Yes, my wife is being held back there, and I need to know why."

"Let me guess. You're William Sanderson."

"I am."

"Your wife threatened the mayor. You may not see her for a while."

"I happen to *know* the mayor, and there's no way my wife threatened him."

"Oh, well let me just run back and get her so you guys can leave."

"Good."

The desk sergeant burst out in laughter.

"Officer," said William, "just get me someone who has some information, please. I'd like to know the charges."

The sergeant pondered his options. While it was fun busting this douchebag's chops, he decided he no longer wished to deal with him, so he went to get the captain. Moments later, they returned.

"I'm Captain Rodriguez. I gather you're the husband."

"I am. Can you please tell me what's going on?"

"That's what we're trying to determine. Your wife tells quite a—excuse me, sir, have you been drinking tonight?" The scent of Woodford Reserve floated in the precinct air.

"No—yes. Some. What the hell difference does it make? I just came from our apartment."

"Can you tell me how you've been spending the last few days?"

"Why on earth do you care?"

"We're trying to ascertain the circumstances around Easter Riddle's disappearance."

"What, and you think *I* had something to do with it?"

"Your issues with the trans community are well documented and Mrs. Sanderson did suddenly appear with Easter Riddle. It's all rather coincidental, wouldn't you say?"

"Oh, for God's sake. I've been in my apartment."

"For days?"

"Yes, for days. Haven't left."

"And there are doormen there who could confirm this?"

"Listen, as much as I'm enjoying our conversation, why don't you just talk to Easter Riddle?"

"We certainly will, as soon as we can find her."

"Are you telling me she's disappeared again?"

"No, but at the moment, we are having difficulty locating her or her parents."

"We were with Easter all day!" cried Ginny, who'd been eavesdropping with the others.

"And who are you?"

"This is my daughter Virginia. And this is my other daughter, Zoey."

"And this is Clover," said Zoey. "She was with us too."

"I see." The captain eyed Clover and the berries in her hair. He supposed it *was* Halloween.

"All right then. And you say you were with Easter today?"

"That's right. All three of us. This is all bullshit. For starters, Mom did not have a *gun*."

"I can confirm that no gun was found at the scene."

"So, *what*," asked William, "have you arrested my wife for? Arriving late to a party?"

"She is currently being held for disturbing the peace."

"You have got to be kidding me."

"However, I should tell you that we are exploring abduction."

"Easter wasn't abducted!" said Ginny, practically screaming. "We saved her!"

"And you girls all claim to have been with her."

"We were," said Ginny. "Since the middle of the day."

"Listen, Captain, can we just please post my wife's bail?" William really wanted to get out of there.

"Bail? Oh, I wouldn't expect that, not tonight. The mayor is breathing down our necks."

"But you said you know she wasn't there to attack him."

"I said there was no gun. Beyond that, a determination has yet to be made."

"We went there to expose the Riddles," said Ginny. "We went there to expose *all* of them."

"We summoned the Furies!" cried Clover.

"The who?" asked a confused William.

"Except things got a little out of control," said Ginny.

"Wait, expose the Riddles for what?" asked William.

"Dad, you have a lot of catching up to do."

"Everyone just . . . *stop*," directed Captain Rodriguez. "Why don't we all go in the back so I can get your statements?"

Captain Rodriguez shook his head. Ellie Sanderson seemed a little unglued, but he didn't make her as a kidnapper, let alone a potential assassin. But he couldn't fully process her and have bail set until the morning. As high profile as this was, he needed to keep her here a bit longer—and he needed to find and interview the Riddle family. The cruiser he sent over to their apartment on First Avenue found no one at home. Where the hell had *they* gone?

He needed to get to the bottom of this.

YOU REALLY SHOULD
LEARN MORE WORDS

I t was timeless in here, with the lights on twenty-four hours a day. Her watch said—there was nothing on her wrist. What had happened to it, anyway? Maybe it came off when she hit the water.

Morning—it must be morning by now.

"Look at her, sitting there, all quiet, thinkin' she too good to talk to us."

Ellie turned her head toward the others in her cell, considering them for the first time. Then she turned back to stare at the wall.

"Hey, skinny white girl, you look like shit!"

Ellie chuckled slightly at that.

"Ooo, something funny?"

The woman, whose name Ellie gathered was Heavy C, was enormous and threatening.

"Yes," said Ellie.

"Waht? Waht so funny, zombie bitch?"

Ellie had been in the cell all night with four other women. She'd kept to herself, staring aimlessly at the pattern of cracks in the wall. So many thoughts competed for her attention that they effectively negated each other like noise-canceling headphones. It was better that way. Allowing her thoughts to coalesce would require her to confront how far she'd fallen.

"Well, Heavy C, if you must know, it's funny on two levels. First, you are correct. I do look like shit, at least I imagine I do as I don't see any mirrors around here. Yesterday was a long day of jumping off bridges and getting tackled by the mayor's security team, and now I've gotten exactly zero sleep because you all have been yammering all night about possibly some of the most inconsequential things I've ever heard. So yes, one of your observations is spot-on. Your second one, not so much."

Heavy C looked confused, but only for a moment. Confusion was quickly replaced by menace. Her considerable bulk rose from her place among the others and walked over to Ellie, leaning over in her face.

"And waht dat be . . . *bitch*?"

"Your assumption that I am white."

"Oh, you white." She gave Ellie a probing shove.

"Tell her, Heavy!" yelled one of the others.

"I'm not white. I'm not anything, which seems to be the problem. Actually, no, that's not right. I am something."

"Ooo, do share, stick lady."

The others laughed, delighted with the growing distraction.

"I'm someone who doesn't care anymore, least of all about sad little bullies like you."

Heavy C was enraged, partly at this Karen bitch's insults but mostly because she showed no fear. Heavy C was used to being feared. Order had to be restored. She swung her shoulder back and took a mighty swing at Ellie. Alas, her size, while giving her strength, also made her slow. Ellie, still sitting, reacted quickly and swung to the side. Heavy's blow landed squarely on the concrete block wall and she howled in pain.

"Fucking bitch!!"

"You really should learn more words."

Heavy C pulled Ellie from the bench, tackling her to the ground. "Get her, Heavy!" yelled the others in approval, but the guards arrived quickly and broke things up.

"Come with us," one said to Ellie. The others shouted overlapping disapproval that their source of entertainment was being led away.

Ellie was steered through a corridor and into a private office to see the captain.

"Are we to have another fun session talking about all the things I didn't do, or did you finally figure this out?"

Ellie had spent an extensive amount of time with the captain the previous evening. She'd been advised as to her right to a lawyer, and while she'd been sure William could roust one from a bed somewhere, she had no interest.

"Actually, we did. You are free to go."

"Just like that?"

"Just like that. Your family is waiting outside."

"Well, then. That was really fun, captain."

As she walked away, the captain said, "Uh, Mrs. Sanderson?"

Ellie turned. "Yes?"

"As far as I'm concerned, you're a goddamned hero."

After Ellie was escorted out to get her things, the captain watched the video one more time.

GOING VIRAL

When Felix Castillo woke up the previous morning, he had no reason to expect that he would be famous, or at least semi-famous, by the next day.

At age seventy, the recently retired machine shop worker had led a decent, frugal life. He'd served in the tail end of the Vietnam War, raised a family, paid his taxes, but had otherwise been but a whisper upon the vast social fabric of America.

He'd never been one to keep with the latest trends in entertainment, fashion, technology, or just about anything else. Felix had never owned a mobile phone, for instance. He didn't see the need to be in constant contact with people. "Oh, that's not for an old man like me," he'd say.

But recently, his wife of forty-five years had died, forcing him to reevaluate many things. She'd always been the glue that bound the family together.

A man who'd never been lonely, suddenly was.

Felix's thirteen-year-old grandson Lucas sat him down one day, insisting on showing him how his iPhone worked. "Look, Pop Pop, we can always be in touch."

A few days later, there was a party at his youngest daughter's to celebrate the arrival of another grandchild, his eighth. Lucas showed Felix how easy it was to take pictures and even film things. "See, you can always keep a memory, right there on your phone."

The next day, his daughter took him to buy an iPhone for himself. He spent the better part of two days learning a few basic functions. He was fascinated by how easy it was. He took to filming everything, from the colorful sugar maple tree in his back yard to passing planes heading south to New York. A blue jay landed on his deck, and he filmed that too. He loved the zoom feature in particular. On the third day, he decided to drive over to Cromwell to see his new grandchild again, and maybe take some video.

Cromwell was over on the other side of the Connecticut River and about a fifteen-minute drive. As he crossed the Arrigoni Bridge, the cars in front of him had come to an abrupt stop. He'd slammed on the brakes to avoid a collision. The car behind him had done the same, effectively pinning him in. He wasn't going anywhere.

He'd seen the people in the cars up front jump out. Much to his alarm, he'd watched as one of them climbed over the railing. Goodness, he should help, he thought. He got out but saw that one of the others, a teenage girl, had already climbed over the rail and was talking to the young boy, who must be troubled. Or was it a girl? Oddly, it was hard to tell.

He thought to call 911, but already he could hear sirens in the distance. Not knowing what else to do, he got closer. Then he took out his new phone and began filming.

That evening, right about when Ellie and the girls were arriving at the Monster Mash, he showed the footage to his grandson.

"Holy shit!" blurted Lucas.

"I don't think we need to use that language."

"Oh, sorry, but really, holy shit. This is huge."

"Well, it's nice that it all worked out for those people."

"No, you don't understand. You need to post this."

"Post it to what?"

"Anything! It won't matter."

As Captain Rodriguez watched, the words were quite clear, and corroborated everything.

> "Easter, come back with us. We'll take you back."

> "What, to my wonderful parents, who wanted me to stay hidden up here? No, I don't think so."

Moments later, he saw Ginny and Easter disappear over the side. Whoever took the video then moved to the railing and pointed the camera down. You could see two heads, floating away.

Then, another voice:

> "Mom, what are you doing?!"

This prompted the phone to swing back just in time to catch Ellie Sanderson leaping over the rail and plunging into the river below. The video now zoomed down to the river, where you could make out Ellie swimming toward one of the others, and then pulling her out. You could see the whole thing, and by the time they got to the shore, it was plain enough that the person she'd rescued was Easter.

Captain Rodriguez called the district attorney, Henry Feldman. There was the matter of the Riddles.

"You're telling me these shit stains knew where she was the whole time?"

"Most of it, yeah."

"All while we mobilized half this city looking for her and they fake-cried for the cameras and asked for money?"

"That's about it."

"That's fraud."

"That would be my take."

"I'll call Judge Manuel. See if we can get a warrant issued right away."

THE UNRAVELING

The girls ran up to give their mom a hug. Ginny winced.

"Oh, Mom. A shower."

"I'll make it a priority, right after I consume some Advil. I'm thinking about a whole bottle. Oh, hello, Clover."

"Hey, Mrs. Sanderson. It's nice to see you again."

"Are you goblincore always so damn polite?" asked Ginny.

"They also have a strong insult game," said Zoey.

Clover shrugged. "It's situational."

"I asked her to come," said Zoey. "We didn't know they were releasing you and thought they might need more statements."

Zoey and Clover were fast becoming inseparable.

"You totally blew up that party, Mrs. Sanderson," said Clover. "May I just repeat, one more time, what a badass you are?"

"Thank you, Clover," said Ellie.

"You know it's online. Everyone in their costumes running for the exits. It's *so* meme-able."

"But we saw *your* video on the car ride over," said Ginny.

"What video?" asked Ellie.

"They didn't tell you?"

"Tell me what?"

"Mom, you're blowing up the internet. Well, we both are, actually."

She thrust her phone toward Ellie.

"Someone was filming on the bridge," said Clover. "They got everything, *including* the part where you play Superman and save Easter."

"Easter . . . Where is she, anyway?"

"They don't seem to know," said William.

"Her parents hustled her out of the party before she could say anything else, but they didn't know that video was going to drop," added Ginny.

"It just hit seventeen thousand views," said Clover, who was glued to her phone. "It was posted last night by some guy with one follower."

"At least the damn city can stand down now," said William. This received no acknowledgment from Ellie. They had yet to exchange a word.

"Honestly, I just can't focus right now," she said. "I need to go home and collapse. Clover, do your parents know you're here? Don't you have school today?"

"Ugh, yes. But can I just say? This has been awesome. Awesome, thy name is Sanderson." She gave a theatrical bow before leaving.

"As for the rest of us," said Ellie, "we have a lot to discuss, not the least of which is where you girls are going to school now. But did I mention I need to collapse?"

They left, and Ellie was in bed by late morning. She would sleep straight through to the next day. She couldn't know how different her world would be by the time she woke up. Views of the video continued to accelerate and the story would dominate the cable news cycle. Clips were picked up everywhere from the *Times* to TMZ. In the strange, instantaneous manner in which modern culture creates its heroes and villains, Ellie became the "Halloween Hero," a paragon of selflessness and a warrior-like Valkyrie, all wrapped up in one.

In the Lenox Hill community, there wasn't a soul not fully aware of the circumstances. Tizzy Addison basked in the reflected glory of being Ellie's friend. "That's just who she is," Tizzy said throughout the day. She practically held court at the Mayflower.

Sylvia Haffred cursed her luck. Bennet Smith called and said that the school was "reconsidering" its donation to the foundation, which was code for "You can suck it, and I hope I never see you again." Then Elton Tribble called from Bedrock. He needn't have bothered. Haffred already knew East Hampton would have to wait for another day and another case. *Those fucking Riddles!*

Duncan Ruggles assembled a hasty Zoom meeting for the board. Having dispensed with the shakedown at the hands of Haffred, they moved on to the matter of Easter. He told the board that despite the behavior of the parents, it was his hope Easter would return to Lenox Hill. Pete Richmond asked whether it was wise to retain such an emotionally unstable student. "I don't think any of us are qualified to make a judgment like that," came the response. Darlene Buckets heartily agreed.

"I also wonder if we haven't been too hasty in our dealings with the Sandersons." *Thank goodness they hadn't yet been counseled out*, was the part he didn't need to say. Perhaps they could walk everything back. All agreed that was wise.

"Lastly, I would like to propose an increase in Padma's compensation. These have been very trying times and I believe her leadership has been exemplary."

No one objected.

The Lovely People wrapped up their Zoom and went back to their lives, content in their virtue.

Later that day, Clover texted Zoey. She insisted that Zoey meet her after school and go to EJ's, the prospect of which Zoey found horrifying. She tried to object.

"But—"

"But nothing. Meet me outside EJ's at four thirty."

And so she did.

"Why are we here?" she asked.

"No questions, Z. Do you trust me?"

"I do."

"Then just come."

They went inside.

"Clover, can we just go somewhere else?"

"We could, but not today."

"Clover—"

Clover put her hands on Zoey's shoulders and turned her sideways. There, Zoey spotted Coco and the BB Girls in their usual booth.

"You know what to do," said Clover.

"No, I don't."

"*Yes*, you do."

She did, in fact, know what to do. They walked over. Coco immediately became animated.

"Oh, if it isn't Doughy and the walking shrub! I thought we'd seen the last of you, Doughy, and I was hopeful about you, too, bush girl."

"Hey, *Coco!*" said Zoey.

Coco laughed. "What?"

In an act impossible to imagine mere days before, Zoey picked up Coco's shake and dumped it on her head.

"Fuck, my hair!" she howled. Zoey and Clover stayed for a few moments to admire their handiwork, then walked out, laughing.

"Badassery now officially runs in the family!" proclaimed Clover.

THE BLUES

Despite the invitation to return to Lenox Hill, Ellie decided that the girls would be homeschooled for the remainder of the year. Zoey pushed back a bit. She had nothing to fear from the Cocos anymore, so there was that, but mostly she thought about her newfound relationship with Clover.

Ginny, for her part, fretted about college. In the end, though, they both relented. Each understood the school's culpability.

In the following weeks, Ellie hardly left the apartment, immersing herself in the necessities of teaching two high school girls. It was daunting, but she welcomed the distraction. She was determined that the girls wouldn't lose any time. She ordered books and joined a homeschooling group on Facebook.

In a way, Ellie was enjoying it, finally realizing her plans to be a teacher. She could do this. And she cherished the time with her girls. All too soon, her house would be an empty nest, a prospect that filled her with dread. She and William would be alone in this apartment.

Other than that, she withdrew into herself, not at all interested in assuming the role of the public hero that she'd become. An organization called 100 Women of Color, on discovering that Ellie was, indeed, one of them, reached out about honoring her at their annual gala.

She politely declined.

Other offers came too. The talk shows all reached out, and the newspapers. The *Sentinel's* reporter, Dina Campbell, seemed almost frantic to land an interview.

She didn't even answer that email.

And then there was Tizzy, who called . . . and called. But Ellie never picked up. Tizzy was so determined, though, that she presented herself one day at 580. Ellie was tempted to not let her up but ultimately demurred. Tizzy's nature wasn't her fault. She was raised in this place.

"I've been trying to reach you," Tizzy said. "Do you know how famous you are right now?"

"I'd rather not be."

"Still, it's like you're She-Ra or something. And I see you're looking better. The bruising is gone."

"Tiz, why are you here?"

"Oh, don't be like that—I have exciting news!"

"What?"

"You're in. That's why I've been trying to reach you!'"

"In what?"

"The Mayflower!"

"Oh."

"Oh? That's all you can say?"

"Yes."

"El, c'mon!"

Ellie gathered herself. She was so tired of being whipsawed by the new, unfathomable rules of hothouse Manhattan culture. She couldn't play by them anymore.

"Tiz, let me see if I have this straight. First, I was on some endless list. Then they suddenly wanted me, strangely right after learning about my background, except then we were in the papers, so they didn't want me because publicity is bad, but now I'm in the papers again and they *do* want me because now publicity is good, assuming it's the right kind of publicity. Is that about right?"

Taken aback, Tizzy said, "I'm sure you're reading into things too much."

"Am I?"

"El, it doesn't matter how it happened, does it? The point is, it happened!"

"Well then, perhaps the *Social Register* is next!"

"I'm sure it is."

"That was a joke.

"Tizzy, you can tell the lovely ladies at the club that while the consommé is excellent, I respectfully decline. I wasn't interested in being their diversity poster child yesterday, and I'm not interested in being their celebrity do-gooder today."

"El, I don't think you understand how hard I've worked on this for you!"

"And I thank you for that."

"But what will people say?"

"Tiz, I'm just going to sweat that one out."

Despite the accolades, Ellie remained in an uncharacteristically dark place. At the core of her despondency was her relationship with William. She hadn't involved him in the decision to homeschool the girls, and he didn't try to interfere. There was a small, unused maid's bedroom behind the kitchen, and she'd banished him there. Oh, he made overtures now and then, and he stopped drinking, at least, but Ellie had hardened to him.

One day he mentioned that Casper called.

"He said he's open to having me back after things die down. I guess the virtue of the wife trumps the sins of the husband," he said with a shrug. He'd hoped the news would help repair things between them.

It didn't.

It wasn't about money, or Will's career. It never had been. In the days that followed, Ellie barely acknowledged him. Will became a ghost in the apartment, with nothing to do and nowhere to go. Sometimes, he tried to make conversation with the girls, but his attempts were awkward. Only Zoey seemed to soften, but of course she would.

Ellie felt like Will had become a stranger. Finally, she told him that he should expect her to file for divorce as soon as the girls felt more settled with everything.

"Don't do this," he said.

"I don't think I have a choice" was all she said, walking away. They didn't speak for several days until Will came to her and said, "El, I know how mad you still are, but could you come with me, just for a few minutes?"

"Where?"

"Just come."

"Fine," she said, tonelessly.

She followed him back to the kitchen and into the stairwell by the service elevator. There, Will started walking up.

"Will, I'm really busy with the girls. Can we get to the point of whatever this is?"

"Just one more flight."

He opened the door to the roof, and there, laid out on a blanket, was a picnic. There was a basket filled with sandwiches, a bottle of wine, and even a candelabra.

"Will—"

"Just hear me out."

"Fine. Say what you have to say."

"I still love you. And I know I've been a fool. Somehow, along the way, my priorities got out of whack. I think . . . I think I thought giving you and the girls a good life was what I was supposed to do, that it was enough to make me a good husband and father. I was wrong, and I hope you can forgive me."

"Will—"

"And you should know I'm not going back to Bedrock. I'll find something else, something that lets me spend more time at home . . . if you'll have me."

He stopped talking, waiting for Ellie to respond. Her eyes were glassy, and he was hopeful he had broken through. After a few moments, she began to speak.

"Will, you betrayed us—not just me but your own daughters. I can't get past that. I think you should find somewhere else to stay."

She walked back downstairs and, grabbing a coat, left the building for the first time in several days. She walked over to Central Park, barely aware of the passing blocks. Entering at Sixty-first Street, the sweet smell of autumn's decay was in the air.

She wandered the length of Literary Walk. It was, she thought, the park's most beautiful place. The warm weather crowds and performers had all left, and the stately elms that lined the walk had surrendered to the season, their leaves blowing about the ground. It was beautiful, still, and sad.

She found herself at the Alice in Wonderland statue next to the model boat pond. Alice still sat there, so graceful on her mushroom, smiling at her companions. Today they were alone, though, except for Ellie, who remained for a bit. A pigeon landed near her feet and strutted around, hoping for a handout.

"Sorry, bird. I didn't come prepared."

The pigeon flew off.

It occurred to her that she'd been recreating that day in the park with her parents and the girls. That was the last day of the "before" time, as she thought of it, the time before things got crazy.

Her phone buzzed with a text. William.

> I told myself I was doing it all for you guys, for
> a better life. I know that's not true now. I'm
> really sorry.

Ellie swiped the message away.

Thoughts turned to her parents, whom she dreaded telling almost as much as the girls. It had to happen sometime.

Her father picked up.

"El, sweetie, how are you?"

They hadn't spoken since just after Halloween, and Curtis knew Ellie's internet fame wasn't making her life better. But he didn't know everything.

"Dad . . ."

Ellie unloaded her misgivings about her marriage, about how work had consumed Will and no doubt would again. About how if Will had been a full partner in their marriage, the girls might not have gotten in trouble in the first place. About how they had been growing apart for years and about the betrayal. And maybe the girls were old enough now to handle a separation.

Curtis considered everything she said. "I know you're not a quitter, and that means you're not doing this lightly. It's a big step, but just know that your mother and I will support you and the girls no matter what."

"Thanks, Dad." She tried not to cry, to no avail.

"Do you want us to come?"

"No, I don't think so. Let me just try to figure everything out."

"One last thing."

"What?"

"Before you do this, ask yourself, 'Did I do everything I could?'"

She paused, considering this.

"Okay."

"No matter what, though, we're here for you."

"I know, Daddy."

Back home, she found Will packing some things.

"Where will you go?" she asked.

"I booked a room at the Gotham."

"Okay," was all she managed to say.

AFTERMATH

Mark and Shannon Riddle were located and arrested two days after they slipped out of the Monster Mash. They had initially fled, with Easter, to Connecticut, but upon seeing a police car outside the house, turned around. Mark was convinced that they only needed to hide somewhere for a short time until things blew over. Heading back to the city, they spotted a large crowd filtering into a hotel.

"I have an idea," said Mark, eyeing the crowd.

"You've got to be kidding," said Easter. "Those are migrants."

"No, it's perfect. It will only be for a few days."

They parked their car on a nearby street and mixed in with the others. They would say they were from Argentina if anyone asked.

It wasn't, in the scheme of things, the craziest idea. But by then, Felix Castillo's video had a quarter of a million views and Mark and Shannon Riddle had become poster children for villainy, perhaps the two most hated people in America. They were quickly spotted by an aid worker, who alerted a nearby police officer. The arrest made the cover of the next day's *Sentinel* under Dina's byline.

While there was sympathy for Easter, loathing for her parents cut across politics and demographics. The Upper East Side set hated them because they'd been duped, milked for their wallets, their good intentions so easily exploited. They could live with all manner of opprobrium, but gullibility undercut their most cherished self-image, that of sophistication. They wanted nothing more than for the entire incident to be forgotten. After a few days of intense gossip and the requisite praise for Ellie and Ginny, events were stashed into a memory hole.

The reaction from the trans community was harsher. Leaving the Sandersons and Bedrock behind, they turned on the Riddles, and their hate burned like New York asphalt in August. Effigies of Mark and Shannon were set alight in Washington Square Park to a cheering throng. The trans were joined by all manner of the LGBTQ+ community and its allies. The furries were there, and the cosplay crowd, along with the demi-boys, the two-spirits, the gender-queer, and, of course, the queens. In the spirit of the occasion, they trashed some nearby storefronts.

Mayor Reynolds might normally have ordered the police to do something, but he was taking heat for jailing Ellie Sanderson. Ellie was now officially a Hero of the Movement, her husband's earlier transgressions forgotten. New York's Finest watched in silent anger as a bench was hurled through a Starbucks window, and the mayor went on to an easy victory on Election Day.

The Riddles vehemently denied any prior knowledge of Easter's whereabouts, and Easter steadfastly refused to talk about it. For reasons known only to her, any previous desire to deliver a public reckoning unto her parents had cooled. Given this, the DA was forced to dismiss the charges.

Lenox Hill and Bedrock both formally withdrew their donations to the Easter Riddle Foundation. GoFundMe returned what was left in the Riddles' account to the contributors.

Easter would never return to Lenox Hill, her tenure there having been less than two weeks. She did, however, post a statement on her socials before shutting them down. It read:

> I am truly sorry to those that I have hurt or inconvenienced. I am also deeply grateful to those who made me see the value of life again, and I won't forget what you taught me. Looking back, I let those around me lead me down a path rather than seeking one for myself. As I move past recent events, I have resolved to change this. I wish everyone peace and love forever.
> Easter . . .

Many speculated that Easter was de-transitioning. Rumor had it she'd left that odd ellipsis after her signature as a clue, but no one really knew. Nor did anyone know where she was. The Riddles had left their New York rental, and their Middletown home remained on the market.

They had all but disappeared.

Ellie, for her part, hoped Easter was all right.

Dina Campbell's reporting on the entire saga would land her an American Mosaic Journalism Prize, awarded for "excellence in long-form, narrative, or deep reporting about underrepresented groups in the American landscape."

Within minutes of receiving the news, she posted it to the Harvard

Alumni Facebook page and signed up for her next reunion. Her landlord, however, hearing about the $100,000 prize, successfully had her removed from her rent-controlled apartment. Even with the prize money, Dina was unable to afford a new lease at current prices and was forced to move back to her hometown of Cleveland. At last word she was hoping to land something in the Metro section at the *Plain Dealer*.

December

BAVARIAN HASH

Weeks had passed and the city had moved on from both Easter Riddle and the Sandersons. It was the holiday tourist season and the crowds gathered at Times Square and the Rockefeller Center tree, as they always did. New York, often dirty and dangerous, somehow sparkled this time of year.

For her part, Ellie rarely went out. Time had slowed for her.

Yearning for some fresh air, she donned a coat and walked upstairs to the roof. It was cold, almost freezing, and the sky was slate gray. But it was quiet, with the noise from the city below blending into a pleasant hum of traffic and distant honks.

From here, she could see over the rooftops of other Park Avenue buildings to the broader skyline beyond. This place, New York, was not hers. Could it still be? The doors were all open now, all she had to do was walk through them.

But did she want it?

The people here were like anywhere else: some good, some not, although most undoubtedly richer. All that money had a strange effect. It worked like an accelerant on people's characters, magnifying the good and the bad. In some, it brought out the madness.

Any evidence of the picnic was long gone, of course. She wondered if Will had ever eaten any of it. Probably not. In retrospect, he must have gone to great lengths to set it up without her noticing anything. The thought made her smile.

A thought, inchoate at first, gradually formed.

Did I do everything I could?

She hadn't seen Will in several weeks, and time apart had mellowed her. Anger had turned to melancholy.

She took out her phone and texted.

Would you like to have dinner with us tonight?

The girls had only been told that she and their father were "taking a break." They weren't stupid, of course, and knew what that portended. Zoey took it hard, and Ginny had become resentful at her father's banishment. But they were both visibly happy when told their father would join them for dinner that night. Their brightened mood rubbed off on Ellie, so she decided to make something ambitious for the occasion, something she'd never tried.

"Tonight, we will be eating Bavarian Apple-Sausage Hash," she said, entering the dining room with a large serving bowl. "I read that it's traditional this time of year in Germany."

"Bavarian *what*?" asked Ginny.

"It's just a recipe I thought I'd try."

"I'm sure it's wonderful," said Will.

As they took turns serving themselves, Ellie took it in. It was nothing that wasn't playing out in a million other homes across America, as prosaic as it was wonderful. A family, having dinner.

A family.

"Look at us," she said, not finishing the thought. Was that contentment she felt? It hadn't been there for a while.

"May I make a toast?" said William, holding up his glass. "To my two beautiful, special girls, and to the best, most loving wife a man could ask for. I owe all of you such a large apology I can hardly express it. I—"

"It's okay, Dad," said Zoey. "Just shut up now."

They clinked glasses.

After dinner, she and Will would talk. Things were not settled, not by a long shot, but they would talk. Maybe there was a way forward.

Ellie wondered, sitting there watching Will listen patiently to Zoey's story about copying the pattern of a Tibetan mandala at the Met, if she hadn't been the fool. It wasn't about a place, it never was. It was about this, right here.

Her roots had been right in front of her all along.

William was the first to try the hash. The smile on his face faded for just a moment before quickly returning. He was trying so hard.

"Mmm," he said.

The girls dug in.

"Yeah," said Ginny. "Really good, Mom."

Ellie tried it herself. It was oddly bitter, and the sausage was like rubber. She lowered her fork.

"It's terrible, isn't it?"

No one knew how to respond. They knew how hard she must have worked on it, but also, yes, it was terrible. Then Ellie did something she hadn't done in weeks: She laughed. It came out as something of a snort, but there it was. The others joined in, laughing, tentatively at first but then hysterically in a joyful release.

"It's probably not too late to order out," Ellie said. "Chinese?"

They all laughed some more. That was probably the only choice on this particular night.

"One more thing," said Ellie.

"What's that, Mom?" asked Zoey.

Ellie held up her glass.

"Merry Christmas."

JANUARY

There was a stop Ellie had to make, if reluctantly. She had to go by Lenox Hill and pick up a few things Ginny and Zoey had left in their lockers. Some notebooks, a sweatshirt, a pair of headphones . . . The girls could have gone themselves, but she didn't want them to ever set foot in that place again.

Reaching the school, she paused on the other side of the street. It was dismissal time for the lower school kids on their first day back from break. Parents were waiting as excited tartan-clad girls streamed out. They wore tights now in the cold weather. She saw the younger mothers, eager faces all, waiting to spot their daughters. For a few minutes the sidewalk and the courtyard were alive with chatter.

In a way, she was jealous of them, those mothers. They were still possessed of blind faith in people and institutions. They still found happiness in all the pleasant distractions of benefit committees and travel teams and holiday concerts. How much easier it all was to be innocent.

The thought vanished as quickly as it came. A cold, misty rain started to fall, and the girls and their mothers quickly scattered. Ellie stayed there, watching, until the last ones left.

She decided not to go in after all.

EPILOGUE

Wilson Girard read the essay a second time, perhaps the first time he'd done that this year. His New York regional staffer insisted he see it. After reading possibly fifteen hundred essays this season, he wished he could pile them all together in the Cross Campus quad and set them on fire.

So much strained virtue. So many overpaid consultants, their hands nowhere near as invisible as they thought. In their effort to give Yale what they imagined it wanted, they all were a blur of repetitive overachievement.

He supposed what bothered him the most about the applicants was that, fundamentally, they were unimaginative. There was no other way to put it. They gamed a system that Yale and its peer institutions had created to great effect.

Perfect grades?

Check.

Instrument?

Check.

Community work?

Check.

Essay about their life's hardships?

Check.

World-changing, conscious-capitalism company started in the garage?

Check.

An ex-Yale professor named William Deresiewicz coined the perfect term for these kids: "excellent sheep." He even wrote a book about them.

Wilson supposed he couldn't blame them, the kids. Or even the parents. People respond to incentives, and seventeen-year-olds were no different. The irony that they were responding to incentives he had no small hand in creating was not lost on him.

But this . . .

This was the rarest of the rare, the four-leaf clover in a vast field of crabgrass: a truly original essay. It almost made his job worthwhile.

Of course, he'd known about the circumstances some months before, everyone did. He'd seen the video. What he didn't know was that one of the principals was in the applicant pool.

She'd even given the essay a title.

Saving Easter.

Wilson navigated to YouTube on his computer. He watched that video he'd seen for the first time back in November. And there she was, getting out on the ledge. This was no sheep. *This* was an eagle! This was courage!

He could just do what he needed to do right there on his computer, but he didn't want to. It wasn't enough. Although applications were now electronic, his staffer had given him a printout of this one, this diamond in the rough. He needed to do this the old-school way because it was somehow more satisfying than clicking a box on the screen.

Wilson reached for his bottom drawer and found his old, self-inking stamp. He let it hover over the application for a moment and then brought it down with a satisfying thump.

"Accept."

Sometime later, and all over the country, high school seniors were hitting Refresh over and over, barely remembering to breathe. Some filmed the moment for social media posts.

Ginny, alone in her room, opened her laptop for the first time that day.

And there it was, in her inbox.

YALE OFFICE OF ADMISSIONS

She clicked on it.

The laptop speakers blared fight music and the screen came to life. *Congratulations!* scrolled across the screen and small animated bulldogs danced back and forth.

Ginny sat back.

"Meh," she said, finally, to an audience of none.

She closed the laptop with a thud.

ACKNOWLEDGMENTS

Like my first novel, *Campusland, The Sandersons Fail Manhattan* is heavily drawn from real life, although the characters and institutions you've never heard of are (mostly) fictional. Yes, the goblincore and eco-sexuals are real things. I'm not clever enough to make them up.

In an effort to get the details as accurate as possible, I relied on the knowledge and advice of a number of friends. They include my early readers: Mike Balay, Judy Lewis, Marvin Bush, Dane Neller, Theresa Melhado, and family members Claire, Sim, and Bill Johnston.

I also wish to thank, in no particular order, Rick Hough, Jane Douglas Reynolds, Bill and Tana Dye, Heath Gibson, John Massengale, Gaby Baron, Rod Hatch, Bert Meem, Paul Rossi, Ryan Levenson, Andrew Gutmann, Alison Feagin, Deb Fillman, Charlie Manuel, Dave Tohir, and Mike and Denise Kelly. Special thanks to *Undercover Mothers* for all their insights. They do great work exposing all the wrong turns our most elite schools are making.

Thanks to my boys, Tucker and Brady, and the women in my life, Kelley and Caroline, who could always answer questions on subjects about which I have no clue—questions like, "What would such-and-such a character wear to . . . ?" or "How would a sixteen-year-old girl say . . . ?"

Not to be excluded are the folks who performed CPR on me when I had a recent cardiac arrest (looking at you, Bart, Genevieve, and others). Without them, *Sandersons* would never have made it beyond my hard drive.

Last but not least, there's my St. Martin's editor and relentless advocate, Elizabeth Beier. It's been great working with her.

ABOUT THE AUTHOR

Kelley Johnston

Scott Johnston grew up in Manhattan and graduated from Yale, where he was later an adjunct professor. From there, Wall Street (Salomon Brothers of *Liar's Poker* fame) and a stint in Hong Kong. On the side, he opened two night clubs and a restaurant in New York City. More recently, Johnston shifted gears and cofounded two tech startups, and wrote his first novel, *Campusland*. His writings have appeared in *The Wall Street Journal* and the *New York Post*, as well as his blog, *The Naked Dollar*. Johnston lives in Virginia and travels to speak to community groups and clubs about the issues that animate his novels.